Diran Adebayo has been hailed as one of the most original young literary talents of his generation. His first novel, the acclaimed *Some Kind of Black*, broke new literary ground for the London novel and won him the 1995 Saga Prize, a Betty Trask Award, the Authors' Club Best First Novel Award, and the Writers Guild's New Writer of the Year Award for 1996. He has also written stories for BBC TV and Radio, been a columnist for *New Nation* newspaper, and a contributor to many national newspapers. He is the current recipient of the Abraham Woursell Award from Vienna University.

Praise for *My Once Upon a Time*

'Not so much a novel subverting a tired genre as one that turns it on its head . . . His greatest asset, beyond his clinical observational skills, is a prose style built around the rhythms of black speech and music . . . an urban novel of considerable style and impact' – *Times*

'Adebayo's work makes its own world while never losing the hard edges of everyday life. His language has a conversational suppleness which can accommodate pathos, bewilderment and moments of beauty . . . The book keeps surprising, never easily giving up its answers or letting the reader settle . . . In the end you're in another country and with the Gods' – *Time Out*

'Garlanded with awards for his first book Some Kind of Black, with his second, the young English novelist Diran Adebayo confirms his promise as a writer of vibrant originality . . . This is a book that sings: its prose a giddy mixture of English and patois, Runyonesque flights of descriptive fancy and the musical cadences of street-slang, is by turns rhapsodic, exhilarating and poignant . . . Adebayo is a real find, My Once Upon a Time is a tale for our times' – Mick Brown, *Daily Telegraph*

'My Once Upon a Time is a contemporary parable in a league of its own'

'This telling

my once

upon

a time

DIRAN ADEBAYO

ABACUS

Published by Abacus 2001
First published in Great Britain by Abacus 2000

BS
Copyright © Diran Adebayo 2000

Extract from 'Heaven and Hell', reproduced by permission of BMG Music
Publishing; 'When We Get By', reproduced by permission of Polygram
International Publishing Inc; 'Til I'm Laid To Rest', reproduced by permission of
Polygram Music Publishing Ltd.
Illustration 'The Evil That Men Do', reproduced by permission of Punch
magazine.

A CIP catalogue record for this book
is available from the British Library

ISBN 0 349 11442 0

Typeset in Caslon by M Rules
Printed and bound in Great Britain by
Bookmarque Ltd, Croydon, Surrey

Abacus
A Division of
Little, Brown and Company (UK)
Brettenham House
Lancaster Place
London WC2E 7EN

Adding one thing to another to discover the scheme of things –
Still searching but not finding –
I found one man amongst a thousand,
but a woman amongst all those have I not found.

ECCLESIASTES, THE BIBLE

For they are the best of us,
Those who love, and believe.

THULANI DAVIS, 'ZOOM'

contents

part two 'to discover the theme of things. . .'

my once

upon

a time

intro/outro

The end was also the beginning in that they both involved this man and a note. The man, to be sure, was changed, but the note was the same:

One man amongst a thousand have I found. But a woman amongst all those have I not found.

He lay with his arm outstretched, holding up his precious scrap of paper, as hot burgundy blood traced their trails around him. Like he was somehow trying to save the thing. And I can remember blankly wondering if the blood would reach and soil his note before his end, or at all, as the girl wept in front of me.

Then there was a tremendous roll of thunder. I turned to the window to be seared by the dazzle of red, gold and green, and I fell.

I often ponder on that last little question, now I have all this time.

part one

*'adding one thing
to another . . .'*

1

a mystery man . . . could it be that I was finally getting overs?

I remember I was reclining in my office, throwing my darts at the board, daydreaming about getting overs, and all the pretty things there would then be for me . . . Just doing my everyday really, when the intercom buzzed.

I scoped the street from the window, but no foreign wagons or anything out of the ordinary down there. Could it be a bailiff, a prospective client, or a stink man come to step on me?

'"Reality Rules"?' The soft burr of a brother came down the line. He sounded pleasant. Maybe he wasn't from these parts.

'Is what it says, don't it?' I replied. 'Who this?'

'I've come to talk business.'

I said nothing. Give a guy a few moments to stew and he tends to give himself away somehow.

'Business,' he repeated. 'I have a business offer.'

I buzzed him up. A client, it seemed. Who knows, maybe one with serious collats. That would be even nice. But never this year.

I draped a piece of cloth over my nasty little stove, pulled some sheaves of paper from my drawers, arranged them on my desk, then cast an eye up to check that all my floppy disk boxes were neatly stacked on the shelf behind me. Along their sides ran the dates and initials of previous clients. They were mostly empty – noting stuff down was the kind of simp's move that landed a man of my profession in trouble. But the labels spoke the language of efficiency to the punters.

I switched on the computer. Perhaps I should have pawned this thing by now, but I was too attached to it. I spent a lot of time on the highway.

I pulled my bottom drawer out slightly, so my bucky and blade were to hand, just in case, and sat myself behind my desk, looking busy.

The guy stood a moment on the other side of my glass door. He ran his eye over its inscription – 'Reality Rules – *cos the city ain't pretty*' – before knocking and entering.

My man was six foot and counting, his hue a rich mahogany, and he carried a good weight easily and evenly about him. He wore a cream crushed linen jacket with matching trousers, and a shirt of deep brown that had an expensive, velvety quality to it. Elegant, but not flashy. I welcomed that.

No doubt any hustler could have rented out some quality gear for the day. I did myself, from time to time. But all bar the champions betrayed themselves still: an excessive fondness for chapereetas here, an ill-concealed brawliness of presence there. But this guy! His abs looked solid but he wasn't shoving them in your face; he looked like he had hardly been feet deep in the strife but he didn't seem simple; he had some grace . . . yeah, class is the word. He looked like one of those broad-backed, top-track, supping-with-the-big-boys brothers.

'Boy,' he said, more a statement than a question.

'Do I know you?' I replied.

There was mild amusement in his eyes.

'I need an investigator. I would appreciate your skills.'

His gaze travelled the room, taking in my disks, my dartboard, designed as a map of the city, and my cabinet, where I deposited my bedding during office hours. He paused, as my more tasteful visitors tend to, by the framed print of a wry old sporting cartoon, *The Evil That Men Do*, before fixing on my knife certificates.

I had these 'defensive weapon' permits for every side of the city, embossed by the area's police authority and renewed each year. My profession was one of the few granted them. I also had a set of the fully fledged private investigator's licences, but these I rarely took about with me. Certain man out there might take you for an informer and step on you with a swiftness if they saw a licence with the stamp of the state. I only used one for my infrequent forays out west – the land of pukka postcodes, mansions by the load, boulevards for roads, and all that good stuff. Officials down that side could get quite particular when some such as I passed through and it was best to come with all your propers.

He went over to the wall to take a closer look and I welcomed his interest for, although hardly a man of means, in the matter of knives I could not be embarrassed. The regulation four-incher that I showed to the authorities as requested was just the start. In the bolted cubbyhole beneath my feet, for all things fight and beautiful, lay my butterfly blade, my Shaolin steel, my blade of many switches, my thin man's knife, my fat man's knife, my 'Six pack? No matter' knife, my rusty 'If the first cut don't do you, the secondary infections will' razor, my little late cut number for when your foe thinks you're walking away, and never forgetting my treasure. My little baby. Its business end was five and a half inches, which glinted differently as the light caught it. Around its grip, in a sheath of intricate bronze thread, was woven a tapestry of some balletic, ancient battle. All that plus a nugget of a cherry-stud on top.

'I would like for you to find me a very special somebody,' he said, turning to me.

'Aha. Well, special somebodies tend to require special rates. We may as well settle that side of—'

He hushed me with his fingers.

'You will be compensated for your endeavours beyond your wildest dreams, believe me.'

Well, obviously I liked the sound of that. Although 'compensated' sounded ambiguous – a trick term maybe. No way was I busting a leg for this man without pure folds up front.

He seated himself in front of me, his fingers brushing against all the dust on the armrest. He studied the soot in his hand, still his genial self, and relaxed deep into the chair, his right foot resting on his left knee. I had not seen a brother sit like that in years. I continued to hunch slightly forward, my weight in my thighs and backside, ready to spring should there be any funny business.

'Tell me, Boy, what do you believe in, heaven or hell?'

It was the refrain to an old, popular song, first recorded, I believe, some time in the nine-zeroes. Folk still sang fragments of it.

'That's easy,' I said. '"We don't believe in heaven, cos we're living in hell."'

'Nearly. That's nearly right,' He smiled encouragingly, and fingered his silver ring. It had a distinctive blue monkey for a signet. 'And the Bible, do you know it?'

'The *Bible*?' I was a little flustered. I didn't want to lose this commission over a trifle. Scripture had only been an optional subject at school, and the Bible had jostled for our attention with other approaches. 'I'm familiar with the Old part. Exiles, vengeance, battles, plenty of trial an' tribulation, I remember. As for the New, well I've never really had any need for it in my line of work . . . ' I trailed off.

'No matter.' He fished in his breast pocket, brought out a crisp piece of paper, and pushed it towards me. 'This is a little something from the Old. Ring any bells?'

I scanned the note. It was written in a flourishful, calligrapher's style on fine, creamy parchment:

One man amongst a thousand have I found. But a woman amongst all those have I not found.

I shook my head and, much as I wanted to hurry on to money matters, I held my fire. For he had posed me some quirky questions, which eventually might coalesce into a riddle. And I have long welcomed riddles.

'Let me explain,' he continued. 'I am a man of means. What can I say? Life has been kind to me. I live in the country. A large farmhouse that looks out over rolling land. Acre upon acre! I have fresh water fountains and tree-lined avenues, cherry orchards, fields of lavender, flowers of every shade and delicacy . . .'

Flowers! Did I look like a man interested in flowers?

'And when the trees trap the gentle west winds and blow them over the apple blossom,' he breathed in deeply, no doubt contemplating all his quality shit, 'trust me, Boy, you've never seen so much pretty green!

'But you know how it is. In the country, there are few of our kind. You get lonely sometimes. We all have our needs, you understand my meaning? I need a queen, a woman from this city. A lady to treasure, to make my blessings complete.'

I lit a cigarette and looked at my watch.

'A lady? Listen, boss, I'll tell you this one thing for free. Why don't you just walk out of here, get to a bar or someplace, flash a few of your folds and maybe one of those flowers you're so keen on, and you'll get all the ladies you can deal with—'

'Really, Boy. You mock me. You know I'm looking for quality, a woman of substance.'

'How much substance? Fat? Thin? One with red cherries on top?' I jested. I was thinking of my knives.

'Oh,' he shrugged. 'All that is of no importance. Simply the lady who would like to take up my offer. The lady who would come to my little piece of paradise, wake up of a morning, smell the coffee, and see that it is good.'

'Well, if you're on the real,' I said, 'let me warn you I don't do jobs by the hour, or half days. This will be a full day's whack—'

'A day?' He laughed. 'I think we both deserve a better crack than that. I may be lonely, but not so lonely! A week, I had thought, should be sufficient, one way or the other.'

He dipped into his breast pocket, brought out a wallet and let his eye wander, I felt a little knowingly, across my disk boxes. 'Perhaps a cover-all fee of one hundred thousand would be in order for your full, speedy attention?'

He spread forty folds on my table, each one a cool grand. I pored over them, I checked them, I believe I may even have smelt them. Forty spanking, spring-clean snaps. What kind, crazy person was this?

'Forty now, for expenses, and to satisfy you of my bona fides. The balance on mission complete.'

I nodded. I could barely speak. A weakness had overtaken me. I even forget to try and harry him for any more.

He eased himself up, gently patting his creases.

'I'll bring you a range, supes. You know, like a shortlist. Five, ten, whatever.' For this kind of money I wanted to assure him value.

He shook his head and gestured at the note. 'Just her.'

He had taken my hand and was halfway to the door before I remembered what I had been meaning to ask.

'This woman. How shall I know?'

'Oh, you will know. I trust you. I'll be in touch.'

And that was that.

I locked the door, stuffed his note in my pocket, then contemplated this mad money in front of me, as welcome as pussy in midwinter. Yeah, looked like I was coming in from the cold.

I reached for my arrows and flung a quiverful into the left, west quarter of my board. Treble after treble. Could it be that I was finally getting overs?

2

some pit stops – musings at the necessaries' spot

As dusk stole over, I slipped my lucky silver coins in my breast pocket and grabbed my don't-leave-withouts: keys, phone, night-sights, and a blade from the collection. Underneath I'd fitted my light, laminated kelvar vest, a defence against cuts and caps from underpowered pieces such as my own antique Tanfoglio, which I eventually decided against taking: it was unlikely I'd need it where I was going and, besides, I was feeling lucky. Looked like Luck was being a Lady to me that day.

And although I was way ahead of excitement in the race to the end, I must confess to a certain tingle then, over and above the money matter. For I would now have the opportunity to head out west, where I was sure this business could be swiftly, classily, sorted. I had lacked the occasion to venture down those pampered parts this last while. It would be like, yeah, a holiday.

I believe I may even have hummed a little something as I killed the lights, felt my way down the stairs and landings, and headed out the back way to my ride.

My vehicle was a vintage Datsun Cherry saloon. Its previous owners had painted the car with a long white stripe that gave it a certain distinction. But, in truth, my vehicle was something of a tank – its edges were hard and its snout long and broad. It wasn't pretty, but then neither was the city.

My street was quiet, apart from a few worker bees scurrying to the safety of their vehicles or the public transportation. They cast edgy looks about them every so often. The disturbances that had mushroomed into the Nine-Fevers and won the election for our current bunch of velvet-gloved hardliners were a while back now but the rumblings, notwithstanding the Minister for Special Duties' loud efforts, rumbled on.

I liked to listen to soundtracks in my ride, tunes and incidentals taped from those old-time pictures you rented out from the single-cigarette stores: the ones with martial monks, swords and sorcery and gladiators, young guns and goodfellas, the odd brother with his hand on the steel, champagne, cocaine and much pain come the final reel.

That day I slipped in a thing written for westerns. This particular project was put together by two out-of-state spaghettiheads, one Leone and Morricone, and should I ever come across them in the next world I shall embrace them warmly. For Leone shot his men's faces up close, the way I liked it. Show me a truth – a virtue or vice – that doesn't reveal itself in a man's eyes. And his partner could knock off a pretty melody, with haunting harmonicas and plenty of space and sweep. When I started it up now, and listened to the grandeur of the accompaniment given to my predecessors in related professions, I must confess a sense of pride. The tunes made me feel large, like a knight riding out.

I turned the wheels round and headed down the sideroad that would take me on to the main, and deeper into the SE10s. The west would come soon enough for me, but first I had this little something to invest.

Cash in hand, cash to grow, clearing my debts! . . . I remember my mind did return wonderingly to my client – why opt for this strange route, and why me? – but you'll understand if my thoughts did not linger there, so occupied was I by my own bright future. I thought perhaps he could not do this himself, too shy or blighted in love before, or that this might even be the outcome of some extreme wager struck, post-port and fine wines, at his private club. He seemed a bit gamesy, perhaps not averse to that kind of thing. Whatever. I wasn't *so* puzzled, actually – I had dealt with one or two of these rich, eccentric types before: they'd throw silly money to have a child confirmed or a lady traced from some fleeting ghetto escapade. Not many, clearly, nor any remotely as bountiful, but their fact was not unknown to me.

The streets began to swell as I moved further south. All kinds of area boys and girls, their lives largely nasty and short. For there were six million ways to die but down here they seemed to step on you just for the death of it. No rhyme or reason, riddles beneath the unravelling of them. Guess that's why they called this side the crime side.

I passed the chancers, the pram-pushers, the boners, the clear and present danger-heads. Behind the bruised shop fronts that leant behind the 'Auction' and 'For Sale' signs, the single-cigarette-heads haggled for credit through the bars and grilles.

On the road I saw any number of derelict vehicles, some with religious-heads inside, their window tagged with 'Father Abraham', 'Exodus' and 'Not Today!' But also the Mr Friday Nights, purring past in their fancy wagons. They hooted plenty. Sometimes to hail up a bredrin but more likely to chivvy the buspass people across the road. Hanging like they were at the top of what passed for a tree in these wretched parts.

The inimitable rasp of the horn and the eddy of excitement that turned the pedestrians' heads could only signify one thing. Sure enough, as I rounded the corner, there he was in front – profiling in the passenger seat of his Jeep, three of his camp alongside – our favourite and most thunderous exponent of the gentlemen's game. Despite the evening's chill, the top was open and the tinted windows down, as the main man leant casually out, acknowledging the folk who hurtled towards him:

'Mas-ter Blas-ter!'

'Ay, Blaster! MB, MB!'

Master Blaster dipped into the money bag that lay on his lap and, with an instinct for self-preservation so foreign to his style on the field of play, flicked out folds to all and sundry. Small denomination bills, I grant you, but largesse none the less. This way, no one would come to rob him and his status as the people's champion was assured.

Folk liked to speak proudly of how he still lived on this side. Although he maintained a place here, I understood that in truth he lived out west. But he always did a tour of the soil that bore him during the build-up to Sports Day, stirring up the juices amongst his homeys for the match to end all grudges.

I felt suddenly hungry and pulled over by Nyam Food as the road bore left into the SE19 division. The front had been granted a fresh lick of green paint. You hadn't really noticed the flaky dryness of the front before but, as soon as you saw the paint you thought, yeah it really needed that.

A few middle-aged care-in-the-community types were muttering by the door. Keeping warm, and seeking a sort of company, no doubt. Further in, area boys, desultory, hands thrust deep in their pockets, dotted the walls. They kissed their teeth from time to time for two were serving twenty. The little available attention was being paid to a man who was defending his, uh, honour.

'Me nah come ah steal food. Me come ah buy food, seen?' he yelled stubbornly at the world, waggling don't-fuck-with-me hands.

I understood he was getting grief for whipping slices of fried plantain from the side tray. Oil stains fast speckling his shirt front, and a drunkard's slur, did not help his case.

'Eb'ry, eb'ry year yuh see me – ah you nah know? Eb'ry year, y'hear?'

The veteran behind the till curled his lip and bided his time. I weaved my way to the front as Mr Eb'ry Year grunted and flung a few inadequate coins on the table. I flashed a fat fold and told my man he could kill the change. Eb'ry Year shot me a keen glance, as if he knew me. I did not recognise him and I ignored his look. I was in no mood for words with a listing man. My server attended me and I was out with unheard-about speed.

Outside, I was chomping on my pattie when a police patrol vehicle, two at the front, two at the back, crept past. I fixed on the shards of glass that covered the pavement beside me – the remains of some unfortunate's car window, no doubt – and I was wondering if it was true that you could step through glass and fire without pain if you did it quickly enough when the same ride passed me again. I glanced up to catch the eyes of my keepers and was surprised to find a face that was female and young. The lady betrayed such a blend of fragility and hostility, that I assumed it must be her first day. The division had probably imported her from the west or even the country, in line with current policy. And although she would shortly be affecting the lives of my kind in ugly ways, I had to stifle a strange sadness. I tried to picture her colleagues conducting the tour. Question: what do they say to you on your first day down here?

Sundays' place was about half a mile further down, in this small, modern, state-sector development. The estate wouldn't quite make a You've-Never-Had-It-So-Good tour by the Minister for Special Duties, but you didn't do much better down here. And I welcomed Sundays his crib, despite myself being currently without one. He had paid his dues, and done as little harm as any after forty years on the crime side.

Elaine, the lady of the house and mother to many of Sundays' lighties, had died a month ago. Of one of those antique water-on-the-lungs diseases that had come again amongst us. He had married her in the hospital on the eve of her passing.

I had steered clear of the funeral, these not being my favourite occasions, but had always intended to pass by today's Thanksgiving do, and now my newly acquired collats meant that Sundays and I could finally chat serious business.

Sundays was my weed man. Indeed, I would cheerfully have purchased all the necessaries I needed to make the load light enough from him, but Sundays was a man of inflexibility in this regard. He had no truck with what he called the poisons out there. His competitors had outdone him with their One Stop Spot policies but Sundays made up lost business with an eight days a week work ethic. Days was toiling in a garage, evenings were for his lighties and serving a motley but trouble-free selection from the SE10s.

I had come to his aid once, as some static crackled around with him changing supplier. His original connection, a man all kinds of slack who could not be reached until he rose at two in the afternoon, had suddenly declared that he would no longer take calls on Sundays. At this, my friend had finally lost his cool, raging against 'Dat lickle raashole! Him seh him don't do Sundays cah him rave on Saturday! An' you see how hard me strive? It don't matter what the runnings is! Sundays is the day the wise man get ahead . . .' And so we had called him Sundays from that time on.

'Ay, rude Boy.' Michael, one of Sundays' regulars, hailed me in the hallway. He may even have been one of the legion of Sundays' family. They bore no resemblance but I had never actually seen Michael pay for anything. And when a bunch of us were sat around waiting for Sundays, which was often, Michael would assume an official capacity, operating the land and mobile phones, and sending youths out to procure refreshments.

We touched and I nodded to his people before poking my head into the kitchen.

A girl sat, head lying on her hands, which rested on the table, staring blankly ahead at three men focused on their game of ludo. They hurled mock battle cries of 'Ai!' at each other as they slammed the dice down.

Around them lay the debris of paper plates and plastic cutlery, the remnants of snapper, rice and curried chicken. By the cooker, Natasha, another mainstay, was monitoring a final pot of stew and giving Sundays' daughter a lesson in dressmaking with a pair of scissors and tracing paper. Natasha's face was set in an unfortunate half-moon, her cheeks fat and long, her upper lip cleft and wont to tremble thickly over red gums. She was plain and poor, of no great anything. And I sometimes idly wondered if I knew anyone with as little prospect of getting overs as Natasha. Who or what would rescue her?

But she was sweet-natured and, I understood, soft on me, and for this I teased her from time to time.

I came up behind her and gave her ample midriff a squeeze.

'Fix up a little something for me, ay, Tash?'

Without turning, she stamped on my foot in mock irritation.

I looked for Sundays about the house, exchanging easys by the bathroom door with a music promoter I had not seen for a while. The long crescent of his telephone receiver scar, the legacy of some troublesome negotiations with one of his acts, rose prominently as he chewed on his food. Age had not withered it. Behind him stood a second old acquaintance, fresh from the house of many slams, shaving off his bird beard (or the Beard of Truth, as it was sometimes called, in a nod to the celebrated growth of a local hero, unjustly incarcerated). Tufty clumps dotted the floor.

A few like him apart, the gathering was mainly 'formerly known as' heads, submariners who rarely troubled the radar screens: guys of an age I hoped to reach, of some wisdom and a healthy fear, who had passed the peak hustling years and now settled for the less fretful rungs of the local economy – doing their trades, fixing goods electric or in wood, and cabbing around a community with no collats.

I finally located my man in a room upstairs. The room was barely furnished and a framed, youngish photo of Elaine, leaning against a solitary bouquet, looked lonesome in the middle of it. Beyond it, Sundays was surrounded by the usual suspects: Michael and Hope, as well as another guy I knew by sight who today was suited up but who usually wore different styles of mesh vest, plus this Latino who occupied the honorary homey niche. Sundays squatted on the floor, the frame still trim and sturdy after all these years. He was tapping the laser display on his scales quick-time, and chastising the eldest of his brood. The son and heir seemed to have had trouble distinguishing his fractions from his ounces.

I took my place to head nods and such, but only Hope actually got up to greet me. He loped over and patted me exuberantly on the back with his good hand, so I knew he wanted something.

'Ay, Sundays, go easy on the youth,' Michael said. 'It been a rough few weeks.'

Sundays sucked his teeth wearily as his young one slunk away.

'Him nah run with no discipline! Me haf to play both mother an' father now, and me cyant have stupidness around me. Time to elevate the game and him nah see it yet!'

A thoughtful silence fell over us as we contemplated the gravity of the mother plus father scenario, broken by Natasha's entry. She slipped me a tray and plumped herself expectantly beside me. She wanted to be flirted with, no doubt, but I was determined to finish my dish first.

'So, Boy, when are you taking me out?' she said finally.

'Oh, soon, baby, soon.'

'Better be. Otherwise you're demoted.'

'How about next week or something? We'll go pictures.'

'It's my birthday Tuesday,' she said helpfully. 'Come to my yard and none of your deep lateness.'

Michael smiled as he watched the unfolding of the latest bout in our long-established cut and thrust, wondering how I would extract myself from this one. The Latino joined him with a little cackle. He was one of those honoraries who never risked jeopardising his position by initiating anything, preferring to wait for the wind to blow.

I licked my fingers, and took hold of the bag of bush that Sundays had tossed over to me. The bush was in fine, grainy pieces, courtesy of his coffee grinder; somehow the draw seemed to last longer this way. 'I can't take you Tuesday, Tash,' I said. 'That's your special day and your special man's got to take you that day, innit? How can I see you on your birthday and we haven't even started yet?'

As Natasha wrestled with a comeback, Hope begged a sizeable piece off of me. I wondered why he could not appeal to Sundays, but no doubt he was already deep in his debt. His eyes could not meet mine but darted around my body and my bag. Not because he was trying to salvage some dignity, but because he was someway ill and did not behave differently at close quarters.

My policy towards beggars was not an indulgent one, albeit I tended to relax on this here, as etiquette demanded in one's spot of choice. However, Hope was another matter again. This guy was so faulty you didn't even want him to owe you a favour. His simp thinking had left him with two fingers short of the monty, after he'd sold some nastiness instead of the Holyfield on what remained of our frontline. After that he'd gone missing until a concerned Sundays had tracked him down and brought him here, where Hope now hibernated, no doubt plotting another quality skank.

But my man had come for me that afternoon, and I had had two helpings of dinner that evening. I was, near enough, happy. I nodded and Hope snatched my bag and babbled like the brook.

'Yeah, yeah, yeah, yeah! Is all we have, you know,' his good hand manoeuvred the greens with a deftness born of necessity, 'looking out for our bredren, sistren still . . .' Hope, the living clear and present danger-head. He would have been better called Despair.

'So wha', Sundays, you expect you get another woman?' asked Mesh Vest.

'Mmm,' replied Sundays distractedly, still breaking down, measuring and bagging his blocks. 'Me feel so.'

'What kind o' gyaal?'

Sundays stretched out on a rug opposite us, his head rested on an upturned arm. 'If she too chatty-chatty, me nah interested. If she too hunty-hunty, me nah interested. Me just need someone who can fit into dis structure here.'

'Ah right,' agreed Michael. 'Someone who can help you keep tings ticking along.'

'I'm on the lookout too, as it happens,' I said and, after an apologetic look sideways at Natasha, furnished brief details of my latest case. And I welcomed this chance to let them know that once again I was in business and in demand. Matters had been rough of late and word would soon get about that I was now living in my office. If you could only give the impression that your stock was rising then a hooligan might step on you tomorrow rather than today. And true, finding a girl was hardly the kind of manly pursuit on a par with my greatest hits but it was gainful employment nonetheless.

'A girl fit for a king in his castle. Me understan'.' Sundays was intrigued.

'You get different, different volumes of girls,' reflected Mesh Vest. 'Sweet girl, sour girl, rub up 'n' ting girl—'

'Him nah want a girl like, say, one of dem Bedouin would have in their harem,' interrupted Sundays, 'concubine, yeah? Him want *quality*.'

'You best fill up your tank and reach far out,' advised Michael, 'cah the women dis side dem too hardback.'

'Ehnit though!' added the Latino.

'If the women are hardback, you don't need to look far to find out why,' retorted Natasha. 'Granted, life run rough for both same—'

'I don't cut you, still,' Sundays gestured apologetically in her direction, 'but what it is, see, most of the girls dem *start* decent, then dem get a man, maybe two or three. And what happen, right, eh, right yeah, is dem get *bad* man. And, from dem adopt the principles and perspective of that man, dem spirit turn, y'understan'?'

'You lay wid dog, you rise wid flea,' agreed Mesh Vest.

'Don't look to her material, look to her sensibility. You don't want a girl that can't give you nuff conversation. Why bother with it?' urged Michael. 'One glorious bash – it's no big ting.'

'Ah true. But still the sexiest ones are the quietest ones,' Sundays insisted. He turned to me, kind of confidentially, 'Dem the ones who pour out the sex on you.'

'A nice, loving, single lady? . . . Hmm. It not easy,' Mesh Vest shook his head.

'Dem *too* nice. Dem tink we're wort'less, rasta, wort'less! Tink we're rubbish,' Hope shouted. He seemed suddenly depressed, but then his eyes lit up. 'Me haf a girl one time. Come back to the hotel now, a lickle dance an' business, a lickle advance an' business, nice, nice! Me nature rise an' me moving to undress her now, slowlike an', an' . . . me find *tings*. The girl haf tings!' He pointed at his own tackle. 'Me jus' box the girl so and kick him bombaclaat out!'

We creased up as Hope admonished, 'Watch out for the lady boys dem!' Hope always had a stream of tall stories which he trotted out with relish and the merest twinkle. What with his recent steep decline, I had forgotten how droll he could be.

Much as I was enjoying the thoughts of Sundays and his people I could not count on so much of its relevance. What knowledge could

they possibly have gained of premier league ladies in their strictly
southside lives? I myself had little form in the matter. Oh, I had dab-
bled for a period, but I found I rarely welcomed the whole
loss-leading business of intimacies with women. Most of the time
now, when surplus built up, I went out and paid for its release.

'So, you haf any ideas? A sniff for someone?' asked Michael.

I shook my head. 'I've got some places though, in—'

'Why don't you go look up the Race Man? Me hear seh him in
town.'

I smiled at the news. It did not surprise me that he should arrive
at this point of general ill omen. The Race Man did not come when
you called, but he was always on time just the same. No doubt he
would already be knee-deep in consultation as supplicants sought
salvation in the one place where they did not have to face the judgement of their peers. But you had to husband your appeals: you were
only permitted three pitches to him in a lifetime. And even then, he
was wont to answer your question with a question, or else a deep
riddle. Some insisted that we needed a Wise One who was more
hands-on, or who at least had his authority recognised by the state,
but they grumbled quietly for, notwithstanding his infrequent
attendance, it was understood that his ears and eyes were everywhere.

I was yet to take up any of my dispensation. But despite this, and
the evidence of the disappointed, I felt someway close to an appreciation of his ways. I had had my thoughts and was certain that the
key to gaining satisfaction lay in the phrasing of the question. No
doubt we would link up once everything was ready.

'Me see him one time, an' boy!' said Hope, eyes twinkling, 'the
brother *deep*. See Sundays' – he pointed to Sundays' three-feet-long
mane – 'all o' dat is like a single lock on him head!'

'You lie!' challenged Michael. 'Ain't no one actually seen him.
Man an' man say all you see is shadow and smoke. Lots of smoke.'

'Yeah yeah,' Hope took the objection in his stride, 'him puff a serious Planet Zion chalice.'

'Where you see him?' scoffed Natasha.

'On the street dere. Live-o, I'm telling you! Me just easing along – taking my mornin' constitutional an', an' this Merc park up an' my man step out. Him hol' a staff in front of him,' Hope rose to re-enact the scene, 'and him covered in robe an' a greybeard that stretch down so. An' him turn to me and rumble, "I have seen many things." Him voice like *thunder*, an' me bones just start to rattle—'

'Is wha' you arks him when you see him?' Michael tested.

He had been cued up neatly but Hope was flummoxed for an instant.

'We reason that day, bredrin. Philosophy, the state, everyt'ing an' everyt'ing. We talk about law: batty law and ganja law. How can batty be legal and ganja illegal, enh? How can man sex man an' lady boy up there and the police dem nah interfere, but still police come an' start wit' we? What kind o' state we livin' in?' Hope thudded the point home as we cracked up again.

'Race Man come an' go as him feel,' groused Mesh Vest. 'Cha! Him nah care fe we.'

Sundays hushed him.

'Me hear seh him a voodoo spirit– like the ruggedest, baddest obeah man,' said Michael.

'What it is, see, he's a man who, like, fed himself right,' Natasha insisted. 'You know how we try an' feed our body in every which way and it never enough? Cos what we really need to satisfy is the soul, and that's hungry still, y'unnerstan'. Feed the spirit and the body will . . . will all right, you know.'

'That's more like it,' I struggled to articulate my instincts. 'We've all got what he's got within us. He's just a man that's made himself more refined than the rest of us. He learns stuff, and throws away stupid stuff, so he's constantly purifying, moving up the chambers. It's like every cycle is bigger and better than the last, takes him higher and closer to nature. So that now he's as old as the hills, and can harness all that power out there. It's like boxing. You don't catch a fighter sexing before a fight, or drinking his dome off. He's gotta triumph over temptations, an' just sip nutrients and carrot juice an' all that, innit? Same way with the Race Man. Every day for him is like the eve of the big fight.'

Hope tried out some boxing moves on the Latino before touching my arm.

'If you go see the Race Man, bring back a blessing for me,' he said quietly.

I told him I would, although I was not sure that the Race Man did blessings, then took my goods, said my goodbyes and beckoned Sundays outside.

With him seated beside me, I pulled my car round to the side of his home for some concealment.

'So what's today's mathematics, bro?'

'Boy!' He shook his head. 'Famine ah lick still. Everyone's waiting for something prime and most of what I can get, or leastways afford, is just commercial. And now Sports Day come up, right—'

'You going to that?'

'Definitely. The boom that everytime.'

'Yeah.'

'But you know dem style! They're hanging on to what they have, waiting for maximum hunger to mount, then make their killing. Tch! I ain't making money serving people no more, you know.'

I knew he was speaking true. Footsoldiers like Sundays did not enjoy times of famine and inflation either. Their cost prices soared and they couldn't make real dividends. Only the big boys would be laughing.

'They're trying to change round the market, isn't it? Cheaper buying bones these days,' I said.

Sundays nodded bitterly. 'Me can't stand it much longer.'

'Just give me as good as it gets.'

'Low grade, you're talking bush at one hundred and twenty, sticks and that gummy silver at one hundred and eighty. Indica and sess two hundred plus—'

'Nine-bars, sir, not ounces.'

'Wha'? You find a big pot of gold?'

I reached down, felt inside my right sock for the bundle of notes that I had taped to my leg, and handed them to him.

'That's fifteen fat ones there, some of the advance my client gave me. I want you to buy me up as much as you can, all sorts. Don't worry, I won't be troubling your neck of the woods, an' thirteen per cent goes your way at anything over ten Ks.'

He looked at me intently as I fired a cigarette, and gazed at the windscreen, and the dark beyond.

'Look, bro, this whole messed-up manor is about to blow – we both know it. All this politician talk about curfews an' prosecuting the peace.' I turned to him. 'It's gonna get worse and it's gonna get worst about here.'

'Ah true.'

'I'm getting out, dread, I'm sorry. This is it, this is my ticket right here. I'm gonna get this girl, collect on the balance, and then retire. Dunno. Even move out west, if things run sweet. Invest in this thing, serve all the soft ones down that side, and just kick back while I wait on bigger plans.'

Two guys took up residence by the shops ahead of us, their hands in their coat pockets, getting their hustle on.

'Yuh see them with their street dreams!' I sneered. 'Gotta hustle in the boardroom, cuz. Like you were saying, elevate the game. Check it. Down here, you get long-time lockdown. Out west now, if even they get you, you'll be loungin' in some open, leafy resting-home for a few months. Long dick style – barbecued wings with all the trimmings, an' hot cherry pie for afters!'

Sundays chuckled. 'I'm with you, Boy. You get the chance, you gotta get overs.'

'No question.'

'But you still haf to find the girl dat fit the slipper! Fe real . . .' He looked thoughtful.

'You know, most women, they wanna be the First Lady to something. Now your client sure sound like something. And you too, yeah, right, you gotta come like something to bring them in, y'unnerstan'?'

He eased himself out of the car, then leant down at the window and patted the wad. 'Nah worry about this. Come check me in a few, y'hear?'

'You think you can handle it?'

He nodded and touched my fists. 'Pro-tection!'

'All right, then. Mind how you go, yo!'

'Give t'anks,' he urged, in righteous fashion, and watched as I swung the ride round and pulled away.

One final pit stop. With Sundays' words in my ears as much as anything, I upgraded my wheels at Sammy's rental to a crimson nine series Beemer. A touch flashy, possibly, but when in Rome and all that. I told him that I would be back for my Datsun in a couple of days. He all but collapsed, gurgling and such, as I produced G notes without fuss and held them to the light to prove they were the Holyfield.

Back on the road, I barely registered the lights stripping down from the helicopters above, or the ground ones patrolling with their taser guns, for my head was set on the west.

3

'I scream, you scream, we all scream, "Ice Cream"!'

My pulse quickened as I approached the bridges, the gateways to everything else. A couple took you east, into the old city, but most took you to the end – or the beginning, you understand, from my direction – of the west.

Aaah, the bridges. Their sight at night! A thousand little lights beckoning the cars on their thousand little missions. You could make fat swerves as the lanes widened on the approach, pick up speed once you hit your chosen one, and smile once again at the pleasure to be had behind a wheel. Even make a night of it as the boy racers had taken to doing on the SW3 bridge, whirling in their customised Escorts and fat-bumpered Fiestas, with indulgent emergency services in attendance. But all the while, your own efforts were dwarfed by the greater majesties around you. The murky expanse of water to right and left. So easy, so near to fall and barely a murmur down there. And the undaunted slabs of cross-stone, with their cross-arches, their rivets, their repetition, erected to govern this expanse, and assert the triumph of men.

So when I am asked, as I sometimes am by some depressed new arrival, to talk of some beauty in the city, I return to the bridges. One such man, who had rashly joined us from his state across the channel, told me that his capital city was full of such stony grandeur, the places of work and rest being blocks of polished white stone. He said that the suburbs, the places where our kind lived, was a different story, but the city proper flaunted untold statues and monuments, while triumphal arches lined the grand boulevards most everywhere you looked. These great projects had begun, he explained, by bull-dozing through the rebellious slum areas of the town a century and a half ago.

Yet it did not surprise me that my friend's pretty city, despite its vaulting ambition, had already suffered much subsequent mutiny and painful rebirths. Here our own masters had displayed less pre-sumption in this matter. Our monuments were scattered, our grand developments half-cut, apart from these bridges. It almost seemed they had built these bulwarks as their sole concerted effort against the chaotic shapes about them and understood they could do little more.

Sometimes I would get out of my ride and stand on one of the bridges. It's difficult to explain but, whenever I stood and looked there, I always got something bigger than what I'd put in. I might gaze up to its lights, and beyond them to the villages that had sprung up piecemeal around the original centres, and that now made up this town. I might think of the rings and patterns of the city, and toss small change or stones below and think of rings again when they hit the water. I might just let the scene – the accidents, the design, the deep – flow over me and gain a sense of how they all played their part in, uh, natural justice. And that the connecting threads were here, right here, if I could just overstand it right.

Most times I would leave those bridges bitterly, frustrated by this peace and power that I did not know how to apply.

I think, when I do finally go to see the Race Man, this is the kind of matter I'll probe him about . . . Have to ask him to allow me at least two queries though; leave space for my beginnings . . .

The circumstances and whereabouts of my birth remain unclear, but my mother later spoke of the night of my discovery in these parts, the night they found me, only a few months in, wrapped in swaddling clothes inside a grocer's bag, and lying in a doorway. A noisy bundle, I imagine. Certainly, I did something to attract the attention of the couple who now stood above me.

'Is it a boy or a girl?' asked the man.

The woman tugged at my tings.

'It's a boy.'

'Oh, then let it be called "Boy".'

Our introductions completed, they took me in and gave me a home, in the general way. And although I was found deep in the city, I like to think, and have often maintained, that I was abandoned there after a start in the country. How else could I explain my slight sentiment for that lady officer before, or my fondness for red cherries?

I parked up in a little lane by the west's end's big theatres and a row of pricey clothes stores. It was strange to see so many young ones around, shopping, giggling and holding hands. Especially the hands – there wasn't much of that on my side.

The place I had in mind was a rather chic little supermarket around the back. Here, after a long day in their local gigs, uptowners descended to pick up a few groceries before hurrying on with their busy, responsible lives. The store, ran the word of mouth, was something of a meeting-point for eligible twenty- and thirtysomethings.

My plan was a straightforward one. I would introduce myself to a few reasonable-looking sistren, get a measure of their situations and their qualities – take them out, if necessary, and then ask the 'best' one to consider my client's offer. Fair enough, I think you'd agree.

The shop was due to close in half an hour. Time enough. I dabbed some drops on my eyes, an instant remedy for my time at Sundays, popped a mint in my mouth, and sauntered in.

I noted with approval the sophisticated, foreign names that adorned the fruit 'n' veg section – shallots, mange-tout and such – and the knee-to-ankle-length coat of superior cut worn by such as the couple I passed, reasoning in educated tones by the fine wines.

I made my stand in front of the mixed salad selection, took my car keys out so they were in view for any interested parties, and waited.

The first few ladies down my aisle were non-starters. One looked like a boy. Nothing wrong with that in itself. Indeed, it was something I often found fetching. But she looked like an ugly boy. Another's figure was hard to tell, under the flowing skirts, but her nether regions seemed to carry about them a lardy blockiness that encumbered her gait. But soon enough a woman who exuded a classy, steely beauty approached. She was well dressed and well upholstered, with curves that were full, if not incontrovertibly child-bearing. Only these qualities did not play in a generous way, as is generally the case. Her air was somewhat severe. I could picture her taking the birch to a wayward maid, before returning to the painting of her nails and the supervising of the dinner being prepared for the big boys, where she would play the charming if no-nonsense hostess.

Not exactly my bag, but quite possibly my man, no stranger to the hard nose of the business world, might welcome it. If business was what he did.

I threw her a winning smile, which got no change at all. She looked through me and reached up to the shelf. It was only when she had deposited her microwaveable meal-for-one inside her tray and sneaked a glance at my still winning self that I saw the set of her face soften a little. Whether this was on account of my evenly distributed

frame or my nine series keys, I cannot say, although I have my
hunches.

'Excuse me,' I began. 'Do you know what time this place shuts?'

'Dunno. Next half an hour, I think.'

'Cheers.'

If she had moved on directly, I would have left it. But she left her
door ajar.

'No, it's just that I'm expecting someone. We're supposed to be
linking up here, only he doesn't know town very well. You didn't see
an emerald Lexus four-wheel parked up outside, did you?'

Her friendliness moved measurable bounds.

'Your friends have expensive tastes,' she said.

'Hey! Nah.' I smiled. 'It's just my boss. He's not in town very
often. He's staying over in a place out west and wants me to show
him the sights. All the quality young, single action. Only I don't
really know the story down this side. Don't suppose I could give you
a ring for consultation?'

'Now that's a roundabout way to do it.'

'Sis, I'm serious. No joke.'

She pondered me an instant, then slipped a hand in an inside
pocket.

'If you're serious, and you, or your boss, want to give me a bell,
then I just might find the time.'

She handed me her card. 'Lincia Forde. Media – Publicity –
Marketing' – I noted the solid midtown number.

'Nice, nice. I'm Boy, by the way.'

She nodded and was gone.

Back in my car, I stored Lincia's number in a safe cranny of my
wallet, next to the note my man had left me. I started the motor and
smirked. A solid start, and now the likeliest bet of the day beckoned
me – the land of Ice Cream.

Ice Cream! I scream / You scream / We all scream / "Ice Cream"!

The ads, with their jingly-jangly catchphrase, had been busting out of the box for weeks, plugging the joys of the state's first 'exclusive, all-inclusive black lifestyle resort'. As I understood it, you could savour many of the modes of behaviour that we were famous for within controlled, secure conditions, thus bypassing the difficulties of any encounters you might have should you, ah, sample the product in its naked form. Deep-pocketed punters parted with a certain number of folds at the reception, depending on whether their stay was for the night or the week, and after that you need never dip in there again. All your needs were catered for.

It was a neat idea, and the latest money-spinner of one Merciless, a champion hustler, wicked like three sixes, and a man whose progress from the street to the boardroom I had watched with some envy. Merciless – so dubbed because, as he'd once boasted, 'Me lose all my mercy and me nah get it back yet!' – had served his apprenticeship as the hard man in a junior mafia, kidnapping and robbing, before getting the rep together to set up a stable of girls in SE13. Then he had disappeared and re-emerged, repositioned as a righteous community radical. The city had been doing all our heads in, he had proclaimed, but now he had seen the light and we should all head back to the root country, where at least we were wanted, without delay. Many folk had agreed and soon the coffers of Uncle M's travel agency, set up to facilitate passage, swelled with lifetime savings. (Even I, when approached by one of his army of fragrant five-year-olds brandishing a flier, had had a moment of weakness, before I remembered who their employer was.) Then once again Uncle M had flown by night, leaving behind brooks customers and a clutch of contracts on his head.

The next we had heard was that Merciless was somewhere in the suburbs, running another stable, but this time of horses, and we had spotted him on the box at the bookies, top-hatting his way around race meetings, sipping fine wines with the high rollers. Perhaps some of them were the real powers behind this latest venture, but he was certainly the front man.

And Ice Cream's star attraction most definitely had his stamp on it: a stable of slammin' hostesses in bunny outfits, sporting names like Crème Caramel, Chocolate Chip, Brown Sugar, Butter Pecan and, my favourite from the ads, a lady whose handle was Morello Cherry. Their uniforms were not the most, ah, dignified, but they looked one hundred per cent more refined than the brawly puddings you used to slip a bone to back in those SE13 days, and, if not these, there would surely be other members of staff, other possibilities, circulating. Given their daily tending of big wheels, my man would not find them wanting.

The problem was to find the place. It was located deep in the W9s, an area that I understand was more popularly known as Notting Hill before the Nine-Fevers. Back then, as was recalled tearfully by longer-toothed associates of mine, it was on a par with the west's end as hustler's heaven. You could have been run out of every hard-core space around, played all your aces in vain, and still make a tidy skanking the tourists of all types that congregated in these areas.

But I had not been down this part for some while, and my street maps were out of date following the redevelopment that had paved the way for the theme park. To have betrayed any ignorance to the officers that pulled me over when I hit the west proper would have been foolhardy. I had already antagonised them with a cheeky reply to their initial inquiry, 'Where have you come from?' A perennial query with such people, and one whose usefulness I am yet to understand. 'Shopping,' I replied before adding, as they checked my seat and my boot for bags, 'Window shopping.' But before they could haul me out of my ride and whatever, I produced my papers, including my PI certificate for the west. They radioed the details through but everything was in order and all they had left was to ask me where I was going. My reply – 'Ice Cream' – brought hoots and halitosis through my open window. 'Bring back a scoop for us!' one leered as I took my leave.

There was nothing for it, then, but to ask the locals for directions. And here was a bleakly funny thing. For I had imagined that my top car and smart-casual attire would alleviate the usual problems encountered when men of my kind accost natives after dark. But these helped me not a jot. Some simply ignored me and carried on; another approached then edged away, mumbling something; still others broke out in a trot at my 'Excuse me', heading for the other side of the road. Like I'm fond of saying, trust is even iller than you think.

But then I saw it. I was driving slowly by the park, half a mile off the main, when there it was in front of me. Perched on a little hill was a giant triple-headed café au lait cone, with a native, nuclear family licking happily from it. The cone and building it fronted seemed hewn into the side, so that it reminded me of a picture I have seen of dead presidents on a mountain. Hundreds of multi-coloured neon bulbs that lit up one after the other in a continuous whirl studded the structure. No doubt the flavour was one of the spotted kind. Rum and raisin came to mind. More bulbs lit up a slogan, 'Salivate – Taste – Recreate!' running underneath.

I parked up by some other rides out front. To my left was a space reserved, I imagined, for the long-stayers and big boys where attendants, in peaked caps and khaki uniforms, took care of everything from stretch limos to family Escorts. I sauntered to join the queue ahead, looking up to get a closer view of the sculpture.

You could not but admire its detail and ambition. I thought to our own public art, and struggled to get beyond the brutally pink and preposterous Elephant and Castle that marked the gateways to the south. But art, I understand, follows money, and I was now in the thick of it.

Not that this was so easy to spot in the crowd around me. The

punters, all native, ranged mainly from late teens to thirties, with a
few female under-agers in giggling groups. These last, hale with the
insouciance of happy homes, were actually the best packaged, in
hipster pants, little tops, and chains draped across bare, puppy fat
navels. But some of the men, in stiff jackets and jeans combos,
looked unsure whether they had come to work or to rave. For the
rest, the best that could be said was that they exhibited a scruffy chic:
utility, rough and ready trousers, sturdy lived-in shirts, necks and
wrists festooned with Aztec accessories. One girl beside me, entertaining her people in pukka tones, had clearly had extensions put in
her hair just recently, only they had coalesced into a single dirty
dreadlock that now hung down her head.

Hardly styles, with their nods to manual labour, that would pass
muster on my side. There we were all about rocking names. And yet
here were the ones who could afford to hang in the west, had steady
eddie futures where they need never get their hands dirty, and whose
incomes were as safe as their houses. While my neighbours, despite
the labels and price tags that they showed, frequently had no fixed
abode. I pondered on the secret of these people's success, and what
clothes had to do with it, whilst I waited.

The only ones of my kind were the two bouncers manning the
doors, whom I eyed warily. For such men in my life had been nothing but trouble. Bullies, brutes and fools, they were the lowliest
specimens in the thug life. Unable to rise above the ranks of
enforcers, they plied the door trade as a convenient legal conduit for
their fuckries and my hand reached behind my right shoulder, to
feel the blade taped there, for routine reassurance.

My two were decked in all the trappings. Black from head to toe,
with walkie-talkies strapped to heavy bulletproof jackets that bulked
out their already sizeable frames, each carried long pieces of lead
piping. They looked dumbly but powerfully into the middle distance, giving the natives that passed them only a cursory glance.

They clocked me with startled expressions, then cranked up a gear. One began thwacking his pipe from one hand to the other whilst the second rolled his neck in preparatory fashion and clenched his fist.

As I came up to the door, this one put his hand up to stop me.

'Sorry, mate, you can't come in.'

'Ah, leave it out, boss.' I tried to move forward again but his hand stayed firm and he brought his weight up.

'You ain't comin' in, all right?'

His partner came to join him.

I blew hard. 'What's the problem?'

'Dress code. That's the problem. It's smart casual, not sportswear.' He pointed to my feet. 'No labels.'

My shoes (a touch like trainers with their half-inch of black springy sole but, other than that, most definitely shoes) had the maker's mark discretely tagged to the laces. The designer had originally made his name in yachtwear for the big boys, but was currently, perhaps for aspirational reasons, heavily favoured by many of us in the south. Apart from this, I was dressed in pressed cotton threads with no labels in sight.

I ran my eye over the queue and let out an indignant laugh.

'Listen, blood, I seen you letting in the livin' buskers and bag ladies tonight, so don't tell me nothing about these.'

'He said, "You can't come in,"' said his second in dull, moronic tones, not meeting my eyes but looking slightly past me, the way such types do. 'Come back with a change of shoes and a girl an' then we start talkin'. This ain't no pick-up place.'

I seethed. My prize was the other side, and here was I having to beg of these fools. I scanned the crowd for a girl who could possibly assist me in this situation. A few of them looked on anxiously, but most seemed expectant and excited, perhaps wondering if this was part of the entertainment. Even if I prevailed on one of them to take my hand, it seemed hardly likely to save me from what these custodians clearly intended to be an extended humiliation.

I faced the pair again. The first's nose was fat and broken, whilst his partner appeared permanently cross-eyed. They smirked and girded themselves, hungry for an incident. I pictured how they must stand here, night after night, dutifully letting in grey after grey, grinding their teeth but mindful of their jobs. Now at last they had someone they thought they could safely make unhappy.

'You're holding up the queue. Better move on, suh.'

'Ease up now, bredrin.' I held up my hands. 'Why you wanna carry on so stink for? I just wanna have me a little drink, kick back, relax—'

'Nah, man,' the second guy was shouting now. 'A club is a club and rules are rules, y'unnerstan'? Bredrin or no bredrin!'

The first man cackled as his second shoved me again.

'All right, all right!' I patted the wallet at the back of my trousers, and indicated a corner wall some yards down from us. 'Come now.'

Bouncer two followed me, lumbering heavily behind. As we turned the corner I pulled out thirty folds.

'Here, boss. A little token for you and your partner, yeah?'

He took the money, then suddenly spun and flung me against the wall, so my hands went up instinctively to protect my face. My fingers grazed and gripped the wall, as he brought piping crashing against my back. I sagged for a moment as he snarled, 'Keep your paws up, tah rahtid!'

There is always a sick feeling in the stomach in these situations, but I was not afraid. I had been complacent for a minute there, but now I was ready again. The blow from the piping had, funny thing, given me all the encouragement I needed. The pipe was hollow. It had not made anything like the impact I would have otherwise expected. These hooligans were ice cream.

The man had plucked my wallet from my trousers and was busy rifling through it.

'Carry on stink? Me show you stink, rich boy! Me bus' up your bloodclaat!'

'Take it an' see if I don't step on yuh head.'

'Ey, fockhead?'

I quarter-turned and cracked him short-arm back-fist across his face, deflecting his piping and kicking him in his tings in three fluid motions. He grunted and flashed out as he buckled, but I moved in straight and kicked his legs from under him. I whipped my blade from my 'blade and jumped on him, my knee under his chin. My first thought was how to send him to the other side of life because, once you had started, it was unwise to leave business unfinished in this town. But the instinct to stick him between his third and fourth and fuck his respiratorial could not be executed with his protective vest. So I brought my knife up to his face and he squealed and sweated whilst I ran through my options. No doubt I could slit his throat and fade away. But then I would have to miss Ice Cream tonight, and lie low for a while. I would prefer to reach, and enjoy, my retirement with minimum heat. Moreover, I am someone keen on proportion and what he had done he did not deserve to die for. So I put his right forearm in a lock and satisfied myself with ripping his middle finger from its joint.

'Shut up,' I hissed, bringing my other hand to his mouth. There was another agonised squawk but his terror and my fingers, now dug deep in his throat, strangled anything more.

'Me from a serious part of town, y'get me? We nah ramp, starr! I'm the southside cleaning services, I'm the *Dirt Devil*, y'unnerstan'? Enh? Cos you don't know how vicious me get when I'm nice with people and dem fuck with me! Me's an undercover cold-hearted man, trust me 'pon dat!'

I relaxed my grip. 'You got people inside the place proper?'

He shook his head. 'We just do the door. We can't go no place else.'

I looked at him. The weakness of the man was there right in his iris. He wasn't lying.

'All right. Hear what now. I'm gonna walk through the front, and you're gonna cool yourself here, and everything's gonna be dandy. And, if your luck's in, we don't see each other again.'

I fished in his pockets for my thirty notes, picked up my blade and wallet and left him, hunched and hand-cradling, to return to the door.

No problem this time. I winked confidently and, though his associate looked at and beyond me curiously, he didn't even reach out for the frisk.

I padded down a thickly carpeted corridor, its walls covered in paintings of grinning song and dance minstrel types, their flattened bodies drawn with flamboyant lines and exaggerated coon features. A small throng was clustered at the reception, attended to by four ladies who stood behind a long desk. They moved briskly in beige blouses and skirts, straightened hair tied back, processing bankers' cards and such. Any large amount of cash they passed to either of two men, also in club beige, who stood in front of what I presumed was a little cash strongroom to the right.

The pictures that bedecked the walls were of a similar breezy and untroubled nature to those in the corridor, although here the accent was more on the pastoral. Studies of woodsmen, Man Fridays and sugar cane cutters beavering away under bright suns. Pride of place went to a beach scene. In the foreground fishermen offered their catch and dark, cheery waiters served drinks on trays to seated figures, perched on the verandah of a plantation-style Big House. I suppose these last were well-heeled holidaymakers, or else foremen and their families. A mauve horizon presided over proceedings. Masters and servers at one with each other and nature.

'Art, sis! You can't beat it!' I said, by way of introductory conversation.

'Short stay or long stay, sir?' No interest in chit-chat, clearly.

'Oh, short stay – short stay, I think.'

'Are you alone or with a partner, sir?'

'Just me, myself and I.' I smiled.

'That'll be six hundred pounds, sir.'

'Six hundred?' I could not believe it. 'Just for a club night? Nah, girl. Say it ain't so!'

'Ice Cream is not a club.' She rolled her 'Don't come to me with your poor, difficult black ways' eyes, and said firmly, 'It is a resort for all the family. Rates are five hundred a day for couples and families, six hundred a day for singles. For that you have meals and beverages when you want, as often as you want, as much as you want, and a room for the night.'

'I don't want a room. I'm just in and out here.'

'Six hundred a day for a single is the minimum charge.'

I looked at her. Was she the flexible type? Was she fuck.

'All right, all right,' I said and reached for my wallet.

I gazed at the roll of honour board behind her as she tapped away at her keyboard. All Ice Cream's patrons and sponsors were there, from various drink and cigarette manufacturers to our city's tourist board. Beside it, a photo of a beaming Merciless with a beaming Minister, scissors in hand, and below it the touching declaration: 'A tenth of all monies from Ice Cream go to projects in the developing world.' I had me a wry smile at the man's consistency. Whatever venture he moved on to, Uncle M always found a place for his favourite charities.

'If you'll be wanting to change, sir, the rooms are first on the left as you go through,' my girl said, handing me a plastic arrow of a key marked 117.

'What – a cloakroom?'

'Changing rooms,' she said firmly.

I walked past the doors marked 'Homeboys' and 'Honeys'. I had brought no spares and I saw no reason to change. I was currently elegant, not flashy, and perfectly happy with that. But I began to understand her urgings as I followed the sounds of music, pushed open a heavy door, and stepped into the Sarah Bartmann room.

Under whirling lights and a wall of jump-up calypso rhythms, one hundred punters danced and ran about in various states of undress. The women favoured bikini swimwear and the men knee-length shorts and baretops, gleaming wet with sweat. Some flung their T-shirts about their heads, shrieking, 'Par-tay! Par-tay!' while others had congregated in a long line and lurched around, one hand on the shoulder of the figure in front, enjoying an ancient ritual that I understand is known as the conga. There were few of my kind there, but those that were seemed immensely popular.

I did not tarry here, nor in the Hattie McDaniel room next door, where a stripper – skin of sable and tackle admirably thick and curling, like plantain – was doing his thing. He had dispensed with his PVC boots and waistcoat, leaving just his leather thong and a giant witchdoctor's headdress. Yelping ladies clambered over one another to knead him with lotions.

I ambled down the Middle Passage, past the crèche and the Rent-a-Dread room – where a member of staff was coolly explaining to two agitated ladies that all the Dreads were pre-booked and they would have to make do with a couple of bald-headed escorts instead – searching for the place most likely to contain my prey.

My ticket was at the end, where the corridor gave way to an arched doorway, topped by the company cone. Beside the door, in a glass case and sloping script, ran: 'Welcome to the All Sorts Brasserie. Come and dine, sip fine wines, and enjoy the company of our delectable hostesses'.

Past the tasteful aquarium, palm tree and potted plants, down some marble steps, and I was in a roomy atrium, pleasantly cool and airy. To my left, chefs stood behind glass counters stacked with fresh fruits, the fish of the day and buffet business, while ahead of me stretched tables for two and larger parties, and a man in black tie tinkling behind a piano, until some more steps took you up again to an intimate cocktail bar, with booths along one side. I settled myself about midway down, at a discreet two-table. I had a good view of the space and my back was to the wall, the way I liked it.

The menu confirmed my hopes. There, under the sponsors' names, and above the motto 'Any flavour, so long as it's black', ran the names from the adverts, adorning little tubs of promise. No actual photos, but no matter. I could make out a couple of hostess types further down and, even as I scanned the card, one of them approached me.

She was styled in the bunny outfit: fitted cream blouse and an A-line gym skirt with a flossy cotton stump on the derrière.

'Yes, sir? What can I do you for?'

I glanced at her name tag and scrutinised her swiftly. Rum and Raisin, eh? I confess I was disappointed. Her complexion was most fair, pre-albino but post a lot else, and spotted liberally with black freckles, as if she had never fully recovered from some infant pox. I ordered a bottle of Veuve Clicquot and a double Hennessy, and asked if Morello Cherry could bring it back for me. I fancied that a little irked look crossed her face, but she nodded and said she would see to it.

I lit a cigarette and relaxed. I had nothing against the boisterousness of youth, but it was nice to be in a room where your company had clothes on. And what company! Here were public figures seated round and about, kingmakers with their current consorts, praise-singers and gravediggers. I could have done without the imminent arrival of some wareseller, limping his way on crutches towards me. Three pairs of shades were pressed to his hair, bangles and bracelets cluttered up his forearms, and he grasped a tray of goodies that dangled around his neck, like a cinema usher. I could not place the limp, but there was something familiar in the face and the frame. Rah – Sinbad!

The last time I had seen Sinbad he had not seen me, but before then we had enjoyed something of an acquaintance. I had first come across the man back in the day during my period running with a small neighbourhood crew. One time, I had headed, with expansion in mind, to the N4s, where I had heard word of a set blessed with the rare bonus of a continental connection. Sinbad – whose tawny skin, coolie hair, fine straight nose and lips like dinghies marked him out as a man of varied provenance – was getting by there as a glorified courier. Glorified because his forefathers had bequeathed him some familiarity in diverse languages and this meant that Sinbad got to travel as a vital cog in their continental capers. But mere cog he remained because Sinbad, this man of many voyages, was forever getting faulty with their business. The passports wouldn't arrive, or the collats would get snatched, and Sinbad would desperately shuttle between interested parties, excusing himself in a blather of tongues, trying to save face and the rest of him from his people and mad Mediterranean brothers.

He was a few years older, but I had felt some affinity for Sinbad during his disastrous runs: just as his blather would fuel his partners' anger, I too aroused suspicion from my crew over a way with words. Oh, my early riddle and puzzle books were indulged as an innocent pastime. But as these were followed by the 'Any Questions' columns and the crosswords in ever thicker newspapers, their murmurs began, and grew as I moved inexorably from the back pages to the front, even to the pink business pages. From these last I would emerge after a concentrated session with my talk of expansion, and could not cavil when my bunch warily redubbed me 'Brains'. Back then I had believed the main difference between us was that I was smart whereas Sinbad was not. Yet even I had not foreseen my big trouble with my people when it came.

'Ay, Boy!' he said, flicking a crutch up and touching my forearm with his.

'Aaaight.'

'Is how long? A year an' we don't catch up!'

He eased himself gingerly down opposite me, used one crutch to hook another chair up to his, and rested his left leg on it.

I was not surprised to see him struggling so. Four months ago two of his more successful associates had come to see me and charged me with finding him. They wanted to see him rather urgently about a matter and had heard that he was holed up around my parts. Obviously I am not one to pester my clients unduly but, what with Sinbad being an old familiar, I felt it only proper to ask for more details.

Their story had his messy mark all over. That Sinbad be pulled over by the police in a routine roadcheck with a bag of phones in the back was not in itself the problem, they freely conceded. Nor even his foolishness in failing to erase their memories, with their original owners' details, thus blowing his claim that he was a salesman. No, the problem lay in Sinbad's panicky exit from the vehicle, leaving his own mobile by the wheel, with all my clients' details available at the push of a button. Next thing now, and my clients are on the end of an early morning visit by those hardcore undercover squads. Boom-boom-crash at the door, wiping the sleep from their eyes, then arms scrunched behind and up, cuffs on, head down. No doubt a few prods of the taser too. They had been released soon enough but were now under scrutiny and the humiliation had not gone unnoticed. As I recall, my clients lived in a respectable district.

The only word they had received from Sinbad was one belated call, two days after the Beast had come knocking, thick with evasions, vague warnings and 'all him Bedouin nonsense'. He would have called earlier, he had mumbled, only he had lost his phone.

We were agreed that fair dos decreed Sinbad must bleed and, having satisfied myself that it was not his end they sought, I had had no difficulty in accepting my clients' commission. Sinbad's behaviour had not been honourable and although more than a mere acquaintance, he was no cousin. Less than a half dozen wanna be calling me cousin.

The mission was a straightforward lost then found number. I had spied him two nights later, in an SE20s flamenco club, fronting as a Latino dance master, and followed him home. Seeing him now, it seemed that my clients had been as good as their word and done nothing worse than shoot off his knees.

'So how's it hanging, star?' Sinbad gestured around us. 'Looks like you doing all right, though!'

I shook my head.

'Surviving still, innit. Just here on business.'

'Seen, seen.' He dipped into his tray and showed me a scrunched-up plastic flower and grinned: 'You won't be needing these then, for any lady friend?'

I peered at the thing. Was it intended as a rose?

'Or this?' He held up a papier-mâché monkey. He pressed a button, and its stringy pecker shot out.

'I'm all right,' I said, raising my palm in a declining motion.

Here was a man practically born with the silver spoon – languages, connections and such – but he had plummeted from siestas and señoritas to bashers and bargain basement baubles. At the end of the day, forgetting all his other defects, the man had no class. Just seeing him made me impatient for Morello Cherry and my Veuve Clicquot.

My eyes darted around the room before settling on his crutches.

'Ah, these! Had a misunderstanding, as it goes. Serious. Coupla bods I did some work for. Lickle raasholes!'

Sinbad smiled broadly, as if proud of his war wounds.

The full-on Sinbad smile, with his super inflatables, was quite a sight. He looked as if he might never close his mouth again. I was reminded of a creature I have heard of from the old country, the Nile crocodile. I understand that this rather laid-back reptile finds the repeated opening and shutting of its formidable mandibles too much of a chore, and is wont to lie mouth wide on the river, in a state of ultrachill, while the petite plover bird – with whom it enjoys a special relationship – comes along and picks its teeth.

'Shit happens,' I said. 'Month or two – you'll be all right, man'.

'Yih.' He leant forward and reached for a cigarette from my packet. 'Fuck knows how they found me. I mean, I'd done left the manor, come down south . . . A little bird reckoned you might know something about it.'

I tensed under the table, ready to assume the position. I should perhaps have simply answered in the negative, but the man was being too cheeky. Was he really going to start something now? Him a crippled trinketeer, and me a fully paid-up customer? My earlier workout of my blood skills outside would ensure speed off the mark this time. At the very least, I would get him slung out.

'That's always been your problem, Sinbad,' I replied fiercely, 'you and your birds – going round, giving it loads. Didn't Mama Sinbad tell you careless words costs lives? I don't go there, suh!'

'Safe, man. You're cool. I ain't beefin'.' He cackled. 'That's my Boy. Same style. You never get a straight answer from him. It'll all come out in the wash, still.'

His smile was not as blank and irretractable as it was wont to be, and left me feeling a tad uneasy. Had I not known him better I would have described it as knowing.

The inestimably pleasing sight of Morello Cherry approached to break up our tête-á-tête. Five foot ten of generous endowments, lips painted salamander, bra straps trembling loosely, all fruits ripe and juicy, voluptuous wasn't the word. She looked like one of those

Amazon types who've got the menfolk slaving under the sun in those twenty-fifth-century films. My millionaire would have to stock up on his red meat without question.

I threw her an 'Enchanted to meet you, I'm sure, Miss Cherry,' but was dismayed by her response. She grunted an acknowledgement, and fixed us with a bilious eye as she all but slammed my refreshments on the table. Then, with a supercilious toss of her shiny, waxy weave and tail, like a filly who doesn't want to race today, she strode powerfully away.

'Safe sisters here, innit?' volunteered Sinbad, unfazed or, more likely, unobservant.

He looked expectantly at me, hoping for the offer of some fine wines. I considered it. The supply was unlimited, and he might tell me something useful about this place over a drink. I nodded.

'Yeah,' he said, after a deep draught. 'All that rubbish out there. And for what? This brother just couldn't be dealing with it no more. Up here now, it's just sweet. No drama, and lodging thrown in. You should move down, I'm telling you. Up here,' his eye burnished with enthusiasm, 'simply being one of us is enough!'

Indeed, the resort seemed an attractive destination for underachievers. For the pain of a few menial chores and daily routines in the themed rooms, Sinbad got a room over his head while Ice Cream was in season. He mustered a little pocket money from the odd tip and hawking these wares. Maybe Hope could get a squeeze here.

I was in two minds about Sinbad. On the one hand, if even a little of his bluster about his banter with the rich and famous was true, then he might provide me with introductions valuable for the life I now looked forward to in the west. On the other, I was of the growing opinion that Morello Cherry's snub was all to do with the low-level company she had seen me with.

There was a bustle on the floor of the cocktail bar, and a chattering crowd gathering at the foot of its stairs.

'All *right*!' said Sinbad. 'Must be that time of the month. Miss Hostess with the Mostest.'

We wandered over to the goings-on, my own self a couple of yards ahead, far enough to say 'I do not know this man' should the need arise.

The hostesses were assembled above us, behind a smirking, bowtied MC. The 'Hostess with the Mostest', he informed us, had become a much loved occasion. An opportunity for their honoured guests to honour those who have endeavoured to make their stays such pleasant ones, and for their humble establishment to remain responsive to public opinion.

'Early heavy betting on Miss Morello Cherry retaining her crown for the third successive month began to look premature as soundings of our pollsters earlier this evening indicated a tight three-way race,' he continued. 'But the winner, by a short head, the new patrons' favourite . . . is Candy Bon-Bons!'

The cheers from the floor threw the frosty response from the competitors themselves into relief. This could have been a stab at steely professionalism on their part, but I detected pure bad-mindedness. Morello Cherry in particular gritted her smile as Miss Bon-Bons was presented with a bouquet of flowers and a giant tub of ice cream.

She looked agreeable enough – a fresh slip of a thing with tons of hair – but I found her resistible compared to the in-your-face assets of Miss Cherry and the dark distinction of Chocolate de Belge on the far left.

'They change into their casual wear and come back soon. That's the best bit. Then you really get to mingle.'

'Is it?'

This safari-suited old man, who had winked at us as we drew up alongside, had been volunteering snatches of background information through the proceedings. I do not know if he had recognised Sinbad from earlier times or if he just wanted to be friends, but he proved himself my preferred kind of business company. Forthcoming and confessional about his affairs, uncurious about my own. I was sure that his face – eyes youthfully blue but lined, like his brow, with furrows of abstraction – had peered out at me in front-page disgrace from recent news-stands, and he confirmed that this was indeed the case. He had been physician to the mighty, peers of the state and the Minister for Special Duties until the scandal had dropped. I forget the details – I think he had self-administered something he should-n't. His wife had left him, his old circles had sacked him, and he had prescribed himself indefinite rest at Ice Cream. He seemed happy but fevered; in need of a second opinion.

Two more came to join us at the bar: a tanked-up Scottish snooker star and his apologetic minder. The player was enjoying a relaxing run-in to the national championships, his first after a two-year ban for violently assaulting officials. We had a moment debating headbutts versus fists and darts versus snooker before he hugged me tearfully and said that we had a fookin' genius in common – one Robert Nesta Marley – and he had been up and down this fookin' joint, looking for some tribute to his greatness, but had found fook-all. He staggered to his feet, tumbled down, grinned and got up again, baying out reggae protest songs of his youth. As he tried out antique moonstomps, his trousers hanging off his arse, and the physician handed me his card, I pondered my habitual popularity among the fallen, and what this boded for me in the long term.

Sinbad took his leave of us to attend to his duties. And just in time, for beyond him some of the girls were re-entering the fray. Miss Cherry had taken up a position in front of us, by the end of the bar. She stood, back towards the wall, in a stretch lace catsuit and sin heels, swaying softly and easily to the pianist's tinklings. She seemed to be dancing to herself, but every now and then she would aim a look in our direction. Emboldened, I grabbed a bottle of bubbly from the tray beside us and ambled up to her. As I approached, she took me in square on for an instant, glared then turned her face away, with a silent sound of kissed teeth. She also turned her body ninety degrees so that, by the time I reached her, I was speaking to her back and quarter profile.

'What's wrong with you? Isn't this the time to mingle?' I said.

She ignored me, continuing to glance back in the direction I had come from, where the lonely physician still stood.

I had half a mind to shake her round myself, but checked myself, wheeled round, took a fresh glass from the bar to add some dignity to my wander and walked back, dazed and confused at this second denial.

Her glances did not let up on my return, and it was some moments before I could admit the grim, inevitable conclusion.

'It's you,' I said weakly to the old man. 'I think she wants you.'

'Eh!'

He looked up at her, then back at me, grinned and went to her, clicking his hands above his head like a castanet player. She beckoned him, slipping her hands on his waist and shaping to his steps.

It was one ugly scene. This native in his Seventh Age, with a smidgen of hair, vanishing lips and skin hanging off at the neck, getting rubs with such prime fitness. As the pianist bashed up the volume she pushed him behind her, and dropped her hands on him again, still dancing but now aiming her sultry looks at a little group of suits who gathered to clap and cheer the pair on.

I could not understand. If this Cherry woman was a hustler, as was suggested by her employment here and confirmed by this performance, then why not hustle me? Just this once I was the easiest hustle in the hemisphere, with a key to riches she could not imagine. If her game was to snare rich old simps and hurry them to their grave, then why turn it on for this younger pack in front of her? And if the young ones were no problem, then why not me? Was some ugly same-kind brand of discrimination operating in what I had been led to believe was a money-playing field?

I slumped into a chair, brought low by this riddle that was beyond me, suddenly tired with this whole crazy place, and started with a jolt when a hand kneaded my shoulder.

'You've gotta laugh, encha?'

'What?'

A young lady, face oval and chestnut, like a lion club, was standing over me. Her emerald eyes were set off by a green, crushed velvet hat that tilted jauntily and a warm grin.

'Look at him. You gotta laugh!'

She was pointing to the Scotsman, still gyrating to his own beat, and I took him in, then the doctor, gasping and tottering as Cherry rode him, doing a donkey wine on his shoulders, and the other punters, running about here when they should be running the country, and I could not but grin a little too.

'That's better! It's a little creaky, mind, but getting there,' she said. 'Cos you can't drink bubbly with a longface now, can you?'

She shook her head and mouthed, 'No, no, no,' in a barely audible whisper, fixing you deep in the eye – her own eyes now, strangely, hazel. The whole effect was soothing and rather compelling. I found myself shaking my head in agreement.

She took hold of the bottle, popped the cork, and poured some into my glass. I peered at her name tag. Candy Bon-Bons! I had not recognised her with her hair packed under her hat.

'You look as if you could do with the top up 'n' all. Unlike some people I could mention. Bladdered ain't the word.' She rolled her green-again eyes at the scene ahead, then moved towards it. I got up to follow her.

She pointed warningly to the grandpa's ticker and he held up his hands in acknowledgement. She hitched up the Scot's trousers, took his arm, and got her 'no' routine going again. A few more words then she nodded her head and mouthed, 'Yes, yes, yes.' He nodded too and she led him off the floor into the hands of his minder, before continuing with her tour of duty.

She was playful but firm with the clientele, quelling the brazen with her breezy, persuasive ministering. They seemed to treat her differently from her colleagues, with something akin to a puzzled respect. There was sometimes a heartiness to the exchanges, but that was all.

I put this down in part to her peculiar brand of casualwear: whereas the others had opted for time-honoured foxy outfits, Candy seemed to have gone free-associating in some gaudy charity shop. She was a blaze of citrus: soft yellow jacket, crushed lime trousers with a hint of yellow, and thick mannish boots. The package could have done with some bedding down in my opinion, but I welcomed its spirit.

I wanted to know more about this Candy Bon-Bons. I waited for her to have an unencumbered moment and then moved in.

'Oowwh hellowww, chief,' she said.

I pointed forlornly at my bottle. 'It says, "Thanks for sorting the longface, now what about the company?"'

'Don't you have any friends?'

I shook my head and mouthed 'No' thrice, after her fashion.

She looked quizzically at me first then, as it dawned that it was her I was mimicking, her face lit up, fell back and laughed with the full-blooded roar of new knowledge. The beauty of it was all in the gap. It was not a gap that someone who spends their days working the angles – a Miss Cherry or, indeed, myself – could have managed. It was a natural-born gap. Whether she was innocent, or even good, I did not yet know, but that gap just made me want to go 'Oooh!'

We found ourselves a table, where she declined the glass I offered; just water for her on duty, she said. She asked if it was my first time at the resort. I confirmed that it was. She asked if I lived local. I said no, not yet. I actually told her I lived in the northside of town. No point in frightening her off needlessly.

I needn't have bothered. She said she'd only been in town six weeks, and hadn't really had a chance to explore it, she'd been that busy. She'd been working and sleeping at the resort and had literally gone no further than the shops at the end of the road. But she had saved up all this time off and she was planning to get out soon and have a jolly.

She talked in a quick high-pitch, with liquidised Rs and a whiney drag to her vowels, which no doubt owed much to her upbringing in some provincial village. I forget its name but it was, she told me, only seven miles from Gillingham, a piece of information that left me little the wiser.

Her home did not sound like the rural paradise of my millionaire. She had lived on a council housing scheme, whose pink towers gave me a gloomy reminder of my own Elephant and Castle. Hers seemed an unorthodox area for our kind to live in, but she explained that she had been fostered out when only a few months old to this native couple in an arrangement that was not uncommon. She had not seen her natural parents since that time and was hazy about various aspects, even which part of the triangle they had come from. Her family had received an official letter, when she was around five, informing them that her real father had been imprisoned then exe-cuted back home. 'Politics,' she said, and for the first time a shadow crossed her face. Correspondence from her mother, irregular before, dried up completely shortly afterwards. It was thought that either she too had been incarcerated, or perhaps she had a new family and just didn't want to know any more. Candy herself had only been told this much by her foster folks a few years ago. I asked her how she felt; she must miss not having them? But she shrugged and said not really, she didn't think much about it, and you didn't miss what you didn't know, did you?

My mind, naturally, went to the similarities with my own beginnings – to my discovery and subsequent adoption. I thought about
sharing this with her, but as it's an unusual story, it might have
thrown us off kilter. I did take the chance though, of telling her of my
mother's premature end. There was more but that was enough, I
hoped, for her to look on me kindly.

She had finished school and then enrolled on a course in hotel
management. She'd been cooling her heels, scouring the job pages,
when she'd seen the ad recruiting women for a swinging new resort.
Career prospects excellent. Must have good interpersonal skills.

'I'm a people's person,' Candy said proudly. 'I like meeting
people, taking them out of themselves, having a bit of a laugh. I
mean, I thought I might do something with kids, summer schools, or
social work or stuff like that. Anywhere, you know, where you're
relating to people—'

'And the people here. What are they like?'

'They're all right. Most of the time. They're like overgrown
babies, a lot of them. Just want more and more of everything.'

'And what's the arrangement for laying on, uh, extras?'

'Eh?' She looked puzzled then leant forward and pushed my nose
with her finger in mock-scold. 'Naughty! What are you like!'

'Candy, man. I wasn't born yesterday.' I gestured to the scene
around us. 'Blatant can't get more blatant!'

'I'm sure it ain't always what you think it is. Anyway, I do what I
do. Let the others do what they do. If you conduct yourself right, you
don't get the hassle. That's why I put my hair up when we mingle. I
do my job properly. Can't nobody say different.'

She looked sad again, made to add something, then checked herself. I pressed her.

'No – it's just that some of the girls are a bit funny with me sometimes. I don't understand. Like I'm stuck up, or think I'm better than

them—'

'Like tonight?'

'Uh-hmm'.

I feared for Candy's future in this establishment. If she spoke true – and I was inclined to believe her – then her unique way of doing things could scarcely endear her for long to either her colleagues or the custom. That she had won this month's 'Hostess with the Mostest' was peculiar enough; either it was the shock of the new or, more likely, Ice Cream had rigged the vote. Perhaps Ms Cherry was getting uppity and demanding a payrise. Whatever the reason, Candy was too outnumbered for her good self to prosper here.

'Let's go for a wander. I haven't even seen half this place yet, you know.' I wanted to stretch my legs and let some present thoughts marinate.

She took me to her favourite room, the Soul Kitchen. It was no kitchen, more a comfy, old-style smoking room, plush leather armchairs and such. She drew my attention to the paintings on the wall and, indeed, the pictures were skilfully drawn, with these sharp lines and angles I have seen in pieces from the old country. Perhaps those Avignon ladies were the hostesses of their day.

I was concentrating on the group of three relaxing around a low table towards the back of the room. There, rolling cognac around a glass, and stretching in an orange suit, was old Merciless himself. Thicker around the waist than before, thinner and greyer about the hairline, the same vulpine features. He unfurled the wrapper from a thick cigar and passed one to a white man so rotund he would have had difficulty moving what I understand the physicists call his point of application from A to B. Their companion was a lady whose profile was most familiar to I and my small circle of newspaper-reading associates. Her family had come to our state in some distress not so long ago as part of the most recent crop of arrivals, refugees from the north-eastern part of the old country. Yet she, like many of her crop, whom we had dubbed 'the desert people', had managed to turn her situation around in no time, so that now her face appeared above several syndicated columns. She used her own rags-to-riches story to drive home her ferocious commentaries, all variations on a single theme: don't feed the blacks.

They were deep in discussion and did not seem to notice us. They talked of rumours of inferiority and a bottom rung, Irish future for those of our kind, an upscale Jewish future for some others.

I wanted to stay, for this sounded like something I should know about, but Candy was keen to leave. 'Politics. I don't like politics,' she insisted.

We walked down a corridor covered in graffiti art with the occasional installation piece lurking to trouble the unready. Candy swore as she stubbed her foot on a doodle-covered fridge then grazed her finger on the crown of thorns that lay on top. 'Pardon my French!' She laughed, which I found ironic, for all evening long – from the veg selection at the supermarket to the Mesdemoiselles in the Soul Kitchen and this Jean-Michel Basquiat corridor – it was clear that French was the very thing we would have to get to grips with if we were to continue running with the big boys.

She linked her arm in mine after that. I peppered her with more questions as we walked, searching out the blight in her. But no, it was all good. Her adoptive parents had given her all the love she needed, her school had been so pleasant and educational she'd stayed 'til eighteen. I asked her to tell me the worst thing she had done this year. I don't know, she shrugged, before eventually plumping for her failure to shut the door more brutally on some guest who had been harassing her around the resort this past month. He hadn't even bought her flowers, much less asked her out. Just groped her glutei when he could. No way did she lead him on, but he seemed to think she was the one that had encouraged it. Maybe she hadn't been tough enough at the outset.

'How about you? The worst thing you've done?'

What could I say? I, who have a gallery to choose from? I tried to think of a yarn soft enough to elicit a sympathetic 'Oh well, no one's perfect' response, but nothing sprung to mind.

'Candy,' I said, 'let he who is without sin cast the first stone.'

'All right then,' she replied. She gathered up imaginary stones, and made to throw them at me, before giggling and gambolling down the corridor.

Question: what store do I set by cuteness in this quest?

We eventually settled in the Original Bad Boy Rap Niggaz Room. Here, deep in the 'Criminology' section, amongst the lookalike Gs and guns and grams, with my back to the wall and Candy buzzing about, I was overtaken by nostalgia.

No doubt this owed something to the surroundings in general and Sinbad's current manifestation in particular. He now had a bandana tied around his head, a mouthful of gold fronts, and, slouched as moodily as his crutches would let him behind a microphone, was flipping gang signs with four others in similar colours. From time to time they belted out tone deaf choruses from hip-hop classics, so fulfilling the dual roles of house band and house gang.

I thought again of my own teenage crew, the CLC. Coming Like Columbians. Oh, I doubt that we are much missed but we put some shit together in our time. All those honed, elaborate schemes: the postman patrol, the tickets caper at the SE19 stadium (how many were in on that in the end? Fifteen? Twenty?). My plans, my name. Hah. A foreign-flavoured name, as was the fashion. My preferred choice was ITNI (Introducing the Nasty Immigrants), but my bredrin felt that CLC rhymed better and sounded grander, plus Danny, our honorary, demurred at ITNI. We hardly rose to the gold-collar 'stocks and shares by twenty years, 'nuff property by thirty' scale we had envisaged, but still . . . We had had us some glory, some donnish team performances along the way. These days, most nobody joined a clique. Everybody was out for self.

'Excuse me,' said an approaching man.

My millionaire! Instinctively I stood up straight. The goatee and monkey ring had gone, and the accent had a different shade of softness but, those aside, the very same.

'This "cream" that they keep chanting about getting,' he pointed to Sinbad and co., 'what do they mean?'

'C.R.E.A.M. Cash Rules Everything Around Me. It's just an old word for money. After bread and readies, but before corn and cheddar and ducats and collats. About the same time as wonga.' If this was who I thought it was, I wanted to be as helpful as I could.

He remarked that it was strange there were so many words for money and only one, say, for love. And maybe not even as many as that, he laughed, in this Rap Niggaz Room. Not so strange, I replied, for cash was fact and everything else was opinion, and I banged the coins in my heart pocket for emphasis. This elicited a second chuckle. The same genial self, love still on his mind . . . my man, without question.

I asked him if he was checking on me, but he looked uncomprehending. I reminded him that he had come to see me that afternoon, but this he laughingly denied and, when I pushed it, steered the conversation firmly to his own agenda. He claimed he was not even resident here, but from foreign, the Americas, and was just visiting our state on a working trip. He said that he used to be involved in the tourist trade himself but had 'repented', and now he had moved his projects away from the commerce end of things entirely. These days, he was strictly about development.

He had travelled a lot, something the information fiend in me always welcomed, but what he had seen filled him with dread. Young ones were leaving their home districts by the trailerload, he said, reaching for the big cities, hoping for enough to send home and stand tall on. What greeted them they could not have foreseen. He spoke of one-meal-a-day people, disease-ridden shanty towns, tens of thousands packed on to hillsides.

If it was not to the cities, then they headed, on islands like his, to the coastal line with its tourist zones. There, they lived on their knees, hustling around the fringes of resorts like these. If only these wretches could understand what riches they had left behind untapped in the hinterland! In the plateaus and gulleys and green of the interior. Land with enough goodness to feed its people five times over. But the tourist operators were only interested in the coastlines, while the government produced food for export and foreign exchange. The goodness would take twenty or thirty years to come through, for the land had not been cultivated in a sustainable way for so long, but all it would take was one generation to show it love.

'I'm just trying to develop a space where, you know, we can be original. For nature ah work,' he said.

His project did not sound a million miles away from Merciless's phoney travel agency, so you'll understand that I reserved my enthusiasm. Still, I liked his passion. He made my brain feel exercised, kinda powerful. I wandered to the side bar and brought us all back refreshments.

'One question,' I said to him. 'If you're so keen on all this work the land stuff—'

'I'm not talking about turning the clock back to Year Zero,' he cut me. 'More a refocus, a redistribution of energies.'

'Yeah-yeah. So what brings you here?'

'Here here, or here as in your state?'

'Both.'

'Well, I am in town principally to look for backing, and as for this place – I thought I'd have a look-see. We have some of these resorts already, but this is more, um, state of the art. You have to track your enemy step by step. Places like this keep me hungry! Besides,' he chuckled, 'I was invited. I'm still on some old guest lists.'

It turned out this double was basically born overs. After some

een recruited by the big central banks and

ears are true, he said to us (just me really;

enly dead on her feet): he'd seen momen-

all talk at drunken parties, so many fates

ig idea.

ks you know. Have you thought about

I mean,' I asked him.

not looking for money. I'm looking for

ntly. 'Why not come with us? We shall

The work will be hard but at least we

r it.'

. But, really, I had this business to sort

e move out west, and the opportunity to

d run a pharmaceutical sideline from home.

short, was the very thing I was planning on retiring

uttered, 'Maybe another time,' and, what with me still

feeling heat from his direction, moved swiftly to bring Candy into

our conversation.

She was awake again, but now hovering around with a slightly furrowed brow, as if she suspected some political edge to our discussion. But they found common ground soon enough, exchanging good-natured banter about country matters.

Perhaps this brother's likeness to my client, and the frisson this lent the pair, had something to do with it. Certainly the more I mused, the more I was sold on this idea of regional black. Candy, this sweet, generous Candy, whom displacement and bereavement had left undamaged, who was so keen to give the benefit of the doubt, no matter how scuzzy the ass or sleazy the environs. I detected a flightiness in her, but underneath that a solid, uh, moral core. She would be loyal, she would be bubbly, she would commend the coffee.

She was a new bird who don't see the hurricane as yet. In the city, but not of the city. A neat little riddle. An

A plaintive cry, fragile and clear like crystal,
the room. I turned to Sinbad's group where a won
in a simple black dress, now cradled the micropho

I could not quite make out her cry, more a
moment alone had put the rest of the entertainment
she continued, with the lush, keyboard chords swoon
I was back in the grip of a favoured old tune from thos

'*Wu-u Ta-ang, yeah,*' she sang.

That's right! The Wu Tang! A musical clique,
ruggedest clans of all.

She sighed and harmonised again, as Sinbad and his pe
against the sweet, rapped over her:

> *Ninety-Four*
> *Taking niggas to war,*
> *A blink of the eye and you're gone, evaporated!*
> *Lose all your strength, nigga.*

'*What do you believe in, heaven or hell?*' came her descant, '*We don't
believe in heaven cos we're living in hell.*'

The heaven and hell chorus, the one my client referred to that
afternoon. I had not actually heard it in so long.

'*We're living in hell, we're living in he-e-ell. What do you believe in? Oh-
oh-oh-oh . . .*'

Her voice struggled a little as she stretched to ring the changes on
the 'ohs', but it stayed honest and flecked with loss and sadness and
all those things I know to be true.

'*Some way,*' she sang, '*I'm gonna end this with a great red cherry on
top.*'

What can I say? This seemed the living sign. I am, if I didn't tell
you yet, a superstitious man.

It was with no mean lump in my throat that I took Candy by the hand, bade a fond farewell to Mr Development, and led her into a corner.

'Candy,' I began. I paused. It had been a long time since I had speeched a girl and this was hardly even your ordinary lyricking situation. 'Let me explain. I'm a private eye, all right? Okay, today this client, this millionaire, came to see me. No joke. He's got the biggest fuckin' – pardon my French – biggest pad you've never heard of. Living country paradise: pure orchards, flowers an' fields of lavender. Only he hasn't got a lady, see. He came to the city to find his lady. He asked *me* to find his lady. Listen, Candy, I reached tonight, my head full up with, you know, this sort an' the next fly sort an' all them strictly surface things. But you – boy! I don't care, Morello Cherry and Chocolate de Belge can't talk to it! You've got the outer, you've got the inner. You're the hottest thing here. Come with me, Candy. You and my client will hit it off, no question. It's yours. I don't business nowhere else.'

She squeezed my hands.

'A millionaire in a mansion! No way!'

'Sright. Believe me. Looks just like the brother we were speaking with. Real decent type.'

'But I've only just started this. I *like* it here. The mixin' and the meetin'—'

'Look, Candy, this whole place is . . . is off-key, y'get me? With my man you can spend all your time arranging fat cat charity dinners and be the most dedicated people's person on the planet!'

'Does sound nice, dunnit? And I trust you. I do.' Her eyes were wide, in silent plea. They transferred all this power to me, but retained another source of dignity. 'Hurr! . . . well I'm definitely interested. I'll have to sleep over it, mind, and speak to my mum and dad, and meeting him might be an idea, but my provisional answer is very interested.'

'You can't have a provisional "very interested". You can have a provisional "yes". Yes?'

And she nodded her head, solemnly, thrice.

I gave her a fair-sized hug. 'Thank you,' I said. I felt excited, truly. It had been a long while and I hadn't felt like that.

I looked at my watch. Twenty to one. I wanted to tighten the grip a little, always good practice when you have someone's provisional.

'Let's cut! Go for a drive, quiet drink in celebration, whatever.'

Her eyes lit up. 'I'd enjoy that. I'll tell you what – I wouldn't mind getting some chips! Can we do that?'

I nodded and smiled indulgently at her slightly curious suggestion.

She ran off to find Créme Caramel. She needed someone to cover for her for the last hour of her shift.

The combination of Candy, exhilaration at the near completion of my mission and the general vibe had left me with a growing rumbling in my tings. Resorts, hotels, bed and breakfasts . . . they tended to have this effect on me. No doubt it had something to do with the way such establishments helped to reduce the expectation of any lingering contact, thick as they were with folk in transit or temporarily away from their lives. You could move swiftly from preliminaries on to the heart of the matter. These days, of course, I like to skip out the former entirely.

I had been pleased to note that the resort catered discretely to the odd good-time girl. For an old hand like me, their demeanour marked them out from the hostesses – no way was I heading down that hazardous route for this small matter – and the bona fide customers.

A pair of them had been standing by the door with their empty glasses for the last ten minutes. I caught their eye and resettled myself about five yards down, looking back into the room. After a few moments one of them – black boots and a soft satin bridal top, a wig and a good solid size – came my way. She had a little story to dignify up the proceedings. Something about her living with her invalid grandmother and losing the housekey, and needing a one-er to stay somewhere and replace it and reah. Some rubbish, in any case. The mathematics seemed a bit steep to me but, then again, this was a pricey part of town. I handed her forty folds and said I would sort the balance on my return, some time around three.

Candy returned and we headed up to her rooms in the staff quarters, four floors up, so she could change out of her work clothes. She had a small sitting room and a smaller bedroom with en suite business beyond. Comfortable enough, if a little cramped.

I stared at a framed photograph standing on a shelf. A gaggle of young friends, smiling on a lawn, in evening dress or formal jackets and ties. You could see the pleasure in their faces in 'getting up' like the big persons they were becoming. A school-leavers' celebration, perhaps. In the foreground, a black group of three, with Candy on the right. I was curious about their story for, although Candy and the girl on the left both had their arms around the girl in the middle and she had her arms around them, Candy and the girl on the other side seemed to be doing their best to keep what distance they could from each other.

Candy kept the connecting door open as she ran back and forth, clad only in tights, bra top and a towel on her head, holding up skirts and such for my inspection.

'Put something on, *please*, lady,' I said. I thought it a little off for her to be walking around like that when she was practically betrothed.

'I'm trying, I'm trying, chief. It's hard to decide—'

'I don't mean that, I mean . . . oh, forget it. Look, it's just chips and a drink. Just throw something on.'

'But we're going out. I haven't been out *out* up here at all. It's an occasion. How about this?'

She held up a short brown skirt. 'Fine,' I said.

But when she reappeared it wasn't so fine after all. Her skirt did not hang properly but squeezed and bunched her buttocks, with the fabric dipping and gathering under the bottom rather than tapering organically down. It was the same with the other skirts and dresses she hurriedly tried on. None made proper provision for high-slung batties and calves, for legs curved rather than straight. There was much difficulty with the femur-tibia tie-in.

'Candy, you need to do some shopping. Serious. Haven't they got any decent garms in the outback?'

'Honestly! Now who's the one who's fussy!'

We finally settled on a workaday baggyish pair of jeans. They did her no justice, but at least they gave her batty space to chill. As it turned out, her hair, when at last she produced it from under the towel, practically covered the problem area anyway. There were acres of the stuff. Very soft, black, fine. It looked like a weave, but when you peered close you could see that it wasn't. It was the type of hair, basically, that would have certain sisters fuming. Only there was a permy thing going on at the fringes which threw the whole package, to my mind, into some disrepute. High-heeled platforms would have felt at home below it.

She seemed a bit defensive about her locks: not, oddly, about the fringes, but the main body itself. She told me unprompted that she had been born with hair, and it had just kept on growing. That it was natural, like her green or brown eyes, and she'd been to see the doctor about it as a kid. Her eyes, not her hair. He'd explained they just reacted to the light. That it was all natural, only some people seemed to have a problem.

'Did I say I had a problem? I wouldn't care if you'd got your hair from a horse's head!' She looked relieved. 'Who's got a problem then?'

It turned out some of the girls had been making little digs. Morello Cherry had even lunged out and clawed at her mane the other day, looking mighty irked when it hadn't come off in her hand.

And that had set her thinking about her last year at school and her aggro with her good mate, Patsy. That's right, on the left in the group in the photo. The trio had come together, really, as a support network for hair, in the days when their hair was picked on in the playground. They had discovered hotrods and relaxers together and, although Candy did not have the same difficulty in managing hers, she had even cut it once in sympathy with the struggle. Unfortunately, midway through sixth form, dreaded reversion had set in for Patsy. Her resurgent curls had jostled with the straightened overlay to produce a moody mess. And, with Candy's own tresses now blooming bountifully again, Patsy got a permanent vex on.

It was a touching tale. They had been brought together and torn apart by hair, Candy's one area of, uh, political experience.

I went to the bathroom to wash my face. On my way through her bedroom I caught sight of her bedside table, where there was a picture of her adoptive parents: her father had a solid jaw and honest worker's hands, her mother a toothy smile and a great, shaggy perm.

One or two niggles, but really there was nothing wrong with Candy that a little makeover, perhaps tomorrow, wouldn't sort.

'All right, let's do this,' I announced as I came back in. 'Are you ready?'

She grinned and nodded.

4

a night at the arches (rumours of a revival are someway exaggerated)

'Where are we headed, by the way?' asked Candy, breaking briefly from her chips 'n' banger in batter.

'Errm . . .' I wrinkled my nose. I was not fond of the smell of cooked food in my car. I frequently ate on the go myself but, as with other bad odours, I did not mind my own – just other people's. 'There's a nice after-hours place I used to go to in the west's end. If I'm still on the—'

'The west's end!' she mocked. '*Done* that. Even as a kid I got to go there. Show me something of the *real* town. How about your neck of the woods?'

I snorted. 'Forget it. There's no point.'

'Why not? I bet there's something going on.'

I looked at her, her pretty head bobbing excitedly to the mix tape she had selected from my assortment. I had told her I lived on the northside. In truth, my knowledge of that area did not extend to

late-night culture and, were we to head up there, I would surely be
exposed. But to take her down south!

'Look, Candy, nothing nice goes on, all right? People haven't got
any money. Man tries to open a club an' some stinkman comes along
an' tries to control it. Ain't no one going out, 'cept those you'd run a
mile to avoid.'

'There must be something,' she said simply. 'Do some detecting,
my detective.'

'All right, all right.' I was a little exasperated now. I reached for my
phone and called Sundays. It was my intention to put paid to her suggestion. Sundays was not one for keeping abreast of the local leisure
scene. I pictured him seeing the last of his callers to the door, getting
ready for bed and the garage in the morning.

I was wrong. Sundays was on the road, reaching for the SE16 rail-
way arches, where Phoenix, a local reggae sound, was playing out. He
must have heard the slight surprise in my voice, for he explained that
he was only passing through to serve some people. 'Everyday seem
like red letter day, an' being that we's in a single-income situation
now, y'unnerstan' . . .' And I was embarrassed, as I thought of my
friend's present difficulties against my own slice of good fortune. I
told him I would see him down there.

I turned to Candy. 'You're in luck,' I said.

I actually parked a few minutes up from the arches, in a secluded,
near empty lot, where I judged my car would be safer. I was a little
worried about the postcodes that glared at us from the street signs, but
Candy saw nothing amiss. She curled her arm around mine, which
made me nervous, as I liked to keep a low profile in these parts.

The scene outside the dance was as good as I could have hoped,
though. I could spot few of the young and turbulent area boys. Most
of the folk that lined the poorly lit alley, drinking and conversating in
little groups, looked my age or thereabouts. No surprise, I suppose,
given that Phoenix had been around a good few years.

I had managed to extract my arm from Candy's, but we still
attracted much scrutiny. People looked at Candy up and down – her
jauntiness, her democratic grin, her distinctive hair and attire – and
could see she was a stranger to these parts. They would flash one
curious glance at me, wondering what the secret source of my power
was, to have acquired a date so rare, before returning to her. I must
admit to feeling, beneath the hardness of my out-and-about face, a
little chuffed.

'Ay rudeboy,' a man leered after us as we reached the entrance,
'tek care o' dat, y'hear!'

'What was that?' she asked, as some sniggered behind.

I handed over the ten folds admittance price to a man sitting
behind a table. 'Nothing,' I said.

'What was that?' she repeated loudly.

'Nothing,' I said, more forcefully this time. 'You've got some
admirers is all.'

She looked unsatisfied but, really . . . now, with all ears and eyes
on us, was not the time for me to give her chapter and verse. She
should be chewing gum, styling above the fray, not pestering me
over some cheeky guy.

'Legs apart, black man,' said one of the doormen, frisking me: a
violent man with a lantern jaw and a lazy eye, I once knew him to nod
to, but he no longer recognised me, something I was perfectly happy
about. I turned to see Candy thanking his colleague. Indeed, that
might not have been the end of the matter – they seemed poised to
begin a full-on conversation – had I not moved vigorously on.

'What was all that chit-chat with security for?' I asked edgily when
she had caught up.

'Just being polite.'

'What for? The man's just doing his blasted job. "Thank you!"
You can't be going round saying that round here. People don't *say* that
round here. You'll just attract trouble.'

'Don't get arsey with me!' she came back. 'Ever since we stepped out of the car, you've been looking so mean at everyone.'

She turned away. I had not meant to upset her. Maybe I'd been too harsh. I was tired and perhaps that was fuelling a new irritability. I apologised and kneaded her shoulder as we walked into the yard proper.

The yard was pretty full, which it needed to be, for the place – with its stony floor and sides – could get quite chilly otherwise and the crowd in fine, somewhat sentimental fettle. Phoenix were rinsing an easy-listening set of old lovers' and devotional 'revival' tunes. Every few minutes the selector bade the massive stand by for a very special guest, but no one was acting impatient. Couples tapped a soft two-step, while guys nodded their heads and fingered their facial hair in philosophical fashion. Even the villains seemed in good humour. A few formed an orderly procession to embrace and bang fists with old Roland, who'd just come out from doing an eight to twelve. Aggravated burglary, I think it was. They'd sent him to a nut-house on the south coast. His body, splayed on a stool, had bloated and his face, tinged grey with incarceration, was fixed in one of those chemical, idiotic smiles. Eight years of being pumped full of shit and I reckoned he was allowed to relax in state for as long as he wanted.

Candy insisted on buying the drinks. She poured the Coke into my brandy glass and clinked it with her Archer's and lemonade.

'Thank you, sir, for taking me out,' she said with her funning sincerity. 'See, it isn't so bad, is it?'

She shook her head and mouthed 'no' three times, before exclaiming, 'Banish longface and meanface forever!' pointing dramatically into the distance.

I laughed. I had relaxed. I had not been to the arches in quite a while and it was nice to be reminded how fond I was of it. We were on the ground floor, but somehow you felt below it, in some subterranean secret cellar, dark and spartan but charismatic too. I would have liked it even more if the upstairs section – more a ramp that wound itself around two sides of the room – had not been closed off. Before, I could stand up there, my back to the wall, and scope the situation below quite comfortably. But I understood that the owner of the place, who had purchased the yard from the railways and now leased it out to promoters on the sly, thought crowd control worked better this way.

'So how d'you get into this detective lark then?' Candy asked.

'Oh . . . well, I had some bad breaks, you know. One or two other things didn't work out too tough. And this – I guess I had some contacts plus, you know, smarts in certain areas. I like being my own boss, keeping my own hours. Like that a lot. That was it, really.'

I apologised once more for my cross words. She said that, where she came from, if you saw another one of our kind in the street or someplace, most likely you'd let on to them. Yeah, I retorted, but that was the sticks – no wonder. It was like, if you were trudging around the desert and you finally bumped into someone else, you wouldn't just ignore them and walk on by. She said I should be my own man and not just bow down to what everyone else did. Only I wasn't really listening at this point, for I had hit upon another intriguing little thought. In fact, I concluded, it might even be that not being polite was the politest thing you could do, if politeness was taking account of those around you, acting to their expectations and such. And I was pleased, pleased with her and at this new neat riddle.

Sundays approached us, buttoning up his coat. He flashed a smile at Candy. He couldn't stop, he said, he was on his way out. I said I'd walk with him to his car.

Outside, he told me that he'd already placed a call with some out-of-towners regarding my business. He felt this was the safer option, but he'd take a couple of people with him come the time, just in case.

'Y'see Roland inside?' I asked.

Sundays nodded. 'It's a shame. Fe real. My man could play foot-ball some'ing bad, you know! A *boss* player. But every time Club come to see him he was away, drinking porridge.'

'Yeah . . . homeboy was foolish, though,' I added. 'He got to believing his own hype.'

At the peak of his career, Roland had been dubbed the Mad Phantom by our local paper because of his penchant for materialising in householders' bedrooms in the small hours and yelling 'Boo!' at them. At his trial he had played up to this image by making sundry peculiar interventions. No doubt he had been hoping to spend a couple of years max in a hospital before taking the rest of his cure in the community.

'He got badly advised,' I concluded.

'Looks like it,' agreed Sundays. He clicked his teeth.

We were silent for a moment. Just the sound of our steps. My thoughts on Roland the footballer, one more for our ledger of under-achievers.

'You ever go down?' asked Sundays.

'Me? Nah – just the odd "discussion" is all. My bredrin couldn't figure it – they used to call me Brains, you know . . . How it would run, say, rads would come an' take me for a ride, buy me burgers an' that and go, "We know you did this, so you better give us a little something else." Battle of wits, man. And I'll just be munching up good an' feeding them bull . . .'

We had reached the car. 'So what do you reckon to my girl?' I asked.

'You tink seh she the one?'

'Mmm. I feel so.'

'She kris, no question. Young still—'

'That's it!' I interrupted. 'Exactly. A new bird. Not tired, or dam-aged, y'unnerstan'?'

He puckered a smile, but made no further comment on the matter before driving off.

On my return I could not see Candy anywhere. I could not understand it. I had said I would be five minutes when I left and she had nodded.

I was wading my way through knots of people, becoming increasingly irked, when I spotted her. She was over by a side wall, inclining her head at the chat of three young men who flanked her. From their swagger to the price tags displayed gloatingly on their garms, they looked more like caution signs than gentlemen. The main guy made confident motions with his hands, leant towards her conspiratorially, a moment by her ear, then stood back and grinned wolfishly. Candy looked touched, like she could blush.

She turned then, and saw me through the crowd. Their eyes followed hers and their main man did not wipe the smirk from his face. Perhaps I was not registering enough displeasure although I seem to remember my eyes screwed a little. At any rate, Candy simply smiled at me, turned back and carried on chatting.

I stood confounded and embarrassed. Why had she not come to me, and directly? What could I do now to keep my dignity? I felt to head for the bar, but she would not be able to see me over there and this whole saga might go on all night. Nothing for it but to hang around at the scene of my distress, light a smoke, and nurse these ugly thoughts.

My cigarette was nearing its butt by the time she sauntered over. I took a deep breath, for calm's sake.

'Do you know those people?' I asked her.

'No, they just asked me over—'

'They asked you *over*. And you went? And you about to be another's?' My words tumbled out in a sardonic rush.

'We were just talking, for God's sake,' she defended herself. 'You left, and I was just taking a wander, an' those guys kinda waved at me to come over.'

'If you don't give off meaningful vibes, man don't beckon you.'

'Please! You know I don't play games like that. They were giving it a bit of chat but they can chat all they like.'

'And why didn't you come back when you saw me?'

'I thought you were gonna come to join us. Didn't know you were gonna huff and puff on your own, did I? Flippin' 'ell!' – she blew hard – 'Am I excused now, sir?'

'I'm just trying to get us a hassle-free evening is all. You can't trust no one. Those area boys are the worst—'

'If I can't trust no one I shouldn't have trusted you,' she retorted, which was pretty comebackproof, really. 'Come on,' she tugged my arm, 'forget it.'

We moved into the main body of people clustered towards the back of the yard, in front of the stage. Phoenix had hooked up some classic – 'I gave her love in the mor-or-nings (and in the evenings too)' I think it was. Candy and I began dancing side to side. I was rather awkward; I had not danced in a long time plus I found it bizarre dancing with a girl who was not, nor could be, your own. She was more zestful, giving it plenty of hips and arms. After a bit, though, I noticed her arms weren't pumping, but seemed to be struggling. Then I saw that two of those same brers were behind her. The leader was holding her upper arm. When she pulled away he reached out again.

'What the fuck!' I moved in and shoved this idiot back. 'What's wrong with you?'

His eyes dropped a little but other than that he did not seem daunted. He kept his hands in his bumblebee jacket, and muttered something, looking a little to the right of me. I caught 'runabout girl . . .' and 'pussyhole . . .'

'So wha', you wan' start someting now?' I growled.

Candy was tugging at my arm, urging me to move on, as the third crew member came up to join his people.

'Look to your woman, star. If she your woman,' cheeked the leader.

These youngbloods, who would barely have cut their teeth on solid foods when I first started splashing my feet in stink waters! They had sniffed out Candy's softness and included me in it. I thought I could take the bit players but the leader – a precociously hard chin, a reputation to keep and who knew what in or under his jacket – gave cause for pause.

A few of the other ravers were now looking on, expecting something tasty to happen. I could spot no one I could count on. I was only two miles away from home, but this was a different patch. For all I knew, these guys might be to this manor born. At the very least, they were prepared to take their chances in the blood game over a girl they had no right to. This told me the brers had very little to live for, and these are my least favourite type of adversary. Whereas I, I had my eyes on the prize, as Candy's insistent prods reminded me.

'Just pray we don't cross again,' was my parting shot. The fool continued to curl his lip as I let myself be led away.

'What a bunch of plonkers!' said Candy. 'I'm sorry, chief, I . . . you were right, I suppose.'

' Sall right. Those fools were looking to dark someone's evening and they just decided to come our way.'

We moved to a space nearer the stage as a great roar went up around us. The doors at the back of the yard had been flung open – this must be the entrance of Phoenix's special guest.

Two men came on first, in traditional Fila caps and indigo gowns. One hugged a long, brown djembe drum under his arm, the other an acoustic guitar. The crowd murmured and fell quiet. We did not recognise these musicians.

We were soon aware, though, of a clippety-hop sound accompanying the slap and brush of the drum. And then the great cheer reprised as a donkey, of all things, plodded through the doors, atop it a rider clad in sandals, knee-length shorts and sackcloth shirt, and bearing the unmistakeable features of Lieutenant Lipman.

This was a coup indeed! How had Phoenix, a middle-ranking sound, no more, managed to secure an assist from a performer of Lipman's stellar status?

Lipman was as famed for his dramatic entrances as he was for his blazing set of vocal styles. He often liked to march in at the head of his own phalanx of uniformed 'soldiers', in keeping with his most frequent persona of an old-country military dictator. Sometimes, though, he would crawl under a spotlight on to the stage, crocodile-style warpaint on his face, rifle and bullet belt strapped to his waist – a buffalo soldier. At the summer open-air festivals that we held when the Minister for Special Duties permitted, Flight Lieutenant Lipman had been known to circle the venue in a heli-copter, in sly mockery of the state's own ghetto birds. He had even once driven a tank up and popped out of the hatch. But this was new.

Lipman dismounted, took a microphone from a stage hand, sur-veyed the scene, licked his lips roguishly, and exclaimed his trademark 'Ah-oooo!'

'Ah-oooo!' the crowd roared back in unison.

'Isn't that DJ Madman?' Candy asked.

'Lipman,' I replied. 'Lieutenant Lipman.'

'That's right. I've seen him on the telly. He chats all that nasty stuff.'

All that nasty stuff! I thought it a mean summary of the guy. True, he did have his standard rapid-fire, gravelly growl, in which he shot out tales of coarse city runnings over deep and dirty beats in long cocksman tradition. But there was also the high-pitched nagging granny and other comic turns.

'Used to,' I contented myself with. 'Word is he's gone all spiritual.

Calls himself a bona fide singer now, DJ no longer. Had to, really. There was all these young ruffneck artists coming up badder than him. The DJ's life is a short one.'

'Don't be so cynical,' said Candy.

Lipman patted the donkey's haunches as it was led away.

'What's with the donkey?' she asked.

'I don't know, you know.' My mind was on it too. 'Probably something to do with his uplift. Like he's more humble, less material now—'

'Isn't it a sweet little thing?'

'Mmm.'

'Yes, my people! Heh, heh!' Lipman stalked the stage. 'Me decide to give you an extra special entrance, in honour of the Race Man arrival . . .'

'The Race Man?' Candy nudged me. 'Who's the Race Man?'

'The Race Man! Didn't your parents or – I mean someone *must* have told you about him.' She looked a bit put out at my disbelieving smirk. 'No? Hmm! Okay, well, say the state runs things in certain ways – laws an' police and all that kind of business, yeah? Well, the Race Man runs things in all the other ways. Or so some say. I mean, no one's saying he doesn't exist, but then you've got some who dispute, umm, how much power he's got.'

Maybe I was not making myself clear, or my explanation sounded too much like politics. At any rate, her brow remained troubled.

'Tell me later,' she said.

'. . . so min' you go pay him a visit an' see my man just drop science an 'dus' up your head,' Lipman was saying. 'Cuh some of we like the living dead – we not *connected* up right, y'unnerstan'? We unstable/Like Cain when he slew Abel/Killing each other . . .'

His guitarists struck up simple chords behind him, as Lipman caressed a melody in his real baritone:

People of the sun, la-la-la-la,
'Til I'm laid to rest
Always be depressed
There's no life in the West
I know the East is the best (yes).

'. . . So let's enjoy ourselves on Sports Day, seen? Go see Master Blaster bus' some big-assed shots. Lick dem fat cats out of sight!'

'Maximum!' and 'Fetch that!' a few roared in happy anticipation, as Lipman cooed an excursion on the version:

'Til I'm laid to rest
Yes, the Rest is the Best
The Rest is the best
and the West cannot test.

'Bow! Bow! Fire! Bouf-Bouf-Bouf! Ah-oooo!'

'So who d'you wanna win?' I shouted above the din.

'On Sports Day? Dunno.' Her eyes dulled over. 'I suppose the West, now I'm living there.'

'What! No way. The Rest is the people's team, man! This is our one chance in the year to kick their arses blatant. It's not as if they're doing us any favours, is it? It's gotta be the Rest everytime.'

Candy shrugged. 'Is it so serious?'

'Sure it's serious.' I gestured around us. 'Listen to that. That's serious—'

My last words were accompanied by two dull, quick retorts ahead of us – sounded like a gun. Folk surged away from the front and we were both buffeted in the mini stampede. I was still looking up and saw a man in Wild West outfit, poncho, sombrero and spurs, with a raised pistol in one hand and a noosed hangman's rope in the other, leap on to the stage.

'It's all right.' I grasped a big-eyed Candy's hand. 'Just the flippin'
HPD.'

The High Plains Drifter was a well-known local figure and dancehall distresser. He'd begun as an enthusiastic amateur who might be
given the odd few minutes to chat on a sound, but he had craved a
greater impact and reinvented himself with this garb, infuriating the
professionals with his sometime interventions.

The surge had died down as people saw who it was. Now panic
relaxed into abuse with elements shouting at him to 'Get off! Get
off!' and 'If you's the Drifter, where's your horse?'

The Drifter didn't care. He brandished the noose, explaining, 'An
outlaw is come to town and me have to arrest him. You's a dictator,'
he turned to Lipman, 'and me's the People's Lawman. Me restore
justice inna de dancehall!'

Lipman, for his part, seemed more than averagely affected. A
haunted look strained his face before it set into a glower and he
walked as far out of noose's way as possible, shaking his head and
waving his hand dismissively in front of it. As the Drifter advanced
towards him, twirling his lasso, Lipman made to leave the stage and
the crowd got really agitated. A couple of shows had been stopped on
the Drifter's account before and they feared a repeat. At last four
burly guys bore down on the Drifter from the wings, and manhan-
dled him away. They weren't worried about his gun; they knew it was
just a starting pistol.

'Me's an artist!' he bleated. 'None of you don't know me. Don't
touch me!'

Jeers rained down on his departure. Me, I felt a little sorry with
him. All he wanted was a little rough and tumble with his hero. Plus
it was Lipman who had introduced these militia styles in the first
place; live by the sword and all that.

The Lieutenant was applauded back and the good vibes returned
as he ran through a lo-fi medley of his fatter tunes. I looked behind;

I wanted to savour this pre-holiday pleasantness. I saw one thirty-something couple that I had noticed dancing together before. Now she was jumping up and down, shouting along, and generally going on a bit brazen, but he was cool about it. He looked on and smiled almost proudly at her. It was nice, how he was tacitly encouraging her to shine her own way. More of the time you'd see couples where one half would appear cowed or worse by the arrangement.

Beyond them though, behind and to the left of the main action, something genuinely murky was going on. My three young friends from before were in a vigorous exchange with a fourth man, about their age and dressed similarly. At first I thought they were all spars until the fourth threw his arms up, as if to be frisked, and the boss-man reached out and pulled the watch from his wrist and a silver chaps from his neck. Rah! I thought, they're robbing him. Their prey did not look happy with the situation, obviously, but he was giving up his goods without fuss. However, just as he turned away, the boss let off a torrent of words in his direction and pulled something from his trouser front – looked like a pistol – cocked and held it, right arm extended up, piece pointing down and lying sideways, in the preferred fashion.

My body stiffened. I could not believe what was about to happen. The leader let off two caps at the poor man's back and he buckled and fell as his assailant, a crazed glow of triumph on his face, bust a couple more in the air in edgy afterthought. They had the short buh-buh of a nine-millimetre.

There was a moment of shocked silence in the place as the music cut out and the realisation swelled from the back to the front. I scoped some cover then turned for Candy before pandemonium broke.

In a more frenzied rerun, folk jostled and hurtled. Candy was no more than a yard to the left of me, but two frantic women had pushed in between us and already a rivulet of fleeing people had formed there. I could not reach out to grab her. I caught her eye and called her name, gesturing to her to follow me.

You hear about these types of incidents often, but this was the first time I had been in the vicinity of one. However, my strategy when bullets are bobbing about is quite simple: I turned, made a couple of bounds and deposited myself behind a protective side pillar.

'Backside!' I cursed as I reached for my own gun and remembered I did not have it. I wondered about the whereabouts of security. They had probably fled themselves, if they were not in on this already. And Roland and his peeps? Where were the villains – where was the Drifter – now we might have some need of them? Lipman and his entourage had disappeared long time ago, presumably through the back doors by stage right, where a good chunk of the crowd were even now struggling to exit, casting anxious looks behind them.

Candy! Jesus! Where the fuck was Candy?

I peered out to the space I had vacated to see her still rooted to the spot; her head was inclined slightly forwards and her forefingers were pressed in her ears, as if she was trying to shut the world out. Her eyes were open but unseeing.

I looked for the thugs. Two of them stood sheepishly, casting fretful, embarrassed glances at the moaning boy's prostrate form. Their boss was bent down, rifling through something with one hand, still waving his bucky about with the other. Then he glanced up and saw Candy's frozen solitary self, no more than twenty yards in front of him.

'Wh'appen, sis? Your man done doss out?' he cackled.

There was nothing else for it. I dashed out and was already a few steps across when it occurred to me that this wasn't the smartest move. I turned my face away and tried to scurry more inconspicuously, until I could grab hold of Candy around the midriff and haul her back with me. Her weight was dead but light enough. The guy took a few moments to register what was happening and then to decide what to do, and I was on my way back before he started shooting. His first shot missed us – I heard a bottle crack to our left and someone scream. His second hit the pillar but by then we were all but completely behind it.

I squatted, pulled my knife from its sheath and listened hard, above the heaving of my own chest.

'Come out, come out, wherever you are!' bade the man.

'Leave it nuh. Come on, bredrin,' his friend implored.

He fired another harmless shot in our direction before I heard them trot then run out the front.

I sat down and slumped against our pillar, flushed and a little nauseous. Candy was sat alongside. She was blinking ahead, still dazed, but she seemed all right. I expelled my dread with a deep breath. '*Boy*!' I said. 'So much for a blasted revival!'

We left pretty much straight after – I did not fancy being part of the imminent wall of silence. We heard the sounds of the police sirens but not those of the more urgently needed emergency services. Candy asked me if I thought the lad would live. A number had rushed to his assistance, but he was unconscious when we walked past him to the entrance. You never know – sometimes those nines can go right through you. I said it was fifty-fifty.

We were silent after that. I fixed my head firmly on the roads ahead, clear though they were. At one point I tried to lighten the atmosphere with a Lipman anecdote. I told her how, at the end of the sound clashes where Lipman battled and, more often than not, conquered other DJs, he would stride out in his dictator's outfit, the medals thick on his breast, acknowledge the applause of the crowd, and declare in his cod old country growl: 'After free and fair elections, I have decided to become President-For-Life!' Candy tittered politely, but that was all.

There is shock always even for me, how much so then for her, but the something in the air was something more. I think we both knew our bubble had burst. At one point, I took my left hand from the wheel and clasped hers in comfort but I remained vexed, and included Candy in it. Those kids, to be sure, were my main target. Why did some hooligan always have to dark up a dance? Those roughnecks, the bouncer at Ice Cream before – half the time it seemed the only thing men asked of me was could I fight. I could be just doing my run-up and down – blood skills was all they wanted to know.

My dissatisfaction with her was harder to anatomise and less substantial, but it was real nonetheless. She lacked some necessary qualification for my purposes. Oh, the fact that she had nearly got me shot back there wasn't the problem as such. She would scarcely have to deal with area boys in my man's mansion – although you had to wonder whether someone this light-hearted could live for long.

I just felt it would be a touch slack were I to set her up with my client (if even she still wanted to be): slack to him and to some of the people I knew in this town. I don't know . . . I was thinking about the dance, and the heart-felt murmurs of approval around us when Lipman came out with his Babylon beatdowns, and Sundays – how he called me cousin because I had come through for him that time. I felt that Candy still needed to be tested. See more of the rubbish out there before she could properly appreciate an offer like this.

'A lady from the city,' he had demanded. I had found him one in, but not of, and this still seemed fair enough in theory. But I feared that, were I actually to turn up with Candy in tow, he would find us both wanting. Perhaps I might still prevail on him to pay up but . . . well, I count myself a man of some honour. No matter, I had pure time left.

Truth say, Candy's strengths were her weaknesses. She had few views, she had less pain. The loss of her natural parents had not undermined her. She was good but like a virgin basically. Somehow I felt I should find someone more deserving.

'I've been thinking,' Candy began as we mounted the hill that led up to Ice Cream. She cleared her throat. 'Maybe it's a bit early for, you know, what we were discussing before. I mean, I am enjoying my work and I've only just started like, as it is. I'd look dead funny settling down before I've even settled in, innit?' she laughed, a little embarrassedly.

I nodded.

'I don't mean to mess you about or nothing. You don't mind?'

'No, I hear you. It's cool. I think you're right.' I smiled reassuringly at her. I was glad that we had both reached this point with the minimum of fuss.

I slid the car into the forecourt where she directed me to the staff entrance.

We stood around awkwardly for a moment, Candy hugging her body in the cool night air.

'Well,' she said, 'it wasn't quite a jolly, was it?'

I smiled. Candy! I would miss her vocabulary.

'I'm fit to drop,' she sighed. 'All right then. You know where to find me and – oh God! You will find out and let me know about that poor guy? If he's, he's all right?'

'Yeah-yeah. Definitely.'

'Good. But give me a call anyway. Let's do something again sometime an' umm . . .'

I took a scrap of paper from my wallet and scribbled on it. 'I don't have any cards left. But this is my number. Any problems you have, or a friend has, let me know. Serious.'

'You will be okay, won't you, about this mission?' she giggled.

'Nah worry. How about you? Tonight. You'll be all right?'

She nodded.

'Take a pill and a brandy or something. Just to knock you out, you know.'

She kissed my cheek and squeezed me.

'Ciao, chief.'

'See ya,' I said, and watched as she, her fine arse and those ill denims, stepped inside.

I parked my car up in the guest car park, ran my key card through a groove, and went in through the main doors. A seated security man woke from his doze and eyed me as I walked down the almost deserted hall.

My good-time girl was hanging around by the booth in front of the lifts with her cohort and a young uniformed liftman. These two were nauseously smiley with me, evidently hoping for some largesse. I was on the point of dipping my hand in my pocket but this man – 'Greetings, sir. Wha', y'go raving? Yes, I can see you like to enjoy yourself, heh-heh! I'm John. I'm here nights 'til eight an' the day shift Fridays. What floor is it, supes? Anyt'ing I can do for you, sir, anyt'ing you *want*, y'get me . . .' – just wouldn't stop. I could imagine him greasing up to all the foolish guests who came here same way and the thought of it irked me. I felt he should show a bit more pride. Let him sweat 'til the morning for my money.

Still, it was nice to feel rich and powerful. I dallied with the idea of asking Miss Good Time's friend up too, for some freaky business. She was quite nice, although her wig, layered and tousled, was most of what I liked. But I was tired. The lift came, and I smirked a good-night at the others.

We padded down the corridor to my room in silence, with me wondering whether the physician or the Scot had ended up on my floor.

Once inside, Good Time took off her top and shoes, and headed straight for the shower. An unusual move, but I welcomed it. Perhaps cleanliness was part of the coup at these uptown resorts. I stripped off to vest and shorts, peeled my sheath carefully off, slid it under the mattress, and put the kettle on.

I always keep my vest on unless I know the other person well. I have this rather disfiguring scar along my stomach.

My preparations for these occasions tend to be quite extensive. Ideally, I like to ingest a combination of uppers and downers, plus various folk concoctions. My recent financial difficulties had unfortunately let me bereft of uppers, but I still had my dihydro-codeine and I popped one of these mid-range morphine pills, then built a spliff, made some tea, emptied a sachet of nutmeg from my wallet into the cup, and slurped back the mixture. I can strongly recommend nutmeg, or cinnamon for that matter, for stoking up desire.

I also called John downstairs, to ask if he could lay hands on any Stone, a gelatinous ointment for the tings that someone at Sundays' spot had first alerted me to. But John, despite his earlier boasts, could do nothing for me.

Good Time emerged, in the cream bathrobe with her hair wrapped in a towel that gave her an air of, yeah, distinction all of a sudden. She looked a little older and sadder now too, with the make-up off and the face flat and business-like, but her skin was still even and unhammered and her frame just this side of big, a way I liked it. I gazed fondly at the way her robe curved up and around her nether regions. When all is said and done, I am a batty man.

She flopped down on the bed and, avoiding my eyes, let out a fatigued sigh.

'D'you puff?' I said, holding the zook out to her. 'Just commersh.'

She took a few half-hearted drags. 'Y'have something cool to drink?' she asked.

I wandered over to the minibar. A notice there said its contents weren't included in the price of admission.

'Y'have champagne?'

'Hunh. All right.' I reached down for a stout for myself and a baby bottle of Brut. No doubt the Merciless mark-up would be fearsome, but if it would perk Good Time up a bit . . .

She gulped her glass down.

'What would you do with one hundred thousand folds?' I said by way of conversation and with my mind on my money.

She glanced up at me, as if to confirm my query was only rhetorical, then shrugged, 'I don't know. Buy somet'ing big,' and yawned.

Point taken. I knew it was late. It must be well after three. I disappeared to do my ablutions, returned presently, and began nibbling about her.

She scarcely seemed interested. She made muted groans and fidgeted underneath me as if she were trying to summon the energy to flee, leaving me to chase her cheeks and soft spots about.

I untied her bobbly bathrobe belt, so that the robe fell around her and she was down to her black stretch panties. I noted with some dismay that her breasts, which I had imagined dense, had flattered to deceive. They lacked a three-dimensional fullness but flopped rather like sacks at the top. I tended to prefer my breasts inside a bra, in any case. I liked the texture and tension of the two together. I had half a mind to ask Good Time to slip back her bra, for I was finding it difficult achieving anything like a bone-on.

My nerves were comfortably unfurled by now, and my tings hummed gently but lacked a keenness. I made a mental note to address the uppers situation tomorrow.

At one point my hand passed over her mouth, and she squealed. It was a different sound than hitherto. It did not sound like pain and I interpreted it, perhaps liberally, as enthusiasm. I put my hand on her mouth again and she squealed some more. I ran my fingers down there – hints of stickiness. Now at last we were getting somewhere.

I slipped off her belt, tied it round her hands, flipped her over so her rump was towards me, and looped the belt through the wooden slats at the top of the bed. Then I put my hand by her mouth and set to, doggystyle, once more.

I don't know, it seemed a little better for both of us this time.

A few more minutes, then my rubber, a shudder, and I expelled. I collapsed gratefully on top of Good Time, untying her hands with a final effort. She seemed asleep already. I nuzzled my head up under her chin and listened to her breath's rise and fall. Her heat and odour had come through much more now. Nice.

Of course my mind went to other girls I'd been in a similar position with. To one, in particular. Perhaps I shall tell you about her.

I wondered how long Good Time had done her thing at Ice Cream; how many business types she would have serviced, Monday to Friday, no doubt, before their weekend wives and rolling country lawns. I had recently read an 'At Home' feature on some captain of industry where he'd said that, what with all the stress his job entailed, it was vital to get some peace at the end of the day, which he did in his secluded mansion. And I did not underestimate his stress, but I judged him a fortunate man to be able to obtain some quality rest. Most of the folk that I knew got home to find little relief from the hectic and the negativity. If it wasn't a red-letter day it was difficulties at dances.

I remember checking on the time and then I fell asleep, dreaming of how life might be when I got overs. I had visions of multimillions, breakfasts in bed, soothing rubs in sunken tubs, and of a land where even the villains were fun-loving.

Brr-Brr. Brr-Brr.

I woke with a start. The room was dark. It took me a moment to figure out where I was.

Brr-Brr.

The flipping house phone! Who and what time was it anyway?

'Greetings, sir. This is John from downstairs. Good morning to you, sir.'

'Uhhunh.'

'Just to say that my shift is finishing now, sir, and I hope to see you before I leave.'

Eight o'clock! I could scarcely believe this fool had broken my rest to say this to me. I felt to mix him down but, more than that, I wanted him off the phone.

'I doubt I'll see you this morning,' I replied, just about evenly, 'most likely I'll see you when you're back on.'

'Yes, supes. Heh-heh.'

'All right?'

'Heh-heh. Good day to you, sir.'

'All right.'

I replaced the handset, blowing hard. I felt tired but I would not get back to sleep now. Good Time was still affecting slumber. She had turned over on her side, her back to me, during the night. The pillow was damp with snail trails of saliva behind her head. I think I may have been dribbling there.

I shook her. A second round was the least I expected for one hundred folds. She groaned and shifted not. I could have made it impossible for her to feign on, but I left it. I couldn't be bothered any more; I was already being overtaken by my customary morning moments of depression and general unwillingness.

My humour revived once I was under the shower. A good break today, and the rest of my life could begin tomorrow. I had the number of that lady I'd met in the supermarket. I'd make sure we bucked up this evening. Maybe even lunchtime.

I donned my clothes with a quickness, keen to be out and about. I counted off the sixty notes I owed Good Time and laid them on the bedside table. I was halfway to the door when a 'Hey!' stopped me.

I turned. Good Time had stirred. She was throwing me a fat-arsed smile, her first of any description.

'Breakfast,' she simpered.

I considered, then fished out a ten from my pocket and handed it to her.

In the right mood I can be a soft touch.

5

if you should stop on the main today

It took me forever to wend my way back south. Traffic was chocka. I had half forgotten how bad it was. I am rarely on the road at this hour.

We were snared up deep in the SW4 old town when I took Lincia's card out. It was a quarter after nine. By my reckoning, she should just have knocked down her start-me-up cup of coffee and would be looking for something to divert her from the work that lay ahead.

She answered my call straightaway, her voice a pleasant, professional alto above a noisy office. She had forgotten who I was at first until I reminded her of her promise to show me some uptown flexing. She said it was a funny time to be calling. I said I made all my best moves in the morning. She chuckled at that.

She held out again for my boss. I said I'd forget my boss, just this once, if she forgot hers. She replied how did I know she had a boss? I said she wouldn't be answering the phone otherwise.

As it happens, I told her, I'm passing by your neck of the woods

later. We should have a drink. She demurred but I pressed.
Eventually she gave me her work address, instructing me to come
round at six that evening. 'And don't give me none of that b.m.t.!'

This last remark, coming after what had been hitherto gentle spar-
ring, had a terseness that I judged wise to take heed of. I surmised,
from her crack about black men's time, that she was probably a frustrated intimate. A lady who considered herself down but who found
herself frequently exasperated by the imperfections of those less
together than her. Slack blacks, perhaps, was her issue. I would have
to come across as competent and ambitious tonight to get her onside.
Let 'driven' be my watchword.

I parked outside Beegal's, a mini-supermarket on the SE16 main,
a mile or so from my office. I wanted to give them my midweek lottery slip, plus pick up some scratch cards.

The day was mild, the street as quiet as it was ever going to be,
although already there were a fair number abroad. Don't ask me
what half of them were doing.

I didn't check for Beegal's too tough. Everything – the punters,
the produce – looked nasty in there, but it was cheap enough and
convenient. Back in the day the place was run by Indians who would-
n't take my cheques. When I returned three years ago, the place had
been taken over by some desert people, and they wouldn't take my
cheques either at first. But after a few months, when they had got to
know me, they did. Unfortunately, a short time ago, there was some
trouble with my cards, so now they didn't again.

It didn't look too bad in there today, and my run to the side
counter was clear, apart from some shorties who burst ahead of me to
ask the assistant the time. What with the grill and glass between
them and the difference in accent, this simple query required a lot of
fussing about the hatch before it was done. The glass was bashed in.
Everytime I came there it looked newly bashed in.

I was checking the printed slip against the numbers I had given him – I did seven lots so it took a few moments – when I became aware of the growing thrum of an altercation behind me. Ordinarily, I would not have bothered with it, but the tones of one of the parties sounded half familiar.

I turned round. I could see the woman standing in front of one of the tills in the main checkout section. She was letting off something bad to the till girl and the manager who had come along: how they were ripping her off and taking people for a fool and could they just explain this to her.

She was pointing at what looked like two bags of potatoes. The manager muttered meekly, 'Special offer . . . it's simple. This is a special offer.' His hooded eyes made it difficult to tell the extent of his anxiety but he cast a sidelong at the security man loping leisurely over.

The incident seemed absurd. From what I could gather it was all over the price of the bags. One was heavier but cost less than the other. Nothing so odd about that. There could be plenty of reasons for it. The spuds even looked different, never mind special offer.

So of course I imagined that the woman was mad, but here was another strange thing. Her voice was relatively genteel and I noticed she hadn't sworn, not in any of the places you would have expected her to. I'm not saying that genteel people can't be mad, you understand, it's just that, well, they tend to hold it down better in public.

I could still only see her from the back. She was wearing a knee-length black leather coat, longer and glossier than the crazy's regulation wear, but a coat so chunky for this temperate day as to be a cause for concern.

A customer, waiting in the queue directly behind, was now adding her own oar. 'Heh. You are disgracing everyone. Aa-ah! Someone call the police-oh!' the customer demanded, turning to security.

Leschelle. It was indisputably Leschelle.

I could see her full now. I was quite shocked. My old, dear friend

Leschelle. Her hair was wrapped in a cheap shawl; under the coat she had on a fluffy turtleneck jumper, brown leggings and flat homely shoes. She looked like nothing she'd ever looked like before. But I had heard that something had happened to her.

She had refused the manager's plea to pay up and move on, so the security was now grappling with her. I thought I should intercede before this escalated.

'Leschelle! Ay, Leschelle. What's going on? It's me.'

Security eased off her as she looked up at me.

'You saw what's going on, Boy, when you were deciding whether to acknowledge me these past five minutes,' came her tart response.

'Look, have you paid?' I said. I found myself looking at the till girl before quickly readjusting.

'I haven't paid . . .' Leschelle made as if to continue but stopped there. She was calming down.

I paid for both bags of potatoes. 'It's not worth this aggro.' I smiled at her. I nodded to the manager, we took the goods and stepped out on the street.

Now that we had some peace, I found myself freshly startled by her appearance: the blotchy leggings, the state of the hair exposed under the shawl – short and bumpy –, I couldn't resist peering to see if there were any bits in it. Outwards, she looked on the verge. Inside, she must have passed it.

I had known Leschelle for how long. We'd been at school together, where she was something of a star pupil. Yet she liked me. I think she was the first one who ever did. Nobody could understand it. We kissed, excitingly, once, in year nine, but nothing came of it. I told her her name was beautiful, and could I touch her there? She told me I could do really well for myself, but the company I kept wasn't constructive.

I'd left school and home shortly after and it was a few years before I saw her again. She was dressed in crisply cut, kinda executive clothes and she'd got a gig in a small consultancy that advised other firms on their recruitment policies. It seemed very impressive. She said she'd heard my company had got worse. Still cheeky.

When I'd finally acquired some qualifications, I'd got in touch. She had her own flat, and was a manager already. She had fixed up a couple of interviews for me at places to no avail. I got somewhere in the end, but I wasn't very sociable in that period, and we'd drifted out of touch. It was only when I fell back here I heard say she was on the slide. The last disturbances had just occurred, there was a new policy of condemning a little more and understanding a little less, and Leschelle's company had been one of its early casualties. No one was interested in her solutions anymore.

'She's gone doolally. She didn't go to a proper college, just a tech, you know. Just so much front!' a penniless but well-educated mutual acquaintance had told me. 'When the whole hollow house came tumbling down she didn't have the strength to cope . . .' Our friend Dean, frequently unsympathetic to those he deemed 'bourgeois', seemed quite perked at the turn of events, but I was sorry to hear it. She had always been nice to me.

'D'you need a lift anywhere?' I asked her.

She shook her head and beckoned behind her. 'I'm just at my mum's. You know I was away for a while, so I'm just waiting 'til I get a new place,' she said.

'Is it?'

'You're looking tired. How's the company?'

'Uh,' I laughed. 'I keep myself pretty much to myself these days — '

'And I heard about your father. I'm so sorry.'

My *father*? I had not seen my father for some years and there had been no recent news about him, bad or otherwise, to my knowledge. I did not probe her further for I feared hers was a mad utterance and, should it prove so, I did not want to deal with the

potential consequences of opening up that can. She might be looking for some kind of emotional crutch and, what with us living so
close again and all . . . There might be no end to it. You have to protect yourself too, don't you? So I just nodded, accepting her
condolences.

'All right then,' she said, and picked up her bags.

'Look after you.' I was relieved that she had not raised the matter
of visiting.

Hunh, I thought grimly as I returned to my car, all those years and
her net yardage had been nil. So much for the girl most likely . . . I
watched her disappear from my mirror. I would go and see her, for
sure. But I'd have to play it carefully.

I gazed at certain others around me with a fresh eye: the dread
with the meaty python coiled thick on his head who shredded my
nerves whenever he approached; the elf-like man who scooted
around on his child's bicycle, shouting 'Rigga! Rig-ga! Rig-ga!'; the
fair-skinned guy in the purple tracksuit who always hailed you, hauling himself jerkily down the road, clutching his personal stereo in
one hand and making periodic stabbing motions, like a conductor,
with the other; the bespectacled shabby-suited man, who looked
down meekly as he made his way up; and the Wynter brothers, the
hopalong twins, who stared straight ahead. They'd been at school
too. They looked young and still with it: quality garms, good hair –
you could see they'd got a home, didn't live on the street. Everything
was in order apart from the blank gaze, and their 'skipping' action,
and the way they never spoke. Once, when I was living up the north-
east side, I'd seen them outside a train station actually talking,
rapping away with a girl. I'd been intrigued by this idea of them
speaking in some parts but not in others.

The worst time was every other Wednesday morning when they
went down to the benefits office to collect their sickness allowances.
They had to be there between ten and eleven, a new rule designed to

stop claimants criss-crossing town for multiple monies, and you'd see them emerge in undignified straggles from Fanon House; gaits fevered, tics accelerated, hastening down, with Hope, my friend from the spot, keeping his distance on the other side of the road, acting like he was scuttling some place else. You could never laugh. Probably everyone here had a connection with someone in that straggle by now.

A pedestrian gesturing frantically at me on my passenger side broke my reverie. I had not even noticed him approach. He was holding out a slip of paper, gesturing that I lower my window. I did not recognise the man. He was in his thirties, agitated, dry, ashy skin, shirt hanging out, jeans; possibly stink, possibly not.

What the hell. I was in that tender mental frame. I buzzed my fancy window down, checking that my car was in first gear – it has long been my habit to keep my ride in first gear whenever I make short stops; presume the unpredictable and all that. I was surprised to find that it was not. I slipped it in.

The guy was brandishing the creased paper. I leant over: 62 Harleyford Road was scrawled on it.

'You know Harleyford Road, blood? Harleyford.'

I scrutinised the man. It was a good mile on from here.

'Harleyford, that's some way on, you know. You gotta go back up the main—'

As I spoke, a second man, who may have been standing outside Beegal's a little while before, came up on the kerb beside us. He was scratching his bald head and looked altogether fidgety. As he passed us he suddenly darted to my passenger window, while the first man moved away from it. Time slowed and my heart missed a beat. The second man – a bit older, someone I'd seen somewhere before – reached to his waist, hitched up his sweatshirt, and pulled a little black bucky from the top of his jeans.

'Boy, we don't like your ways!' he spat at me, cocking and gripping it sideways.

I checked my gears. A blank instant – I could not recall how to drive – then I took my foot off the clutch and hit the gas as hard as I could.

'You too dark!' he shouted.

There was the briefest pause. He was angling the gun up, beside my open window, on a line with my face. Then the car lurched, wheels burning, and shot diagonally forward as a volley of shots shattered the glass behind me. My mind was tight on the worst moment that I knew lay right ahead, as the car rocked on itself and dipped in speed. I kept my head down as far as I could as I skidded and wheeled frantically left.

Bam, Bam!

The glass on my right side got hit and I waited for the softness at the back of my head, *Bam!*, then the car surged again and I was away.

When I was a good handgun and a half's distance away I changed up the gears, glancing behind me. I could not see them, nor hear the angry heat of a car in pursuit. I kept going straight. My heart was still thumping, my body clammy and flooded.

The immediate thought was to turn the car round and return to the scene. That way I would give myself the opportunity to take the offensive, or else to find or see something or someone that could furnish information. Find out what the fuck this was about . . . But without my gun it would be too dangerous a move. My birds might not have flown.

Who were they? The shooter I had seen somewhere . . . In the head! In the fuckin' head, tah raas! That meant extreme malice. And but for that little, late adjustment I was finished.

It was our custom to have our funerals with the coffin lying open and the face exposed, for mourners to file past. So to come to off a man's head – well, that was deeply dark. *You too dark*, he'd said.

I had to get off the road. The right side window behind me and most of my back window had gone, my front right and side left were cracked. I was pretty conspicuous.

I considered seeking temporary refuge by a friend's, but I am a proud man and there might not yet be cause for it. I did not fancy sharing a room with Hope at Sundays'. In the end, I decided that my best bet was to return to my place. Apart from anything else, I needed to get my gun. And even if my foes did have a home address for me, I might get to spot them first.

I chucked two lefts, then continued up a parallel sideroad, my eyes and ears alert for sirens and anything else, parking a kilometre or so on, a street behind the brown-bricked block of units that housed my office. The units were originally part of a refurbished council estate that had been sold off to insurgents during the gentrification that preceded the Nine-Fevers. After the burnings, the council had had to buy them back, divide them up and lease them out as low-cost units, the new plan being to encourage local businesses. As much as the cost, it was the fact that there were two routes in and out of this one-time estate that had appealed to me.

The connecting yard did not look part of the estate. An entrance, sharp right after a corner that you could easily miss, past the big metal bins, a few stationary vehicles, over the grassy bank and past the bollards, then I was quietly mounting the black iron steps of the fire escape that ran up the back of my building. All clear so far. Blade in hand, I tried to turn my key silently, but it was impossible so my sole recourse was the crash-bang approach. I counted to lucky number seven, a swift turn, then I kicked the door open, a moment's pause for whomsoever it might concern to show their hand and I tumbled across the floor.

The place was as I had left it. I retrieved my piece and peered out the front blinds; everything seemed in order down there. One final, dirty, knee-raking tumble outside my front door, a wary wander downstairs, and I was done.

I fell back into my chair. I had a dull pain at the back of my head, a headache of the tense and nervous kind. I reached for my morphine: two would probably have done the trick but three is a good number for me as well. I let the sweet sensation of still life hug me a moment. I felt better; but I was not out of the woods yet.

Information was the key. My first call was a breathless 'Here's the drama!' recount to Sundays at the garage. He had to tell me to slow down and start again.

It was when I came to the gunman that it suddenly clicked where I'd seen him before: at Nyam Food when I'd set out yesterday evening. The thievin' Mr Eb'ry Year . . . I did not know the man from Adam. There was nothing I could think of between us. Sundays did not know him either, nor had he heard my name raised recently in connection with any dispute. An unnecessary question on my part, really – if he had heard anything, he would have told me already – but I had to ask. He promised to ask around, and get back to me soonest. He said I should move out until this matter was sorted. I said yeah-yeah.

Next I belled this guy who served at Nyam Food. He remembered Eb'ry Year: he came to his take-away every so often, no fixed times. For sure, he'd give me a shout when the man came by again. Okay, the moment he stepped through the door. He was cool. He didn't ask me why or anything. I wondered if he'd heard yet about the incident.

I tried Dean, my bourgeois-baiting friend, as well. He and Sundays got to hear much of the local chat. He might even have chanced upon the scene by now, and picked up something useful for me there. I cursed him as I heard the continual dead tone of a disconnected phone. He didn't have a mobile either. No doubt he was still about his daily perambulations, but I wasn't about to brave outdoors just yet.

I came off the phone with my thirst for facts hardly slaked, but altogether more relieved. It was just warming to feel that there were people on my side. You get quite paranoid when someone is trying to kill you.

Who could it be? If it was not Eb'ry Year or his colleague directly (and I was certain I'd had no dealings with either one) then either I had somewhere injured someone connected to him or else a third party had put him up to it. A contract, pure and simple.

Boy! Well, one thing was for sure. If it was a contract, the person who was employing them would have to be dirt poor. They were hardly Premier League. That was reassuring. They had even come on foot. Or did they? That, at least, was something I should be able to check.

I got me a pen and a pad, and headed it 'Enemies?' I arrowed 'Old Cases?' north-west from it, and due north I arrowed 'CLC?' After a pause I added 'Prisoners?' I was thinking of anyone who'd recently come out. Someone who had been away, drinking porridge.

But when I thought about it, a man didn't need to come out to get a job done on me. And, in fact, my enemy might not even have been inside at all. He might just be out there, always have been out there, nursing this grievance.

That got me low, thinking of it like that. '*We don't like your ways, Boy,*' he had said. Again, that could be anything. What had I *done*?

I really did not feel well. My brain was leaping about, I could not keep it still, my head was still hurting and I felt jittery all over. I went to the bathroom to wash my face.

I had to penetrate this puzzle. On my return I crossed out the 'Prisoners' category. It got me nowhere. The way I now saw it, if I had done or stood accused of doing something to somebody that merited getting shot in the head for, then most likely I would remember it or else I should easily be able to dredge it from my memory now that my mind was turned that way. Hindsight might be required, but whatever I'd done would have the hallmark of a major incident. Therefore my enemy was known to me.

This felt like progress.

I turned once again to 'Old Cases' and 'CLC', adding personal and professional in two sub-categories underneath, and 'Eb'ry Year' in an unmoored bubble in the middle of the page. Old Cases! To have even had some to be worried about would have been a fine thing, but work had been even thin for a while, and the little done had been footling. No need even to peruse the brief details I'd logged on the computer. A couple of still missing persons, bits and pieces for lawyers and councils (finding, then serving X an order. Not work, granted, to make me popular, but I'd never had any grief doing it. My prey knew I was just the messenger. And not even debt collectors get shot in the head). Oh, and Sinbad.

Sinbad! Could it be? The thought had had no preparation but it took me only a few moments to assemble the data and wield them into a powerful force. Why not Sinbad?

That unprecedented look he'd given me at Ice Cream, like he was scheming but wasn't saying. Crafty, no question. *It'll all come out in the wash, Boy, still.*

On the face of it, it seemed absurd. Sinbad, the original faint-heart. But every worm can turn. Perhaps he had decided 'Enough' and had started with me. He had contemplated his gammy legs, and my part in them; he had grown tired of being picked on.

There was the cause. At the time, when I'd extracted a 'moderate prejudice' pledge from his associates, I had felt I was doing Sinbad a favour, but obviously I could well appreciate how he might have a different point of view.

The pedestrian assassins, the botched job – pure low-level Sinbad flavour. Plus he'd been staying down this side when I tracked him – plenty of chances to link up with an Eb'ry Year. It would have required some high-quality nerves to have handled himself so amiably when we ran into each other last night but, hell, he was a villain. That was his job.

Sinbad – one can smile like the Nile and be a villain, I scribbled and circled, before lighting a steadying cigarette.

Personal/professional. My CLC I considered but was inclined to discount. True, it had ended both bloodily and inconclusively, both cause for pause, but that was so long ago now, ten years and more. Out of our original five, Danny and Bassie had turned fellow travellers, but only TK had turned outright enemy. And TK was inside, TK – I had not raised him up for a time. I could not believe he would come for me again.

My powers of concentration were fast fading, but I knew I had to fix my mind on older cases, those from the earlier part of my five years in this game. I'd locked a lot of those days deep away, and did not go there often.

Hunh, my government days . . . A man had come to see me about eighteen months after I'd first moved into these already straitening premises. A Ministry man, with a well-greased offer. He wanted me to attend the initial meeting called by a new clutch of 'agitators' at the local recreation centre: a public meeting, a two-page report, a fat cash fee, simple. I had asked him why they didn't go down themselves. He had thrown up his arms and smiled thinly.

I was no fool. I knew the coup and had – like I said, under different circumstances, with a different breed of official – been approached before. I'd had the longest thought, then rung him up and said, 'No "who was there", strictly "what was said".' 'Done,' he'd replied.

Well, it had progressed pretty much how you'd expect, from public to private meetings, from those of a political or cultural nature to villainous assemblies. No retainer, no codename, I kept as much distance as I could. Of course, it was not possible to keep to the no-names policy, but I hope I can say that I betrayed few intimacies. Sometimes I confused or else sprinkled morsels over two pages, and sometimes I told them of matters – the neighbourhood mood, say – that I judged they, for everybody's sake, should know. And I protected too. A few had caught trouble, but none of it had been major and none of them had been friends.

Boy . . . but it was poor though, the poorest. This I do not deny.

You may wonder how such behaviour squares with being a man of honour, and there is very little I can say to this. Except that it had been done to me before. Perhaps at the start, with my foundling beginnings, and certainly once, brutally, after. And, well, if I wasn't a man of some honour, I wouldn't feel a way about it, would I?

All our dealings were supposed to be confidential, but you never knew. There could have been a slippage, even a sly leakage. I had refused to play ball in the end, after all. But surely they would seek to reinveigle me first?

No, I came back once again to Sinbad. Like all the top people, I have my hunches . . .

Something was burning. Aaah, shit, my cigarette. Its embers were smoking, merrily singeing my thigh. I slapped it away. Those cfs must have knocked me out for a minute, and it had dropped from my hand. Now I had a two-inch circular hole in my best black trousers. Damn! Days like these . . .

My head hurt less; I felt more spacey now, plus this new grogginess. Too fretful to kip, but it would be good to get more comfortable. I pulled my bedding out from the drawers where I had dumped it yesterday and stood there a moment. I was wondering where to place it. I didn't want it anywhere remotely near the front door, only there wasn't much choice with just the one room and a hole-in-the-wall bathroom. In the end I deposited my mattress behind my desk, in the back left-hand corner. I stripped off to my vest, and lay down.

From my position I could see the top part of my door, and my senses waited for sounds or shadows behind the glass pane. My gun was to hand, and my knife in its usual position. You, at least, have saved me before.

My eyes dropped after a while, my head drifting where it wanted, to sweet, lulling scenarios: Sports Days past and future, me playing a heroic role . . . I clearly must have, but you know when you don't feel that you've fallen asleep at all . . .

Cars. Hearing cars. In the dark, in the back, on the floor. T-shirt and shorts . . . Shaking, shaking, I cannot stop myself. It sounds like I've been sobbing but I'm only trying to catch some breath.

If I don't keep quiet, they may do it here.

Two in the front. What can I do? Just teary outlines. Slipping in and out, in and out. I'd like to rest now. In . . . trying one last time:

'TK, just call him, man. Just—'

Rings raining down on my face. Out.

Say something. Please tell me something. If they said something, I might be able to talk our way out.

It must be soon now.

Baby bro alongside, retching, terrified. Pleading 'Forgive me' with my eyes.

The ring man steps out and opens the back door. He punches my face.

Thinking quick, I know this place. The shoppers' overflow spot, where the cameras don't reach. He is inclining his head.

And we're hobbling towards the railings. Hear the car start behind. I'm trying to reach my upper back, reach the knife. Need to stop and arch, but we're only safe when we're hobbling, when the sport is good.

And I'm there, rubbing my back against the stakes, scrabbling under my shoulder.

Car halts, he's shrieking, and I'm scrabbling, scrabbling . . .

Quarter past five! I jumped up, dismayed. I was supposed to be at Lincia's within the hour.

I'd been asleep the whole afternoon. I couldn't remember my dreams but I knew they'd ended bad. My stomach, that old sore, was starting on me again.

I was damp with sweat too. I did not think it was drama-related; I wish it were. For some years now, situations that I used to handle, to my remembrance, without sweat have had me perspiring in spades.

I think I may lose ounces in weight every time I lie down. I went to see a doctor, who was no help, but a Net respondent believed there might be something wrong with my 'sympathetic nervous system'.

I scurried about, getting ready, trying Dean's number again (still discontinued), slipping on my black trousers, spotting the burn, and rummaging for another pair. I was wondering what to do about the car: It would be a risk venturing out in a vehicle that was known to my enemy, but I could think of no other one I could lay my hands on in the next few minutes. It had to be a quality ride, too, for Lincia. I couldn't go back to the rental company and hire a new one, or even get my own back – they would want to see their nine series first, in its original state. Anyway, the place was ten minutes in the wrong direction.

I decided to take the car down to the glazier round the corner where – notwithstanding his attempt to charge extra for what he seemed to regard as aiding and abetting – we did a hurried, makeshift job on the major casualties, replacing the back and the left side windows.

I had to get a listings mag too and it was twelve minutes to RV time before I set off proper. I would be a good fifteen to twenty late, no question. I prayed she did not storm off, cursing my parts.

Now that I had slept on it, I no longer regarded Sinbad as a sure-fire bet. I realised I'd completely forgotten about the bouncer from Ice Cream. The odds on that fool being able to turn a contract around in eight hours on another side of town seemed longer than a politician's nose, but how many half-forgotten fuckrey incidents were waiting to be taken into account?

This kind of trouble sure concentrates the mind. Thirteen years ago, after I'd suffered my other near terminal encounter, I'd understood it as the start of the rest of my life. Like the loudest of wake-up calls, not surprisingly. And I'd most definitely rung the changes. Gone to college, done the straight. Now I was back in the manor I had fled from, getting stepped on again. Like Leschelle and her return to her mum's, my net yardage had been nil.

It was extraordinary to me, really. I'd always had a high opinion of my talents, and had assumed that, sooner rather than later, my achievements, my lifestyle, would be commensurate with that opinion. There were excess amounts of things I could do or had a skill for over and above the left-handed matters: my knowledge of natural and ancient history – Name me the spot on the globe – was extensive, my syntax in perfectly good order, my mental arithmetic a legend in certain quarters. I finished my sentences. I could have been, I don't know, a doctor of something. Even a Merciless-style success would have been enough. And I could work with my hands too, I could scope the colour of men's minds, talk a bunch of talks . . . plus the city. I knew this city.

The knowledge and the hunger was there, but somewhere between these two and the execution was a dulling.

Not always so. The first twenty years of my life, until the break with CLC, I think my speed was quite good. Notwithstanding some useless schooling, I armed myself different ways and selected routes that did not do disservice to my abilities. But since then, now that I looked at it square, my progress had been alarming. There had been some good, elevated times – the first few months at Roswells, Cosmic-Cosmic – but I hadn't managed to hold on to any of them. True, I could point to the harshness of others in certain instances, to being abandoned here in the first place, to all the cards of a dud hand. But I am a firm believer that there comes an age by when, no matter what the hand, the big boys and the genuine pretenders should have sorted their shit out.

Someway I'm gonna end this with a great red cherry on top.

It was still possible. Finding this girl would be the dream lift-off.

Might have to review my ways. Take today. Okay, the morning's drama had been upsetting, but I could have recovered in time to have got another car, made further enquiries regarding the matter, and still have been prompt for Lincia. Instead, here was I inspecting my watch and cutting through traffic like a crazy man.

There were a whole heap of cautious drivers alongside, frustrating me. I kept looking out for other black drivers to slip behind. I could always rely on my kind in a rush.

I think the pills were partly to blame. One, even two, would have been fine; I'd been shot at, after all. But the three . . . that was what had knocked me out, seen off my afternoon. Could it be that I'd spent a good part of my second phase in a daze? I didn't think that my pharmaceuticals themselves were the problem, but perhaps I had unwittingly placed them between me and the problem.

I'd been prescribed morphine when I was hospitalised following that first big trouble. The pain had been something else. I'd been gashed on my left side, plus haemorrhaging from my stomach below. They'd had to cut into my stomach and drain the blood out before they could even start on my side. They'd put me on diamorphine for the weeks I was there and a course of cfs when I left. Never completely knocked them on the head since.

Boy, what a big-arsed mess that had been. To get stepped on for things I hadn't done, hadn't said. Ironic, of course, in light of my later. Probably even TK didn't think I had bitched; he just seized a rumour, a Boy and his rides with the rads-rumour. He, he'd been a real error of judgement.

That guy he'd sent . . . Deep asleep, I thought I was dreaming when someone broke down the door, shouting 'Police!' He'd sprayed me, then kept crashing his bat down. Only when those rings came glinting did I know for sure what it was about. Gold shell-like spirals that twisted up to points. Utterly distinctive – could only be the man from the wedding . . . Now that – to invite your tightest to your cousin's wedding and introduce him to the man you're sending to end him – *that's* dark.

I'd got him though, in the end, courtesy of my blade on the bed's blind side. Only been keeping it by me a week. TK and I'd been having cross words and I just fancied something was brewing. But then had come the chilled-out wedding, and after you're not as watchful as you were.

I'd managed to grab the knife and surprise him with a lunge. Very close, very messy, but I was on top and used my last strength to stab him again and again and again. He struggled in vain to stand. So much blood, making a mockery of my own, but it was the movement of his bowels that I most remembered. Him sitting and shitting his last breaths away.

I told the police a piece of the truth, which was that it was self-defence. They didn't take too much convincing, given my condition plus all the stuff that he'd brought: the bat, the Mace, the cuffs. I later found out he'd planned to do some shit to me, then dump me in the supermarket car park.

He was the first and, to my knowledge, the only man that I've killed. Which is something, I suppose.

It was ten minutes to the bad by the time I turned to Lincia's road. Nowhere free to park, so I put some coins in a meter and dashed across to Barclay Towers, not the grandest in a street lined with stone and glass peaks, but a mighty building nonetheless.

Long-toothed security eyed me from an alcove on the right, but I had no business with them. Unfortunately, I had to stop at the list of companies by the lifts to ascertain the floor of Lincia's company, and, sure enough, an insistent 'Excuse me, sir' pulled me back. I had to spend a precious minute filling out my details at the desk before, twenty-one floors later, repeating the exercise at the reception outside Lincia's office. The receptionist buzzed through and said Lincia would come out for me.

My relief veered towards irritation when, ten minutes later, she still hadn't materialised. I suspected she was playing hardball. I'd been late for her so she'd be tardy too to ram home the point that

time costs money. Either that, or she was using her woman's prerogative to its letter. I blew out – this might be one of those prickly,
cat-and-cat evenings.

I scanned the journals on the low table in front of me. *Management
Today* had, perhaps, seen livelier issues, but an interview in the paper
on the lives and loves of one Darren McIntosh, a football star, kept my
attention. He'd recently had a kid with a native lady – I think she was
an athlete – and the interview was part of a wider piece proclaiming
that the number of my kind who were married or cohabited 'out' had
now passed fifty per cent. Fifty per cent! I had not imagined the rate
was quite as high as that. Fifty per cent made me feel embarrassed.

Miss Don't Feed the Blacks had devoted her column to a profile
of Merciless, extolling Ice Cream and the spirit of enterprise. The old
villain was pictured by his horses and a dog he was entering for
Crufts, a sensationally mean-looking hound called Congo.

Folk in suits criss-crossed the space from time to time. I guess the
company office space extended across both sides of the lobby. A
gang of four came out from the left positively chortling; they must
have been making mad stacks to be so bubbly and we hadn't even
reached midweek. One of their number was an unprepossessing late
twenties brother and he caught my eye for one long, startled
moment. His look, anxious bordering on the embarrassed, was one
that I recognised very well: that of a once or usually orthodox type
discovered in an unorthodox situation. You might see it in the neighbourhood on the faces of people stepping out with an unhomogenous
partner – although presumably that example would soon be ancient
history in these new fifty per cent times.

They moved to a big map of the world, dotted with flashing
bulbs and multicoloured marker pins, on the wall behind the
receptionists. The brother seemed somewhat discomforted but
tagged on nonetheless. The most exuberant of them, a bearded
five-bellied figure who carried the swagger of seniority, shifted

a yellow pin from the Siberian steppes to the Gobi Desert.

'I'm sorry, Zeke, it's off to the Gobi you go,' mocked the bossman. 'I don't know what we're going to do with you. Next no result and you're off the map!

'We had a session at Madame Zsa Zsa's last night,' he continued to the receptionists, inclining his head sorrowfully at my friend. 'You know it's slappers' delight down there, and still he couldn't score. What are we gonna do with this one, eh?'

'You fancy the K.A. tonight then, Zeke? Time for do or die at the last chance saloon,' cackled a sandy-haired fellow.

'You're not doing so well yourself,' was all Zeke could muster.

The third man breathed out contentedly and prodded at a pin in California: 'I think you'll find that I'm still in babe heaven . . .'

They carried on past and I got up too shortly after. I'd begun to perspire again, for some reason, and needed to wash my face. Zeke's shelling was continuing in the Gents. He was adjusting his clothes in the mirror that ran the length of the room, while his boss's voice boomed out periodically from behind a toilet's closed door. You could hear the man grunt, followed by the splash of his dumps dropping, and then his eager resumption. I fancied Zeke wanted to leave but felt he couldn't until his boss had finished his business. I felt for him. I am no fan of this practice of holding conversations whilst passing excreta.

Lincia finally emerged, some twenty minutes after my arrival. She wore a black linen trouser suit and a cautious smile. The braids framed a face that was as I remembered; not turn-head classic, but altogether agreeable.

'Sorry for keeping you. I just wanted to finish for the day.'

'It's cool. I got to catch up on some reading.' Relaxed, but with a hint of the driven. Solid start.

'Lincia, O light of my life,' the boss was back, 'coming out with us? Just the one. Nothing dangerous.'

She shook her head and indicated me, a tad apologetically.

'Oh yeah. This is he, then. You will take care of her, won't you? Or you'll have the boys to answer to.'

His tone was jocular but he and his cronies had a good look at me. I was fast developing an unreasonable hatred of this man.

'A nice-looking place you got here,' I said to her in the lifts.

'We're one of the top five you know, in what we do.'

'That big, bearded guy – is he your boss?'

'Umhmm. The head of my section.'

'He seems to have a relaxed grip on the reins of power.'

'He's all right. A little of him goes a long way.'

'I can imagine.'

It was still light when we came outside, a clear sky and the merest nip in the air. Pleasant weather for a date.

'So what's the plan?' I asked.

She shrugged.

'The indecisive type?'

'No. I'm waiting on more information.'

'I'm keen on information too,' I said breezily. 'What else is there to do?'

And I told her of the hours I spent accessing sites on the Net, increasing my worldly knowledge.

'Do I take this?' I said as we came up to my car.

'No, it's just a walk where we're going.' She peered more closely at my ride. 'God, what happened here . . . and there?'

'Ah, nothing really.' I shrugged. 'I screeched past some kids earlier on, musta nearly knocked them over. Had to stop at a light further on and they ran up and pelted it with stones an' that.'

She screwed her eyes at me, an unconvinced curl about her mouth.

'So what d'you do?' I asked as we walked on. 'I mean, the card says "Media – PR".'

'I'm a media buyer,' she said. 'I have a list of clients and I look at

the media that it would suit their product to advertise in. I match up
the client with the outlet and see the campaign through.'

'Serious?' I was impressed. 'Long-dicked, no question.'

'What?'

'Nothing, nothing.'

'And you, Mr Mysterious One. What do you do?'

'Me? I'm self-employed.'

'Self-employed?'

'That's right.'

'But, at the same time, you have a boss.'

'I work for people from time to time. And this week it's for this guy.'

'Doing what exactly?'

She had led us into a small, descending alley where, halfway
down, I could spot the lit lanterns and benches of a bar. This part of
town, on the borders of the City, was old and the alley, with its flag-
stones, lanterns and the sloping script of the tavern sign, had a
medieval feel that I welcomed. You could imagine shadowy deeds
being done in times past: the clink of sword from scabbard and the
rush of horses' hooves . . .

'You wouldn't want a man who revealed his whole hand on the
first date, would you?' I replied.

'Excuse me! You say you're a freelance something, you work for
bosses who come in and out of town. You've got a nice car, except for
some strange marks on the bodywork, bullet holes for all I know. I
think I'm allowed to be curious.'

She stopped outside the bar door. I pushed it open and followed
her in.

I liked what I saw. From the outside it could have been your
everyday, all-corners-style pub but inside it was indubitably a
winebar, catering to a smartish crowd. They sipped their drinks
perched on log stumps, while oak beer barrels and a standing suit of
armour continued the medieval theme. It was exactly the kind of

establishment I liked to hit when I made sorties into town. You could meet solicitors or insurance types here, folk who could give you work. I used to work joints with Vee, an old friend and one resourceful lady. It was easier to wheedle your way into others' company if you came as an unthreatening couple. But she had only gone and got married on me. Just recently, I had been making less successful sorties with Dean, but he couldn't really do the smart, urbane part; he was always odds-on to say something rude or otherwise embarrass you.

Lincia asked for a glass of white wine, and I thought I'd follow her lead. If things went well we could go for a bottle.

'You were saying?' she said, as we sat down.

'What?'

'I said I was curious and you were about to explain.'

'Oh. All right. This guy this week – he's got a tourism business. Not tourism, more development really. He wants me to look at the books for him.'

'So you're an accountant. Hmm. Really?'

'Yeah, I studied it.'

'Where?'

'East Bank University.'

'East Bank? You lie!'

'Umhmm. You know the East Crescent site? Just up by the market—'

'I was there as well. Did communications studies.'

'Yeah? I did my AATs down there, first off. Then this company that recruited me, Roswells, sent me back there evenings to beef up my skills—'

She whistled. 'Roswells – we do a little something for them. They're quite big.'

'Umhmm. Hundred partners.'

'They must have liked you.'

I shrugged. She knew all these places. I would like to have bolstered up my credentials but I would have to be careful. Still, I was glad that I had told her these parts of the truth. It allowed us to dip into a shared history and soon stories of our college and the lives of its infamous were flowing. We had not overlapped, but this did not diminish her enjoyment of the coincidence. She could hardly meet many East Bankers in her quality of work.

She mentioned a couple of guys from Roswells, and asked if I knew them, or was in touch with anyone there. I shook my head to both. I could see she was waiting for me to elaborate but I preferred not to go down that troublesome route. I searched for a line more likely to nourish this sense of a bond.

'You know how it is,' I said. 'When you leave a place like that, all of a sudden it feels like a million miles away. What *you* see and deal with, compared to what your old workmates are seeing. Sometimes, even when you're there, there's that contrast—'

'Tell me about it! I just bought a flat, right? Whole six-month song and dance. Endless meetings with the blasted banks and trying for tenants and – anyway. So I'm steaming off to my colleagues and they're all really sympathetic, saying they had the same hassles, but when you check with them more now, turns out half of them got a nice leg-up to get their places. Daddy put some money in or paid off debts, or Grandma dies and leaves you something tidy in the will. You can't compete with that. I had to do it all myself, plus I've got a child on my hands too.'

'Is it?'

'Umhmm.' She fixed me in the eye, gauging my reaction. If children weren't a problem for my client – and he had not said so – then they weren't one for me. As long as their dad wasn't around, obviously.

'Boy or girl.'

'Girl, thank God.' Lincia grinned. 'Asheema. She's only four, but you'd think she was a big person already. She speaks very proper.

She says things like, "Mummy, the TV's getting on my nerves!" or "I can't do that cos it's against my conscience." The other day I was effin' and blindin' on the phone, right, she goes, "Mummy, don't swear!"'

'And where is this new Lincia-Asheema residence?'

'Oh, east still, just. I'm on the riverside.'

'Yeah? Must have set you back some.'

'Some. A lot of my workmates live out west but where I am you get more space for the money.' She took a gulp from her glass. 'You know, we don't all have to be living in some rubbish area where the schools don't work and the only cinema's some stinkin' fleapit – you step through the door and the rats come to say hello!'

I had to laugh at that.

'You know what I mean, though? Too many of us are set in that same-old same-old mentality, looking through the wrong end of the telescope, not seeing the bigger picture.'

'There's so many nice things to be done out there,' I fed her.

'Thank you. I work hard, I do all right, why shouldn't I have a nice place and do nice things? I *like* nice things.' She considered me a moment then shook her head. 'Some people – take my child's dad, right? Nothing so wrong with him. He wasn't a runaround, bright, popular, could do all sorts. But he just likes getting by at work and hanging out with his same-old stagnant "boys" from the manor – pure "East-East-East".'

'Boys, man.' I shook my head too, sympathetically. 'A couple in your life is all right, but, from they reach a certain critical mass – you're finished.'

'Critical mass,' she repeated, turning it over. She seemed to like it.

'So tell me about these nice things you're keen on.'

'Oh. I have this sort-of socialising group, me and my girlfriends, and we go to health clubs or the big tennis tournaments, or go see a show—'

I pulled the listings magazine from my jacket. 'I come prepared, you see.' I flicked through it. 'Theatre, maybe?'

She smiled. 'Nothing too heavy, mind.'

'No-no. I'll find something . . . romantic.'

'Please!'

There were a clutch of big west's end productions, but I didn't know anything about most of them, plus the ones I did, like the Shakespeare plays, looked quite heavy. I'd been thinking it was probably better for us to see a black show in any case. That was the most likely to provoke reaction, give me the swiftest sense of the candidate.

And there was quite a lot on offer there too. But when I checked it, well, never mind heavy, they all looked downright depressing: *Women on the Verge of a Nervous Breakdown, Waiting to Explode, Playboy, Black Men – Is There A Cure?* (tickets include entry to after-show discussion), *MsBehavin'*, a musical – Aaah! This looked more promising. The listing included a photo of three women in evening dress, perched on stools around a bar. 'Ever wondered what divas say when the lights go down and there's no-one around? *MsBehavin'* is a sistren's conversation for everyone to tune into! Hit songs include "The One that Got Away," "We're in Business, You're in Crisis" and "Cos I'm Tired (Mighty Tired of You)". Jesus!

'Anything?' Lincia asked.

'Plenty of stuff about boys and girls. Nothing that you would quite call feel-good romantic. God, I didn't know relationships was such a big ticket right—'

'You kidding? That's been the issue for how long? Where've you been? You "been away" or something?'

'No, not at all.' I was momentarily backfooted by her use of the left-handers' euphemism. 'I just hadn't, uh, noticed. It's been three years since I, you know, was in deep with someone.'

'Three years? That's no time. It's been more than twice that and I haven't met a brother who didn't have feet of . . . tch,' she shook her head, made a 'forget it' gesture. 'Years. If it doesn't happen soon I'm off with my boss and done!'

She grabbed the magazine from me and flicked across a few pages.

'You know what I was gonna do tonight, before your call? This friend of mine is having a dinner party for eligible singles. It's his second one. He calls them his "waiting to exhale" evenings.'

'Like that old film?'

'Yeah, cos that's what we're all waiting to do. Set eyes on Mr Right and go "Ummmm!"' She exhaled dreamily.

'So what happened first time?' I was intrigued.

'Oh, the men were – didn't really do it for me. I was still gonna go though cos, you never know . . .' She returned to the magazine. 'How about *MsBehavin*? That's supposed to be good.'

'Let me have a look.' I reached across.

I was now thinking it might not be such a good idea for us to see one of these shows. It would be a high-risk move for certain. On the one hand, her frustration might be so oiled as to ease my path and hurry her into accepting my client's proposal. On the other, two hours of *MsBehavin'* and she might just want to strangle me and my kind.

I came across a bold half-page ad towards the back of the magazine:

CITY CIRCLE
presents
The Sports Week Ball
(Eve of the eve!)
Get in the holiday mood at our exclusive boat party.
Celebrity guests.
Complimentary wines and cuisine. Carriages at 5.
Dress: Formal.
Venue: *Seabreeze*, Albert Bridge

'Know anything about this?' I asked.

'Oh yeah, 'nuff people are going to that. Master Blaster's supposed to be reaching. Making a little speech, doing an auction – all sorts.'

'Why don't we do that then?'

'Are you offering?'

'Sure.' I looked down at the ad. Eighty folds a head. Rah! 'My treat.'

Lincia beamed. 'Why, thank you! Times must be sweet for freelance accountants.' Cheeky. 'It would be nice. Don't think I can, though. I got a sitter for Asheema in, but only 'til eleven.'

'Why don't you just bell the sitter and get her to stay over, if she can?'

Lincia made the call and the matter was sorted. She made a bid for me to stump up the extra readies for the sitter, which I resisted. We settled on going halves.

'Hmm. We could reach for the first dinner sitting, but it won't really get going 'til after eleven. That's when the boat's actually setting off.'

'Hear what,' I said. 'Why don't we pass by your exhale party, chill there a while, see your friends, then we can head down to this thing.'

'Sounds nice. Gonna be mash-up tomorrow, though. Might have to wangle the morning off.'

I was pleased with how things had turned out. This 'exhale' evening was just perfect: I would meet a whole bunch of options there, quality back-up should Lincia prove a non-runner.

It wasn't far. We took my car down, stopping off at another fancy supermarket to purchase some provisions. 'We bring something savoury, you bring something sweet,' she explained, ogling a counter's selection of Thai curries. I roamed and came back with a packet of cheesecake, a bottle of rum, and some milk.

Her friend's drum was a few minutes on, west-central rather than west-west. We parked in a pretty mews street, and sauntered down to no. 14.

6

exhaling

Exhaling. Do I *have* to talk about exhaling? Je-sus. The main problem with it, as I was saying to Lincia in the drive down to hers after our swiftish in and out, was that barely anyone was actually up for exhaling. Oh, you could sense some of them wanted to – especially with this one baldhead – no doubt we'll come to him. But they weren't really going about it in a way best calculated to achieve it. Weren't playing the percentages. You gotta indulge and dig out that best side; shit, you gotta give some to get. Okay, I don't have so much form in the matter but how much form does it take?

We'd arrived to find two grim-set ladies intent on calling an end already. They were in the kitchen mixing down host PJ, this fogey-ish, late-thirties light-skinned guy, clad in stripey shirt and tight-battied jeans. One of the women was busy rewrapping trays of grilled fish in clingfilm, stacking them in an icebox, and adding the odd gruff endorsement to the flow of her slim-nosed friend, who was buckling up her overcoat and couldn't believe how they'd got messed around again. How he'd portrayed this top evening and promised they'd have no complaints this time and what had he come up with? More no-no rubbish guys, and who *was* that funny-looking one who kept coming out with foolishness?

'Oh that's Kwame,' PJ had piped up, in joltingly pukka tones. 'I met him or rather he met me the other day. He's uh, he's different. He's the wild card.'

'Do me a favour. Don't play that one again,' growled the doggie-bag girl.

Lincia had introduced me to PJ, Lola and Stella in the coat. PJ was a management consultant. They'd dated once, a while back, she'd told me. Stella was quite tall and elegant, Lola cuddly-pretty. The ladies had considered me, casting the briefest of smirks at Lincia. I'd felt a little as though the honour of my gender was at stake and had found myself standing as straight and as broad as I could. Your eggs are safe with me, I'd smiled at them, before leaving all to catch up while I inspected further afield.

The situation in the spacious sitting room was as ugly as the complainants had indicated. There was a sprinkling of my kind among ten or so women. You couldn't even really say the men were sprinkled for two of them, reasoning in old-country-inflected tones, were engaged with each other while four women were grouped unconnectedly beside them, desultorily picking from the savoury selections, disappointment etched on their faces. Three other women sat on the cream sofa: one had arms folded, the second was catatonic, and the third, intricate rows of orange beads curled about her twists, seemed to be having trouble surmounting even the introductory hurdles with the brer who sat on the floor in front of her. She was going, 'Guess I'll have to call you the Shadow then? Or Mr Nobody,' and he was firing back, 'That's right! That's my name,' body hunched, staring down, the picture of petulance. He looked like a guy ordinarily on the agreeable side of regular: dainty chin beard, little round specs. I could not imagine what had transpired for him to be withholding even this particular.

Though the situation was probably to my advantage, I remember I did feel for the ladies at this point. They had really dressed up, they had sorted this top food. The only man they were getting any interplay from was one at whose sight I doubletaked. *Dean*. Rah! No one less likely . . .

He'd got up when he saw me, to the transparent relief of the girl whose ears he was burning. Old Dean – with his difficult pitted skin, his frayed twenty-year-old clothes, his singular points of view plus the habit of rolling his neck and shouting at close quarters – could be quite disconcerting to the many he accosted on the street, never mind the stush.

'Dean, man, my poor righteous teacher, who let *you* in?' He still had his trademark pink and white checked washing bag of a rucksack slung over his shoulder.

'Kwame. Kwame tonight,' he'd muttered, moving us out into the corridor.

Kwame. He liked to go for an old-country handle in sophisticated company. I called him Rip quite often myself, after old van Winkle, for it was my contention that he had been sleeping all these years. I'd told him that tonight I was an accountant by profession.

How he had managed to remain so stagnant was a mystery that perplexed me even more than my own thwarted progress. He'd left our primary school to go to the one decent secondary in the borough, and gone on to gain entrance to a solid old university. Even then he'd seemed a touch eccentric but we'd naturally assumed this was a by-product of his large brain. He had failed to do his duties at college, though, flunked out, and since then essayed the odd aborted assault on the workface. I remember him completing a course for teaching English to foreigners, for example, only to find no joy securing a post at the private colleges where out-of-state fat cats sent their kittens. He had been ill served but clearly something was ill adjusted in there too. What it was had never come out between us.

Turned out he'd met PJ just the other day. PJ was advising some friends setting up a business and politics magazine and thought that Dean could do something for it.

I could picture the scene. PJ the commuter, making his dry-arsed way between two points of safety, getting pounced on by Dean. PJ at first perhaps reaching for his change then being gradually won over by this shouting man and his forthright opinions. PJ in the grip of a big idea . . .

I told him I'd been trying to bell him after my drama earlier. His eyes had widened. He could not believe it was me that had been involved. He had heard the screech of tyres and shouts and hurried over. Beegal's Mr Jamba, sweeping the glass from his front, had said he'd seen nothing, but others claimed they'd seen the gunmen running down a sidestreet opposite. Some of these same onlookers had also maintained they'd witnessed a several-second firefight. Nonetheless, I felt now quite confirmed in my view that my hitmen were cut-price pedestrians. He could tell me nothing about them, though.

I'd sketched him in too on my case and asked whether he had any recommendations from present company. He couldn't say as yet. 'They think they're all that but they're just "Bailey's girls", most of them,' he'd smirked, referring to a creamy old neighbourhood favourite.

Dean may not have had a job to speak loudly of for all the years that I had known him, but that did not stop him being, after his fashion, a snob. I'd wondered if he knew of his role here as PJ's wild card.

I'd led the way back, my plan to take over this so-called party. Raise the vibes and see who rises to the occasion, was the thinking. Flush out the coffee-nosed.

My first move had been to edge up the volume on PJ's *Sisters of Swing Vol. 30* compilation. It was either that or Haydn and those guys. Lincia had strolled in, come over and nodded. It had to be done, she'd agreed.

She had brought a pack with her: her friends' humour had light-ened measurably with the entrance of some more males. PJ made some fresh introductions and folk sat up and restocked on this and that. Feminine eyes darted newly about myself, and, I imagine, the other unknowns with good skin. It had felt like seconds out, round two, but all too briefly, unfortunately.

With this whiff of battle, of competition in the air, I accept that I may have allowed a certain personal dimension to creep up on me that next little while, but I do not see how it could have been other-wise. To be sure, my mind remained on my client, but of course I could not talk to that business directly, and, even before I could deploy the indirections that I favoured, there were these other broth-ers to dislodge. Mr Handsome Gleaming Bal'head in particular.

He had eased himself down among the floor rugs in the central reservation, beside myself, Lincia and three of the livelier girls. He was this graphic designer cum amateur boxer, and was simpering modestly as they chortled, 'When's your next fight, then?' and 'When you're done there, pass by my work, I've got a boss whose head needs a thump-up!' It did not surprise me, amid so many mild cor-porate guys, to see this weakness for the full-blooded.

'What weight do you fight at?' I'd asked. He didn't look all that big to me.

'Light.'

'Light,' I repeated. But this fact diminished his spotlight not a jot.

'I used to do martial arts, you know,' I'd said.

'*Is* it?' That got their attention.

'Especially this "capoeira" style. Kinda kung-fu meets dance. That's the lick that, it's got everything—'

He had nodded. 'That's non-contact, though, innit? More like gymnastics.'

'Depends who teaches you. These days mainly people learn it to keep fit an' that,' I'd conceded, 'but originally the slaves developed it in Brazil to hone their combat skills. They could hold razors between their toes.'

And I'd stood up and arched back, tensed my arms, and run a couple of capoeira twists and twirls past them. I'd tried to execute them with due elegance, to draw the observer to its balletic rather than its breakdancing aspect, but I'd been too cramped in the small space at my disposal, landed awkwardly on my right foot, and found myself taking a fall and rolling over less than tidily.

'Haven't done it in a while, plus you need the music,' I'd muttered, clambering up, righting a rolling Pyrex bowl, and noticing, with some alarm, that I had lost Lincia and co. They were back exchanging trifles with Bal'head. 'It's the fighting art for connoiseurs,' I'd trailed off, defeated. His sly 'non-contact' jibe had perhaps been the blow that had sunk me.

PJ wasn't slow to stride over, scoop the bowl from beside me and plop it back on a low table. As if to compensate for the precipitousness of his move, he'd begun patting me on the back.

'How are we then?' he'd inquired hollowly. 'Have you been fed? Have you been coffeed?'

It had irked me, being patronised by a man whose dinner I had been trying to save, but I'd taken his hint and settled myself down on the sofa with some mullet. Tuned into some others' chat, and tried a more conventional tack, only to find that I had had to repel more questions than I could put. The ladies were just as Lincia had been initially with me, but with bells on, hitting me with initials then supplementaries on a few of my facts: 'So where d'you say you live again?' 'The south-east, south-west *borders*?' 'Accountant? You don't portray yourself as one.' 'East Bank? Oh, all right. When was that then?' Their good stuff – gossip about the big names this radio reporter had interviewed, or the beautiful people Stella had come across (she worked for a cosmetics firm) – they'd aimed at each other and the friend who called in on Stella's phone.

Perhaps it was paranoia, but I felt small, a little shut out by most all. Like I'd been dismissed without due cause. I was perfectly entitled to call myself an accountant if I wanted to. I'd passed three-quarters of the AATs, hadn't I? And it wasn't as if mathematics was even the half of what I knew. I just wished I had, you know, all the propers to show them that.

They weren't so clever. Stella, in particular, irked me with the blatant assaults she committed on the word 'portray'. 'You don't *portray* yourself as one.' I'd noticed it first in the kitchen. Portray! Her one big word.

It just seemed as though, whatever it was that I might have had to bring, they'd already somehow weighed and found wanting. If it had been just a reluctance with my admittedly possibly shady self, I might have allowed it, but even the old-country-accented geezers, whose chat was solid and whose credentials – one of them a banker – were impeccable, were getting little change. They may well have had an all-round polish, something else to discuss besides their favoured politics. No doubt these girls, glugging their Bailey's, thought those ones were too 'bush'.

As for Dean/Kwame/Rip, he was generally being studiously ignored, which was further condemnation as far as I was concerned, for he was a man of cheeky but rarely less than piquant conversation. At one point Lincia did engage with him. They were arguing, obviously – he'd just asked her friend whether she'd ever thought herself a 'tragic mulatto' – but at least they were talking.

I went to investigate the girl who'd been dozing on the sofa earlier when she began waxing with my Africans. Her features – squat and powerfully built, like a bison, but a not unattractive high-cheek-boned face – had a familiarity to them and, as she continued the discussion, dropping names of dignitaries, I remembered where I'd seen her. One month before, our one feted African leader had paid a brief visit to these shores. Space had been made for him to tour my humble neck of the woods in the company of the Minister for Special Duties, and we had lined the streets by the recreation centre that afternoon to greet him. Buoyed by the general euphoria, the man with the snake on his head had lifted his python and began shaking it around. Two-twos, this squat, suited woman with an official's badge on her lapel, had materialised and pointed frantically towards the snake-man. Three policemen had come running and, after some struggling and juggling, managed to drag man and beast away. She had stood there impervious while elements shelled her. Even I, with my loathing of serpents, had added my stone's worth: one of our own iron-fisting one of our own on a day like this!

She had hardly enamoured me then, on that occasion, and didn't make up for it now. The three had discovered a mutual admiration for the old country's ageing strongmen and I came with my Lipman impressions and some else, to only the haughtiest acknowledgement on her side. I could see that she was soft on the banker, and that he was indifferent.

I was now of the view that it was smartest to pursue the devil, so to speak, that I knew. Lincia seemed as quality as any, less objectionable, less hard work than most and, from what she had told me of her history – how she'd weighed PJ and some others and found them wanting – I reckoned her gettable. It was a view that strengthened with the one decent conversation, Dean apart, that I had.

The once sullen man with no name had approached me, flexing his arms karate-style. He'd seen me doing my party tricks before and come to tell me of his own abiding interest in the ways of the East. His youthful interest had been sparked, like mine, by the rituals of the arts – the bowing before and after, the graded dans and

dignity, all that ancient fragrance – but now he was coming more
from the spiritual tip: he'd been a Buddhist for some years and from
time to time went on these country retreats; long periods of reflection
with the monks interspersed by bouts of what sounded like flagella-
tion. He'd have these baths there and lie down on a slab afterwards,
where a cohort would beat him with a bundle of big, soapy towels:
'It's like a film that seeps through your skin; your body just disap-
pears. Plus if you've got that mental stillness there already, ah, it's
just sweet!' And I'd nodded encouragingly, thinking of his stillness
and my bridges.

His name was Ken. Canto Ken I called him. He was a sound
recordist and I'd said to him that, with his solid job and peaceful vibe
then, so long as he was keeping stumm about the flogging, I *knew*
there must be 'nuff girl wanting to slip a ring on that finger! And he'd
snorted and said he didn't think so. When I enquired as to the problem, he'd smiled sourly. 'You know, everybody's got layers,' he said,
'and that's fine. Someone like me, I've only got, say, five layers. But a
lot of the sisters I've tried with, it's like they've got fifty. And just
when you think you've got through – Boof! Down drops another one
to unpeel before the two of you can progress. It's like the twelve layers,
or labours, of Hercules. It's almost as if you've got dates willing for it to
fail so they can say, "Oh yeah, I tried it, and it ain't happenin."'

He looked quite upset. No doubt someone had been mugging
his mind only recently.

That had been the reason for his dis of the orange-twisted lady. 'I
just thought, Aah, how about if I turn the tables this once? Make
myself impenetrable.'

I'd sympathised, though of course I could not help thinking that
he had allowed his 'history' to prevent a new start just as much as
anyone.

I was certainly getting an introduction to what Lincia had earlier
called the issue, and could only hope that come a few years time,

when I might myself be in the market for a provider of uptown seeds, the air would have cleared somewhat.

I took Canto Ken's number. He thought he might have my client's Wu Tang 'heaven and hell' song deep in the vaults of his collection. The original clan, he told me, were these renegades, these 'fallen angels' cast out by the Shao Lin temple of monks, great strivers after physical and mental perfection. Interesting.

The intervention of Dean's bag had furnished us with a convenient exit point. A shocked yelp had suddenly cut through the room and I'd looked up to see Lola holding the edges of a dress that was spattered in peppersoup, while Dean brought the culprit to rest and rolled his neck apologetically. She'd glared at him and hurtled towards the bathroom.

We'd taken our goodbyes, resisting PJ's proposals for parlour games. Mr Bal'head too was making noises about leaving – early night and all that before the weekend bout. I'd closed the door to an unseemly five-cornered scramble for lifts in his ride.

Exhaling. That was exhaling. No wonder my client was paying for it.

7

a ball on a boat – the dream team turns nightmare ticket

'A premier pied-à-terre you got here,' I congratulated Lincia a few
minutes into our stopover, the little voice in me wondering whether
that was the right expression or, perhaps, a potato. Whatever, I had
wanted to get something in early, mindful of the great efforts she had
exerted in acquiring the place. And I meant it too, although the flat's
stature could only have been enhanced by the spectacular view of
our river's quays that we'd glimpsed as we'd driven up to the gates of
her fancy estate. As it was, her fifth-floor apartment was situated on
the wrong side of the block, and instead looked out over their little
park of a backcourt: lanterns, well-scrubbed lawns and stone terraces
that finished with a pond at one end and curled round to the forecourt, the entry gates and the guard-booth at the other. I had not
realised that these secured estates, so common in the west, had penetrated as far as here. Beyond the gates were some warehouses and
offices, half of them bearing 'To Let' signs.

She handed me a glass of some peach-tinged soft drink and we headed back to the sitting room where the babysitter, a gum-chewing teen, had her feet up in front of the movie channel in a manner that suggested more of a personal connection than simply business. Asheema was already in bed, and Lincia disappeared to take a peek at her and have a quick wash and change.

You couldn't glean much about Lincia from her surroundings: white walls, black Formica surfaces and a few, low-key furnishings in light, natural woods; the flat looked pretty much how it must have when she moved in. The sofa, where the sitter reclined amid assorted rugs and cushions, looked riotous by comparison.

There were just the odd extras: a couple of handsomely mounted posters of shows in the corridor and matching empty blue vases on a table, beside a dinky globe that I twirled around, feeling slightly chilly.

A tarted-up Lincia returned, cradling her daughter. Asheema, a plaited, sleepy-eyed thing in her nightclothes who gave me a close, morose look then, when I approached, squawked and buried her face on her mother's shoulder. Hers was a relatively modest negative response; normally, when lighties see me, they start bawling, for some reason.

'Asheema – it's a lovely name,' I said.

'She's just tired,' explained Lincia. 'Come on, sweetheart, say something to Boy.'

'Are you taking my mother out tonight?' Asheema enquired, as if she feared the worst.

'I am indeed.'

'Make sure you bring her back safely.'

'Yes, miss,' I nodded.

'A little star or what?' Lincia hugged then watched her scuttle away. 'I tell you, her dad was well wrong-footed when this one popped out. He was so sure it was gonna be a boy. He says to me he reckons God gave him a daughter as a payback for all the girls he'd distressed in his life. Now, when Asheema gets to that age, he won't be able to rest thinking about all the sweet-talking raases running after her.'

'I thought you said he wasn't the runaround type.'

'I said not when he was with me, he wasn't.' There was a defensive edge in her voice. 'But there's a before and after, ain't there? My girl will be too smart for them, though. She's dead clever. Head like a sponge.'

She was sending Asheema to a private primary school on the other side of town, but the school would only take her for one more year and Lincia was already fretting about what to do with her next. I could not make any specific recommendations but we both agreed that local provisions, notwithstanding this fancy estate, would be the death of someone with a head like a sponge.

We made our way into the front corridor. As she slipped her coat over her black chiffon dress, she pointed to her wallprint of a dance company's 'groundbreaking, dazzling' production of Shakespeare's *Antony and Cleopatra*. The cast looked pure United Nations.

'Did you catch that at all?' she asked.

I shook my head.

'You should have. It was the best night. These friends of my friend were in it, and a bunch of us went down. I love dance.'

'No, I've just been real busy,' I muttered as we stepped out.

'You seen any Shakespeare ever?'

'Sure,' I answered emphatically, opening my passenger door for her. If Lincia wanted to go down this cultural road, I would defend myself to the hilt. 'Plenty.' Her face looked enquiringly of me as I keyed the ignition, and pulled round to the forecourt.

'My favourites are the ones set in . . .' I stopped myself. I'd been about to say 'ancient times', but I realised this did not sound very sophisticated. In truth, the only two of his plays I could produce any sort of spiel about featured antique Romans and the like. One, *Julius*

Caesar, I had read, amazingly enough, at school; the other I had stumbled upon during my times with Cosmic-Cosmic, to whom I owe much of my knowledge of such matters.

'I like the ones about legends the best. You know *Troilus and Cressida*?'

She screwed her eyes at the traffic ahead. '*Troilus and Cressida*?'

'Umhmm. That's the beautifullest right there.'

'Are you sure he wrote that one?'

'Yeah-yeah. And he was on some big-arsed bleakness when he did it.' I was pleased that now I would have the chance to impress her. 'Okay, you know that famous old-time war between the Greeks and the Romans? I mean, sorry, the Greeks and the Trojans? Okay, you got Troilus and Cressida who are lovers in the Trojan camp. The thing is, this whole war is being conducted like some gentlemen's sport. Like cricket, basically, if you know it. It's all, you know, top-notch codes of honour and breaks from battle for tea and feasting in the enemy's tents an' so forth. True, the Greeks are pretty devious behind the scenes, but your Trojans are livin' Knights of the Round Table. And Troilus, he's like that to the max. To begin with, Troilus is like, "Oh, I'm a lover, not a fighter!" He calls the warlords "fools on both sides"—'

'Have you got a tie, by the way?' Lincia burst in, leaning forward, staring at my open neck.

'Oh yeah. In the glove compartment. I've always got a tie.'

'Good.' She fell back, and I returned my concentration a moment to the road.

'Where was I? All right, the Greeks capture one of Troy's key people so the Trojans do an exchange and send over Cressida as the deal. She gets interfered with, you know, messed about real bad and she finds herself meeting these rampant Greeks half way. She loves her guy off but she has to stoop low to survive. Now Troilus – when he hears he just loses it. He rushes out to battle, spitting fire, he don't

care if it's Cressida, the Greeks or his own – he's gonna do the lot of
'em! So this guy's life gets shredded, then Troy itself goes up in
smoke—'

'And does he kill her?'

'Oh – Cressida? Urm . . . I don't quite recall now, actually—'

She tutted in exasperation. 'So what's your point?'

'Well, my point is that when a situation hits the fan – a certain situation you have to encounter – it can fuck up even the best of us. I
mean, people are always going on about somebody's character. "Oh,
what's he like?" "Is he a good sort, bad sort?" whatever, when in fact
more of the time a person's real character has got fuck all to do with
how he ends up behaving in a certain situation or how his own life
ends up.'

'That's not true.'

'What's not true?'

'It's not true. That your character doesn't affect what happens to
you. It's how somebody portrays themselves in a situation that probably decides what happens *next*, and that's where your character
comes into—'

'So how about unfaithful Cressida? Or Troilus? A sweet lover who
starts coming like a beast. What was his true "character"?'

'That's different, though. That was strange, extreme conditions.
It's not a normal situation.'

'I disagree. I mean, okay, it wasn't normal in the sense that there
was this mad war going on, but it was typical in the way that here's
this key moment in this guy's life where his character is counting for
nothing compared to these other factors. He's already lost his inner,
his real self during this war, this situation that came along, and suddenly got so big and personal on him, you see what I'm saying? I
mean, obviously your personality is gonna affect those around you,
family and friends, whoever, and, who knows, the Race Man may
have a few words to s—'

'You don't believe all that crap, do you?'

'I – I prefer to be on the safe side.' I smiled. 'Anyway, what I'm saying is that in terms of your life's big shape – are you rich or poor, jobs, options – your quality of character don't tend to have much bearing. Cos I reckon the majority of people fit within the same broad, average range. Hear me out,' I begged as she started to protest. 'You've got those who fly off the scale, you've got the few big brains out there, you've got the odd out and out stinkman. But more often than not it's the same broad range – even the nicest person is irking somebody and even the laziest gets off his butt at some point to find work. Our differences aren't enough to explain away how different people's lives actually are. And that's where situation comes in.'

'So how about the ones who go from the till to the boardroom?'

'Them,' I chuckled, 'a sprinkling of them are bona fide stars, but mainly they just ran into a good situation.'

'Maybe they actually ran out and got the good situation. Maybe they sat down and planned it out, fired off applications and rang round, and all that comes back to character.'

'I thought we've already established it's not just the special few who get off their asses!' I countered. 'You know, there are so many variables . . . you may need all of them to run your way—'

'Nuff times people do get the job, or do get what they want, then they fuck it up still.'

'That's true.'

'And that's character.'

'Can be. But that's some cases out of how many millions? It might be that you only get one bite at the cherry and the next man who succeeded was lucky enough to get three. It could be that the timing wasn't right for you; "If I knew then what I know now" type of thing; it could be that general politics undermine you, the way Troilus has to hand over Cressida. It might even be that yes, you are this top person who gets handed this top opportunity and, this time round, character is gonna be all that counts. The only snag is – and this is why that play is so dread – you've had an *earlier* situation that was so overwhelming that it's completely undermined what you once were and what you would have been. That earlier reality just ended up crippling you, the same way it's destroying your top city with its top principles. Maybe you even saw it coming, and you did your home-work, got yourself prepared, but this thing – oh, it was so strong and you were weaker, and now it's too late for this new, good situation to make the difference. Imagine if the god of love had passed by noble Troilus's yard at the end of the play and said, "So wha'? – I trust you and Cressida are still up for this altar business?" The little devil's gonna get sent packing with a lot more than just a flea in its ear, innit? That's why I always say to people, "Don't tell me what he's like, tell me first what's *happened* to him."' I gave her my QED smile, happy that I had started and finished with Troilus in the circular style I have seen deployed by many a top debater.

'Well,' she shrugged, 'I still say, "Show me anybody who's forty, and I'll show you the bed they made for themselves."'

'Oh I say it 'n' all – I agree with you. Definitely. If anything, I drop the age down to thirty-five—'

'So, what's the problem then? What's your point?'

'Well, that folk don't see the balance right between cha—'

'Oh no, not again!' Lincia shook her hand at me firmly. 'You've had two gos.'

She brought out her face mirror and tweaked her make-up. 'God, I hope they haven't pissed off without us.'

'What time did they say again?'

'Eleven or thereabouts. It's coming up to half eleven now.'

'We'll be all right,' I said.

And we were. Clusters of partygoers were still hanging around the riverbank and on the walkway that ran alongside the waterfront

development above us. Lincia could hardly contain herself, got out
and cooled her heels halfway between myself and the nearest guests,
waiting for me to do up my tie.

It was good to be back by my bridges. The Albert's lights were on,
though they were too close to me and there were too many folk
around to be at their most affecting. I gulped in; the air was fresh, the
air was good up here.

She greeted a couple of acquaintances as we sauntered down the
row of restaurants and shops. I handed over the damage to a City
Circle Promotions lady who sat behind a low table, flanked by my old
friends Security, at the walkway's end. Beyond them, a steep wooden
bridge took us down to the boat.

A few of the guests were standing in a small deck area at the back
of the boat, teasing a bunch who had come down to the quayside to
hand out fliers for other events ('We'll bring you some fish in the
morning!'). But most, a good one hundred and fifty, were congregated in the large lounge room on the lower of the boat's two floors,
sipping the complimentary wines. Everyone was certainly dressed to
impress – the ladies had come in gowns and dresses with lacy frills,
satin, taffeta an' ting – nevertheless, there was an inconsistency of
tone, which I put largely down to the wide range of jackets and suits
that the men were sporting.

At eighty folds a head, I suppose a lot of the guests there must
have been right high-fliers – 'That's Monica Alexander, the chilli
sauce queen,' Lincia whispered to me excitedly, 'the Minister for
Special Duties made her Business Newcomer of the Year . . .' – so I
was quite amused to see that their manners were nothing to write
home about. Some waiters entered with trays of fried chicken,
samosas and nibbles for those, like us, who had forgone the dearer
dinner-inclusive ticket option. As soon as they set the trays down,
there was a mad, unseemly dash towards them, with words and
elbows flying about: 'What you doing?" 'Can't you just hang on a

minute?' 'Paula, Paula, pass some down here then!' I passed one unfortunate, who'd been knocked down, examining her foot and flicking bits of pastry off her front. The waiters looked quite bemused at the dogfight.

We set off from the shore with a cheer, as City Circle people walked around handing each of us Dance Cards. They were marked '1', '2' or '3', with a blank line by each number.

'You've all got your dance cards, you know what they're about. Don't say we don't give you every opportunity to get to know each other!' announced the promoter, standing on a raised dais at the top of the room. 'Meeting people, making contacts and whatever whatever – that's what tonight is for,' he laughed. 'So, ladies and gents, if you see someone you like, ask them for a dance and get them to sign your card. That's for later. Right now, we've got some star cabaret for you, and after that, well, we ain't even begun yet, I'm telling you . . .'

Hamma and Decka, a well-known comedy act, came on to do their unfunny thing. While they prated, my mind went back and forth over my Lincia decision. At some unconsciously reached point, probably during the Great Food Rush and my realisation that I was unlikely to meet some spectacularly classier lady here, I'd settled on her. Of her type – and it was, for all my little jests, a perfectly good, thinking, progressive type – she was fine. The two could go places; she could hold forts, no problem. There was that briskness, a certain sharpness in her manner that I avow I didn't greatly care for, but I put this down to her territory. I'd seen it in others at PJ's that evening and during my own corporate sojourn. Besides, I thought it a touch absurd for one with, ah, moments such as mine to be holding his nose at such a trait, which had me wondering if my distaste was not, perhaps, gender-related, and it was this nagging worry that helped to seal my decision. Let no one say that Boy has a problem with strong women.

We'd have to build up the vibe again, and then I'd hit her with it. Gotta leave myself enough time to spring those contingencies if she deals me a no-no . . .

I asked if she wanted to explore the ship and we took out, up and along the top floor, which boasted, I noted, a little casino and a games room.

'You happy with the turn-out then?'

Lincia shrugged. 'It's the same old faces, most of them. Me and my friend Stella, we used to do all of these events, the medics' ball, the lawyers', these City Circle dos, and there's a bunch of people you see time after time. You know that Duncan who came up to me? He's wearing that same brown suit every occasion I see him. I *know* he wears it to work as well! He's such a fraud. One time, we were all coming from something in a cab. It came to, like, two nuggets each. You should have seen how long it took him to extract the shekels from his pocket.'

We had come down to the back of the lower deck by now, and here we halted by the rails, looking out to our company on the river, and the house lights and the silent shapes on the northerly bank.

'And there are never enough guys. New ones, you know. My phone's gonna be ringing about you tomorrow.' She smiled at me.

'Yeah?' She had a sexy smile. Her lips were full and packed with juice. 'I'm still trying to get a fix on the kind of guys that appeal to you. I mean, your kid's father sounds a bit different from these bods here, or the PJ—'

'Someone who can support me, period. Someone who's gonna add, not subtract to the equation, and that equation includes Asheema and me—'

'Seen.'

'He'd have to be pulling in fifty K minimum, for starters.'

'Fifty K?' I whistled.

'Umhmm. And I'm talking solid money, not sometime money.

Asheema's gonna need money for her schooling for the next ten years. And then there's fees for college. And what if she wants to be a doctor or a lawyer? That's extra years to subsidise—'

'It's a fair whack, though.'

'There are people out there on that kind of money. I've *dated* guys on that kind of money. You can't expect me to go backwards when I should be going upwards. Why settle for less?'

'So what if you really checked for a guy, his head was screwed on and he was ambitious and everything, but say he was still making his way up?'

'Look, I've done the "really check for" thing. It don't last, man. Me and Asheema's dad – six years and done. And it don't even need to be about anything. I just don't think human beings are designed to . . . dig each other for much longer. That seven-year itch thing is true. And seven years max ain't enough to design a life around.'

'Hmm . . .'

She looked expectantly at me. 'Say it, say it,' she said.

'No, no, I was just thinking you're tough is all.'

'Just realistic.'

'If you were a queen you'd be Lincia Ironheart!'

She smiled and jutted her jaw out towards the river.

'You need a millionaire, I reckon,' I added, and I would probably have continued and hit her right there with the offer but for the sound of clapping that broke in from the lounge behind us. Lincia wanted to return to see what was up.

A communications entrepreneur, Martin Dubay, was on the podium. A man who had started working for a cable firm and then gone his own way, putting the Net to new uses. I generally had time for what he had to say but I must admit I thought he was applying some unction a little thickly that evening. All this guff about how we guests were the new middle class, the pioneers, the shining examples: how we should large up our chests because we were achievers, the mere fact that we were here proved that.

I thought that a bit much to say on the strength of eighty notes and, as Lincia had commented, what would be some of the guests' one suit. I snorted and Lincia frowned at me but she was tutting too when gremlins troubled City Circle's great coup: a live link-up with a hotel on one of the islands, where a similar do was taking place.

Dubay had introduced the link-up by calling on his guest of honour to join him; there had been some whoops and hollers and the clink of bottles, then Master Blaster, as billed, had emerged from the ranks of his followers. He'd taken the stage, where he was handed a glass trophy, City Circle's Community Award. MB, it turned out, was last year's recipient, and the idea was that he would 'present' the award to his absent successor via the Net. However, and I do not know if the technology they were using was Mr Dubay's although I imagine it was, we could only make out various bodily parts of those on the other side. And even these bits – three heads and shoulders above a table, the chin and microphone-clutching hand of Dubay's counterpart in the foreground – kept jumping. Dubay was shouting 'Can you hear us, Carl?' and Carl kept going, 'What, what?' through a loud crackle and hiss. After a minute of this, I could hear grumbling amongst my fellows and the first cry of 'Cha! Eighty notes, nasty samosa, dry comedian – an' this!' was posted.

Luckily the Blaster's own rather weary tones brought all to respectful silence. He said he would keep the trophy safe and warm until the winner's return. We had a few more seconds of gesticulating hands then the picture fuzzed out.

Master Blaster looked of a mind to step down but Dubay pressed him into announcing the winners of a prize raffle for City Circle members. As one who had followed Master Blaster and his exploits closely over the years, I could see he was not in the best of ways. He looked down, shoulders hunched, smirking. At first I thought that perhaps the aborted link-up had offended his high standards but, with the way he was slurring his banter with the winners, it was clear that liquor had mashed up his head. He was known to overindulge from time to time. With the winners clasping their envelopes and waiting for guidance, Dubay fired off a scattergun reel of questions at MB, eager to compensate for the damp squib of the link-up. But MB only mumbled thickly and threw twisted grins out to his corner. 'I ain't really doin' no full-blown interview right now,' he piped up eventually. 'I came to hang with my peeps. With my *peeps*.' There was a truculence in his voice and Dubay did well to desist. MB stepped down to his customary good hand, the raffle winners slid off behind him, and the presentations were concluded in rather peremptory fashion.

Some music broke out from the PA and the crowd circulated once more. I picked up one of the event programmes and glanced through it, feeling surplus to requirements, while Lincia dealt with a few more who accosted her. Two of them were clearly friends but one seemed a straight-up interloper, who, bizarrely, appeared to consult some notes from his pocket to aid him in his patter. I swear, even the driest of guys have a keen nose in these matters. They can sniff the hum of a first-date no-lockdown situation from fifty paces and will mosey up, bent on entryism.

'You should introduce me to some of these folk,' I said, as we walked on. 'I mean, just your friends, not the, umm, not the others.'

She gave me a quizzical look and then slipped her right hand around my left. 'You're the one who's in pole position, you know,' she said.

And we continued in this rather sweet manner to the bar. No chancers troubled us then.

I was keen to head outside again, find a quiet spot and get my speech on, but Lincia wanted to chill around the fringes of the celebrity corner. I couldn't actually spot any celebrities there apart from MB and this other female athlete who'd recently come off a four-year ban for taking steroids. I looked at her face closely. There was pure hair coming out of it.

The main man seemed most happy to be back with his peeps, dousing them with a bottle of bubbly like a racing driver on the podium. I was dismayed.

'I don't know what the bredrin's doing. In thirty-six hours he's gonna be on the field of play, for the biggest day of his bleeding year. The guy should be in a quiet bed, resting up,' I exclaimed.

She made no comment and I realised that someone else was claiming her attention: a burly baldhead from the Blaster's camp who had slunk up on her other side. This time I was more concerned, for this man might be here on behalf of his boss. I came up right alongside and asked Lincia if she wanted a top-up. The beefcake gave me a gracious nod of defeat and returned without quibble or even so much as a mark on her card. I'm not sure if this incident set off the old, competitive, hunter-gatherer in me, or whether I was trying to say something that I imagined she would second, but I began muttering about how I didn't know what City Circle were doing giving awards to MB. Lincia wasn't having it.

'Listen to you! What have you got against him?'

'I've got nothing against him. I love the brer – how he plays; I've seen him handing out his money in certain places – he's safe. It's just that this place is supposed to be about promoting pioneers and MB's just an old sports star like we've always had—'

'Actually,' said Lincia, 'he got the award for this cheque he gave to help send three young guys to college.'

'Is it? I didn't know . . . Well,' I added by way of a parting shot, 'maybe his college kids can help write next year's programme. Have you seen this?' I pointed to the games room's billing on the invitation: '*Your sure to enjoy our superiar extras!*' These guys must have gone to pissin' East Bank, spelling like that—'

'Boy! You're so bad-minded! Stop knocking everything.'

'I'm not bad-minded,' I replied, stung. 'I was—'

'What did East Bank do to you?'

'Oh Lincia, you were there, you know what it was like. It was full of gangsters. That's not college. Will you be happy if Asheema ends up at East Bank?'

'It got me on my way. And it got you into Roswells, didn't it?'

'That's just it. It didn't even . . .' I paused. I didn't want to go down this road. 'It didn't really get me in there,' I trailed off.

She was peering at me intently. 'What did happen at Roswells? You never finished telling me. Something happened, didn't it? Tell me. What did you do?'

'What did I do? Give a brother the benefit of the doubt.' I shook my head. 'I don't want to talk about Roswells, man.'

'No, let's talk. You're the one who was saying people weren't talking at the dinner. Well this is what I want to talk about.'

'All right, all right.' I blew hard. It was fair enough. 'Okay, but let's go out somewhere. I'm claustrophobic in here.'

We headed out to the deck.

'Go on then,' she urged.

'Well, I had to hustle to get there in the first place. You know, it took me a year of banging my head on doors to get anywhere when I finished East Bank. I was just getting a couple of days here and there – doing a payroll, just rubbish really. The funny thing, Roswells had turned me down already. And I had just sent them a second letter – I was dead broke, just frantic, by now – this letter asking them what would they advise me to do for me to be capable of getting a gig there. And I got this letter back,' I laughed at the recollection, 'saying did I want to come in for an informal chat. I couldn't believe it. I don't know if it was – actually, what it may have been, I found out, was that the executive who saw me had just met and married this girl from the South Seas or somewhere—'

'Come on, come on,' Lincia cut in. 'You haven't even got to Roswells yet.'

'I'm just giving you the whole flavour, you know. It's important. You've gotta see the context. Anyway, so I prepared like it was a full-on interview. Got advice from this friend, I beefed up my CV, you know, plus whacked on some voluntary work . . .'

Her eyes smiled but she shook her head in light admonition.

'. . . and they, they offered me a job. They had me on this nine-month probationary period. I was working flat-out everyday, believe! Not going out, not seeing people, just *on* it. Didn't want to fuck up.'

We had come to the door of the games room by now. I raised my eyes to her, she nodded, and I ushered her in. There were only a few guests inside what was a fair-sized room. These were mainly grouped around a roulette table, complete with croupier, but there was also a pool table and some video arcade-style contraption, to which we gravitated.

'Come the end of this period they put me on another low-pay, six-month probation. Boss goes to me: "Oh, you know, you've gotta put in the air miles. Shame the old CV wasn't quite Rolls Royce" an' reah reah reah. And then they sent me back to East Bank to do this course. You think they send the juniors they're looking out for down there? They got fixed up at the City Institute and invited to brain-storming retreats in country hotels! Boy, I was brewing. I didn't know what they wanted from me. I mean, I wasn't really movin' with 'em, doin' the bevvyin' an' that – and that may have counted against me.' I shook my head. 'The johns there were different to the kinda black-hearted ones I was used to. I never really knew where I was with 'em. Hunh. They used to speak with their lips shut. After a few months, I got to feeling funny about the way my own kept clattering about!'

She threw her head back and laughed. It was a good move, I decided, telling her this story.

'D'you want a go on this, by the way?' I asked, pointing at our videogame, an electronic shooting range. We had a gun at our end, the infra-red beam type, and the top half of an animated hoodlum figure flashing on a screen ten yards ahead.

'Be my guest. We're getting to the crunch now, are we?'

'We are most definitely getting to the crunch.' I had to put some coins into a slot, and then the image began to veer from side to side, making villainous noises. She stood beside me as I took careful aim.

'But the main problem, the incident, ironically, was with the one other black guy there. He wasn't even in my actual department, he was doing reconciliation and what have you, on the real fast track. Funny-looking geezer, actually; a brow ridge that came together and eyes that were bulging so there was this constant look of surprise on his face. Looked a bit like an alien, but we got on all right most of the time. I did get a bit irritated with him sometimes, I admit. I suppose I thought we should have . . . some big pact, but he didn't really; he didn't call the situation the way I called it. Okay, so one day, end of the day, we had this big argument. He'd just had twins with this white girl from the office and they were giving the kids names from here. This guy, right, came from Africa, but his surname was Williams or something so now his children weren't gonna have anything in their names to connect them up with their "before". And I was saying he shouldn't mess with their names that way. Names are a serious thing. That's your whole history right there. With the right name it don't matter where you go or what you do, you're always connected. Just fuck 'em if you get teased in the playground or people can't pronounce it. I said his kids would hate him for it later on, when they felt able to say hello to that side of themselves. 'Til now I don't know how this discussion got so heated, but other things came in and, I just got into a zone and, uh, it came to blows.' I turned to her to illustrate, leaving the game, where I had racked up a mighty number of points with surefire head- and breastshots, still squawking. 'I had my man in a grip like a python, and he was yelling. Then the head of our team came and . . . I didn't really hit him, but there was a definite laying-on of hands. And that was it. I was out . . .'

'Just over a blasted name. It wasn't even your business.'

'Yeah.' I pondered. 'I guess I'm pretty sensitive to that stuff. I was adopted myself, and I don't even know my own shit so . . . I mean, 'Boy'! What kind of a name is that?'

'You know you've told me more about yourself this past ten minutes than you've done the whole evening.'

'Maybe.' I shrugged.

'So what then? Your references couldn't have exactly been glowing.'

'Ah, well now we get to the good bit. Hang on,' and I went to fetch two chairs, 'you need to be sitting comfortably.'

And I told her. I told her it pretty straight. How I'd become a private eye – 'I knew there was something. Just knew it,' she murmured – and how two days ago this millionaire had walked in with this offer. She listened, rapt, leaning forward and nodding occasionally, which encouraged me. I took a deep breath when I came to the bare bones of the business, counted to three, then seven, and dived in. She stared at me at first, and I repeated the offer. 'Nah, guy. You trying to tease me?' she said, although I think even then she was half daring it to be true. And, when I took her through it a third time unblinkingly, her face flushed up and a grin came puckering through.

'And all the time I thought it was you! I thought that was just foolishness about a boss.' She took my arm. 'Oh well,' she added.

'There's always divorce . . . So, what are your thoughts?'

'My thoughts are . . .' she gave a dazed shake of the head, 'I need to go to the toilet.'

'Okay. I'll meet you on the back deck – the romantic section.'

She threw me a nervy playful punch – quite hard, actually – and scampered out. I had half a mind to purchase a bottle of champagne and conceal it somewhere in anticipation, but I adjudged it better not to tempt fate and instead took a slow gander around the roulette tables – the crowd was thickening and if all went well we could relax there later – then on to the deck.

I could hear stray, mainly excited, bits of conversation about me, the clatter of women's heels on metal steps, and always the gentle slurp of the engine. I wondered what speed we were doing: two men, striding briskly along the riverbank, were just about keeping up with us.

We were wending east across the midtown bridges – past one of my favourites, so brilliantly caparisoned – and I peered up to my left, seeking out the spot by the refurbishment plaque where I'd stood more than once.

It was weird to stare at a memory, old shadows of yourself, receding into the distance. I fired a cigarette. I had never seen my spots, or the water, from this vantage point. Surely this was a sign, of new horizons, new possibilities?

Come on, girl, do me this favour. Lincia! She was all right, though. Stern, maybe, but all right. She'd thought I was the one after her, of course. 'Oh, well,' she had teased. Hunh. I wonder if she did like me that way. I wonder if we would have got on.

Bad-minded, she had cussed. That had sent a chill right through . . . Too sharp a reminder of Eb'ry Year's 'You too dark'. Tomorrow, maybe even tonight, I would have to attend to this thing, before it came back to attend to me. It seemed odds-on that someone would die before this matter was resolved. Tch! Made me feel faint to think on it. Always the same: you're trying to move on, and some old shit drags you back down. Like Lipman and the High Plains Drifter. I wondered if it was possible to somehow bypass this trouble; to leave it behind me, too, in the distance.

Bad-minded did seem a little harsh. I mean, I knew I had a downer on a lot of things but she, if anything, had just as much. In certain areas definitely. Like that six years and done remark. Lincia Ironheart! Lionheart.

One of the dons that cropped up in my sword-and-sorcery films was old Richard Lionheart. He was forever dying of some arrow in a tent, surrounded by his knights, having spent his lifetime battling heathens, chasing the shroud or grail of his Lord, and it suddenly touched me how my mission had about it a chivalric flavour that was not dissimilar: I was being asked to find a good woman for a good man, which made me, well, perhaps not necessarily good, but it certainly placed me on a superior level whilst I was about his business. Thank God I had made no moves on Candy or Lincia myself. It had never even occurred to me to do so, I realised with some relief. I would be able to look my client straight in the eye and know that I had acquitted myself honourably.

I reached into my pocket and took his note out in some excitement. It fluttered in the breeze.

One man amongst a thousand have I found. But a woman amongst all those have I not found.

Funny thing, I had not really examined this note properly. I had assumed that the 'man' was a reference to my client and the 'woman' a reference to my quarry. But who then was the 'I' in 'have I found'? Surely that was my client, which would make me the 'man amongst a thousand'. Perhaps I was not meant to take this note so literally, but I was surely supposed to draw some aid, to understand something from it. And this, this fitted. If I am the man, this man . . . Could it be? I stared at the rich, old lettering. I had been selected to complete a task in the great tradition. A pride I had not felt in some time percolated through me.

High heels were approaching. I looked up the steps. Lincia was bearing down. She was smiling.

'Girls!' I laughed. 'You took your time.'

'I've been thinking.' She shook herself. 'It's a bit parky, innit?'

'Do you want my coat?' I was all about chivalry right then.

'I'm okay.' She smirked at me then looked away.

'And?'

'Are you really for real?'

'For real, for real, for real. Yes?'

'Yes – to a start of negotiations.'

Oh, Lincia, please don't get complicated on me. 'Meaning?"

'Meaning this is all too good to be true. This millionaire – how do you know he's a millionaire?'

'He gave me forty thou in cash. The Real Deal Holyfield.'

'And how do you know there's more where that came from? You don't know anything about this man. He may be trying to launder the money or something—'

'Look, Lincia, I've seen excess amounts of badness out there. The stinkmen – their shit is there right in their iris. This man now – he's different. Straight up and copper-bottomed, y'get me?'

'How come I don't see or hear about him on the circuit then?'

'Maybe he doesn't check for your circuit. I don't know. I think he's out of state a lot. Doing that development project, like I said.'

'So he told you about that, did he?'

'Not exactly. Someone . . . ah, forget it. It's just a hunch, really.'

'And I'm supposed to get hitched on a couple of your hunches?' she challenged. 'Look, bring him along to my office, say, in a couple of days. Tell him to bring some recent bank statements, business details, financial projections. You know, bona fides basically. And some proof he isn't married. I'm not raising some woman's pickney, you know.'

I considered. I did have a number for the guy. I just prayed he wouldn't be too irked at this request for proof. 'All right. I'll call him first thing tomorrow. I'm sure it's no problem. My man's legit.'

'Then we're fine.' She smiled breezily.

We went back to the ballroom, with me not altogether elated, you understand, but relaxed enough to accompany her to the dancefloor. The PA was playing bouncy, soft R 'n' B numbers, no Lipman or anything that could remotely upset decent folk. Lincia was quite nimble on her feet, tapping out dainty four-steps. She was one of those people who don't look at you when they dance. She barely met my eyes, preferring to glance over both of my shoulders as if there was some better prospect behind, or else stare in blank fashion into the middle distance. The only time she engaged me was when this hit cover tune 'Who Do You Love? (Are you sure?)' came on. She brought her face up to mine as the chorus kicked in, stuck her ample rump out, dangled her arms down by her sides, and chortled 'Who do you love? How much money does he make?' hurrying the end to fit the metre. I did not find this quite as droll as she seemed to, but I recall we took a time-out in pretty good humour and the evening proceeded perfectly well, for a while. Our guards were both plenty lower than hitherto and we entered upon some free and frank discussion, oiled, no doubt, a little by brandies on both sides. She interrogated me closely on aspects of my life and I found her pertinent in various instances. She said I'd been a fool to let the brother at Roswells rile me ('Why does he have to be like you, or me? I'm sure he's got a lot of fans in his world'), and declared it a shame that I hadn't given that world another go, bad references or no, because we needed as many as possible inside, infiltrating.

Unfortunately, we had this tendency – and I had noticed it already on less sensitive matters – towards concluding many exchanges in uneasy fashion, leaving behind a sour aftertaste, so that conversations that should have to'd and fro'd attractively instead induced the ill feeling of spats. Perhaps it was an error for me to provide, as I did under her probing, a pretty honest sketch of my missing years, between sixteen and nineteen, when I was doing most of my badness. She certainly enjoyed the tales of some of my crew's more memorable capers, the delicious football stadium scam in particular, but she used my information against me, drawing a harsh parallel between my abrupt departures from both CLC and Roswells. 'Your usual tactics are fuck-up tactics, isn't it?' she pronounced. 'That's how you propel yourself forward, by burning bridges.'

She pondered me, like I was a potential good cause. 'I can see you could do well, but there's some rough edges – a self-destructive element there. What's *that* about, I wonder?'

'I can be perfectly constructive where it's something I really want to do.'

'What *do* you want to do, Boy?' She leant forward. 'I know it can't be bailiff business and spying on naughty wives the rest of your life. What do you *really* want to do with yourself?'

'Well . . .' I considered, 'there's no particular thing. But I would really like to achieve great purpose, a path to glory. I mean, what I fear is not doing something special before it's all over.'

She nodded several times. 'You know what I'm gonna do for you? There are a couple of people I know here, and definitely one of them is in an employing—'

'Ah, don't *go* there!' I cried. I could not believe she could so misunderstand me. 'Haven't we been through all this already! I don't check for those workplaces, simple.'

'Look, Boy, I'm trying to help, all right?'

'I know—'

'You've gotta start somewhere. This PI business isn't gonna take you where you say you want to go. I just can sense this, this tussle in you and I don't think you're gonna lay it to rest until you've tested yourself again in a proper arena.'

I stared at her, the vision of her meek colleague Zeke and their boss on the toilet in my head. Could she really not see beyond her pumped-up little world?

'The niggerati ain't the only bunch that's saying something, you know,' I growled. 'I got people down southside, they may not have the suits to say so, but they could come down and reason with these heads here. Learn them a thing or two about reality—'

'Reality? Reality? Surviving, innit! Reality!' she mocked, shriller by the second. 'So this ain't reality too? Or is it only reality when we're being poor. What do they do, these people?'

'What do *you* do? Jesus, Lincia, humble yourself a minute! "Media buyer", "campaign planner", whatever – face it, it ain't brain surgery. You just make phone calls and do meetings all day.'

'Well, excuse me! It don't make you a genius ripping kids off their pocket money and flaking out of work. What kind of rubbish is that?'

'I'm not disputing that. But I'm raising my chambers now, watch me. In ten years' time, what are you gonna be doing? More phone calls?'

'I'll be a pampered housewife, won't I?' She smirked. 'And if not, I'll probably be an exec, and then you'll see me make my big noise. I certainly won't be messing around moaning about "reality" like a joker. Nah, guy. And those sorts think they're so strong and proud and it's reality that's beaten them! There are different kinds of strength, you know. Sometimes it's about just doing the job—'

'But what happens when you *lose* the job? Even say you knuckle down, but still lose it. You go straight back down. That's what a lot of you people don't see—'

'Let me finish. Right. And sometimes it's about holding it down and biting your lip and having the hunger to come through.'

No chance for a comeback, for her attention was already directed above me. I turned round to see the memory-aid man who'd marked her dance card upon us.

She got up now without so much as a by your leave and cooed me some triumphant final words: 'Remember, the right end of the telescope . . . I'll be back.'

I lit a cigarette, smarting, as they trooped off. What's her game now? Is she trying to rebuke me for my jibes by this loud endorse-

ment? Or just covering her angles, in case my millionaire doesn't
come through? I know he'd signed her card but that was then. Shit
had changed since. And even if she needed to dance with him, she
could have gone about it in a nicer way. Face it, man, that girl just
ain't nice.

I strode over to the bar. I couldn't be sitting waiting like a sad one.
More dealings with my man, and I found myself an observation spot.

They were not the gainliest of dance partners. He was a thudding,
hulking specimen, with next to no moves. Mind you, I knew there
are girls around who just like big men. That was cool. My client was
a good size too.

And good luck to him, when they linked up. Cos I don't know
what you were thinking about back on the deck there, Boy; you two
wouldn't get on at all.

I wish I hadn't slipped in that crack about 'reality': she'd seized on
it gleefully and run with it . . . I tell you, that's why I don't bother
explaining myself to people. When you do, you just end up in a
mood, cos they most never appreciate what you're trying to say. They
take your bits and pieces and make plenty from them, and leave you
feeling well irked. That's why I prefer guys. Guys don't fuckin' care.

The one lady I found I could chat freely with, and leave with all
my bits intact, was Cosmic-Cosmic. We'd have had a good laugh at
something like this, no question – if she could ever have found the
clothes to get in.

I snorted, thinking back to Lincia's six-year relationship limit. I
hadn't said so then, what with my matter at a delicate stage, but I
thought it was bollocks. The way I saw it, being that it was so hard to
find someone that you could explain stuff to, and who'd still be up
for you, someone who touched and brought out the positive in you,
well, when that special someone did come along, five, ten – no
amount of years was enough. You always want it to be there. Ah,
shit.

I could not even say for sure it was love, nor did I find myself needing exclusive rights, but there was a sweet dependency that grew and when it was gone a part of you that was animated and comforted in particular ways with that person was gone too. You don't see that bit of yourself again. It's like a little death. Cosmic- Cosmic, even TK . . . to add to my big deaths. The big deaths I probably could not have prevented, but the little deaths felt avoid- able, a stupid waste, and were a continuing source of irritation to me. No one would look at my life and think it, but I am something of a perfectionist.

I wondered if Lincia suffered from little deaths. It was hard to imagine her entertaining such an investment, a belief, in people. I don't think she believed me. She didn't even really have faith in him.

She doesn't believe, she doesn't believe . . . *What do you believe in, heaven or hell?*

I trace the start of my sinking feeling to then. By the time of our return to the games room a short while later (she'd come back to our table and I'd let her stew for a few moments before emerging), uncertainty was overtaking me.

The air of unconvinced pleasure that had settled about the roulette tables played its part. The croupier-cum-banker was having a difficult time persuading some nervous punters to play for real stakes rather than the joke chips they had used hitherto. One was demanding a breakdown of the banker's cut before he got to see any of *his* money, whilst a City Circle man was backfootedly explaining to others why the cost of the bet had not been included in the price of a ticket. The banker, as bemused as the waiters before him, reduced the minimum stake down to a single nugget in a song and dance that lasted five minutes. And though some of me wanted to shame them all by dumping all the expenses I had left on me on a stack of num- bers, more of me wanted to be shot of this toytown, and of this ungenerous girl, now badgering me to dip my hands in my pockets yet again, and all of me that was here. I could scarcely believe I had envisioned, when I got overs, prancing around at dos like this.

All too clearly now I saw the juice in the riddle my man had set me. For I had come with money, and talked of money, and found me this money-minded girl, but such, surely, was not quite what my client had intended. He was a high- not a mean-minded person; I could not pretend I did not know.

What had he said? 'A woman of quality. Someone who can smell the coffee,' I recall. Nothing especially particular. Something more? I should have jotted some notes.

Should have spread my net for other girls here, too: who knows, found me one of indisputable quality, who'd maybe wandered down by accident. Covered my angles, like Lincia.

Oh, we sniped anew in there, as we stood out some rounds amongst the onlookers. We resembled nothing so much as teenage siblings, hurling all this familiars' baggage on one another, just beyond the age to actually fight about it. The funny thing was that, in between times, Lincia was perfectly cheerful. There was an elasticity to her; she didn't seem to take anything to heart. In other circumstances I might have found this trait appealing, but that night it only added to my discomfort. There was so much at stake, could she not see that?

Our final spat erupted from one of her bounce-back attempts at small talk. She'd been happily observing how she wouldn't need to deal with PJ's exhale parties anymore, and we'd then fallen to discussing some of the guests in his house. She made the preposterous claim that she preferred one of the earnest Africans she'd barely said a word to rather than pukka PJ or the bal'head glovesman. Some swords later, I was saying how she made me laugh cos she didn't know herself; that she veered erratically between PJ types and red-blooded homeboys, and she'd probably even entertain me, if I could rustle fifty grand up front. But whether it be a PJ Tuesday or a Roy Thursday she was a hustler as much as I'd ever been, and the way she'd eaten up my proposal proved it.

'I can't believe I'm hearing this!' She'd been fixing her gaze on the game in front during my shells, but now she stared at me. 'Do you want me to do this thing for you or not?'

I shrugged. I had also been surprised by my words. You know when you say something and that's the first you're finding out that you just don't care any more.

'All right then, I won't.'

'Fine by me.'

'Good.'

I believe she added something like, 'And what does this make you, anyway? A pimp or something? It's about par for the course,' and I replied, 'Not if I do it right,' eyes roaming, not wanting to look her in the face, when I saw him.

My client was there, right there. Standing, arms folded, black tie and burgundy cummerbund, behind the croupier, behind the crowd on the other side of the table, by the door. I was in shock; I just stared at him. He smiled and gave me a half-wink, an encouraging flicker of the eye, then turned and headed out.

'Wait here,' I said to her, and all but dashed to the door, heads turning about me.

There was no sign of him in the corridor. I searched up and down – on the deck, in the ballroom, the toilets, I even checked the river for this mysterious man – but nowhere. Eventually I found a quiet spot in the air and took a breather. I was sweating, I noticed.

For sure, it was him. The graceful gait, the goatee, shorn when I'd seen him at Ice Cream, back. So that wasn't him at Ice Cream, unless a man can regrow a goatee in a day . . . Well this was definitely him. The silver ring on his finger. He'd even winked at me.

What to make of this latest appearance? In truth, I was a little frightened. He, and something too much like him, seemed to be able to, uh, locate me at will. Fortunately, he had not seemed unhappy with me. It felt most like, like a gentle reminder: of his flesh and bone, his bona fides. Of his expectations. That this business was real and I could still play a quality role.

It served to stiffen my nascent resolve. I wasn't too fazed to find that Lincia had disappeared by the time I returned to the casino. I thought perhaps she had decided enough was enough, but she came back, having seen to more dance card matters, with her rubber self, and – what with our chatting to some people, and me even bumping into someone I knew – we managed to spend a perfectly pleasant last half hour before the long night drew to a close. So much so that I, weak as I am, got to thinking it would be unwise to be too drastic, and perhaps I should mull on this matter 'til the morning. For her part, Lincia appeared to have completely forgotten about our calling-off and, indeed, reminded me, as the boat pulled in and we filed out on to the quay, to ask my client for his particulars.

My car greeted us with a nasty surprise. The engine coughed tubercularly to my start-up and then shut out. I rekeyed the ignition three times and tried the choker too, to no avail. We exchanged a frown.

'Maybe the battery's flat,' said Lincia. She turned and looked around us nervously, as if fearing that others had spotted our difficulty. 'D'you leave the lights on or something?'

'I don't think so.' I stared forlornly at the lights on my dashboard, tried again a few times with the choker, then got up to have a look. No doubt it was something to do with my afternoon's drama. Old Sammy would give me pure grief when I returned this ride to him.

There were various possible causes: a leak in the exhaust where the bullets had grazed, the left back tyre looked a little flat too, and a big metal plate by the engine was smouldering. Lincia poked her head out of the window to ask if I could sort it. I said I could try.

I took off my jacket, took a cloth from my car, and set to with my oil and water cans. Lincia joined me presently, shivering and agitated.

'Bang in front of the boat as well! How long is this gonna take?'

'I don't know. Not long, one way or the other. Must have been this afternoon. Those kids.'

She skinned her teeth, wrapped her coat around her tighter, and looked around and beyond me, like we were dancing. 'You know it's five o'clock in the bloody morning?'

Don't start now, Lincia, just don't start now, all right.

She went off back in the direction of the boat and fell in with four friends who were walking back to their car. I toiled with the jack, got some grease on my shirt, and watched in disgust as that group left and she buttonholed another. Every so often she glanced back at me. I could not make out her expression, only her big hair and her big coat that she filled promisingly well. Now that I had no time for her, I wanted her girth to grow and all the bits of her body to sink.

You killed it, girl. You killed what made you attractive. How I could have decided that even sweet Candy wasn't right, and then, twenty-four hours later, been considering giving it to your stush-arsed self, I just can't figure.

It took me about fifteen minutes before I tried the engine again. It spluttered, but came through. To my unsurprise, Lincia trotted over. I buzzed the passenger side window down but kept the door locked as she came alongside.

'Deal's off.' My voice was deceptively level. 'Finito. You cruelled it, lady, good and proper. I would drop you but, well, you know, it is five o'clock in the morning.'

She stood there disbelieving as I pulled away. Twenty yards down, I stopped and leant out. Her mouth was still hanging fatly. It was worth it, for that moment alone.

I hit the gas, ran my hand across my brow, and puffed my cheeks. Sometimes, like I said, I get into a zone.

8

the race man cometh

I lay in bed awake for a good while before I actually rose. There was only the half-inch of dull light poking out below my drawn blinds so you couldn't actually see what time of day it was, but the clock beside me said 11.30 a.m. I had slept pretty well – deeply, not too much sweat – but had woken up to a bad five minutes.

There was a shape, the length of a human frame, on the right-hand side of my coat pegs, by the door. I had no recollection of replacing my brown coat there when I'd returned earlier. The bulb on my bedside lamp had gone so the only way of allaying my suspicions – short of throwing a knife or shooting at it – was to make the potentially perilous journey to the light switch by the door. This I did eventually and, well, it turned out to be nothing, simply my coat, but I did find that my stomach, which had started on me yesterday, was now hurting considerably more. Its left side had the grating, bruised soreness of a cracked rib. I'd always insisted it was my ribs but the professionals maintained it was my stomach, which made historical sense, I suppose. After rubbing some mentholatum there, and inspecting again the discoloured, winding, tight passage of my scar under the bone, I'd returned to my bed and found that lying right on it provoked a brutal numbness that allowed me to turn my mind to other matters.

I was, well, depressed certainly, but more rueful. It was a shame that I'd left Lincia with that inelegant vent of spleen. I did not regret my decision but its execution could have been more gallant. I hoped she got back all right.

It occurred to me that she and Candy were flips of the same coin. Whereas Candy did not see the negative, Lincia had no real feel for the positive. 'What do you believe in, heaven or hell?' he'd asked me, and I'd returned with the lines of the song, and he'd gone . . . he'd gone, 'That's *nearly* right . . .' didn't he? Why?

Tch. This teaser was beginning to slide like grease. I should really have taken some notes.

My phone rang a couple of times. I checked the scanner and left it. It was this City geezer: he would come over all friendly for three bogus minutes and then try and get me to put some money in pension plans and such. A bit cheeky of him to ring during office hours. I don't like being disturbed by foolishness when I'm on the case.

Two cases. Sinbad, te raas! Would have to go a-hunting him today. Should really have disappeared from this place 'til that had been done.

The approach of noon, and another half-day gone towards my deadline, got me up. The pain was back in full effect but was swiftly forgotten when I saw the state of my finances. I'd had it in mind to pop out – take a recce and grab some provisions – but leafed through my wallet to growing alarm. I only had a couple of one-ers left there. Jesus! Where had it all gone? I hadn't checked on the amount before I set out yesterday, but there'd been at least a monkey in there, plus some extra notes stuffed down my socks.

I went to the cubbyhole by my desk, where I'd stashed the remainder of my client's retainer. A puny four thousand folds was all I had left. It seemed incredible but when I totted up all my outgoings – fifteen Gs to Sundays, the deluxe hire car, the night at Ice Cream and entertaining Lincia – plus the dollars I'd earmarked for unavoidable debts, it just about figured. Thirty-six grand down in two and a bit days . . . and no tangible progress. Boy!

The shower was as sobering as you might imagine. For the first time, failure reared its head at me. I decided, after much yeaing and naying, to go and see the Race Man. It was worth it – I felt stuck and I just couldn't afford to mess up on this. There was the small matter of my death to discuss as well. I felt better almost immediately and easily resisted an involuntary step towards my cfs. Today, at the least, I had to be pure.

Finding his whereabouts was a little less than straightforward. When he came to town you'd see folk from his band of helpers pop up on the main drags of our various neighbourhoods. I'd glimpsed a woman with a dyed henna bob and an 'RM' sculpted in her hair standing outside Ziggy's record store yesterday, but she wasn't around when I drove down there. Sunyiatta the pamphleteer was there, of course, but he was locked in conversation. An elder in a white robe looked a little peeved that I hadn't come for him, but told me that I could find my girl in the local library.

I was intrigued at the thought of a first inkling into the reading matter of the Race Man's circle, but she was bookless when I found her. Her hands lay on the table in front of her as she stared into space, beyond the pensioners opposite – meditating, no doubt. Her henna love did not stop with her hair – her trainers and canvas jeans were coated in it too – more evidence, perhaps, of the Race Man's famously broad mind.

She replied to my query by giving me directions to another library on the north-east side. Now I have heard say that his supplicants are frequently sent around and about – no doubt to shuffle the wheat from the chaff – so I stressed to her that I was quite serious in this matter. But she insisted that all she knew was for me to go there. There I'd meet a man.

'The Man. Or a man before the Man?'

She shrugged.

So I filled up my tank and was off again. I took some quick back ways to bring me to the SE11 main, jooked a left there, and headed for the new Northway. It was funny: I was trying to prepare what I would ask of him, the particulars of my plea, only my mind kept going to what I might say in defence, in reply to his, uh, admonitions. And I don't know if it was that, or the fact that my route took me up the hill past what used to be my old school and the cemetery where my brother and mother lie buried, but I got to thinking on my family years.

My father is still around. When I say around, I mean around as in alive rather than around and about, for he remains a frequent traveller. I know that he still maintains the tiny house where I grew up by the SE4/SE15 borders, and that he pays the rent on it – I call the council occasionally and they confirm it's happening on the regular. I also know that he's sometimes actually around because he still knocks up Haroun, our old dry cleaner, for these sweet pencil cigars the old man has smoked since my bro died. When he comes, Haroun calls me and I, well, I don't do anything. I keep meaning to, though. The calls have been very rare just recently, maybe once a year. Which doesn't mean that my dad isn't in town more often. He might be around but finding himself able to resist the cigar temptation.

His nerves-soothing cigars became the one indulgence in what was a most serious-minded household. Neither of my parents were the type to chat idly and my father, who treated me like a big person from early, largely confined himself to stern instruction: 'Be careful what you say,' he would warn me, 'for the angel of death may be circling over the house.' And, 'If you are not gaining knowledge, you may as well be dead'. Or he would lock his arms around my mother in one of their contented moments, customary but bizarre to me, and turn and say, 'When you come to marry, be smart-oh. Heh! Be very smart. Because your work life will be difficult, it will be troublesome, and you cannot have war at work and then war at home!' waving his finger emphatically from side to side. Ha, the old man.

Both our rooms, even a rack in the bathroom – were crammed with books, and we spent most of our quality domestic time with our heads in them. Fables, philosophy, mathematics . . . My father would emerge in his travelling suit and case, and set me and little Junior tracts to read and problems to solve by his return.

Two things I never understood about this obsession with books: how, with all their knowledge and wisdom and gravity, we could remain without money. I didn't see why the old man had to be for-ever donning his Sunday best when it didn't seem to do us any good, and my mother was also one of those high-activity low-return types. She devoted her energies to local concerns, petitioning this, organis-ing that, nursing people, projects, little sales and festivals, voluntary work a lot of it, I guess, like rich ladies do. She was certainly much esteemed but we, we did not even have a front door to call our own. We rented from this other family and we had to go through their sit-ting room to get to our box portion. It was ridiculous. And it was a nasty place, musty and damp and discoloured walls. I'm sure that contributed to my brother's death, although they said it was some-thing else.

The other matter I couldn't figure was how they could be so keen on learning yet send me to the worst school in the neighbourhood. It was the smallest, and probably not quite the baddest, but definitely the all-round worst: fuck-all facilities, teachers on the brink of break-down, plus all the usual pressure, you know, from schoolmates. At other schools, you had the pressure an' that, but if you were strong, you could still come through, *and* they were nearer to us. My mum was a sometime teacher, plus on these parents' committees an' blah, she didn't need me to tell her. But when I'd ask them about leaving, they'd say, 'Oh, you have to stay there. It's not up to us,' which isn't true, is it? This is why I tell my friends that my folks were a rum pair. My friends would be thinking that my folks were simply further along a gradient that they were familiar with – a little more heavy, perhaps. And I'd go, 'No. There's something more going on here.' At the end of the day, there was stuff about them that just didn't tally . . . like why didn't they have children of their own, for another instance?

The day they brought my bro home was just the best. It was late afternoon, I remember, and they came home unexpectedly. I was supposed to be doing some work and I had just enough time to restore the books and dining table from their ping-pong to their rightful positions, when in they strode. Dad beaming, Mum cuddling this crying tot in her arms. They found him, they said, just like me. And the funny thing is that he really did look like me. You'd think we were blood, no question.

So I had a ping-pong partner at last. That, and chasing his crawling, screaming, ecstatic self behind the settee. I see them both so vividly.

The wretched day that it happened was another late afternoon, like that first time. For others, it was the time when kids' programming makes way for the early evening soaps, but we were listening, my dad and I, to 'The Ten -Isms of Human Thought' on the World Service.

We started hearing the faint sounds of a hubbub outside. A bit closer, a bit louder and it was definitely a woman screaming. We could hear the neighbours pulling down their windows and I went to take a peek from ours. But I was more interested in the sounds of the soaps than anything else until the shrieking woman turned into our street.

It was my mother. She had come from the doctors, where she'd taken him cos he'd been sick that morning. She was stumbling under the streetlamps, clutching his form then hugging him to her shoulder, just wailing terribly. And I stared at her with all the others, so sick and weak, as she came to the door.

Things fell away after that. My parents seemed defeated. My old man's travels and his books brought him ever diminishing joy, 'til one day he flung these last away from him, and cried that it was still no better; he had not profited anyone and what was lacking could not be counted. I, no question, added my load to their weight: bunkings and exclusions from school, gracing the final entry in its caning book, hanging with these older ones at the other site; and there were clashes . . . My father and I started having these big-arsed arguments. He'd be banging on about bills; about how everything had to be paid and accounted for in the end, did I not know that? 'The bills are your own, the bills are your own!' he'd shout. And I'd fling back that, if we're talking about earning our keep, his Sunday best never seemed to pay for much around here. He should have hit me. But he never did. He'd just look crushed, the way he did when he threw his books.

It was around this time that I met T'Kalla. I'd headed on a long wander, one mid-morning lesson (such a rubbish school, believe. All I got from it in the end, of all things, was a certificate of attendance), through the park, and found myself by the place for EDBs. The Institute for Educationally Damaged Boys was this kinda secured institution, run by these unpleasant ex-army guys, and even though TK was thirteen and had been there for some time he was still rarely allowed out. They needed a reliable after-hours purveyor of ciga-rettes, liquor and what have you and I became, for a commission, that boy. And, when he could go out, we'd go around, get up to things. Over a couple of years he met a couple of my spars, I met one of his, and we formalised links into the CLC.

He was a sharp sort in certain areas, especially with people. He liked to tell me of all these tales then protracted silences he spun around their psychiatrist. A true nutter, though. I saw that soon after I met him. We were standing down the road from his keeper when these two young geezers drove past, winding their windows down and hurling out some racial. Unfortunately for them, they had to stop behind some other cars as the lights turned red twenty yards up. TK, who had grinned twistedly to my frown just before, registered this with the flicker of an eye and was off like a tracer. It took me a couple of moments to see what was going on and I jogged after him. He got to the passenger side, hauled this guy's head, and yanked it up and down the window frame until it became a bloody mess. I tell you, I thought he would take life.

That was TK in his purest form – opportunistic and lacking in pro-portion: all the stupidness, indeed, that so beset crimes of our kind. I should have knocked it on the head right there; rather, I let it flour-ish. I even stayed at his EDB place a few times when I was AWOL from home. The police and whoever bring you back time and again, then, after a while, they don't.

I remember my immediate ambition was to return home, dump a sack of money on the table, and scream at my father, 'Here's the bal-ance on your bleedin' bills!' Not that I would advance these 'debts' as a justification for my CLC runnings. I did what we did because I had no big problem with it. And, while my voice carried big weight, we behaved to the best of my conscience: no grief to anyone we knew or had a connection with, no (physical) grief to anyone who hadn't put themselves in the game. Play it long and, where you can, hit the deepest pockets, the insurers and the state. I would like to think that, between these principles and the elegance I endeavoured to bring to our capers, there was some class in it.

Acquiring and selling on was our metier: hospital supplies, car parts, tickets, passports, social security cards – different volumes of cards, different styles of fraud. Plots which, like most of the best ones, lent themselves to preparation from a prone position. Give me an hour and a pen and a pad, I would say, retiring to the sofa, where I would set to work with my graphs and pie charts and cost-benefit analyses.

One thing we did, though, during the swing of our stadium caper, shook me up good. It was a big derby game that day and all us touts were doing good business. This unfortunate kid – your original callow, country youth – was standing lonesome in the bustle outside. Two bredrin met his searching eyes and told him the only seats available were in the executive stand at fifty notes. He blanched but didn't baulk at that, so they led him around the side to our next set of people, who took his notes and peeled him a ticket, and guided him to the turnstile where I was stationed with a steward. The kid was starting to lose it by this stage and, when we sternly informed him that his ticket was a fake and he would have to fork out a further forty to be allowed through, he crumpled, broken. I remember breezily chatting to him whilst we waited for the steward to bring him some change – about what a boss player so and so was – when I saw that his eyes were brimming with tears. He kept on blinking, unable to look at me, so bewildered at the turn of events. 'My sister. What am I gonna give for my sister?' He was in such a state. It was my cheeky custom to have my photo taken with the patsy at this juncture, for my personal collection, but I didn't even think of trying that this time. 'Jesus, Boy,' it sunk home then, 'you're an A-grade cunt and no mistake.'

I suppose it was then that I began actively reconsidering my week-to-week, not that I'd ever contemplated this kind of hustle as a long-term option. The occupational hazard of the left-handed life is the company you end up keeping. That was the main reason I urged us to avoid pharmaceuticals: the dividends might be top but the people were rubbish. When TK, who had started to hang with

stinkier fry than I could justify, came back one day with wild
unconstitutional talk of an armed – his idea of playing it long was
taking tools up to the Midlands – I knew that this number was up. I
tried to pull away before it got ugly but not, as it turned out, without
difficulty.

I never knew if or what my folks knew of my activities, but whenever I saw them after certain events, like that stadium episode, the
through door would be bolted and their faces to me changed. What
am I saying? For sure they knew. My father, after all, was the rum one
who, rather like my millionaire, could even find me at will. I'd be
changing places, this base and the next, but a letter would reach me
every time. Something to the point, in his neat handwriting, generally saying, 'Go and see your mother'. Hunh . . . So the time when he
was garrulous enough to write, 'Go and see your mother. She is ill,' I
guessed something was seriously up.

She looked more sad than anything, when I saw her, propped up
on their bed, my dad pacing forlornly about. So I told her what I
thought would cheer her, how I'd finally put all this confusion and
uncertainty behind me, yet she still looked so sad. And I couldn't
understand, because she didn't look so bad, and she told me she'd
been getting the shakes, plus a few headaches, that was all. And
that was it, the last time I saw her before she died; she had a haemorrhage, one afternoon, shortly after.

One devastating, cheating haemorrhage.

Her funeral was well attended. She got a headstone too. For
some reason, Junior never did.

The way I saw it, I got saved and, probably, punished. Saved
because managing to survive the man that TK sent was a miracle,
reward, perhaps, for changing my direction. Punished because I did
not change in time to have any impact on my mother's condition.
Those head pains she'd been having, blood pressure; worrying about
me could hardly have helped any . . . Just got a feeling that this mis-

sion I've been charged with is becoming another one of those 'big play' situations – I mean bigger, even, than the hundred thousand fee. I really want to be right and on time this time.

My exit from the Northway brought me to a part that was not the most prepossessing the north-east had to offer. Further up, in fine three-storey houses, lived some who'd got overs, but not quite here. Here, many of the houses were divided up into bedsits, filled by the transient and the needy. To the east and south of them loomed a couple of infamous estates whose features, warren-like with exits as numerous as the Patels, made them an ideal home for those who craved some privacy from the police. I used to venture here on the regular during my document-shifting days (this was where I'd first met Sinbad, actually), but had not had cause to come here for a while.

The area had a pretty similar profile to my own, but I'd always detected a milder public tone, reflected in the slightly higher life expectancy of its residents. I couldn't tell you why – perhaps the water was different up here. Or the fact that it was greener, with better transport links: folk could get out, cool off, come back . . .

I had never been to the library, but I found it easily enough. The place was shut – a sign blamed cutbacks – but I saw a small animated group gathered on the grassy knoll outside. One of them, my age but with a skullcap and beard that gave him an air beyond his years, was clasping a small shiny staff, and it was he I approached in expectation. He was perfectly friendly but merely gave me a fresh set of directions. I was quite exercised by now and my voice was raised when I told him this was no joke thing. He nodded gravely then repeated his directions.

It was only when I started off again that I realised I'd been asked to describe a circle: 'Straight on for two blocks, take a left for one block, another left and head down for three blocks . . . a final left then drive slowly and you'll see it.'

Despite my reservations I did as I was told and my last left took me, peculiarly enough, not by the library or any familiar sights, but to a narrow, unnamed alley.

As I crawled along I noticed a small bill poster on the dark curtained window of a semi-detached house about a third of the way up. The image on the poster, the snarling mask of a human-like creature, zig-zag incisions down its face and great, staring eyes, was the same as the one I'd seen atop the gentleman's staff a few moments earlier. I parked and went up to take a closer look. Beside the poster was a smaller two-inch square notice in black ink: 'Caution. Race Running Wild Inside'.

I knocked on the door. The door opened, to no one behind it, so I stepped in and nearly fell over at the sight.

I was inside a splendid, cavernous, grand hut of a hall. I say hut for the floor was soft underfoot, with lengths of straw covering a rich red clay, but the walls were hard to the touch, not plaster or stone but some mineral with dazzling seams of deep green, red and gold stretching as far and as high as you looked. The place's dimensions, at its top a gently curving minaret, seemed far larger than anything you could have imagined from outside. There were fifteen to twenty – fellow supplicants, I presumed – sprinkled around the sides at the bottom end of the hall, and I made my way towards them, taking in a row of framed portraits and the warm, fertile smell of earth.

That smell! It had an utterly distinctive quality to it: a real partic-ular sharp sweetness – oh I can't precise it, but I was sure I had smelt it somewhere before. Some memory deep within me. A comforting smell; I am content in the memory.

I stood there a few moments just trying to place it, raise the image and the sounds to go with it, 'til I realised how many were looking at me, and walked on, my face breaking into a broad smile. Image or no image, I sensed this to be a true recollection. And where else might I have inhaled this but in the country? I *must have* started there; now I was sure of it.

All the low wooden stools were taken up so I joined a few others on the floor. Most, not surprisingly, looked preoccupied and a few were close to tears. I could see no official types or ticket system, so I asked a woman sitting cross-legged beside me what the procedure was. She shook her head and returned to fingering her comfort scarf.

Two burly minder types, perched on a bench opposite, gazed impassively across at me. I got in into my head that they were Lipman's people, and that he was in the inner sanctum, taking advice on the High Plains Drifter.

What noise there was was coming from a deportee who was shaking his arms in front of him, crying that they were coming for him today, and he needed to be seen directly. There was also a stout mother who was chiding her son ('Lee, shut your raas before I slap yuh . . . Lee! Don't make me tell you again, you know . . .') with language I deemed improper for what was probably a holy place. From the conversation she held in between, I gathered that Lee's schooling wasn't going well, and she was seeking some salvation for it here.

I started as a section of the back wall slid open and a man and a woman in matching crisp mauve prints stepped from darkness behind into our antechamber. They went to the deportee and managed to calm him, and I followed them over to introduce myself. They said he would see me shortly. At this the deportee, presuming gazumpage, started howling again.

The panel slid open once more and a flashy-looking brother emerged, blinking at the light before slipping on his shades. The burly ones hurried to him, making way as the helpers steered the deportee past. Not Lipman, as it turned out, but perhaps some other celebo with a problem.

I took a closer gander at the portraits, trying to relax. They were really quite something: a metre high some of them, in acrylics, ochres, dyes and God knows what else. These dudes were his favourites, I supposed. There were few from our state, more's the pity, but many of them I recognised, like the one of our late lamented old-country statesman, grinning in a trademark safari shirt. He was one of several bona fide leaders on display, but there were also nurses, poets and peacemakers, trumpeters and track masters, largely cast in heroic scenes. My own favourites was one of a most dapper geezer, garmed in eighteenth-century epaulettes-and-breeches business, leading a rag-tag brigade against a mighty troop in French colours; and an engraving of a more modern brother, with sombre great-goggle eyes, his hand resting on his chin, and the inscription 'Nobody knows my name' going across it.

The deportee returned, after a short while, altogether happier. In his hand he clasped a slim blue envelope and I too was heartened at the sight of it: the Race Man had such a formidable reputation as a riddler extraordinaire that his furnishing of assistance as practical as a set of documents was something I'd barely hoped for.

Now it was my turn, much to the silent chagrin of some others and more unlovely vocals from the mother. I gave an apologetic shrug at my elevation up the order and went with my escort, the male half of the duo.

He stroked the wall and the section opened. We stepped through and I could see nothing for a second, just the flash of his hand in front of me, before a lantern flickered on the left side of this passageway.

My escort was mid-thirties, kindly eyes, clean-shaven, normal-sized cranium, nothing remarkable about him. I felt to ask him a raft of questions – how he got the job, for one, but my heart was thumping, and the passage was short.

'This is where I leave you,' he winked at me as we came to a stout mahogany door. 'Enter in your own time. No need to knock. Oh yes—' He pointed to my shoes. I took them off as he disappeared somewhere to the left. After a few paces he was shrouded in dark-ness.

I girded myself. It's all too late now anyway, B, so relax. He isn't going to eat you.

I took the handle. The door was heavy enough – it took forever to shudder open. Inside was as murky as out, but this was more a pea-souper of a fog, akin to the spread-out from dry ice. I inched my way with old cautious instinct along the side of the nearest wall. After a few moments my vision began to adjust and I could make out a finely threaded golden stool. It seemed quite far away – I could only spot it because it gleamed. The place felt big – there was no ceiling that I could see – but it was impossible to tell how this throneroom compared in size to the antechamber. Beside me hung more pic-tures, this time of landscapes, the sun, moon and stars. At one point there was just this empty frame, and I remember pausing by it, won-dering what that was about, before I padded forward in the general direction of the gleaming stool.

After ten or so paces, with the stool big in front of me, I stumbled into something, stubbing my toe quite painfully. I peered down: it was a small, pretty, tawny red chest, terracotta maybe. On its top was engraved in a calligraphic hand not dissimilar to my client's: 'B I B L E – Basic Instructions Before Leaving Earth.' At its front was a keyhole . . .

'Can I help you or are you just passing through?' a large voice rippled. I flinched, as much from my guilty thoughts as the surprise.

'I'm sorry. I – I didn't know—'

'That's all right. What can I do you for, Boy?'

I did not know where to look. There seemed no particular source point to the voice, which itself – I mean the voice – was unnerving enough: it spent most of its time within a low, sonorous frequency that filled the room, only in some moments it came like the bass of a man, at others the alto of a woman, and still other times, later on, I found it tripping with the lightness of a child. I decided to fix my gaze on the stool.

'May I just say, sir – may I call you "sir"?'

'If you must,' he intoned.

'May I say, sir, how privileged I am to meet you after all this, er, time,' I burbled, 'and, when I think of all that philosophy you—'

'Every black man is a philosopher,' he cut me, 'every prisoner is a philosopher. Being a black man is like being in prison. Discuss.'

A minute in and already a riddle! I had not been misinformed. I bent my mind to the task. 'I don't quite know the word for it, sir, but the way you linked those bits up, it ain't right, is it?'

He chuckled. It sounded like a series of staccato intakes at the back of a vast throat: 'Just your average, faulty syllogism. It has a plausible sheen, but it stinks.'

'Right, right,' I nodded. 'Yeah, I love puzzles, crosswords, all that. That's how I relax.' This wasn't going too bad. My man seemed most approachable. Would it be cheeky for me to ask . . . 'Do you ever get to relax?'

'What's this? Boy concerned for my welfare? Heaven forbid!' he ho-ho-hoed. 'No – not relax, as such. I have to prepare, as you know, endlessly. But preparation is often relaxation, when it's done right. Funnily enough, I was just blitzing through some old crime and detective shows, getting myself up to speed with you; *that* was about as near to no-brain activity as I'll be getting this millennium . . .'

He had this intriguing new line on this classic pulp fiction: how it was actually about the devil, which is the strange light shining out of the brer's suitcase at the end, and miracles and being redeemed and so forth. I must have seen that movie a few times and I hadn't seen that.

That apart, he didn't much care for my childhood favourites. I was meekly backsliding on *Hart to Hart*, conceding that at most it had sentimental value for me, since it came on during the hours of a

Sunday when all four of us might be sitting together in the front room, when he said something which pulled me up right there.

'I knew your parents. Both sets. Excellent people. I'm so sorry, of course, about your mother.'

'You knew them? What, know as in you know about everyone or know know?'

'Know know. Your dad could be a little . . . fraught at times, but they're up there with the very best.'

'But they, they never told me!' I was staggered.

'You didn't hang around all that long to give them the chance, did you?' There was a sharpness to his voice then, the merest hint of a growl.

'No, guess not.' I shuffled uncomfortably. 'I don't suppose any of them can be too pleased with the progress I've made, if they're still watching?'

I suppose I was fishing for, if not a compliment, then some word of encouragement, but there was silence. I looked down into the distance, as if that might avoid his gaze.

'Sometimes I think I'm a terrible man,' I admitted. 'Then other times I say, well perhaps it's too soon—'

'It's a high form of science,' he sounded mellow again, 'to know your inmost nature and then despise it. But we are all better than our worst acts. Self-abuse is necessary but not sufficient, and should never be so much as to overwhelm.'

'That's it, sir, that's it. Bang on the button.' I was heartened – I did not think it too fanciful to hear some encouragement there. 'And when I think of it, I may not even have put myself about so poorly, given this city's fuckreys—'

'Oh, forget about the city!' The Race Man boomed in exasperation. 'Just like your dad. City this and city that. Hunh! That was all we got from him after he'd been down there a while. He took it on willingly – did we force him? Yes, it gets tasty, and yes, it gets nasty, but it isn't relevant at the deep end of the day. The city is a poor excuse for a better man, do you understand?'

'I hear you, I hear you one hundred per cent.' Those lines about my father intrigued me, but a return glance at the empty frame on the wall steered me towards a query of greater personal consequence. 'Still, I just reckon that if I could get to spend some time away from here, you'd really see me fly. If I could maybe find something that involved travelling—'

'I thought you just got offered something the other day. Hard toil, but you'd get to see the country, other countries—'

'Oh that.' I remembered Mr Development at Ice Cream. 'That was a strange thing . . .'

Just then I heard a cough, a little laugh having trouble restraining itself, of a timbre totally different to anything the Race Man had yet produced. It was like someone else was there in the fog.

'. . . But no doubt you know all about that,' I trailed off. 'We are alone, aren't we, sir?'

'I'm all you need to worry about,' he replied.

'Aha. No, that brother's project was something deep. But well, it just sounded like voluntary work, kind of. My mum did a lot of that, you know.'

'If you say so.'

'I was thinking more . . . well I know this sounds too cheeky, but do you think it's still remotely possible . . . I mean, I would love to work for you. I'm dead hot at riddles, got good general knowledge, college degree plus university of life—'

'Not one for small asks are we? Do you really know what that would entail? How much, for example, trustworthiness? Do you?'

'I think a lot, sir. Definitely, I can imagine, a great deal. Still, if you let me – I know that before I've uhm . . . well, I've uhm . . . what I'm trying to say, sir, is that I promise, if you let me, I wouldn't let you down.'

'Oh, Boy. You . . .' he sighed in his gravest tones. I could feel the hard gust of air, '. . . yes, you are welcome. For your family's sake, and for a few of your multitudes. Complete your present mission and then we'll see.'

'Wow, that's just amazing, just blinding news! That's made my day, week, everything!' I cleared my throat, beaming. 'This mission—'

'Look, the clues are there, you've had them all. Keep your head and your heart, heed the Bible, and you should come through fine.'

I glanced automatically at the chest by my feet. 'Same old Boy!' he chimed. 'Always looking for short cuts. And what do you think you'll find there? Tablets of stone? A woman's name? You have all the information you need now, I tell you.'

'A pointer would really help me. Like . . . well, like a name?'

The silence was emphatic.

'Maybe there's a particular district I should be homing in on? Or an age group?'

'Remember we were talking about *Hart to Hart*?' he began finally. 'The basic problem with the series is that it never knew what it wanted to be. Was it romance, or was it detection? Was it straight, or comedy, or *Lifestyles of the Rich and Famous*? What I would say to you, Boy, is, if you're going to do romance, make it the spine of the story.'

'Make it the spine of the story.' I waited for him to continue. 'That's it?' I said when he didn't.

'That's it.'

I felt a little shortchanged by this, and determined to extract something more while I still could. I obviously meant to ask about my beginnings, but it dropped down my mind for something else. 'Thinking on the bigger picture . . . Sometimes, you know, when I'm standing in certain places, I feel I get a glimpse of it and then it's gone. I wonder if you could give me, give me a pointer to, umm, to what I'm supposed to be doing – like a guide to best behaviour. I mean, how do you do it? How do *you* do it?'

I thought I heard a yawn from him. He certainly sounded bored. 'I'm sure you know quite nearly as well as I. There are no surprises. God don't like ugly. One's striving must simply be to live the best life one can. You are life; deeply linked to all that lives. Which is why I cannot dismiss your Mr Development's business, or your mother's before, for that matter, as mere "voluntary work". The earthly degradations he combats is something that I actually feel. Not in the sense that I don't have a nice view out of my window or my street doesn't have trees, no, I'm truly *feeling* it, do you understand? You know the story of the butterfly and the avalanche.'

The stories of him being as old and as earthy as the hills went through me, as I pursued a burning query: 'You mentioned my mother and, as you must know, she died, as did my brother. For no fair reason that I can see. So I wonder – I mean, stop me if you've heard this one before, but I do worry about the logic, the fairness factor, in this "life" of yours – of ours. I mean, maybe it doesn't operate like that and I do recall in the bits of the Bible that I read – not this one, the other one – that it seemed harsh and unkind in places—'

'You ask me if it's fair! If it's kind!' he thundered. '*You* who might have died several times over! Yes it is kind. And fair. But when you sin, somebody somewhere pays. Bills have to be paid. That is natural fairness. The kindness lies not least in that it is not always the debtor who pays. The sinner may still be saved. A second chance – is it not so? As to your losses, I have no hand in matters like that. But for every sacrifice, there is a great miracle. I have four hundred working on my side, against two hundred on the other. And that, too, is natural kindness.'

'I'm sorry, sir, I didn't mean to – it came out completely wrong.' I was terrified. The walls and ground had rumbled in his rage, as if a train was careering underneath. 'I suppose I should be going—'

'Soon,' he said. 'Between now and then, no more undercooked questions.'

That was definitely the low point. I was cowed for some period after and, if anything, he got to putting more of the questions, probing me at some length about certain rumours of a revival of spirits amongst my kind. I was most flattered, and marshalled the week's evidence – from the bouncers at Ice Cream to the dance at the arches and the exhaling party – to give him a considered, if pessimistic opinion, thinking how much this was like my old reports for the state, only for better.

One issue I did raise was the hit out on me. There was quite a pause – in my anxiety I felt that I could dimly hear the great churn of his cogitations – before he said that he'd tell me what, I didn't even need to worry about that side of that matter at the present time. 'Just complete your task. After, everything is possible.' Naturally, I was massively relieved, even more since it suggested that he was no longer irked with me. I took the opportunity of confirming that I could return here post-completion and offer my services. 'Much better that you come, than that I should have cause to come and find you,' he intoned with some traditional opacity.

'Enough,' he announced, and I bowed my head at the stool then, impulsively, repeated the gesture to the fog above, turned, gave a respectfully wide berth to the BIBLE, and headed to the door. Almost there and I was turning again at a footfall and a distinct rustling sound behind me. Surely there was someone here?

'Goodbye, Boy,' said the Race Man firmly. 'Your client, at least, has every confidence in you and remains convinced that there will be a happy ending for all three parties concerned.'

I was all abuzz as I redonned my shoes outside. Without actually being able to put my finger on a piece of wisdom unambiguously useful for present needs, I nevertheless felt my whole future had opened up. Revitalised, no question. All thoughts of retirement were banished – I was now set to be a travelling soldier in a mighty cause. Who knows – within a few years I might even be the Race Man's trusty lieutenant: bringing information, assessing rumours. I was welcome. Despite everything. He'd stayed any execution of the Eb'ry Year contract, he'd had time for me. I'd lasted thirty minutes longer than the deportee.

And that stuff about my folks. How he knows them, knew them. . . Rah! Who'd have freakin' thought it? I was a blackhead with connections.

9

mambolikin'

I drove south a few blocks before surrendering to the strong inclination to revisit and linger by the hallowed ground. But I could not find the place when I looked for it again and gave up after a few minutes, parking the car down a quiet sidestreet. Safer though I felt after the Race Man's tip, I kept the ride in time-honoured first gear.

My phone was flashing – messages. I would not attend to them until I had laid bare the heart, the romantic heart, of this matter. Ordinarily, I might have tugged at it over a drink, but I was still all about purity and the need for big match fitness. So I took my tennis ball out from the front and spun it to myself a while, then got out and pottered around the block, stopping by a newsagent and glugging on a bottle of water. I did have me a couple of cigs eventually, unenjoyed as my head darted about, fearing his roving eye.

The water made me think of Candy. She'd liked her fill of it. Now she was the romantic type ('*Make romance the spine . . .*'), no question. See how she'd jumped at the offer. Blatant, rudeboy! Huh. Did he mean for

me to return to her, or someone like her? Good, unsullied? No require-
ment to be unsullied, just – romantic. Sullied like, like me. Could it be?

My romance, *my* romance the spine . . . What romance? Well that
was easy: there had been only one.

My foot skidded in some pavement nastiness as I pondered very
carefully, my notion growing shape by the moment. The Race Man's
words seemed an emphatic reminder that my business was to engi-
neer a love match; to find someone who was capable of setting my
client off in such a fashion, one who could reciprocate such feelings.
Only I was the one charged with picking for my man. It followed that
the one who'd be right for my client would be the one who touched
something that deep in me. Then there would be an almost-romance
for me, romance for him, romance would be at the spine.

Now this someone might be no one I'd ever met, someone totally
new I could endeavour to find in three days, but I found this less
likely than the possibility that this person, or the person that could take
me to that person, was already known to me. The latter chimed with
my growing overstanding that this case had something to do with me.
Moreover, if they were not known, then I was basically in the same
position as I'd started out from on night one. Which would make an
irrelevance, a plump red herring, of these last couple of days, scarcely
the type of thing that happened in this higher chamber of riddle. No,
what was needed was within me by now, garnered this week or before.
You have all the clues, he'd said. If that was so, and this was all about
love, then where else could I turn to, go through, if not her?

Excitedly, I tapped my last numbers for Cosmic. A slim chance –
I knew they were old and, sure enough, the occupants at her old
home number had never heard of her whilst a guy at my last-known
daytime number abruptly informed me she didn't work there anymore. No matter, I had another idea for contacting her. I hurried
home, my notion now well and truly airborne.

I played the messages on the phone. Lincia, staggeringly, had

called. 'Give me a ring when you get this, please,' she had left in
tones that were busy-person cold rather than the big chill you'd at
least have expected. I don't know what that girl thought she and I
had to speak about.

Dean had called and called again as I was heading back down the
underpass, which made, between the pips on his payphone and my
struggling mobile, our moments of communication brief. He'd heard
a bit more about my Eb'ry Year, though: real derelict sort, low-level
irritant. No one Dean spoke to knew where he lived exactly. Folk
hadn't heard of him shooting off gun before but it didn't surprise
them too much. He wanted to know if I was gonna head down to the
morrow's big match. I said for sure, business permitting. He said
he'd come check me in the morning.

Past the pink elephant and the streets were a mid-afternoon, pre-
rush hour quiet, until I got to the market area just down from the
hospital, where a heap of police cars were blocking up the place. I
thought at first that someone had been ended but it turned out they
were just checking drivers' tax discs. It was a blatant cheeky thing to
do, with extra customers down there buying provisions for the holiday. If I were one of those traders I'd sue them for disruption.

Once home, I headed straight for the computer. A chill went
through me at the thought that, as likely as not, her cable line would
be disconnected by now, so rendering this exchange impossible (and,
if the account was still in my name, dragging my credit rating down
further). Still, I could but try and, after a couple of minutes to cogi-
tate and subdue my pride, I e-mailed her:

> Salutations, O custodian of the superior poetical nation,
> If you're not presently lounging at some high-falutin'
>   planetary location,
> This still boyish worker bee,
> Requests the pleasures etc. of your company.

No response came directly and I hovered around the computer until I forced myself to turn my mind elsewhere and realised that the pain in my stomach had gone and that I was starving. Most all there was to be cooked was tuna and pasta which, for once, I welcomed. I didn't really feel to eat meat today.

With a tin of peeled tomatoes and spices there was enough to work with and – after what was an arguably foolhardy stroll out my front door for the sake of some cream – I fashioned a quite satisfactory meal. I lingered a while, savouring the therapy of home cooking, turning hopefully every so often to the computer, before I grudgingly accepted the need to pursue alternatives.

I drew up a personal ad. It was a course that had first occurred to me even as the client had left me that first day but I had since then neglected. I thought the advert needed a little extra, something that gave an indication of this unique proposal. I scanned my little row of books for inspiration and was quickly drawn to my favourite: there, atop my puzzle-easing thesaurus, the *Encyclopaedia of Epics* that Cosmic had presented on my birthday three years ago. Her inscription (*'To my man with the twilight allure – Still feeling it! C-C. PS, look under 'C' for 'Cyrano de B' – who says you can't be a lover and a fighter too?'*) brought the story right back and, though it was not exactly applicable, it helped me on my way. Yet even as I typed the ad, my thoughts were more about how all roads were returning me to her.

'Wanted! A romantic girl for a curious boy, who needs must sing the praises of another . . .' I reckoned it read all right but could not bring myself to despatch it to the site for such matters. I feared that that might mess up my Cosmic karma. Then, with my positive frame beginning to tire, a smiley-faced envelope trotted his way along the top of my screen and I rushed to access my post.

Yes, yes! My girl had left me something. A nonchalant 'How are you doing, cherub?' message, like this wasn't our first words in seventeen months. A few exchanges later, and I'd arranged to pick her up from some east-central hall around five.

I arrived before the turn of the hour feeling – from the water in my hand to the freshness of my socks – quite full with purity.

A lady preceded me up the stone stairs of the building and pushed open the door as I peered through the porthole window of the hall that we came to.

The place felt like an old school and this room – with various youths jumping on mats and trampolines – its gymnasium. The lady had joined a few other parent/big sister types that lined the wall at the far end where a class was taking place.

I could not tell if the one adult there was her at first – she had her back to me and a large lumber shirt over her butt; certainly the garb, mauve tracky bottoms and spanking white trainers, was not unknown to her. Until she turned and, notwithstanding some infernal mask on her face, there could be no doubt. I poked my head round.

'Okay, I'm the boogieman. The big, bad boogieman. He's your worst nightmare come to life, and he's come sailing through your bedroom window. I want you to give me some *fear*. I want to be *feeling* it,' she was exhorting as energetically as her languorous out-of-state tones would allow, clunking towards her charges with that slight flatness of foot, and halting before one unimpressed shortie. 'Come on, Ara, you're scared: what do you do when you're scared?'

Ara, mindful of the smirks around him, replied in a head-down mumble.

'Say what?' Cosmic unhooked her mask and craned her head forward. 'So what if it's kids' stuff? Kids' stuff is good.' Her gaze travelled his classmates, about a dozen ten- and eleven-year-olds, mainly blackheads, before alighting on me. Her hair was much trimmer than before. She signalled ten minutes.

The big persons did not look convinced by this kids' stuff. A couple frowned and checked their watches, whilst one who joined me in the corridor was even wondering whether Cosmic was all right up top. I assured her, with as much conviction as I could muster, that she was.

I had some sympathy for her. I gathered that most of the children were at these competitive schools where they were very much in the minority. These after-classes, according to the council and the brochure, would build up confidence and self-projection in social situations. 'I thought he'd be doing public speaking,' the mother said to me. 'Learn more sophistication in a supportive environment, you know. Last week she was telling them to make noises about what kind of breakfasts they'd had.' She threw a look of concern at her Ara, who stood amongst a hard core of resistors as the rest howled and slithered about them.

The doors opened shortly after and class and company filed through. The odds on my girl feeling in front of a full house next week looked long.

I went back in and could not see her for a second, 'til I heard an 'Urrr-rhurgh!' of frustration behind me. She was beside the door, struggling to clamber up one of the thick ropes that ran down from the ceiling. No doubt her intention had been to swing on it and jump on me. Instead she dropped down and ran towards me, wrapping her arms around my middle and resting the side of her head on my breast.

'Oh Daddy, Daddy, Daddy!' she cried, like a melodrama queen. 'Daddy went and left me for so long!'

She often called me 'Daddy'; partly, no doubt, because she was perverse that way, but mainly because I would come with these fatherly things like how she should get a proper job.

'My hands are hurting from the rope.' She pushed out her lips in a childish expression of dismay. 'Daddy's got to kiss them better.'

I looked at them. She was a light-skinned woman, and her palms could get truly red. More of me didn't want to kiss them. I didn't want to get sucked into the same old bullshit. I hadn't been seeing her for a reason, obviously. On the other hand, not to kiss would be to hint at a hurt that I did not wish to display. I kissed them. She beamed, took my hand and led me out of the gym, turning right down a corridor instead of a left to the stairs and exit. She grabbed my watch and inhaled sharply at the time, in unconvincing alarm, before tugging me along more firmly.

Twenty minutes' wait, three minutes in, Daddy this and Daddy that, and I'm being forcemarched to I don't know where. Jesus, Boy, see how you surrender to this girl!

'So who was late today, you or the kids?' I asked, in a bid to wrest some control.

'Oh – a bit of both.'

'And your hair – whassup with your hair?'

She patted what there was left of it. 'It's my victory cut.'

'Victory over what?'

'All the victories to come.'

'You look like Lady Lesbos.'

She smiled me one of her murky swinger's smiles.

Our destination was a music room to which she had, clearly unwisely, been given the keys. I helped her make away with a micro-phone and, as an afterthought, a music stand. One of the mikes at the bar where she was hosting a spoken-word gig that evening had been playing up last time around, she explained. I said I didn't know she was gonna be busy tonight. She always had time, she replied, to spare for Daddy.

She could see I'd got thinner. Stress and pharmaceuticals I told her. The two when I had money, just stress when I hadn't. 'You're lean, man. Like an African hunting dog. Big shoulders still . . .' she massaged them and I could not stop myself simpering, 'but knotty.

That's where you put all your stress, that is. Did you know' she asked, 'that "stressed" said backwards is "deserts"?'

'Yeah?'

'Almost.' She paused when she came to the knife, regarded me ruefully and ran her fingers down its outline. 'That's not mine, is it?'

'No.' She had brought me the red cherry knife from one of her travels. 'Yours is in a safe place.'

She nodded and stepped back. 'Well, deserts or whatever, you look all right on it.'

'It's amazing what water can do,' I replied, offering her the rest of the bottle. I was pretty sick of the stuff.

We stowed the stands and her overflowing bags in the boot, she grabbed my final cigarette, and we were off, Cosmic laughing as we shared a "here we go again" look.

When she laughed big belly fashion, her hand would pound the floor or another hard surface; when she got vexed her bottom lip would just stand hanging out – characteristics she shared with others I had met who had grown in the old country. Her dad was a rugged old chieftain there, with diverse import and export interests, her mother a scion, I believe, of some high-class family from the Viking climes of our continent. When her folks separated, she'd gone up there to join her, before travelling to our parts then across the big water in pursuit of an expensive education. When I'd first met her, she was artifying around town, which she'd continued to do, in between yet more courses, courtesy of a now wearying father. So even though Cosmic personally never seemed to have any money, in her bigger picture she was rolling in it.

'Well,' I began, 'I'm pleased to see you finally joined us in the land of honest toil—'

'That's not fair—'

'Although you'd be pushed to claim that getting kids to fall about was likely to put the economy back on track. And I *know* you got them snaking around just to wind me up—'

'So what d'you think, what d'you think?' she laughed.

I glanced at her. 'Since when have you cared what I think about matters artistic?'

'That's not fair either.'

'All right. Well, being that you asked, and skipping swiftly from the creative to the service side, I would say that you've gotta be careful. The customer is always right, you know. You gotta pitch it on their level. Those people, they're just your above average, anxious parents. If they're not seeing blatant benefits to their kids, they're gonna run—'

'Then fuck 'em. I mean, it would be a shame but, you know . . . I only get a coupla folds a head for them anyway. It's the council that stumps up the bulk of our fee.'

'Aa-Aa! Spoken like a true businesswoman.'

She handed me a florid card. Her name was down with a couple of other penniless veterans of her scene, among masks and painted faces and a staff with a snake curled around it. '. . . words – sound – power,' it read, 'Mambolika – Creative Consultants.'

'Mam-Bo-Lie-Ka.'

'Mamboleeka,' she corrected.

'Whatever,' I passed it back to her, 'it's another pissin' snake.'

Where we were headed wasn't far away, maybe a mile and a half further north, but the traffic was ugly at this hour and it had taken us near twenty minutes before I went over the big roundabout and down EC1's main drag.

The neighbourhood was distinctive, with its spacious but generally blasted look: weathered greystones and coshed warehouses, their lettering long-faded, full, it was true, of character, an ancient web of sidestreets and the odd dinky little square. Back in the day, I understand, the area had housed the wholesale goods of fruit and veg folk, manufacturers and the like. More recently, monied creative types had pounced on the derelict buildings, converting them into roomy living-cum-workspaces, and the area into a haven for their kind. The cyber café, which we passed, was where my working self had first tracked her down. She herself, she casually told me, had just found a flat in the area: a typical Cosmic 'I can't buy cigarettes but I can rent a conversion' kind of move.

We pulled up about halfway down, outside a bar with a glass frontage and a vertical 'MOJO' neon sign. Cosmic stuffed the poem in my pocket. 'We must talk,' she said airily, stepping out.

'We must,' I replied.

Clutching her bits, we went through the side entrance, where a small reception committee awaited us. The manager – looked Greek to me – and a braided brother, who turned out to be a musician, included me in their look of mild irritation. The event wasn't due to start for a little while but there were staff and the band to be briefed, furniture to be shunted, ting an' ting, and Cosmic was the first member of Mambolika to rear her head.

As she soothed and sorted, I faded away – easy enough for, notwithstanding the neon outside, inside our fondness for gathering in dark spots was honoured. Most of what light was to be had was concentrated on the little stage up front, where a guitarist, drummer and keyboard player perused the running order that Cosmic had handed them. Behind them a pixillated video screen projected a series of mildly disturbing close-ups – Petri dishes that resembled bits of anatomy and the like. I glanced into the back pool room, before depositing myself along the central, rather fine horseshoe bar.

There was a fair sprinkling of heads of every hue about me already. Students strangling pint glasses, earnest hand-rolled tobacco types, and others who looked like they'd rarely encountered a tax form. A few glanced warmly in my direction. A couple I'd probably met with Cosmic a while back, the others, no doubt, were simply being liberal. I smiled tolerantly in return, enjoying the rarely tasted bite of straight orange juice.

Nothing could faze me at these spots anymore, but when I first experienced them I was two parts intimidated and one part derisive – an over-reaction fuelled, no doubt, by my knowledge that I was there under false pretences. Some four years ago, while I was doing my sometime business for the state, my contact approached me. He wanted me to slip inside a new so-called radical group, the Point Fivers. He had given me a date and an address so I'd tootled down to the cyber café up the road, not knowing what to expect, and found myself among all these pretty freaky fauna. There was reciting and testifying and any manner of touchy-feelying, guys with lo-fros beside six-foot female bal'heads in boots, and a Brother Scorcher, stripped to his waist, hobbling around the stage with a ball and chain. I was sat at the end of a row of cheap chairs, wondering if people got paid for this, my ears pricking at the periodic references to the Point Fivers in the performers' introductions. At every mention, an enthusiastic cry of 'Large up!' would come from my right and I looked to see this caramel girl sat by a sidetable. Her hair was short and straightened, with dinky ringlets at the front, and she was wearing a black, sleeveless, bust-flattening dress. Her darker companion sported a similar dress, in cream, and matching hair. I peered more closely and saw that they were linking hands. No great surprise there, by that point of the evening. I was more taken, I recall, by the flair they'd displayed in their package.

Anyway, soon after the light-skinned lady was called up and I was quite hyped in expectation of something singular and brazen – particularly when she was handed a top hat and cane. Unfortunately, she soon dispensed with the hat and the cane turned out to be some spiritual ancestors' cane that she trailed as she hit us with this stodgy poem about five centuries of struggle. All these big-arsed images: 'Mama Africa, stubborn beast of burden / Inheritor for certain, pure global vision / Your hips bring forth nations / Cosmic-Cosmic . . .' The crowd intoned reverently but I thought that shit was, well, dry. It didn't smell lived, you know, and, not meaning to be low level, but it didn't fit the promise of the girl. Still, despite her same-old, she had that real something – charisma, I guess, and she put that across.

I saw her a few times over the next weeks, tracking her to different venues, pumping up the hours on my invoice. The fourth time, she accosted me, and we got talking. It transpired that the Point Fivers were simply a bunch of mixed-race folk in her field who came together every so often to reason over their roots and wring out some appropriate art. Nothing, in short, for the Minister to be fretting about. (My own unreported surmise was that my employers had confused them with the Five Percenters, a very different kettle of fish.) She must have asked me what I thought of her stuff, and I came out with this crack that it was all very Cosmic-Cosmic. Truth say, I don't rightly recall if she ever quite uttered those words, but her friends certainly found my take droll, and gazed at me with new scrutiny; an aka was born directly and I remember the little gust of pleasure at being acknowledged by these creative types.

You don't often get to meet interesting people on cases, just raasholes all round, so all this was a real other trip to me. I invited Cosmic out to dinner where I ended up telling her the true deal. I tell you, she hadn't shown any especial interest in me 'til then, but after that, she was all over me blatant. She reckoned it was all very exciting and dangerous and chic what I did. And poor – I think she was duly appalled by the source side, but she welcomed something dark in the folk she was fucking. So we'd get it on, then off, and on, then off again until eventually I just couldn't stand it any more.

Brother Scorcher came in, fully dressed this evening in a cream fleece top. He ambled over, accompanied by two others I also knew – Steve and Mira, this real pleasant girl. Steve nodded to me warily: nothing personal, he was just one of those reserved types.

He'd been the first person, actually, to make me realise that this scene wasn't quite as chilled as I'd imagined. A 'facilitator' rather than a performer, he'd wrap particular artists up in a package and present the project to our favourite Minister or sympathetic companies for sponsorship. Nothing wrong with that, only with Steve you felt he was less about truly checking for the talent who provided his daily bread and more about manipulating a scene. I used to watch him watching the performers, a sneer hinting about his mouth. You'd only really see him perking up when he dealt with the funders, Cosmic had once noted, like he preferred dealing with folk who were somehow scared of him. It did not surprise me, then, when he told me he'd moved the focus of his business on, elsewhere. He'd just come down, he claimed, to show some love.

I would have preferred not to buy him a drink, but that would have been a declaration of war, seeing as I was getting them for the others already. His eyes flitted to Cosmic and co. toiling with the new microphone, no doubt storing the sight for a good gloat later.

I looked around too; there were no awnings or banners to tell or remind the punters whose gig they were at. I knew tonight was basically a trial run – the event was free, with Cosmic hoping to show the manager they could attract a good, spending crowd, and so ensure future bookings – but still. I would have to speak to her.

She was looking great, though. She had changed into plucked eyebrows, a black evening dress, pencil cut and glittering, plus one of her fancy black hats. She looked a bona fide star, the only earth-bound rumble those white designer trainers she still insisted on; rarely have I seen a name so coveted be so ill used. In truth, her appearance had never again been without difficulty for me as it was that first time. Off stage, she went for those mix and match, down-at-heel fashions so beloved by products of our older universities: cardigans and Indian pants and men's shirts and boots. Couple that with her slimness plus all her, uh, habits and some would have been surprised that she was so much my girl. But, like I said, she had a style.

She bounded down from the stage, jiggled her hands in front of us like a runner, to signal her trepidation, took mighty gulps from first mine and then Mira's glass, grinned, mouthed 'Five minutes!' and dashed off tugging Brother Scorcher.

The place was about a third full now, which I thought was all right. No doubt another quarter would drift in during the gig, running on some grisly combination of ours and artistic time.

The three musicians took their places: a young ponytailed saxophonist, with curls where his sideburns would be; DJ Dizzy, an old-time intimate of the circle, handling the decks; and the braided guy, settling stage left, legs bent, cradling a drum shaped like a pestle and a mortar. I didn't think they were coming with full horsepower today. There used to be a guitarist too.

A mighty gong sounded, and Cosmic and Scorcher emerged from the wings with six or so others. They came to the front, holding hands, heads bowed, as the drummer got to work.

'We deal in words poetic and sound power. Words poetic and sound power. Poetic . . . power,' Cosmic intoned.

I braced. I had seen her do this holding-hands warm-up before, backstage, and it invariably ended with the group hugging up and such. I feared she had decided to export this business and, any moment now, we'd be asked to embrace our neighbours. I had no major problems with this, but on the whole I'd rather not. Cha! Too late to exit now.

Luckily Cosmic reined herself, and she and her fellows confined themselves to maintaining their contemplative posture, as if they were summoning up the gods, while the lights dimmed further. I think they were waiting for a complete blackout, but when it dawned that that wasn't going to happen, they scurried off severally.

First up was this folky singer. The voice was a touch ragged but

what I heard of it was all right. Mainly I was conversating with
Mira. She worked as publicity officer for Vanguard – this outfit
catering for unpopular poets and performers and Cosmic's former
employer – and had just returned from some lame event out in the
sticks. A pensioners' afternoon library club – only three women
and a dog had turned up, she said. 'Lets hope it was an arts dog,' I
consoled her.

She had had a tough time at Vanguard, no two ways about it. It was
a thankless task trying to procure any coverage of the acts Vanguard
patronised, and then the rubber pay cheques from the board on top!
Her forthcoming kid had made up her mind: when she re-emerged
she was gonna find a new gig, 'something holistic but paying'. I was
pleased to see another convert to the real world campaign I waged at
these spots.

With a twinkle in her eye she enquired whether I'd heard about
Cosmic's glorious exit from Vanguard. Cosmic's last day had begun,
in not unusual fashion, with her late arrival. As she was interrogated
by their superior over the whys and wherefores, it seemed that
Cosmic, said Mira, had finally lost the will to come up with stories.
'Oh, I resign!' she had shouted and walked out, her work bag still
slung on her shoulder.

The devil must have heard us, for she came on a few moments
later to deliver two husky-toned pieces, wry, closely observed numbers some steps up from the flabbiness of her apprentice style, before
returning a little while later with Mambolika partner Eclectic to per-
form one of their regular dialogues. Cosmic was really the foil,
feeding stray thoughts to the monstrously brained Eclectic, who'd
grab the bait, run and shimmy with it. She complained of a hungry
belly so Eclectic offered her some words 'because words are like
food. We digest them.' Then he, a barely corked bottle of fizz with
his ceaseless pacing and his too small suit, was off speculating how
different words might taste, and words in space; might that be a

place where they'd be allowed artistry and not anthropology, and anyone for astrophysically correct texts? One for the connoisseurs, no question, but the mass of us, including a couple who stumbled in having lost their way, still got into it enough to shout, 'Yeah, yeah, yay, yo!' whenever he requested. I mean, Eclectic was a cocky son of a gun, but when people put their shit together in a way, you go to their side for the duration.

Theirs and an acrobatic turn by Scorcher were the highlights of the main part. After the break it was open mike time. Most all the amateurs who stepped up, clutching their notebooks, came with some out-of-state affect or handle, abetted by an MC Cosmic whose own accent had been receding to ever more exotic shores the longer the evening went on. This aspect had always saddened me; it had seemed that the passion was strong yet their own voice timid, but tonight not at all. I understood, I think, finally. They were all in the business of concocting a dream, these people, of some other, fantastic space that they brought to life every time they gathered. And she, she and her easy, stink-free, shamboleeking life were a kind of dream to me.

'All right, y'all, it's that time of the night where we like to free up the style, and invite you bad and brave to come stand and deliver. An' you best come warm, otherwise we'll be sending you back in a box! No, seriously, anyone with any processing to do . . . Our theme tonight, boys and girls, is "war". You know this morning I was leafing through the paper, looking for some good news to get me out of bed, but all I could find was battles here and massacres there. Anyway, one of the articles had this statistic that blew me away: you know we've only had two hundred and sixty-eight years free of war on this planet in the last four thousand? A piddling two hundred and sixty-eight. That's a man's world for you—'

'Go, girl!'

'— so we got a theme, do I have a beat?'

She turned behind her to Dizzy, who threw down a brooding bass-heavy rumble, punctured with screeching strings.

'Ai! Ai!' Cosmic padded around as if in pain. 'I got a theme, I got a rhythm I can ride, I'm just waiting for my volunteer. A soldier . . .'

Nobody came forward. 'Better make that a conscript!' someone laughed.

'Come on . . Aha! I spy with my little eye a man with experience of the rough and tumble.' She was looking dead at me. 'C'mon baby, let me feel that hinterland I hear rumours about,' she goaded as a hundred eyes turned my way.

I shook my head fiercely, discovering, as I did so, that I was actually in the mood for once. I'd been feeling really mellow, recollections of the Race Man's job offer running through me and everything. And I would have done it despite, you know, my first time and all these people, but the stuff just wouldn't come together in my head.

'I can't go first,' I stalled. 'Three's my lucky number innit?' I immediately regretted adding that last part, as cheers to my right indicated that someone else had picked up the gauntlet. I faced a nervous few minutes fearing Cosmic would come for me again. Luckily, Scorcher got up third and kicked something round and profound, and, with the Greek barking that they were running thirty minutes over, Cosmic brought the proceedings to a close. She invited me plus amateurs up to the stage, where I played a somewhat fraudulent part in the huggy curtain call.

We milled around in buzzed-up but aimless fashion afterwards. Folk were looking to continue the vibe without spending any money doing it.

I buttonholed the manager and ordered up bottles of the house's finest. A couple of C notes would hardly deepen the financial hole I had dug for myself, but it could give some poor people a good time. Moreover, this would forestall any need for the group to repair to Cosmic's place nearby, now that mouths were desert dry.

Cosmic approached as I was distributing the bubbly and kissed me powerfully. 'What a downlow sweetheart you are!'

'I'm maturing,' I replied, clinking glasses, 'like fine wine. This—' I gestured around us '—then talks.'

She nodded and squeezed my hand tightly. Nice, although not as reassuring as, perhaps, she intended. I knew she could be squeezing me at eleven then disappear to jump on the next man's bones come the small hours.

I kept a close eye on Cosmic's toing and froing, trying to determine who she was presently sexing. A difficult call, what with her lazy hands and varied history, but you could generally tell. It was such scrutiny that had first alerted me to her ting with Steve, which more than irked me at the time seeing how, by her own admission, he was such a cunt. Handsome, though, I suppose. And leaving now, which warmed the old cockles. She and Eclectic shared frequent glances, but theirs was a long-time special relationship, so I fretted not. Nor too much about Miss Dizzy, who was sniffing around my lady. I knew that Dizzy was quite hardcore in that direction but Cosmic, at max, was just a dibber and a dabber.

You may think I sound the jealous type but I can honestly say you won't find someone less so than I, so little so that I've sometimes wondered whether it was ever, truly, love, for me. Competitive I could be, but not jealous. She passed by others during our time together and – though the fact was never pleasant – I'd kick up no great fuss about it. How could I? It was most natural. I had been elsewhere myself in what passed for earlier relationships and, if I didn't this time, it wasn't because I had converted; I just hadn't, I don't know, hadn't happened to do it. When she tried to excuse her behaviour one time, I replied, 'I don't even need to hear that. All I need to know is "Is it me more?" and "Will you stay?"' She'd say the first, regularly enough, but never the latter. So every time she became suddenly uncontactable, I never knew if she was coming back. I tell you, that sense of suspension can be almost worse than the real thing.

Dizzy and Eclectic plus one other unidentified male were still not shaken off as we headed for Cosmic's at closing-up. Once inside, she slumped tipsily on to the nearest rug so, with Eclectic not the type, it fell to me to play host. But I was determined to make the others' stay as uncomfortable as possible, and offered them nothing. The four of us ended up fighting this bizarre war of attrition over the dozing form beside us until, with Dizzy muttering that it was too late for her to get home now, I outflanked them, calling some cabs and deploying my dollars to silence their objections. I allowed myself a winner's wink before shutting the door behind them.

Cosmic was still slumped as I made my ginger way through her flotsam to the loft's kitchen area, coffee in mind. It was difficult to tell whether she was even messier than I remembered or if her usual amount was simply spread over a bigger space. Competing with her bits were numerous artworks that friends had donated her – dainty figurines, floor compost arrangements and abstract paintings, the largest one daubed, like her wallpaper, in frenzied reds – so that one lurched through a battery of visual events.

'How did I do, Daddy?' came a yawn.

'Oh, safe, C-C. You and Eclectic kicked it, no question.' Great. Coffee, but no bleeding milk or sugar. 'You know, you really shine when you're up there. You bloom in front of fans.'

'And why didn't you come up after I begged you? A star would have been born—'

'I don't think so.'

As I padded back out, a coffee for her and a mango juice for me in my hands, I snagged my sleeve on a hook from one of her figures. The mug was jerked forward, cascading coffee all over her scattered smalls. Cosmic hooted.

'You know why that happened?' she enquired merrily. 'Cos you're such a hustler. Even in a room you're trying to cut corners. Instead of walking straight, you thought you'd take a sharp left and bam!'

'But you welcome it,' I said, wondering where to start in my search for a cloth.

'Sure.'

'So what's the problem?' I turned to her.

She only held my gaze for a second, then looked away. I hadn't meant to go down there yet again but – you know.

'Because, like I've said, underneath all the hustle and all that evidence to the contrary, is a nice guy. And once I saw that, I couldn't . . . I don't want to mess around a sweetheart.'

Which begged a few questions, not least why she didn't consider being nice to a nice guy, but I didn't pursue them. You can't force someone, can you?

'I thought I might hear from you today, actually,' she said.

'Yeah?'

'Unhn. You know what day it is tomorrow?'

'Sports Day.'

'Yes. But the date, dickhead. Come on.'

'Jesus! Junior's . . .' It was Junior's birthday.

'Aha.'

'I can't believe that. I was even thinking about him, and the whole family, so much today. And when I put Sports Day down in my diary this year, I said, "That's Junior's birthday." It just slipped my mind—'

'Have you got a headstone yet?'

'No.' I felt so embarrassed about that. 'No, I haven't.'

'Oh, Boy!' she scolded. 'Still. What's your problem?'

'I don't know.' I shrugged and sucked my teeth. 'It's not what you think. It's just . . . fuck it, man, the thing is, when my, like, my faith is weak, I just think they're gone. That's it, why bother . . . The other times are like "yeah! I really feel to do this", 'cept that those times don't seem to last long enough for me to get it sorted.'

'And how's your faith currently?'

'Oh – right now,' I smiled, 'my faith is strong. I am being cared for. Guess who I went to see today? . . . The Race Man.'

'No!' she screamed and sat up. 'Really? Tell me "Yes, really".'

'Yes, really.'

'Mama Mia!' she jumped up and scurried around for a pen and a pad. Her foot sent a micro-cassette recorder skittering across the floor. She picked it up and considered it, before looking back at me.

'Get comfy, Daddy.' She indicated the rug. 'Come and tell little C-C all about it.'

And so I joined her there and recounted my week, starting with the Race Man then peeling back to the beginning. She sat in silent animation most of the time, pausing me only to extract further detail and, when I described Lincia as a pure 'Monicca' type (Money – Condo – Car), to make a note of the expression.

'You know,' she said thoughtfully, 'I'm sure I met this girl. I'm pretty sure it was Barclays Towers we went to . . . Me and Mira were trying to get some sponsorship for this festival we were working on. We had to make a presentation in front of this girl and two johns. Was her hair in a bun?'

'Braids—'

'Braids in a "no nonsense, no dollars for you today" bun! I tell you it must be the same girl.'

'Very possible.'

'Isn't it weird,' she continued, 'how this case has taken you right back up all these avenues in your past? What's *that* about?'

'You mean like Lincia and East Bank?'

'Umhmm. And your old song, and your parents, plus this Sinbad you think is trying to kill you.'

'Yeah . . . No, you're right . . .' I had reached a similar conclusion, pretty much, only I hadn't put it in quite that succinct frame.

'Definitely.' A bare ten-minute overview and already she had grasped the heart of the matter. Cosmic! She was such a smart fucking girl. That's why I loved her.

I'd been so frequently fooled. She'd notice and store such stuff about me – like Junior's anniversary or how I cut corners in rooms – that, you know, you'd think she loved you. But it wasn't that at all; just the wheels of her big brain whirring.

'That's what he meant when he said you had all the clues, surely?'

I nodded.

'But why these . . . reconfrontations? What's that about? What does he want you to *do* with this past?'

'Do it better, d'you reckon?'

'Maybe.' She paused. 'So what are you gonna do?'

'I don't know. Will you help me?'

'I'll try. Of course.'

'I thought – if it's cool with you – I thought I could maybe stay over. It should be safe by mine but that Eb'ry Year was such a retard he probably hasn't got the Man's message yet.'

She kissed her fingers lightly, leant forward, and ran them along my lips. Then her rather serious expression broke into a grin, and she got up, took care of the main lights, and produced some candles. Perhaps for Junior's sake, perhaps for ours.

I was quite excited. What a dapper move to seek her out. It felt like strides we'd made already. Who knows, I just might solve this case and win me the best by-product in the process. A future – Cosmic and me, could it yet be?

You know how your mind runs away with itself. I had visions of the two of us, in a loft out west or wherever, and our seeds, a-painting and a-scribbling away . . . Ha! The mixed-race factor would certainly shake up the gene pool. Rah! What happened if she produced some ruddy-haired throwback for me? No matter. We'd give it all the support it would need.

She was busy domesticating her bed and its environs, by the back wall. Her stereo was also there, and I ambled over to attend to the sounds.

She asked if I had any smoke. What with my concentration on purity, I had forgotten all about that. After due deliberation, I built one. Perhaps it wasn't the purest of moves but, if certain rumour were true, even the Race Man was a puffer.

We topped up our beverages and headed for the bed which, like pretty much everything else Cosmic had to sit on, was on the floor. There we lay on our backs, smoking, humming and playing with the clothes rack that stood above us. The rack was so positioned that she could literally get dressed without getting up, and I believe she did so frequently. We flicked her motley garments down with our feet, dextrously but messily, so vitiating her earlier good work.

Quite a good game, if something of a fire hazard. We didn't play very long, though, for she jumped up shortly, took two of the candles, and sauntered to the bathroom. I went back to her music table. I thought we could listen to this 'Gunslingers' compilation I made for her. I was rummaging when I chanced upon a cassette box with 'Wu Tang – Various' scrawled along its spine. I scanned the cover in hope and there it was, third song down – 'Heaven and Hell'. My client's song! Now, finally, I could listen and discover if there was anything to be discovered. One problem – I couldn't find the tape itself anywhere. I tried a couple of the unmarked tapes scattered about, but all they gave me was atmos and scraps of spoken word.

'Cosmic –' I dashed to the bathroom, cover in hand. She was lying in the tub. 'You've got the tape – my client's song. Where is the actual thing – do you know?'

'What, the tape for that?'

'Aha.'

'I don't know,' she sounded unconcerned, 'I haven't played or seen that in years. Didn't you give me that?'

'No,' I snapped, 'of course I didn't.' How could she not remember the ones I'd done for her? And how could she not have the tape?

'Don't worry. We'll get hold of a copy. Shouldn't be difficult.' She splashed about. 'You coming?'

I considered. I didn't think it was the smartest idea, definitely not while I was still figuring the role she might play in my matter, but I put down the cover, undressed, and came. I sat at the taps end, she at the other. It was a smallish tub – there was about the length of a Cosmic leg between us, a leg whose foot she was now running along my flaccid member.

'Cosmic, don't . . . C-C, enough already!'

'Is it tickling?'

'Umhmm. Among other things.'

'I'm sar-ry!' she said insincerely, then splashed forward, resting her head on my scarred part and lying on her side so that her blackest bits, her curving spine and behind, invited me. I kept my hands to my side and fought the good fight. I thought of the water, being blessed by water, and the rectitude of the Race Man. For a while, with her head poised on my tummy as if she were checking for a pulse there, I fought well. But then she pushed against me so that I could really feel that old, welcome weight, tugged and tweaked at my nipples and sweet spots, before turning to face me with too wicked a grin and . . . well, moments later, I submitted to the rush within me. It feels as if you are obeying a physical imperative but, really, all it is is mental weakness.

One nagging matter I can plead in my defence. That first time we'd messed around we'd endured a marathon, incomplete inter-course. You know, when you go on and on, but you simply can't achieve the result you crave? That was me, that first night, and I was scarcely any better on the second and third either. No question it was nerves. I got them under control eventually but by then, I believe, Steve had already snuck in and, although when I've brought it up she's hotly denied it, I've always believed that the reason I couldn't lock her down was because she didn't like my fuck.

So a bit of me always felt I was one premier performance away from sorting this situation. Tonight I encountered nerves of the opposite kind. Our first deep kisses and holds and I was all ready to explode. I was more than usually grateful, then, when she forced my head downstairs and I could attend to her pleasure while letting mine simmer. I gained a second unexpected respite as she pushed me away to impatiently hunt for a penetrative position. We scrabbled about the bath bootlessly for a while, trying to find a grip that we could sustain. Eventually I sat down across the bath, feet dangling over, and she clambered down and sat on top of me. However, when I was way into my final surge, I was undone by a sudden sadness at the probable futility of the whole exercise, which somewhat subdued the ejaculation. I do not know if she could tell.

Later, as we cradled in the long-curdled bath, Cosmic asked me, 'You know when you got the advance, and you went and you gave however much it was to Sundays for the weed—'

'Ummm?'

'Are you still gonna – do you still wanna spend it like that?'

I snorted. I'd been turning over the same question, this last day and a bit. 'Uhuh. I mean, I haven't told Sundays yet but I don't think I do anymore. How can I when I'm gonna be working for Old Greybeard? I don't think he'll appreciate that kind of moonlighting somehow . . . I just wanna be out of all that now, get this, uh, get this achievement monkey off my back – get back into a team! It's all to do out there, and in here.' I tapped my forehead.

She dripped candle wax on to my shoulder then picked away at the crust. 'It's good. I'm impressed. At how you've moved. I like people who've taken issue with what they were prepared to be.'

'What? Like from "Romane Romanum" to "Cosmic-Cosmic"?' I jested, a reference to her youthful gems, studded with Latin tags, which I had once discovered. 'I should show those to the world. Fuck your credibility right up! So let me get this straight: this liking me more means wanting me less, right?'

'Stop it! I wasn't looking for a love affair,' she replied tartly, her head turning away from me. I caught a glimpse, too, of that characteristic absent look passing her face: as if she were away in a place where those last words were being accorded their full, brutal text. Sometimes I used to wake up from a heavy doze, after we'd sampled one another, to find her gazing the same way and I'd just know that wherever she had gone she was building up the case against me.

I conceded defeat then, finally. These little things don't lie.

Back under the quilt, it was she, for once, who was snoring, and I who was brooding: angry that I had again let her get to me, wondering how I could regularly give of my best without the power she would give me, trying to stop the resentment from drowning me, and turn my thoughts where they should be. The connection, the way through, must have been waiting some while, champing at the bit, for when it came it burst through, fully fledged and galloping.

'C-C!' I shook her frantically and flipped on the side light.

She stirred slowly. 'Ow!' she groaned, when I prodded her in the breast.

'Cosmic, Cosmic, hear what! You know how I'm that much mad for you, an' you ain't really interested? Well – that's cool now. I understand. It wasn't meant to be with me. But with him. You're meant to be his. Cosmic!' She scrunched her eyes and dabbed a damp brow. 'Don't you see? This is doing it again. Only doing it *better*. Make romance the spine. Heaven and hell. You had the tape—'

'The cover. I've got the cover.'

'Cover, whatever.'

A smile flickered about her and she reached for my cigarettes.

'It all fits,' I continued. 'He's got the money, but you're not money-minded, which is how it was supposed to be. But just think

what his corn can do. He can fund you a place, a Mambolikin' building, a base for all of you. No more scrabbling and scraping from
project to project, gettin' dissed by Lincia and the big wheels. All
your shit can happen now.'

'I thought you might ask me before, actually. When you were
telling me about the case.'

I shook my head. 'I didn't know before. Only now. I just had a
hunch you could help somehow, that was it. Will you, please?'

'This is a bit more than help.'

'I know you will,' I goaded her. 'This is the kind of mad shit you
do. You don't care. Plus you get to cheer up the old man into the
bargain. No more dowry worries.'

I could see her mind imagining, the appeal growing.

'Think of the story – the poem you could get. The all-round
coup!'

'I'll tell you what. I will meet with him, your client. And we'll see.'

'Yeah? Dapper, C-C. You just dapper for that. Thank you!'

'Can I get some sleep now? Some of us have to work in the daytime.

She flicked off the light. I nuzzled right up and kissed her on the
cheek, temple and nose. After some minutes of content a doubt stole
up on me.

'Cosmic.'

'Ye-e-es.'

'You could love somebody, couldn't you?'

'Ummm,' she drowsed. 'It has been known.'

10

sports day

I awoke to the sound of early morning doors below. I felt clear-headed and quite stocked with beans for the shortish sleep that I had had. I could even almost recall my last dream. A pleasant one, it felt like.

To my left side, on the floor, lay a version of my customary bedspread: a couple of cigarette halves and papers, a half-drunk glass of juice and a banana skin, the remains of a midnight feed, my bracelets, bits of tissue, and stuff. 'Nestbuilding,' Cosmic called it. I would have to find somebody anew who would allow me my stuff. Start all over, if at all. But it was right to do it; to free her from me.

I thought perhaps I should wake her. She rarely took on work that required an a.m. attendance, though. I was just running through my own plans and appointments, if any, when I suddenly remembered what day it was.

'Hello? Hel-lo?' This time I licked her ear. 'You know it's Sports Day? No work day. It's Sports Day, man!'

'So it is,' she yawned. 'That's a bit of a bonus.'

'A *bonus*?' I was incredulous. 'Girl, wha' you talk 'bout? It's numero uno.' I jumped up and waggled my rump: 'Nu-me-ro uno day of the beautiful year.'

I jumped off the bed and buzzed about. 'Can't believe it, I ain't never been so ill prepared for Sports Day. Calls have to be made, bets have to be placed, gear has to be got.'

'I take it you're going to the game, then?'

'For sure. Have you ever known me not to? And you're coming too—'

'Ah, please—'

'I'm not hearing that. Come on down, honey. Come on down. And then we'll see my client after. He may even be down there. *Everyone* will be down there.'

My phone brr-brred. 'This'll be the first of the "link-up link-up" calls.' I pranced over. 'Come on, it'll be boomy. Look at the day!' A young sun was scaling up her southside windows. Indubitably spring-time.

My scanner warned me the caller was ringing from a payphone. Dean, I surmised correctly. I said I would meet him by mine in an hour or so.

Cosmic was persuaded easily enough, if less by the prospects of the game than by the great sprawl of humanity that would attend it. She could take some photos, she said. I was not surprised at her initial reluctance: these days the great game, Sports Day apart, was even less popular than her favourite artists.

I charged about excitedly before cooling my heels for the lady. I gazed in wonder as she threw her wear on: wide black felt trousers and the white trainers, a floppy-eared cap over a heavy working man's jacket and a rucksack on her back. Today, with the weather turned, she was coming like a polar explorer.

The stadium was in the north-west, only three or four miles along

the top of the city from Cosmic's, so she queried my decision to head
south first. But I had to change into my best and grab those essentials. One thing, in particular, was crucial.

The car started directly. There had been no problems with it since
that night with Lincia – another good sign. I slipped on some sweet
mood music. Old timers: dreamy dub from the Upsetter and the
silky keyboard strains of D'Angelo:

> *Oh, when we get by, when we get by,*
> *when we get by with love . . .*

We hummed together and smiled, alone in our thoughts. Yes, love
was a fine thing. But I was entering a higher chamber: I was making
a sacrifice.

An excess amount of traffic, as behoved a Bank Holiday. It would
be even worse going the other way. No matter, I was happy enough
speculating on the residents of the rides about me; their everydays,
their weaknesses, their allegiances on Sports Day. We – Miss Arctic
and my shaded flashily motored self – were subjected to our fair
share in return.

Dean was pottering about in the yard outside when we pulled up.
I was relieved to see he hadn't been bucked up or anything. I'd forgotten to warn him how it might be safer to wait for me around the
corner. I did take my Tanfoglio out from under my seat and stuffed
it down my trousers, just in case.

I greeted Dean warmly, my arm across his back. He and Cosmic
got on safe too, despite their frequent debates. No one else had
called for my popular self, so I guessed it would be just us three.

The place was undisturbed, which was a bit messier than I would
have liked, what with guests being there. I made some tea, gratefully
stacking the sugars, and busied myself. I resurrected and dusted my
cream, brown-rimmed conch, which Cosmic grabbed greedily from

me; I took my green-red-and-gold-stringed whistles from my coat stand and slung them around my neck; I emptied a half-bottle of Hennessy into my hipflask; I shaved and applied a smattering of eau-de-toilette; I donned some light trousers, a striped sports shirt and matching jacket, to be zipped up if the colds came. I lingered a while, hoping to supplement my dress with a little something, a hint to the connoisseurs that I, too, was one, but could not discover anything quite right.

Dean, his only departure from his customary fashion-defying attire a battered maroon cap with the Rest's crest on it, quizzed me about my forecasts for the game. I pooh-poohed his suggestion that Master Blaster would again prove the difference.

'The skills are still there, granted. But is the hunger? I question his hunger, his preparation for the big score right now. Nah, guy. Put your debts on the little men. Today's when a whole heap of them come through.'

He was surprised when I told him I hadn't placed any bets, then surprised further, after I'd explained about the drive for purity, that I still found the need for a flask. But I reasoned that, on Sports Day, I might be allowed to get away with the one if not the two.

One final act. I moved with all due gravity to my long wall and there, beside my certificates, unhooked my prized cartoon print. Nearly a century old, its panels recounted the cautionary tale of a player who suffered a bad game and a worse aftermath.

Cosmic wandered over, smiling. 'That's the one,' I said, pointing to the 'I haven't seen you since' panel. 'That one just kills me!'

I'd acquired the picture in part payment from a mid-town cheese I chased some money for. Straight off, I'd taken to it. It had accompanied me to every Sports Day.

'What's up?' Cosmic asked.

'Hey?'

'You look pensive.'

The last man was in and with only one run wanted—

Smith, of all people, dropped a catch.

He stole away—

but his sin followed him.

He decided—

to leave the country.

After many years he returned.

"Good heavens, Smith, I haven't seen you since you dropped that catch at the Circle."

"Yes, I once saw him play when I was quite a lad. On that occasion he had the misfortune to drop a catch."

THE EVIL THAT MEN DO.

'No, I was just thinking about the picture . . . and my client. How he stood here, had a little laugh . . . And you? Everything still cool?'

'I think so. A bit nervous. Should be an interesting day, one way or another.'

'No question.'

I slipped the picture inside a transparent cover and this I stowed under Dean's bag in the car boot. I left the rest of my goodies with Cosmic at the front, replaced the bucky, and we were off.

Although the cartoon was my kind of talisman for these occasions I could not claim any great returns from it. Out of the four Sports Days there had been, honours had been evenly split. The match itself had been the brainchild of the Minister of Special Duties when he was a young, thrusting parliamentarian. Indeed it was the Sports Day concept, hatched after the last big disorders but one, which had effectively launched his reputation as a dab hand when it came to matters to do with our kind. I understand he saw a high-profile contest of the gentlemen's game as something that might help in the regeneration of, ah, civil society. A day to instruct the lowers in codes that were courtlier, a day to sublimate the tensions between richer and poorer. The new holiday had not prevented the last trouble, but, our man's crew had been re-elected nonetheless and he elevated to the new ministry with a brief to come up with more big ideas.

His original suggestion – of an annual encounter between the west and the rest of the city, with proceeds going to fund the sport's redevelopment and related projects in our poorer parts – had seemed a modest enough proposal, condemned by many of us aggrieved as the wettest of sops. It was true that, at the height of those fevers, a demand that attention be paid to the lack of recreational provision had featured on our wish list, but someway down the order. Indeed a boycott was called that first year, and only averted when the State had promised a committee for some of the graver issues. The controversy had whetted the appetite and a good-ish, albeit largely western, crowd had attended the premiere to witness a dramatic victory by the Rest: sweet confirmation for those of us who had maintained that, for all the west's fancy clubs and the collats that allowed them to enjoy a fully professional league, we had the juice to take them.

That improbable result and its new heroes had made the event on our side and our numbers had swelled the second time around, aided no doubt by the introduction of diverse incentives and relaxations: discounted tickets, a blind eye turned to music, plus the holding of a special lunchtime lottery. The event continued to have its detractors – 'Bread and circuses. It's like "Let them eat cricket",' groused Dean behind me – but even most of these still put in an appearance so that the event had become a not-so-baby carnival.

I had eased my gambling worries. I figured that if I lent Dean the money and got him to place the bets under my direction and then maybe we shared out the winnings, that wouldn't be so bad. I stopped off for some newspapers and Dean rattled off the bookies' spreads for me. Some of them were so delicious I all but gurgled off the road.

'The one clever bet they've got,' I mused, 'is the Crab.'

'*The Crab?*' queried Cosmic. 'I think I've heard of the Crab. Isn't he the one who had to make way for Mas—'

'— ter Blaster. That's right.' I grinned, happy that all the talk that had once raged about the pair had pricked even her great indifference. The Crab, a tubby, genial native approaching his dotage, had been running one of the few remaining academies for the sport on our side when he was appointed captain of the Rest for the inaugural occasion. Folk, until now largely ignorant or else fond of the fellow, did not welcome his elevation. The heat on the Crab had risen as his modest contributions paled beside Master Blaster's brilliance, and the captaincy issue had provoked much media debate, until the Crab decided to resign, so averting a threatened boycott of Sports Day 3.

He was still in the team though, and remained a difficult bet to call. You could always have a flutter on him on 'The Fat Boys Index', which estimated how often the rotund players' girths would involve them in some comic incident – sell him high and make your little change, but he was the type who could really fuck you up on the per-centage points tally. The PPs – based on a complex calculation of a player's scores, his errors and his contributions in decisive match moments – were the most lucrative bets on offer and should have provided oodles of cream for a man who knew his game and his arithmetic. But my underestimation of the timeliness of the Crab's quiet contributions had often undone my other good calls. Today I might just give the Crab a wide berth. Depending, to be sure, on the pitch.

'Everything's provisional,' I turned to her, 'til you see the pitch. Your pitch is your situation, the environment you've gotta deal with. You see, C-C, pure philosophy in this game, trust me!'

We had reached the west's end now, various shoppers about attending the Sports Day sales, heading for the underpass that would take us north-west. I would have welcomed Dean or Cosmic taking over at the wheel, allowing me to peruse the papers, but neither of them had really reached that stage. No matter. We descended and, after a little lesson in horsepower, emerged not five minutes later.

Traffic slowed to a legal canter at the first signs of the police. They were in a wave-on mood, even for a fancy ride like ours. I tooted my horn playfully at them, then again at all those who'd fes-tooned banners and scarves across their windows. If they were reaching for the match, they were my friends.

Dean expressed surprise at the number of natives displaying Rest stickers. Cosmic told him not to be so prehistoric – they lived on all sides, didn't they? 'This is the new state, negro,' I smiled over my shoulder at him. I was concentrating on where to turn off, plumping for the exit before the stadium's. Any nearer and I would put the ride at risk, given the thieves that would be circulating down there, if I even found somewhere to park at all.

We pulled up in a sideroad and joined the other knots walking down. For once, I was with the early birds. I gazed anxiously at the skies. The sun had gone in but the weather looked to hold.

We ignored the right on to Pavilion Way, its leafy, spotless boulevard a reminder to us that, despite the stadium's 'neutral' location on the borders of west and north, this was truly an away-day. A right instead on to Luckhurst Lane, where the old gasholders that skirted this side loomed as comforting as ever. Here was the stand, the more cheaply priced Concrete, that formed our customary enclave.

Here, too, the first heady flavour of the public parade: ladies with traffic-stopping styles striding out of triple-parked rides, young bloods with chaps gleaming, the traders, the touts and those of no fixed, benevolent purpose. Hunh! Me and my old CLC gang: we'd have made a killing on a day like this.

Two solitary protesters, an apocalyptic lady with a loudhailer and Brother Sunyiatta, liberator of the State Museum's Nubia Papers, interrupted our paths to the ticket booths. Dean started trumping up a debate with the latter before I chivvied him on. I was all about one matter right then.

Past a perfunctory security – the excess crowd cover made these excellent times to settle scores, yet enemies traditionally called a truce on Sports Day – inside the perimeter and no time to savour the moment, for I was impatiently beckoning them onwards. Later for our seats; now for the spot.

I halted us about a hundred yards down, under the great shadow of the Concrete stand, by the last of a row of food and drink stalls. This one was probably the shabbiest of the lot, with biscuits, bottles of beer and spirits and a dozen miniatures perched on a sloping, peeling table top. No fridge, no cooking facilities, but a tiny radio and a tiny muted TV, once colour, now a sludgy brown, around which seven or so craned forward, silent. A couple more lounged on the steps of the plain blue van that was parked behind, or else leant against it. The crowd, mixed but in the main men of my kind, were of the same greyer generation as those at my other favourite spot. And, in the midst of them, fiddling with the radio knobs, stood the burly form of Franklin, ex-player and purveyor of warm beer to the connoisseurs.

He frowned at the noise of our approach and gave the merest acknowledgement when he saw that it was me, then frowned again as the giant video screen that loomed above us entered his eyeline and returned to tweaking his dial. He might have been more forthcoming if I was alone, but it took him a long time to adjust to new faces.

I shooed us in, and peered with the others.

'What's—' blurted Cosmic.

'Sshh!' Heads stared as I pointed at the small screen, 'The *pitch* . . .'

Two commentators were standing on the twenty-two-yard grassy strip that would host the duel of bat and ball. They prodded and poked it, brows furrowed, and dug pens in to assess its consistency. The camera cut to a short, wizened figure standing by the boundary line – the groundsman whose work, whose big day this was. Not for the first time, he was shaking his head, a drawn, hunted look about him.

The pitch, the radio voices confirmed, had seen healthier incarnations; its colour uncertain, its covering uneven, in some places a moist muddy soil where the ball would land and all but die, in other patches dry and parched, already breaking up, with crazy paving lines jagging through it, where the ball would lift and rear like a fiend. Just what had happened to the venerable groundsman, they lamented, as their telly counterparts held up divots from the track in stupefaction. Various pukka-toned possibilities were raised to account for this surreal stinker of a strip, his third in a row, with much citing of current ecological fragility. The derisory hoots from our end indicated that my fellows had reached a different consensus.

But none of us said anything just yet. It fell, I knew, to Mr Franklin to issue the first, great opinion of the day; we would no more dream of denying our host that due than we would sneak a glance at the big stadium screen, with its crassness and frequent moments of non-cricket, in his company.

So we waited as he rose, cracked open a beer and passed it towards me. His gaze did not break from the TV where a blazered Master Blaster and Montague, the perennially doleful West skipper, were tossing up. And he waited until Montague had called the coin right, elected to bat, and cast one last anxious look at the pitch, before snorting, 'Me nah know why him look so, when him get what him order. "Mother Nature, Mother Nature," dem say – more like Doctored Nature!'

A chorus rushed to join him on the conspiracy tip. How could this ground, divisional headquarters and home to the major league's champions, a ground that had lain unused since the previous season, deliver yet another foetus? True, they'd called in the groundsman from out of town, but he was hardly out of state, was he? He knew who his masters were. But why fuck up the pitch, dissented one, when both sides would have to deal with it same way? Because, retorted others, this evened things out: lay down a dodgy track and any fool team had a chance. Why d'you think they'd won the last two? At the end of the day, Franklin decreed, Big Man Nuh Cry and, besides, he had a hunch that the pitch wouldn't play as badly as it looked.

I grinned; play not yet begun, in my hands a complimentary warm beer, and moot points fizzing through the air.

I made drastic revision of my betting card – redistributing in

favour of the Crab's limpet-like virtues – and passed my phone over
to Dean to make the call as I took us up to the Concrete. We purchased some cheap binoculars before going down a dark little tunnel,
up some stone steps, then into the light and the heaving cauldron.

'Lordy!' Cosmic halted to take in the panorama. She had hitherto
maintained a look of mild amusement, but now she pushed out her
lips and nodded, impressed.

The sun had returned on forty thousand and more ramming the
stadium, making not so much noise at this stage, but certainly a hum.
Most of the space still to be filled was, naturally, in our stand, with
patches of green still on the Hill, the grassy bank where the most rau-
cous of the West's support tended to congregate. We made our way
up, past a party of schoolchildren and a row of Ladies Club types in
happy hats, to the top tiers where my back would feel safest.

We were just settling down when the eddy around the ground
swelled a little and clapping broke out amongst the Members Stand
at the Pavilion End opposite. I peered ahead then up to the video
screen to see the Minister for Special Duties himself making his
entrance, wearing a white carnation in his buttonhole and the usual
treacly grin. He waved in lordly acknowledgement then ushered his
guests onward to the spanking Three Gs balcony, primest of vistas.

The cheers that had greeted his arrival were not as loud as they
sounded on my car radio, where I normally heard them. I wondered
whether this was to do with media trickery or, much better, a sign of his
party's decline. Certainly, the sounds from the stands to right and left,
home to mixed-up allegiances and kinds, was no more than a murmur,
while some irreverents on the Hill made slack-arsed moonies.

The real roar came a few moments later with the emergence of the
players. First Fuller and Montague, the West's opening batsmen,
blinking at the light, fiddling with their protective armour, swinging
their lengths of willow in preparation. Then our guys, the Rest, the
strutting, gum-chewing Master Blaster at the head of his cohorts.

No doubt that their livery did not quite possess the dignity of yes-
teryear – a rash of sponsors' names covered their coloured underlays,
blue for the West, maroon for the Rest, so that they resembled racing
drivers – but they were our doughtiest still, the crack troops in these
proxy wars: the bald, barrel-chested Barber and the lean, whippet-
like form of Whispering Death, that most lethal of bowling artillery,
flanking their skipper; longer-toothed these days, but never less than
fearsome. To their right, nattering with the Crab, Syed, our pocket
battleship; known as the Dervish for his whirling swashes of the
blade, his main responsibilities lay behind the stumps; then our
puckish, bristling middle order, Hunte and Barlay, best man at
Master Blaster's wedding and the blackest white man you ever did
see; the enigmatic figure of Harper, who could stroke like the gods
when the mood took him, following behind. And in the last group,
Yat-Sen, our left-arm spinning Chinaman, underused but uncom-
plaining, leading out the little men.

'They're not very athletic, are they?' said Cosmic, enjoying first
use of the binoculars.

'That's the Crab you're looking at. He's allowed to be tubby. He's
a veteran.'

'Good bums though, some of them.'

'You'll be seeing a lot more of that when the batsmen take strike
at this end,' I advised her.

The West's Hillites struck up their first taunting chant of 'We are
the champions, my friends,' and, cheekier still, 'Land of Hope and Glory',
prompting the Barber, who had taken position by the boundary
below, to turn and shake his fists at us, a manic glint in his eyes,
urging us to respond. Dean surmised that he'd been baking it up
again, a reference to the Barber's suspension for substance abuse,
which had so cruelly robbed us of his services last year. We answered
with a somewhat tentative 'The Rest is the best / Oh, the West cannot test';
we didn't have the numbers just yet.

More winning song came from the Nutsman, come to pay his first
visit of the day. His natties were packed under a giant striped top hat,
and over his shoulder the body-long brown canvas bag, stuffed with
every known nut in the world. He had all these ditties for a pitch,
'*You grow big on nuts and honey | All that's missing is your money | Nuts!
How many? Is it any?*' and crooned them, his right palm poised by his
ear in anticipation. He slung some up, while Cosmic snapped some
photos.

The umpires were in their places, the clock was on the hour,
Montague had taken guard and Whispering Death was pawing at
his mark. I locked my friends in a tight embrace, then took out my
cartoon and kissed it.

It was only then, with Death already on his way, that I remembered about the pitch.

His first ball was a quality loosener – good line, good pace.
Montague fished at the cherry blur as it sped past his outside edge.
The third, a throat-high lifter, had their skipper prodding the track
suspiciously. Another bowler, the Barber for example, might have
seized this opportunity for a mid-wicket face-off, but the Whisperer
returned to his mark without a glance. He was as undemonstrative a
player as the easy, gliding approach, a model of frill-free economy,
from which he took his name.

The next two breakneck deliveries the hapless Montague did
well to miss, but the sixth was the original jaffa. It pitched on the line
of his middle stump, swerved away and ripped out his off. The field-
ers and two-eighths of the ground high-fived and jigged merrily. The
rest was silence.

'Is he out?' asked Cosmic.

'As out as it gets,' I shouted above the whistles. 'Bowled – violation
don't get more ultimate. And he never even got to touch the ball!'

Their next bat in, Premedasa, was someone I was actually rooting
for, partly because of his out-of-state lineage and partly, I

think, because I saw something of myself in his arrested progress.

Despite making a stack of runs for his league club, Premo had signally failed to get going in the big representative games. His technique was ordinarily flawless – beautiful balance and shots of classical rigour – so the problem had to be a mental one. I remembered hearing how he'd bang his head repeatedly on the dressing-room wall before these innings and how it'd struck me that, at the highest level – it could be a cricket test or a striving for great purpose – you are dealing with the stuff that can make you mad.

He would not be tested just yet, though. It was a fresh over now, so the dapper, neckerchiefed Fuller would be first to face our Barber.

Aaah, the Barber! I turned to Cosmic. Where to start about this singular force? Where the Whisperer was silky smooth and liked to pitch the ball up to take wickets, the Barber came pumping in, arms flailing, limbs gangling, and much preferred taking heads. And where the Whisperer was quick, the Barber was in the ninety-mile-an-hour bracket, a league of his own. Rumours about the man were rife: about how his dad was a juju man, and how the Barber himself kept effigies of Montague and some others; that he relaxed by listening to hate tapes on his stereo; that he breakfasted on broken glass.

One thing was certain: after his enforced year-long absence, the Barber would be raring.

I settled for drawing her attention to the newspaper headlines ('The Barber Cuts Today!' and 'No More Mr Nice Guy'), confident that his actions would shortly speak loudest.

In he thundered, medallion dangling, finding his favoured bodyline straight away. Fuller, though, was able to work the ball away for a single, bringing Premo down to the striker's end.

Immediately Master Blaster, directing operations from the slip cordon that fanned out alongside the Dervish, called up two more into close catching positions. I peered at Premo's visored figure in the video screen, scrutinising his body language, wondering about the thoughts in his head; a flashback to his two previous failures, perhaps, or maybe his mind was wrapped around the two-fifths of a second he would have to see and play the ball, a fraction that, given human reaction speeds and such, was a little less than mathematically desirable. Perhaps he was just preparing himself for pain.

In Barber pounds again. Premo steps back and his virgin delivery raps him on his bat handle, sending a jarring pain up his left arm. The West's physiotherapist bounded down the pavilion steps and hovered on the edge of the ground but Premo wisely declined his assistance. The Barber did not take kindly to physios disturbing his rhythm.

'No front foot for you today, Premo!' a wit admonished a few rows below. 'You shoulda left it at home!'

His was the only crack. Folk were too locked into the tension below. Before we had been all about skipper Montague versus the Whisperer but Premo versus Barber was more visceral still.

For, although the gentlemen's was a team game, this one-on-one business was the heart of it. Unlike other games I do not care to mention, where individual battles are swiftly buried under group exertions and where the faulty are given opportunities to find redemption, in this a man had no false modesty, no untold chances to hide behind. It was brutal, but honest and honourable, the way a knife is to a gun. Here, every moment, a man was in danger of meeting his fate.

A solitary, doomy drum rolled from the Concrete while pigeons wheeled away into the light. This was no place for birds of their kind, as Barber came again: feet splayed, chest inelegantly open, he hurls it in.

This one's short too, but a bit wider, and hits a damp patch that squats it up a little. Premo takes a flinching pace away then jabs at the ball involuntarily. It flies off the outside edge straight into the frying-pan hands of Barlay in the cordon.

I could not share in the hollers of my neighbours but blew a wistful Morricone note on the conch as my weakness, the very image of a mugged mind, made his disconsolate departure.

'Caught in what we like to call "the Office",' I confirmed to Cosmic. 'Also known as Death Row. I got plenty more where that came from, you know.'

'Give a damn!' she laughed.

Cheers at last rang out on other sides as new man Green hooked his second ball imperiously to the boundary. A typically forthright response from the West's top bat. The Barber stood there, hands on hips, and glared at him, only to be dismissed with a 'Fetch it!' wave of the hand.

'*What?*' The head ball hooked and now this! Never had Barber been baited so.

The batsman then blithely tripled his impertinence by calling to the umpire and pointing at his adversary's medallion. I shared a look with Dean and keened my ears to the radios about us. Green, it would appear, was complaining about the distracting glint of the jewellery. Barber stomped about and gesticulated fiercely before eventually being persuaded to remove it.

The Barber's walk back was ominously slow and he turned, still muttering imprecations.

The catchers crouched, the crowd went 'WohhHH . . .' We all knew what was coming. This ball was fractionally less short than the previous, and again Green squared his shoulders and made to pull. The problem was that it was appreciably quicker. The ball skidded through the surface and speared towards the batsman's chest. Green, realising that he was both high and late on the shot, tried to sway away, but too late. The ball struck him a sickening blow over the unprotected heart, the raw sound like the blast of a shotgun, and Green crumpled to the ground.

A hush descended as officials and players rushed towards him, all except the Barber, who glowered at the prostrate from halfway down and snarled out a recommendation for hospital food.

After a few anxious minutes and endless replays of the incident on the video screen, the physio and the stewards managed to lift the semi-conscious batsman on to a stretcher and carry him off the field with a few of our guys in solicitous attendance.

The Barber, meanwhile, had returned to his mark, where he stood, fingering the medallion he'd taken out from his pocket in what some may have deemed an inflammatory gesture.

Cosmic and Dean started one of their debates. Cosmic reckoned the Barber was your playground bully, pure and simple, while Dean replied look, this was the game, the Barber wasn't breaking no rules. You could even argue this was the point of the day, and he didn't know why the Minister was pretending to be so concerned, seeing as he now had the villain for his pantomime. Much as I could see the merits of Dean's case, I found myself coming down on Cosmic's side. During my youth, the height of my playing days, I'd functioned mainly as a slow finger spinner, and it was no more than I owed my trade to rail against the speed merchants at every turn. Of course, there had been no proper teams at my school so a kindly teacher had pointed me in the direction of a local club. This still being the days when the game retained some appeal for teens of my kind, the team was stacked with mini Barbers while I barely got a look-in. There, in the outfield, desperately twiddling my fingers, trying to gain the captain's attention, I was first made painfully aware of what it was to be one of the little men.

I used the lull in the proceedings to school Cosmic in the game from the little man's point of view: the state of Zen that could be achieved in the outfield, the guile and deceit of the spinners' craft – lashings of connoisseurs' candy. If I could really make her enter this passion of mine, I decided, in the sudden arbitrary manner I am wont to, then everything would be all right, not just today, but beyond.

Today, to be fair, was looking covered, with the West a paltry five for two and one critical, their plan to make early runs on a deterio-rating pitch in ruins.

Our stands began to fill to numbers hitherto unreached before lunch as the young ones, who liked to spend the morning profiling around the perimeter, came flooding in, sniffing blood and history. I was a little brusque with one who badgered us for a blow-by-blow account. He was just the kind of low-level typhoon-lover who used to deny me a bowl.

The Nutsman, sharp as a tack, had returned, his stock magically transformed: '*Nuts nuts! Mix-up, mix-up! Whisper nuts and Barber nuts. Special Barber rates. How many – did I hear twenty?*'

The Cosmic bridgehead seemed to be secured: she hailed him and took the catch he slung her quite admirably, then quizzed me on various aspects, from vital statistics to leg before wicket, as the con-test entered a less dramatic phase. The West were not without their physio-calling alarums but they gritted it out until the Whisperer rapped Dooley, Green's replacement, on the pads, patently adjacent, with the final ball of his spell: thirty-one for three.

His dismissal broke me out of my trance. I sighed. Time for work. I had that call to make.

I stood up. I thought it best not to make it here, in front of her and all this hectic-hectic.

'All right, C-C. I'm gonna do this thing. You still up? Speak now or forever hold your peace.'

She gave a slow smile – slightly muted, slightly opaque – and flickered a nod. I kissed her, winked at Dean's look of enquiry, then trotted off.

I went back through the tunnel to the quieter perimeter area, and leant against the fencing that ran behind the stand. A few punters about, getting their lunch in early, even Franklin's doing a little trade up ahead.

I was going through my wallet for my client's number when I heard a distinctive clunk-clunk from the other tunnel that led into the Concrete. What is that noise, I was thinking, like someone on . . . on crutches. Crutches!

I dashed to the tunnel, then along it, pulse speeding. Could it be?

It was. Sinbad. Dragging himself to the top of the steps, breathing hard. Between his sticks and his dangling tray, it looked heavy going. No need for the blade or anything; if need be, I'd start by kicking his aids away.

Too late to back him into a quiet corner, but if I could get to him before he reached the safety of numbers . . . I came up behind. 'Yo – Sinbad.'

His head turned, fearfully, then broke out wide, 'Ay, Boy. What you saying?'

He was innocent in my shooting; I saw that straight away. There had been no dissembling, no momentary panic when he'd seen who it was, his initial anxiety no more than the glance of a man who keeps bad company.

'It's all good, blood,' I replied. 'And yourself? Like the shirt.'

'Ay?' It was a yellow safari number. 'Heh heh. I'm all right, you know. Gonna get paid today, that's for certain. Ain't got no licence or nothing though. Don't matter.'

'You planning to stay on at Ice Cream?'

'For sure. Full-on – proper name, tax deducted, the works. That's my route back to the registry!' he laughed. 'Gonna get me a pension out of this shitstem at least. A man's gotta look to that, star.'

'Yeah . . .' I was only half hearing him, tuned in as I was to my own relief, a relief that, curiously, was mainly to do with our own inconsequential relationship: that our dealings – and his condition was a reminder that I was the guilty party – were untroubled and we could still go anywhere in them. We were hardly about to become bosom but it was just nice to feel we weren't fucked up.

'Saw you chilling with that sort the other night,' he said.

I smiled then, thinking he might mean that good-time girl, shot him a querying look.

'You know, that fresh hostess—'

'Candy.'

'That's the one. Fine, fine, *fine*, and real mellow with it. The others, they think they're all that but, when I see her now, we just chat every which way. You sexing that then?'

I shook my head.

'I'm there then, rasta, I'm there! She should be reaching as it happens—'

'Is it?'

'Uhmm. She an' her businessman people. Hope so.' He patted his tray. 'Shift loads o' this, more 'n likely.'

I looked at his goods: tired-looking T-shirts, batteries, the unfurling monkey and binoculars busted at the bridge. I took these last, handing him a fifty-fold note.

He grinned then tutted, 'I ain't got no change for a Megarratt. You got some—'

'Take it. Just take it, blood. You're cool.'

'Yeah?' The crocodile smile. 'Respect to that.'

'Safe. I'm just been caning it with the bookies today,' was my little tidyover. 'Whisper's come good for me already.'

'I hear the Barber ain't joking neither.' He turned to face the game, and I took my leave. I asked him to greet Candy for me and wished him luck with the repairs down below. That was as far as I dared go.

I turned back as I went down the stairs. He was busy investigating my note.

Old Sinbad! Forever surviving . . . That was a smart hunch and no mistake! Puts me back to square one on that matter but, still, definitely good news.

I returned to the fencing, my client's number in my hand. That immaculate, antique hand of his. Reassuring, despite my never having encountered quite this arrangement of digits before. I could scarcely believe we hadn't spoken since that time in the office; he seemed to have been around rather a lot.

'Hello?'

I could hear the buzz of voices and the hiss of the radio commentary.

'Hello – sir? It's Boy here.'

'Boy!' He sounded most jovial. 'Good to hear from you. How's tricks?'

'Not so bad.' For sure they were cricket sounds. 'Umm, if you don't mind me asking, where are you exactly?'

'Up in the Tavern. About a six shot away from you.'

'Hunh!' I snorted. 'That's a – well I suppose it isn't such a surprise. Had a feeling you might be. You weren't at a boat party the other night were you?'

'Don't think so. I get so busy I don't always recall,' he replied, 'and I have no recollection.'

All right. If he wanted to play it like that, that was his prerogative. Let me get to the core. 'About our business. I take it you're still interested?'

'Oh yes.'

'Right, great. Well I've got somebody for you. And, urm,' I cleared my throat, 'depending on the two of you getting on an' that, I think it can run.'

'Was it that delightful lady sitting with you?'

'Ah-hah. She's a, a friend. She's a poet.'

'A poet! Boy, you surpass yourself. Congratulations.'

'Same to you.'

'Go back to your seat. I can wave at you both.'

'All right,' I laughed. My man was really quite chilled for a big wheel. He liked to drop in on a game when he could spare the time, he told me. He had a pass for the Three Gs, but he preferred the atmosphere in the mid-priced Tavern stand. I asked him who he was supporting but he would not be drawn. 'Do some detecting, my detective,' he teased, which I thought I'd heard somewhere before.

I had reached the others by now and, after a useless moment with Sinbad's, grabbed the other binoculars from Cosmic and scoured the Tavern. 'It's him!' I mouthed to her, pointing at the phone.

I eventually spotted him, standing up in a green shirt. Too indistinct to be sure it was him. Except that he'd said so. And he was waving.

I asked him to hang on, thrust the glasses in her hand and gestured up. 'Can you see?'

'Where?'

'Green shirt, goatee. Just taking off his shades, walking forward.' My client bowed slowly.

'Yeah – I think so. No he's gone. Someone's standing in front now.'

'Let me see!' Dean grabbed the glasses but put them down after a moment, shaking his head. As did Cosmic, most fiercely, when I asked my client if he wanted to link directly. But he was booked for lunch, which was just around the corner, anyway, and after that he would be popping in and out of the ground. He had no wish to disrupt our spectating, he said, so why not all meet at the Tavern bar at the match's end? Our tickets, technically speaking, did not allow us there, but as the day went on you could gain access to all but the most exclusive sections.

Cosmic was staring at me accusingly when I put down the phone. She struck out at me and I gathered her in my arms. 'What's up?'

'He's here, bloody *here*. It's actually happening, already. You didn't – it's like you jumped me!'

'C-C, it's just a drink, plus I'll be there and all.' Dean, whom

Cosmic had clearly brought up to speed, was singing 'I'm getting married in the morning' behind. I wished he wouldn't. 'He's mad for poetry, especially the unpopular kind. Think of the projects, baby.'

'*Ding Dong, the bells are gonna ringgg,*' Dean purred in her ear, and she turned to pursue him down our row.

Nervous energy: only to be expected. She'd be all right come the night.

Howls from some local Barber-lovers alerted me to Master Blaster's introduction of wily slowhand Yat-Sen into the attack. I don't know why they were cussing MB: Sen's deployment in this last over before the interval, with no time to find a rhythm and the batsmen in extra-cautionary mode, indicated that the Blaster had as little faith in his abilities as they. There should have been no path to glory, but my man found it with an exquisite three-card trick. He drifted two deliveries away with the arm, then flighted one that gripped the damp pitch and broke wickedly back, leaving his victim's leg-stump leaning drunkenly. Fifty-five for four, effectively five, at the close of the session. At this rate they would not even complete their allotted fifty overs.

We waited for the crush to diminish as our neighbours left to get fed. A few acquaintances of Dean and mine came past us and we got caught up in small talk. Cosmic hovered, eyes flitting, on the lookout, I imagined, for some familiar faces. This wasn't really her crowd, though. For the first time, she seemed a touch bored.

'Here,' I said, slipping her my flask. She had a good glug on the brandy and grinned. 'C'mon, let's get some nyams.'

We sauntered down in the opposite direction of the swarm, over the advertising hoardings then along the boundary line. A celebrated soprano, cast of rainbow cherubs in tow, was taking up position on the field for the official entertainment. They would all be introduced to the Minister before starting on their medley.

We had to step aside smartly for Father Joel, a bony ancient clad in an athlete's vest and shorts and clutching a maroon standard, to pass us on the first of his customary furious laps of the ground. This year, though, the Hillites, who liked to stay on during lunch to heckle him, had come armed with a rebuttal: beery cheers went up as a topless young woman, brandishing a West flag, emerged from their ranks and made a beeline for Joel. Six stewards, no doubt mindful of the Minister and party even now making their entry, dashed to apprehend her and we were in danger of being caught up in the scrimmage, especially Cosmic, who had whipped out her camera. We survived unscathed, but not before a debut appearance on the video screen.

We took a right at the end of the Concrete stand and walked through it to the perimeter. Here were the sweetest food stalls. I thought we could start here, then take a leisurely stroll around.

The day's attendant action was shifting up a gear with the arrival of our town's champion sounds. King Jamo's were setting up at the back of the Concrete stand, which explained the mad crush we suddenly found ourselves in. The throng extended to my stall of choice, so we purchased our curries and what-not a few places down, walking on to Franklin's to eat. Here the line tallied with my own: a top start but, what with the pitch and our brittleness in recent years, far too soon for our fat ladies to sing.

'So how long does this luncheon thing go on for?' Cosmic tittered. She found the lunch concept highly tickling, the tea to come even more so. 'Are you really telling me they settle down side by side and go, "Pass the pot, old bean!"?'

' 'Sabout the size of it.'

'They hate each other though! Where's the Barber gonna sit?'

'But that's it, that's the point. Half these guys,' I gestured at the area boys around us, 'ain't exactly thrilled to be crossing paths neither. Then there's the sounds – north, south, east – a lot of them've got beefs too—'

'It's a derby game all ways,' Dean cut in.

'Thank you! Only today we forget that shit.' They looked at me doubtfully. 'Maybe not forget, but today we elevate it. Make it *beautiful*, man, for real.' I threw up my hands in only part-explained pleasure: the stiff-arm stance of the batsman, the straightened arm of the bowler, these orderly wars, like *Troilus and Cressida*, nature curbed and made nobler . . .

'I can hear a "Mine Eyes Have Seen the Glory" mood coming on,' Dean mocked, sharing a pitying glance with Cosmic. 'Hey!' He nudged me, eyebrows indicating behind me where, squatting by Franklin's truck, playing no part in proceedings but watching all with a dull glaze, was the late great Everton Burnett. To see the stains on his coat front, his matted hair and ill-kempt beard, you would scarcely believe he had once been a hero dearer than Master Blaster in our hearts, a place he had seized with a matchwinning century on Sports Day 2, capped by a vault into the Concrete to lead the calypsonians and King Jamo's in song. At a time when music was still banned, his gesture had seemed thrillingly pointed, but it was probably no more than youthful thoughtlessness, of the same kind that saw him jump at the offer of a fat-folds transfer to the West. It wasn't even the defection that so vexed people – Everton was not the first to chase the wong – as much as its savage timing, on the eve of Sports Day 3. His form plummeted shortly after and he'd been forced to beat a hasty return to our side to find most every door, be they sporting or social, firmly bolted. 'This is what we do to traitors down here,' Dean gloated to Cosmic. I could only wince at the reminder of it.

It was not the first time I had seen him; a few times I had even approached him, the still thirsty fan. More often, though, I would nudge and point and pass by on the other side. You may think such condescension absurd and I would be the first to hold up my unclean hand, but I'd been knee deep in reality out there; if my only responsibilities had lain, like his, to a dreaming then, well, you would not have found me wanting.

The sight of him twitching at the trumpet blasts of the Jamo theme, as if in involuntary recollection and I couldn't stand it any more. We moved on.

We had just turned the arc of the stadium on to the Tavern side when the view ahead stopped me in my tracks.

'Shit!'

'What?' asked Cosmic.

There was Lincia, with two girlfriends, one of whom I recognised from the dinner party. I looked away tactfully as they approached, but Lincia just came straight on up.

'Excuse me—'

'All right?' She actually sounded quite friendly.

'Can I talk to you please?'

She walked away, a few yards to the side of our company. I gave a shrug of a smile to my friends and followed her. I didn't want a scene.

'So you didn't get my message?'

'Yeah, I heard your message.'

She waited in vain for me. 'Have you got anything to say about the other night?'

I shrugged. 'Probably shouldn't have run off like that. How about you?'

'I was probably a bit uptight. It happens, you know what I'm under. But we seemed to be doing all right, 'til you had to dark me bigtime!' I curled my mouth ruefully. 'So what's happening?'

She didn't ask it like a general enquiry. 'About what? About the offer?'

'Umhmm.'

'Well, it's been—' I glanced sideways to Cosmic '—it's been taken up elsewhere.'

'What! That light, little . . . thing you're with? Surprise, surprise—'

'Oh, don't start there, Lincia. You know it ain't that. It ain't that at all—'

'All right.' She lifted a pacifying hand and screwed her eyes over. 'Sure I've seen her somewhere before, you know. What does she do?'

'She's a poet.'

She continued staring, then turned her head back. 'Listen, call me this week, very soon. Will you do that? There's someone I know who's sweet on you, so you'd better call anyway.'

'Is it?' We were rejoining the others now.

'Think so. Unless maybe she just needs an accountant.' She smiled.

Cosmic took my arm as I pondered, almost wistfully, Lincia's receding form. It's funny, when you haven't seen someone in a while – it can even be for a day or two when it's been a long week – and you see them again, you tend to forgive them their faults if they're just quite nice.

We spent most of the afternoon session in the Tavern stand, partly, I suppose, on the chance of running across my client, but mainly because the vibe there was quite excellent, much the sweetest I'd seen it. In previous years the Tavern had functioned as a somewhat subdued borderland before the buttoned-up home support beyond, but now it had a sound of its own and, even though we got there at the tail-end of its set, with the players due to re-emerge at any moment, the little joint was still jumping: tens of twentysomethings, mainly native, were out on the perimeter asphalt, twirling to breezy, Latin grooves. The bass may not have shuddered enough for your average Concreteer, but the tunes were fresh and, with spliff seemingly as free as the moves, it did not surprise me to see a few of them pondering at the fringes.

We followed as a core of enthusiasts helped the sound offload their essentials on to a sturdy table, then carry it to a new residence on the right of the lower tier. I purchased a bottle of rum and an ice bucket, and we toasted our new vantage point, forty-five degrees from the wickets.

The disapproving stares that greeted the sound's arrival from the Panama hat brigade in the stand to the left were something to behold. You could tell it wasn't the music, all but restricted to the gaps between overs, so much as the surprise that these people hated: they had lived their lives to avoid surprise, had probably chosen their neighbourhoods for their lack or surprise, and had today paid good money only to have this surprise thrust upon them. Their trusty Tavern, so long the shock-stopping buffer, now turned!

Luckily for stadium relations, our friends soon had enough on the pitch to distract them. They finally got a surprise they could enjoy when, with the fall of another wicket, none other than the earlier stricken Green came down the pavilion steps.

He received a tremendous hand, from I as much as anyone. A mythic moment, no question. His gait did not quite bustle in his usual manner, and he carried some extra padding around the chest, but when Master Blaster predictably withdrew Yat-Sen to bring the Barber back into the attack, Green unflinchingly stepped into line.

His defiance seemed to fire up the cowed Fuller, and the two set about the makings of a stand. The Barber, straining for the extra pace to see off this undead, lost direction, and Green crashed him twice to the hoardings.

Master Blaster, the Crab and a couple of the other senior players convened for talks by the bowler's end, their subject, it could be safely assumed, an arithmetical one. Do they let Barber continue and use up his complement of ten overs or, with the West now look-ing as if they might stretch to their full allotment, save his barrage for the dread task of the finish? And, if not Barber still, who? Sixteen overs in the innings remaining: setting aside seven for the front line, that still left nine to be juggled amongst the little men. I scribbled some permutations furiously. Aah! such mathematics in this game . . .

Cosmic was getting restless: no doubt the liquor – we'd emptied my flask and caned half the new bottle already – had something to do with it. First she tried to drag us across to abuse our neighbours then, when I proved unwilling, opted for a dip in the paddling pool by the boundary ropes below.

I must have watched her peel off her layers and disappear with some dismay, for a young white guy sitting near pursed his lips and shook his head sympathetically: 'Cricket – it's a relationship killer,' he said.

'Yeah,' I replied, then smiled as I saw the meticulous scorecard he was keeping. Soon he, I, and some others, fell into vigorous debate on the Yat-Sen question, and I was pleased to receive a fairer hearing than might have been granted me in certain quarters.

Green finally went, driving a ball into the Crab's midriff, where it stuck. Caught and bowled, plus one for the Fat Boys Index.

The applause that accompanied the batsman off the field was deafening. Tomorrow's poster boy cradled his helmet to his chest and kissed its crest before tottering a moment – a touch hammily in my opinion, but it was sufficient to produce a final crescendo, the last hurrahs for many for some while as the Whisperer, finding once more the lovely shape that had so graced his early overs, rattled through the tail.

The West's innings closed on a mediocre hundred and forty-eight. With the pitch clearly playing easier, they looked seventy or eighty runs short of making a match of it.

Dean and I made our way out of the stand. Cosmic, in a T-shirt and someone's towel wrapped around her waist, had her limbs held by four revellers who were 'bumping' her into the pool. I didn't know it was her birthday.

'Your girl, man – she's definitely some'ing extra. Pure "Read all about it!" You sure she's the marrying type?'

'I hope so, cuz. Hope so. Huh,' I snorted, 'it's funny, you know. You can think about something a whole lot and then, when you actually come to do it now, you kinda do it on a whim.'

We drifted into one of the side amusement areas that thrived in the footwells of the coliseum on Sports Day. X amount of betting and gaming stalls, all jostled together, with the innocents and the inveterate pottering through, gave these places the feel of a market. Many of the games their hard-eyed custodians demonstrated – counters juggled under cups or else tied to bits of string that you propelled pinball style up a board – were home-made, cottage-industry side benefits that I remarked on to the cynically minded Dean.

I was efficiently relieved of some change – you couldn't win on those things – before slipping away, leaving Dean behind. I had an RV with Sundays back at the Tavern.

I had buzzed him a little earlier, in the midst of his exertions around our home quarters, and recommended him a visit to this side: we needed to speak and here, with the acrid smells of hash about me, I judged a sweeter-flavoured weed man might be welcomed.

Cheers rang out from inside as I walked back. Our reply must have started. It made you tingle, hearing the shouts and not knowing what they were about.

The Tavern sound had returned to the asphalt outside, which I doubted popular demand would let it leave. I passed near to Cosmic, who was sitting on a low wall, wet, chatting to two white guys, and indicated to her I was going in. Her companions were trendy sophisticated types, the kind who might have studios in lofts off her roundabout. I don't know what they could have said but she was suddenly slapping her palm down hard in maximum-amused mode. I tell you, cool white guys can get everything.

I scoped the top tier – no sign of my client. Sundays and his youth Kamahl were there already when I came below. I remember thinking that Sundays did look a little . . . not quite irked, more kind of agitated, but I thought nothing more of it, putting it down to the short wait, and greeted them warmly. Kamahl was wearing a sleeveless top and I was amazed to see how much bigger in the arms he looked these days. 'Me have to watch how me talk to you now,' I chuckled.

Their rundown and the scoreboard told me our boys had been fiercing it already. Twenty-five without loss after three overs. I kept one eye on proceedings while Sundays hit me with this rather startling proposal.

It was to do with my client. Sundays had come up with this idea for a private million-dollar black school, where a bunch of celebos and notables would put in the money. He was hoping that my client could act as a broker figure, bringing together those needed. He had it all quite detailed: the school would be one more practically than academically orientated, and would run off the interest generated by the initial pool of investment. The pupils would also work the area, say, for local firms, and build accommodation to rent out, so the place would eventually pay for itself. I listened, wondering if he was being completely serious. I mean, he had a lot of ideas. We had kicked around quite a few in the spot in my time, but obviously nothing had ever come of them.

'I don't know man,' I said. 'I'll try, but I don't know if he can do this, you know. I don't know he's hooked up with the celebo scene in that sense, where he can be calling on the Master Blasters an' that an' bringing them to the table.' A scheme like this, I was thinking, if it could work, someone would have done it already. 'But I'll mention it – I'm seeing him today, as it happens.'

'Nice, bro. You see a place like that, and everybody's getting something out of it.' He pondered his son ahead, clucking his tongue. 'Boy! Me just can't wait for the yout' to start realising themselves, you know—'

'Yeah, yeah . . . Not a man *move*!' I burst out as Mensah spanked a ball disdainfully through the covers. The West could ill afford these four-shots so early in the piece.

Sundays turned away and contemplated our fellow Taverners. He still appeared someway out of sorts, but I had seen nothing yet.

It came from almost nowhere. I remember looking at him watching the crowd, and coming out with some crack about all these things I kept slipping his way, and how it seemed like I was the one keeping his head above water these days, and next thing he was putting it to me blunt.

All this don't come with no joke, cos he wasn't catering to that aspect right now. He'd had too much joke today already. Idiots trying to slip him Monopoly money, or lay him a watch, or a ring, cos they're short. And no, blood, he's not finding it funny when he's having to rush about in his car, kids in the back, when he's carrying, and there's bere rads and state man everywhere. Did I hear? Joking done long time.

I was stunned. He'd never had that tone with me before. I improved a bit when I realised that the cause was not so much me as the general, but we had barely begun to return to our usual keel when his phone went and he walked off, speaking to it and nodding to me, his son trudging behind. Telling him about my change of thought on our business clean slipped my mind.

I felt winded, too disturbed to register the fall of a wicket and the excited, pre-Master Blaster eddy that swept through. I could see that it was probably no more than my friend's bad day, but could not stop myself trawling through our history, searching for signs of fault-lines.

Cosmic returned, looking as lean as I felt sobered. She slumped heavily across me, her hand grasping mine as if, after testing the waters abroad, she wished to reassert her power at home. I tried telling her about my little incident but it mainly elicited a yawn. She squirmed a little across the seats, licking watery droplets on my lap. I pushed her up; I thought we should hit a bit more of the Grand

Tour then head back. Sundays' outburst had taken the shine off our present surroundings and, anyway, she could lie more comfortably along the uninterrupted stone of the Concrete.

Master Blaster had started like a train with a plane to catch, continuing the brutal early assault. The one hundred and fifty needed for victory could have been reached at a canter but the plan seemed to be to humble and break the spirits of any remaining resistance with this flurry of disrespect. The West's attack shook their dazed, sweaty heads. Lacking the sheer fear factor of our spearhead, they compensated by concentrating their efforts on the corridors of uncertainty, where a ball with the necessary line and length might trouble a batsman into error, only today the corridors seemed shut.

We were skirting the edge of the field, the hoardings and the odd cameraman to our left, the boundary ropes and the play to our right. I'm not sure it was a strictly legal move, but I nearly always did it, and I'd seen others occasionally, too. The buzz was just the sweetest: near enough to fill your nostrils with the tangy cut of the grass and around you the serried ranks stretching up, everyday types hunched intently, or else swopping judgements like lords of the earth.

We attracted a couple of anxious glances from the surprise-fearing tendency, but our progress continued unimpeded. In these situations, it always helps to have the unthreatening promise of a girl with you, even though this one was swaying a little and burbling nonsense rhymes about honey still at teatimes.

Mensah was undone seeking to repeat a six-shot. The ball twirled in the breeze and the fielder did well to scurry round and hang on to the catch in the deep.

It was enough to break the stoutest Western heart to see the departing Mensah crossed on the pavilion steps by the sun-hatted, sauntering form of Harper. MB may have been more feted but, by my and most heads' reckoning, Harper was the most prodigiously endowed of all. To see him play was to feel that, yeah, maybe we were made in a certain image after all. He nothing common nor hurried did with the blade in his hand; he didn't appear to 'do' at all. With MB on this day, like any other, batting was a loud business; you could almost hear the 'seconds out' bells of the prize fight as he waited at the crease, gum-going, bare-headed, hear the assertion of his will as he smote and subjugated, but with Harper now you got no sense of effort. He seemed more an instrument, the played-through not the player, and I could have stared rapt at the lines of his play all day. He announced himself with a few flicks and caresses before easing himself into double figures with the deftest of 'day after tomorrow' shots, leaning on a late cut with the ball all but past him.

I was torn between rushing back to the Concrete, the only side to be, really, with these two doing their thing, and making a first-time bid for the Three Gs a little further up. It would be a coup to pass through there, plus its photo-finish view of the field and its frame sloping below, such as might bring Cosmic back, so to speak, onside.

We got to within gobbing distance of its gates before stewards, shadowed by boys in the most serious state blue, advanced to halt us. They inspected our tickets and insisted we turn right around, not even allowing a contrary Cosmic to take some snaps at ground level. But not before I got a good gander upwards, where quite a sight awaited me.

There, beneath the club honour boards, amid the rows of ruddy-faced patricians, suited and booted, guzzling their gins or snoring soundly, some familiar faces: Merciless, in banter with a retired great; in the rank beneath, unsteadily plunging two glasses into a Pimm's bucket, Miss Don't Feed the Blacks; and there, towards the foot of the balcony, two down from the Minister and three from the soprano, the beady eyes and sour, saturnine features of Caesar, the man who bought me.

He was the one who'd first approached me and, right up to last year's end, the only one I'd seen during my dealings with the state. I'd guessed he was something pretty serious but to see him now, deep in the Minister's entourage, bursting in on my day, so to speak, was a shock all ways. I just stared, my stomach clenched up. He actually glanced down at us; I was sure that he would recognise me, but once he'd confirmed that security had the situation in hand he returned his furrowed brow to the game. I was relieved he hadn't spotted me, but upset still. Here was a man I had shamed myself for and yet, outside the one-to-one confines of business, we clearly all looked the same to his scuzzy ass.

I mean, I ask you – what a shabby crew! Evacuate the honours board, the ex-players and, maybe, the soprano, drop a bomb in there, and who could complain? Seeing them then, seeing him especially, reminded me how much – more even than the lustre Harper and Blaster were covering us in – how much I wanted to win.

About fifty yards into our journey back, as we passed a grassy bank that catered to the overspill from one of the high-priced stands, I heard a high-pitched someone call my name. I looked up to see old Candy, standing up amongst a pile of recumbent guys: sprawled out amid picnic debris, chanting and guffawing, they looked like cocky, fast-money uptowners, as Sinbad had indicated.

She was beckoning us up. I hesitated, and signalled her to come down. Didn't really want to get caught up in that group. But when I told Cosmic it was Candy she excitedly pushed me up.

Well, she was looking mighty fine, I must say. All her hair up, same sparkling grin, little top and dinky skirt, its back still unsatisfactory, but legs that were toned and shapely. I gazed a little disdainfully at her crowd. The only other girl there was Crème Caramel, entertaining a couple at the back.

'What brings you, Miss Mostest, business or pleasure?'

'Hey, shut up, you!' She played to punch me. 'Nah – business. A bit of a bummer working on the holiday – thought I might get it off.'

'That's a shame. Otherwise I'd say, "join us".'

'Don't think so.' She rolled her eyes behind, where a few were shouting, '*If you hate psycho Barber clap your hands . . .*' 'Not unless they can all come.'

'You all right?' I asked. She'd had a bit of a grimace there too.

'Just about.' She leant forward and whispered, 'A few liberties, like we talked about before . . . What time is it anyway? Rum and Raisin is supposed to be taking over at half time.'

'Half time!' I snorted, as Harper drove through the covers to post the century. 'We're all but done already.'

'What a cow! I bet she's taken a sickie.'

'You should have too, child,' rebuked Cosmic, a veteran in such matters. 'You gotta get with the programme.'

Cosmic seemed to have clicked right back into gear and she prompted a sit-down on the grass, at the edge of the group, where the two began swapping introductory material. It was funny to hear C-C's patter to a new recipient – she was such a fibber. A couple of anecdotes involving her friends that she had once regaled me with were now tales that had involved her or something she'd read about in a paper. As it turned out, though, I was the one who was nearly exposed. Candy mentioned that she had, staggeringly, ventured south again, to visit an old friend of her folks, and when she said the name of the area – the SE24s – Cosmic goes, indicating me, 'Aah – that's just up by our mutual friend.'

'I don't think so—' Candy turns to me, '—you're north, aren't you?'

Cosmic smirked at me, but didn't give it away.

Candy's southern sequel had proceeded a hundred per cent more pleasantly than the première: an evening chewing the fat with her aunt had been punctuated by trips to a hush-hush twenty-four-hour chips and liquor store and the discovery of delicate out-of-state pastries, like nothing she'd ever tasted before. 'It was the best!' She puffed out her cheeks and stomach. 'I was that big by the end of it!' I nodded as I lay down and looked at the clouding sky: she was right, that was a safe spot; I used to pass through and sample the little late-night scene; too long neglected.

'I'd better go,' she added with a sigh, as a couple of her clients hovered about us, impatient for an 'in' or else the continuation of the attentions they were paying for.

She invited us out to this south-central club that she and Crème Caramel were hitting on their night off tomorrow and we promised to try to make it. 'Give us a job, eh?' she tugged at me as we parted, a week's wisdom on her face. Cosmic jumped in with a plainly unrealistic Mambolika proposal. She seemed quite beguiled with Candy. I had my suspicions.

'She's so fragrant.' Cosmic shook her head as we started back. 'And you installed me instead! I'm very flattered. And all because she wanted to take your hand at the dance.'

'Come, man, that wasn't it.' I shrugged. 'I mean, you know. She's top, but, you know . . .'

'Funny guy,' she said, as if I wasn't there. 'Funny guy, funny game. Are you sure, Daddy, are you sure you're sure?'

I looked hard at her. What was she playing at now?

The twenty-minute tea break had started by the time we returned to the Concrete. The custom seemed even more absurd on a day like today, but it provided a convenient enough moment for the occasion to move into its final celebratory phase. King Jamo's had racked up its levels and been joined by Hot Buttered Soul, which played everything from the islands to the old country, in a lusty clash. The great calypso singers, Django, Lady Law and the Mighty Cockerel, were also being glimpsed and excitedly talked about. Their time would come.

All the Mr Friday Nights had made their entrances now, decked in their proudest get-ups, bedecked ladies on their arms: more natives than before – the honoraries joined by the brave and curious and those who just fancied being on the winning side . . . So many local heroes! Begetters of dances and expressions that had ruled across town. Jonny Holder, who'd first propelled 'dark' into its current usage, then daringly flipped it, so that the word meant quite the opposite in some parts for a while, before his original resurged with undeniable force. And Mr Bodywork, gyrating his double-jointed cross-dressed self, at his place in front of Jamo's, getting away with it as only he could.

We found Dean looking on at the folk dancing in the aisles under Bodywork, reasoning with the Nutsman. He held out his hand for some spattering rain to hit it, and I glanced up to the skies: it would be too cruel . . . But the west, where the weather was coming from, was clear. This would be no more than a passing shower.

Kuti, Cosmic's hometown sound, kicked in, and I took her into the pack for a slightly strange little session. I was – aaah, tch – conscious of how this was quite possibly our last free dance, and I was searching her face for recognition of that, but she was gazing away, gripping me real hard on the back, digging in, her cheek pressed to the crook of my shoulder. She didn't say nothing. One of those times when I couldn't reach her.

Ten rain-affected minutes later than planned, MB and Harper re-entered the arena. A few more moments and both were walking back, Harper after guiding an innocuous delivery elegantly but unerringly to point, Blaster the victim of a phenomenal pluck – a fitting end to what had been a blistering seventy in even time-exhibition from the Don. He could not resist a little victory shake of the fist before dipping his bat, to us first, and then to the rest of the ground, departing with every side standing.

None of us were fretting. Four out of ten wickets down now, but only twenty-five more needed. And no likely end to the fireworks either, for new men Hunte and Barlay were hardly slouches, as a

couple around me were gaily testifying ('Ee! Hunte's a bad-boy
player, though! He don't care, he goes on rampage, trust me . . .').

But then the funny things started. Not exactly funny; a little rain
tended to lively up a pitch so it was no surprise to see the ball darting about again, as it had in the morning session. The zip in the
wicket extended to the field as the West, scenting the slimmest of
lifelines, scurried and flung themselves about, saving singles and
halving twos. The corridors were reopened and troubled repeatedly
and we found ourselves suddenly becalmed, five runs coming off
the next five overs.

I would have welcomed this fluctuation if I wasn't ever so slightly
worried. My fellows were less anxious then irked. Not connoisseurs,
they found this new state of affairs puzzling and had little time for it.
An uneasy teeth-skinning murmur grew amongst the groundlings in
our stand, the mood summed up succinctly by one: 'Ay! Get on or get
off!'

Hunte looked up then. The screen showed tense eyes above the
visor, like he had heard. I braced myself, for I was afraid and, sure
enough, he flashed out at the next delivery. The ball, a near corridor
cherry, was not wide enough for the chop he was attempting, and it
clipped the underside of his bat, ricocheting down to kiss the off-
bail.

Barlay was next to go: trying to hit the hide off a ball that wasn't
really springing to greet him. The Dervish joined him directly, succumbing to a suicidal third run.

Jesus! Pure madness out there.

One hundred and seventeen for two had become one hundred and
thirty-five for seven. Thirteen still needed. Montague was clapping
his hands and chivvying, his teammates puffing out their chests and
extending traditional gestures of grit. Their fans were starting extrav-
agant waves. These thirteen would be the hardest to get.

'Sore afraid, furthermother, sore afraid.' I glanced to Dean.

He snorted derisively at what had befallen us. 'So what's the SP on the Crab? Can he get us there?'

'Should do. He's got them Mr Freeze-like nerves.'

'Umhmm. He don't exactly fill you with confidence though. All that poking about . . .'

Beside us, Cosmic, who'd been reading and doodling a while, gathered her things and stood up decisively.

'Where you going?' I asked. I'd already grown resigned to the fact that my passion was striking no chord in her, top brain though she be, but her leaving was another matter.

'Aaah,' she shook her head mendaciously, 'just gotta pop out for a bit. Little while.'

'*Cosmic*, man!' Now what? 'This is gonna be over soon. We've got an RV—'

'I know. Relax. I know.' Looking away – look *at* me. 'When's this end?'

I threw up my hands. Fuck the end anyway. There was still work in progress here, and that's what I needed her, I needed us three, to be concentrating on.

'Tell you what,' she continued, 'I'm just around. I'll either see you back here, or else outside the Tavern ten minutes after this finishes.'

No grin, no reassurance there. I stared at a practised opaqueness, sensing that this was probably a really bad moment, but amidst my fear there was a surge of anger that she was subjecting me to this now, at this critical, all-hands-on-deck juncture.

'You got your ticket then?'

'Umhmm. Can I go now?'

'Whatever, lady. You always do what you do. Yeah, bro, it's true,' I turned to Dean, 'my man ain't the prettiest. Crab's more your thievin' type of player, but we can use that right here . . .'

I didn't see her go.

I couldn't decide what to do with my cartoon. I was now of the mind that it carried as much ill fortune as its subject but I could hardly throw it away. Eventually I decided to slip away myself for a moment, in body if not in concentration: it would separate me and the talisman plus acknowledge the 'watched kettle never boils' principle that had brought me some joy in the past.

I spent a melancholic little spell by Franklin's, bemoaning the indiscipline that was undoing us. If we lacked the strength of mind to withstand even the pressures of this one-day pyjama version, how much less the rigours of the five-dayers of such fond memory? When I mentioned to him how some had heckled Hunte and Barlay, he went off on one breathless about the youth of today. How it was instant this and quick money that with them, and no wonder the game was tottering. I nodded sympathetically, thinking of mentioning Sundays' school idea, till he pointed me a Carnation Milk tin, where he stored invader-repellent acid, and I fell subdued at a reminder of my own low parts in these matters, desperate to get overs.

On the video screen we were inching our way towards the total. The radio voices kept us up with the arithmetic. Eight runs were needed by the Rest, three wickets by the West. Even money. The most exciting finish in years, they burbled.

Montague brought his field in, as trusty carthorse Haigh started his penultimate over. His first up was a real backbending 'effort' ball, full-pitch, travelling along an off-side furrow and the Whisperer, relatively correctly for a tail-ender, stuck his front foot out and across. Unfortunately he got his bat tangled up in his front pad, whose base the ball hit resoundingly.

The West jumped up as a man. 'How's that?' they put the question. Umpire Sammy Beckett, a spectacled, painstaking sort, peered long and hard before raising the dreaded digit. The Whisperer stood stunned and disbelieving, then turned, swatting the wicket with his bat as he walked.

Franklin shook his head. It was a marginal decision at the very best. But Beckett was known to be bowler-friendly.

I dashed back, my insides aflutter, to find the mood changed dramatically. Nothing overt, apart from some fierce looks thrown over at the Hill, but you could just tell: if this was grudge before . . .

Yat-Sen came out to join the Crab. 'Little man, I need you now,' I murmured. I summoned the gods, the Race Man, all the big hitters.

He negotiated the first ball successfully and even cheeked a single from his second. I was a bit worried about that, but the Crab managed to scamper another and so retain strike for the next over.

Below us I saw our calypsonians, with the High Plains Drifter an unwelcomed interloper, gathering at the edge of field: poised to run on, garland the victory in song, and lead our stand's triumphant charge on the pavilion. Beyond them the Hillites, with their facepaint and tattoos gleaming in the twilight, threw out an eerie counterpower.

Another single left Yat-Sen only needing to last out two balls from the over. He opened the bat face on the last delivery and our sharp intake of breath turned into a roar as the ball beat the in-field and scurried away to the ropes: a boundary now would tie the scores.

But anyone looking closely, and with a child's grasp of physics, could see that the ball would not quite reach the boundary. They should clearly settle on the two, leaving the Crab on strike. But Yat-Sen – I don't know, man, I think he was just too excited – completed the two, turned and pelted down for a third. I do not blame the Crab for responding – the fielder was picking up the ball, his teammate was yards down already, and any hesitation might have proved fatal for his own twenty-stone frame. The upshot, one heart-stopping dive in the dust later, was that Yat-Sen, insanely, would be left to deal with the final over.

Dean couldn't see my point. Only two were needed. But Yat-Sen's average was two, I told him, and he had got four already. Why push our luck?

Double digits would be continuing their wait for him: Yat-Sen contrived to keep Haigh's first delivery away but come the second and – perhaps overexcited again – he shaped to open the face, aborted the plan with no alternative provision, and succeeded only in dollying the ball back to the bowler.

Delighted roars cascaded around a good half of the coliseum. The Minister, with Caesar by his side, clapped and spread a saccharine beam. Horrible, horrible. And then the boos as last man Barber, medallion restored, sallied forth.

Lord above! Barber with a bat in his hand. He was as rustic as Father Time, as unrefined as Hi-Wine, a joke thing, pure and simple: Barber with a bat, and the groundsman starts reaching for his roller.

Montague signalled for two men to retreat to the fence, while others crept in like carrion. Their senior pros clustered around Haigh. The Crab called his partner for talks too, before pottering haplessly back to the wrong end.

The Barber brandished his willow broad and high, like a club, as Haigh quickened his weary limbs one last time. The silence was awesome, and then slow-motion.

The delivery thudded into the track and halfway down; it seemed that Haigh's flesh had finally cried 'Enough!' and pulled him short – he could surely not have intended it. Of all the variations that might have come his way, the headball was about the only one Barber knew anything about. My stand rose as one as Barber rocked back and swished his bat across his torso to smite the cherry to kingdom come.

Only the ball wasn't recognising that at all. It had landed on the damp edge of a crack, and squidged in, slowed down, and was now proceeding at grubby, grasscutting height. Enough time for Barber, through with his shot, to turn back to the leather he thought he had long despatched, and gaze at it with a startling blend of curiosity, fear and loathing before it ever so gently, but blatantly still, rapped him on his foot.

The West's appeals were drowned in ten thousand others. Then the longest moment, until Beckett let out a sigh and raised the boniest, ugliest of fingers.

It's difficult to recall the whole scene exactly those next few minutes – you're so locked into your own private, disbelieving zone. Little sequences penetrated occasionally – the West players grabbing their stump souvenirs, cavorting and hugging, the Crab and Barber staring at one another whilst their wickets disappeared around them, before the Crab dropped desolately down and drew his legs up. I remember wondering when the sound systems had fallen silent, and then the Hillites' taunt of 'You're not singing anymore' suddenly impinging. Noticing, too, the calypsonians gone.

It took a long time for folk to file away, to leave their grief. As if something might change by our staying there.

Aah, it was bitter, a real heavy feeling. You start backtracking the game: there had been moments – Harper and MB at the crease, making that corrugated beast look domestic, before this implosion dashed honour from our hands. Oh, I know that victory is a moody, one-handed god, but not even *honour* . . So shabby! We'd done the flashy then dropped the dolly; proved pulpy-headed, a collective bunch of Premos. It was as if all the worst stories were true. I was crying. Jesus. I'm crying.

'Come on, bro.' Dean put his hand on my shoulder.

'Yih . . .'

I remember too the public address sounds dully penetrating as we got up, and the crowds flocking across the ground to the presentation area on the other side. But what actually snapped me back was the sight of a man tearing through at a right tangent. He was running like he was being chased, and so it proved, three men thirty yards behind. I could only see the back of him but something about the suit – it just looked way tight, especially with him trying to move so fast – rang a bell. He turned once to check on his pursuers, and I made out the

features and characteristic arm crook of Hope, my friend from
Sundays' spot. He was too far away for me to do anything for and, in
any case, shortly disappeared over a hoarding and into the bowels of
the stadium. His pursuers, athletic, younger, appearing to be gaining.

I hoped he'd be all right; it looked serious. Huh. Didn't take long
for the truce to done.

We arrived at the Tavern no more than fifteen to twenty minutes
after the game's end. Cosmic was nowhere around – I'd hardly
expected her to be on time.

It was a pretty grim scene, the punters there being mainly on the
other side. They were out on the balcony or clustered around the TV
screen to start with, so at least that was something. We got ourselves
some shorts and a table by one wall, with the length of the room in
sight.

We weren't the most talkative, though I did fill Dean in on my
Race Man encounter. However, his periodically expressed scepti-
cism was not exactly what I wanted to hear. I walked off three or four
times that first thirty minutes, through the bar to the balcony and
down to the tier below. I'd return to see him still shaking his head.
After a while my mind began turning from Cosmic to my client. He
had said he would be here by now too, hadn't he? Maybe, just
maybe, they'd met up en route, and even now were talking up a
little something.

My phone rang. My mind leapt ahead. *Sorry, Daddy* (little giggle).
Don't be cross with me. Yes, you are! I'm feeling that from here . . .

'Boy?'

'Hello, sir.' My client.

'How are we doing?'

'All right, you know. We're doing all right.' I exchanged a look
with Dean. 'Not brilliantly. My friend – that's the lady I was gonna
introduce you to – she's just popped out for a bit. Not around just
yet.'

'Oh, but she will be soon, I hope?'

'Oh definitely. Urmm – but you're around?' There was no background noise from his end this time.

'Umhmm. I can be with you in a minute.'

'Great. So what I'll do is – I think the best thing—'

'Just call me when she comes.'

'Will do. Yeah, no point wasting your time. I'm not keeping you, am I?'

'No, no, I can wait. See you later.'

I felt relatively relaxed the next ten minutes, before I got up for another scope, this time venturing out on to the deserted perimeter area and then on to the field. You only caught sight of the faces in the little packs of revelling figures late on in the dark, so I was concentrating more on gaits. I just wanted to find her now. I didn't care if she was bringing bad news or whatever.

When I came back this time, Dean got up, gestured at his watch and threw out his hands. 'I've gotta go,' he said.

'That's cool.' My voice was choking up. 'You can get back all right?'

He nodded. 'Listen, I've got some time tomorrow, for a change! We'll go out. We'll nail this thing.'

I nodded. I couldn't look at him.

'Experience, bro. She's a joker ballbreaker – you *know* that.'

'Yeah.'

After he left, I considered the situation realistically. She wasn't coming. She'd all but intimated it with as much clarity as I would clearly be getting this day of the week. I really grew to hate her those few minutes, as you can imagine, but not focusedly so. I was too numbed for that, battered by the brutal collapse of all my hopes.

Shouldn't have slept with her; just knew it. See how soon punishment come.

One thing for certain. Not a trace remained of whatever foolishness I had for her. For me to feel like that, and for her to know so, plus my position in this case, and to still do me this way! Breathtaking, man, breathtaking. Boy – can you pick 'em!

And she ain't finished with you yet. Ninety minutes later and you're still . . . pleading.

For the umpteenth time, a hemmed-in punter eyed me, eyed the chair my leg was propped against, and approached.

'Excuse me,' she said, 'is that free?'

I got up. 'All yours,' I replied and walked out, head as high as I could, trying to remember the whereabouts of my ride.

11

all the worst stories

At Netto's you could get breakfast all day: three medium pancakes, sausages and scrambled egg, a slab of buttery breadfruit or dough-bread, a glass from their selection of sorrels and juices, and a nugget back from five.

You have a little gander by the café-high front window, step in, walk down the aisle to the far end, grab a tray, join the queue (not so long in the pre-lunchtime) and find yourself talking across the counter to two Turks and two desert people. Discussions are generally short and to the point, for a shared language is not on the menu.

You see the Turks toss the pancakes and what-nots on the hot plate and grill, you get your plate stacked by their partners, you proceed efficiently down the line.

Walking away and there's a pleasant range of options: you can be in the smoking or non-smoking part; with others, one amongst the clutches of bargain-conscious young ones, perhaps, or the little groups of working people in their overalls and basic suits and ties, or by yourself; you could leave a tip, you didn't have to; you could rush in and out, or ponder the day through the window.

A place as good value as this and you'd expect it to have one of those write-ups from a fashionable magazine pinned up on the door, or to slip in an application for one of the Minister's 'City Challenge' grants and move into the nice street in the neighbourhood set aside for such successes, but Netto's had never seemed interested in building up its profile. It remained our little secret.

Neighbourhoods are funny. This particular street – right on the borders of the manor really – had for a long time been the first port of call for new arrivals to these parts of the city. Every ten years another group were settled in the same complex of public housing and always a few would soon enough emerge to work their way up through Netto's. There had been Latinos and Chinese and now these; when the Turks went on holiday, more desert folk came to replace them. And it didn't matter who the incumbents were, they all served pancakes just the same.

To take your seat there was to feel that you were scratching your mark respectfully against a great, sturdy tree. It was soothing, a soothing end to an invigorating morning.

I had stirred a little before eight. Didn't feel too grim, despite the hour and how low I'd been getting in last night. I'd had just enough focus then to fire off that ad I'd done across a few sites. Cursing my stink for not flying it a day ago, cursing her. Nodded off at the keyboard still in all my things.

Waking had brought a rough initial quarter of an hour, obviously, but I'd quickly resolved not to let the disappointment dominate me. The relief of a light headache showed the way: I'd washed my face, glugged the rest of my juice carton, found myself re-enacting some of the more pleasurable moments of the day before and, when I checked back, the head pain had gone.

I extended the remedy. Let me not even think about my matter for a while; instead enjoy the little things, then come back when I'm fresh. I opened the curtains and the windows, threw some darts, had a long shower. It was then, remembering Candy and her new-found pastries, that the long-neglected Netto's had come to mind. Yeah . . . Eat well and be happy. See people, live a normal life. Get out before midday. Change the routine, the style of attack.

I dressed, if not exactly leaping about, at least in a relatively positive frame. Okay, I now had under forty-eight hours to find the girl, but I would not panic. There was still time enough. A glance, a chat – thirty minutes might be time enough.

I would stay calm. What do you do when you reach an impasse? Go lateral on the business. All the way across and all the way back. Strip every last mutha down.

So I'd grabbed some smokes and a trusty pen and pad, slipped on some shades and stepped out into the milky sunlight, taking a long, bridge-then-back walk to Netto's, resifting as I went: the facts from the comment, the strategy, my whole agenda.

Did I even still want, or need this case? Forgetting the contract, forgetting my word, strong but not compelling, forgetting even about getting overs, cos if I did do this, and things panned out, well I'd be beyond all that. I'd be off with the Man, more than likely. Speculation, perhaps, but with grounds: '*I like you, Boy. Complete your mission then we'll see . . .*'

Travelling, researching, adjudicating, welcomed – weekly councils and fine flowing robes – that would be the lick, that's the light reminder! Scaling the chambers . . . Who wants to get overs when you might get to live forever?

So I *had* to do this, and do it well – simple. It was the same as I'd known it on the first day, only deeper: a true red cherry opportunity, with a test attached. Double-sided, probably connected (comment, but fair again, I'd hazard).

Slipping sideways, for a minute, into the mind of the chief exam-
iner; picturing the Race Man as a grand hirer, say, or a team coach
scouting out a potential buy. What would he be looking for?

I reckoned he would have seen something he could work with in
my five-day form: hunger, long hours, dedication. I had been, uh,
human, clearly, plus short, perhaps, of the smart, real killer move,
but there had been showings of initiative, times when I had picked
up the ball and run with it. Felt warm, joined some dots. He'd
even said I had all the clues so he couldn't say the work was beyond
me.

And the girls? Okay, no joy yet, but I could hold my head up
about them: nuff man would be even happy to step with any of those
three down an aisle.

Hmm, the girls . . . There had been method there, but not
enough, perhaps, to pass muster. I'd gone for Ice Cream and that
supermarket that first evening when I wasn't really up to speed and
Cosmic – yeah, I'd worked that out, I was just wrong. Two fairly
basic notions and just the one, more considered . . . experiment. Not
exactly a scientist's tally: they'd have a thousand of those dishes up
and running.

Where was the toil, I could hear him cry, the time and time again?
The unglamorous poundings at the rockface, the steady accumula-
tions of data? It's not always the season for flashy moments in the
sun; sometimes it's about grinding out results over the hard winter
months. Western grit.

Systematics was my weakness, systematics the new key. I would
show him I was an all-round player.

And so a little before midday I found myself filling up at Netto's,
waiting for Dean. I had found him just up from the main, challeng-
ing a God-fearing man with a microphone, and asked him to join me
here. He had volunteered yesterday, I remembered, and a scientist
rarely moves without an assistant.

He came soon enough, and joined me at my two-table. I got up to get us some coffees.

'Have a look at that,' I passed him a noted-up slip of paper entitled *Campaign*, 'especially from a systematic point of view.'

'Looks good. Plenty to be getting on with,' he nodded on my return, going down the list. *Electronically* (it read): *Ads – newspapers, lonelyheart sites, love zones, wanted columns.*

'I've already done that,' I explained. 'Fired some off.'

By foot (car): Colleges, day centres/crèches . . .

'Crèches?'

'You know what I mean. Those kinda places.'

. . . Libraries? Shopping centres? Friends/family of people we know . . .

He reckoned it would be hard to get a look-in with the shoppers. They'd be running about and think we were pollsters. The one I was more doubtful about was the friends of friends option: mix business and your personal world and you can get locked into the consequences of a case for ever. I had wanted to steer clear of that road, and the Cosmic experience had hardly endeared me to it. Still, beggars and all that.

. . . The street (Dean's friends!).

'You talk to everyone, man!' I slapped him on the back. 'Finally there's a use for it. You're my secret weapon.'

He smiled a little sourly and passed my notes back to me. 'It's good to see you reclaiming the streets though, after your shooting drama,' he remarked. 'You must have a lot of faith in Old Greybeard.'

I nodded. 'If the Race Man says I don't need to worry, then I figure I should be all right. The third eye don't stop still but yeah, it's good, good to get out. Sometimes you gotta absorb the sound of the herd, you can't just stay locked in to the sounds of your head.'

'For sure. Otherwise –' he made a popping noise, and a cloud crossed his face. I guessed then, finally, that it was the sounds in his head that sent him out so. It had been so long and I hadn't pressed

him, on what he was doing and how long he expected not to do it, I'd
lost sight of the concern, the fact that it was still an issue. I wondered
whether, if we carried on not talking there would be a flashpoint one
day, like there'd been with Sundays, and just how long could even
the strongest hold their shit down.

'Listen, when this is over and I've come through cash-friendly,
we'll take a little trip someplace hot. Come back, start life number
two.'

'I don't think so, you know, right now. Thanks still.' He was looking away, clearly not wanting to pursue these areas. I felt pleased,
though, that I'd tried and that, at the least, I had articulated certain
things with certain people during the length of this case, clarified key
matters.

'You know, whatever happens,' I said, as we got up, 'this has been
a good one for me.'

We covered much ground that afternoon, starting in our little
patch and moving out, up, and across. I had my *Yellow Pages* with me,
and we must have ticked around twenty possibilities straight off. We
hovered by the railings of day centres, sipped coffee in college
common rooms, initiated banter with those behind counters, looked
for a friendly eye in a traffic warden or a passer-by, fishing all the
while. It helped greatly that Dean had no shame; he'd impose himself on anyone, he didn't care. Quite a few we ended up speaking to
were women he'd buttonholed before. Unfortunately about half
these number clearly thought he was mad, and they carried this mis-
trust over to me, especially when we pulled up sharp in the ride and
jumped out at them. The way it would generally work was for Dean
to start, then for me to try to calm them with a couple of minutes of
unimpeachable sanity and my crisply shaven profile, before one of us
steered the chat into relationship territory. Dean might go, 'So how's
your man. You still in that?' and I would follow with a couple of supplementaries. 'Say there was a guy, this real pleasant, lucky guy . . .'

I quickly found that it was better to stress, pretty much to invent, imperfections in my client and his situation, rather than harp on its comforts. That way, much as I wished I'd done with Lincia, we cut less slack for the chancers, more for the pure in heart to shine. By the fourth lady, a bank teller in her lunch hour, gone was my client's mansion and even his stable abode. He'd gradually become – not so strange I suppose – Mr Development, his goatee-less double. 'This man, this dream man, he *could* settle down, fucked-off crib all o' that, only he prefers to travel about, see, doing really important work. You've heard of development, right? Now say there was this situation, this offer on the table . . .'

Of course it was not everyone – if they even let us get that far – we gave full treatment to. Some disqualified themselves quickly, perhaps blatantly insincere, their carotids and such pulsating, or else someway prosaic, underpowered, struggling to fuel the leap to match the grand offer lurking under the topsoil of my patter. One was already content.

The likeliest we found in that long opening spell was this librarian, Funmi, encountered taking a cigarette break. Our age, modest organic-style clothes and clogs, big brown eyes, and single – as we established through that corny old joke about libraries. Very winning, very considered she was; you know, one of those people who seem to have thought about everything. So much so that I even found myself running my client's 'What do you believe in, heaven or hell?' query past her. She'd frowned and, invoking her biological observations of this world, addressed herself sceptically to the next: she'd love to, but she couldn't see much beyond this brief ironic interlude, then the soil falling over our heads. I feared it were true, but it made me too sad, thinking about two of the people in my life. Still, we exchanged numbers and I asked if it might be possible to meet with her again, perhaps at short notice. She said we could find her here most days around this time.

Back in the car Dean pressed Funmi's case strongly. When I mentioned my heaven and hell worry, he accused me of muddying the
issue with trivia.

'It's not trivia,' I retorted. 'It was my client himself who brought it
up.'

'So what did you say to him?'

'I told you. That Wu Tang song—'

'And what did he say?'

'Well, he said, "That's nearly right", actually.'

'So what did you want – what did you need her to say?'

'Dunno,' I muttered, 'maybe not to feel sad.'

'What?'

'Nothing.'

'So we're back to your hunches, right?'

'No. Just trying to be thorough the best I can,' I defended myself.
I yawned. 'D'you remember the Wu though? They used to have
those martial arts-style videos. Battle with their sticks round a giant
chessboard—'

'Yeah-yeah.'

'You know the original Wu, these Chinese fighting monks, were
supposed to be these exiled fallen angels. This guy at that "exhaling" evening told me.'

'Does that help us?'

'No, no, I don't think so. It's just a, you know, neat little concept.
Once were angels!'

I did call that Canto Ken I'd met at the exhaling evening. Popped
into a couple of record stores too – no joy. Came out and found Dean
now outside the car, clogging up the pavement with three others.
They seemed like long-time acquaintances, but you never knew.
He was pointing his eyes meaningfully at one of them, a dinky ruck-
sack-on-back lady with delicate, fine features and short, moody hair.
I lit a cigarette and she came towards me.

'Boy – Wiwa,' he introduced. 'Wiwa – Boy.'

'Hi.'

'You got a cigarette please?'

I gave her one. She hovered a short, impolite moment then disappeared behind. I shook my head. Another grabby bohemian, I didn't think so.

She returned, some seconds later, as I was flicking through a newspaper Dean had picked up. Sports Day was all over the pages front and back, and I was making noise at an especially mischievous Master Blaster story when she peered over my shoulders, rolled her eyes in bored fashion, and disappeared again. So now it definitely wasn't gonna happen.

We pressed on, approaching a good ten or so more in points north and east before, with twilight closing in, Dean bade us homewards. I offered no complaint: we were both of us whacked, plain talked out, plus I had the electronic side of my system to attend to still. We had accomplished as much as we could in the field.

The later batch had been mainly scoped in bars by their offices. One stushed-up establishment had had one clock of my typically attired friend and barred the doors. Aah, we had suffered certain indignity, sweated plenty today. I hoped somebody somewhere was watching.

I'd taken a couple more numbers to triple my amount but, really, I thought that, if anything, my librarian still had the edge on these two. And with her, still, those reservations . . . you'd think I was being dead choosy but it wasn't even that, although I was certainly trying to do my side honourably. I was jut finding that, seeing so many in one day, even the preferred were tending to slide into one another, into the same bracket of eligibility, with no one really standing out, shouting out at me, the way that, say, Candy or the others, to be fair, had all once shouted. And true, I was trying to go easy on the hunches, but hadn't my client told me I would know when I found her?

I hadn't called him. I knew I should have. It was my one glaring omission today; from last night really, when it became clear. Tch! Couldn't face it then. And now, now I wanted to come with some good news.

We were just south of central when my eye was caught by a banner headline on a news-stand, 'Exclusive! Master Blaster Transfer Sensation.' Wha'? I had to pull over. There had been some such speculation in Dean's paper, but I could not believe it was true.

The evening edition confirmed it. The Blaster was moving to the west's club champions in 'the sale of the century' and would now play for that division in representative matches. The fee was undisclosed but it was understood that the deal would make him their league's first seven-figure batsman. 'Now the Blaster Truly is Bionic,' page 2 blared; 'Who Can Stop Us Now?' crowed page 3; 'From the Streets to the Stars,' by Miss Don't Feed the Blacks (pages 4 and 5).

I walked back in a daze, staring at the evidence – MB, in shades, snapped sliding into his jeep for the press conference, while his minders pushed the cameras away – before tossing the paper to Dean and switching on the car radio.

A lot of the stations were carrying the press conference: '. . . well ummm . . like I say, I felt it was ah, time for a new challenge an' ummm . . . no, money ain't the motivation. I've done as much as I can here ummm – I hope the fans dem understand . . .'

I carried on pressing channels. Now I was hearing it I couldn't stand it.

'Did you see this?' Dean asked, holding up the paper.

The inside pages were carrying a story on the imminent closure of the Prince Picture Palace, our neighbourhood's once grand cinema-cum-concert hall, still our largest venue. Its demise had been frequently rumoured, with its owners baulking at the bad publicity attending the clashes that cursed some events there, and, sure enough, the paper quoted Mr Prince blaming 'local forces' for his decision. Various potential 'saviours' of the site were mentioned, chief among them this guy who'd already refurbished two other establishments on the same successful street. Even Merciless was in the frame, for an Ice Cream 2.

'I tell you, man,' I shook my head, 'when they come to lay it on you, they lay it on thick.' I was still trying to find an MB-free zone. Even the strictly music pirates were holding impromptu phone-ins. I was just about to scoot past one static-thick station when Dean told me to hold it.

It was the PPP, not the Blaster, that was the issue on Southside Radio. They were interviewing people outside the venue. It seemed that an unhappy number had clustered there a short while ago. A few missiles had been hurled only seconds before police had come screeching round the corner. Three had been arrested.

'It's hotting up down there!' Dean nodded.

We kept the station on and scanned the streets as soon as we passed the pink elephant. Difficult to say quite where it was going, but there was definitely a vibe abroad. A lot of busy pavements, voices raised, huddled folk stabbing at newspapers then staring hard at cars that drove past. An increased beast presence too, of the marked and unmarked kind. They could hardly have been thankful for the mild evening.

I dropped Dean by his nasty estate, thanking him heartily, then up the side on the park, on to the main, to mine, summoning what energy I could for the evening leg. I was thinking maybe I should drop my car off at the rental's at some point, get my own back before they shut for the night. I had seen some familiar faces when we were driving just before but I couldn't toot them, no one would've recognised me in this piece of fanciness. The air had the whiff of local forces and, if the place blew, this guest ride might prove a liability and my own a wise reinvestment. It was not as if these wheels had brought me much joy anyway.

Jesus, MB, how could you *do* us like that?

I spread out the sofa and collapsed on to it on my return. Sparked a spliff – I reckoned I'd earned it – and monitored the sounds outside to my left: past the front yard and my companion block, back out to the lights. That was where any drama would be coming from.

Sat up pretty quickly, Blaster thoughts putting paid to any rest. I'd been slightly fearing the encounter with my messages, but the number of replies, four on my e-mail, five answer services, was some good news that put me right back in the swing of my matter. I made myself comfortable and hit those calls.

It was a much more straightforward process than our trudgings earlier. These respondents were as focused as I; most were no strangers to the market and had a fair idea already of the type they were seeking. There was still the odd joker – one who got quite taken with my voice and declared it was I she loved, another who cried and swore that I'd abandoned her and our issue – but these were swiftly despatched.

After an hour's bashing, I'd managed to contact all but one of the nine, dealt with two more enquiries, and discounted seven. Of the three that remained, Yvette – all bleary weekenders and 'me an' my mates' – was just lacking a little gravitas, and might easily be bored by months in the country. In Debbie I could detect – beyond the sad facts that she divulged – a depression that still had some curve to travel. Which left just Mona.

She sounded great: rich, alto vocals, she worked for an ex-offenders' housing trust that, she said, like good development, was more a cause than anything; she approached heaven and hell squarely from the punishment tip, which was likely to endear her to the Race Man, and she believed in him too. There was proper concern at the thought of my client's frequent absences but she was sure they could arrange something. I didn't tell her he was a millionaire.

So, Mona, and Funmi, my librarian. A straight-up two-horse race? Hmmm . . .

A little something was bugging me, to do with that sense, gleaned over the last week, that the solution was someway to do with me. I'd been concentrating, during my exploratory conversations, on interrogating via pointers recalled from my meetings with the client and the RM – the hard facts of the matter. All the rest – my opinions during the case, the points I'd reviewed with Cosmic and others— was mere speculation, to be fair. But I knew some must count for something too, or the best authority would hardly have commended me for my progress (fact). I had to make space for fair comment then, somehow embrace the two . . .

I thought I had solved it when I flashed upon the blinding idea of drawing a graph. I'd bounded up to dig out a ruler, coloured pens, fresh paper, thinking, *Just like the old capers, only better*, and drawn my perpendicular lines, marking 'candidates' at the top of my vertical axis, with a 1–10 scale along it, then 'key words' by my horizontal. To Mona's and Funmi's names I added Candy's and Lincia's, more to assure myself of the others' pre-eminence, but also because they hadn't ruled themselves out the way C-C had.

'Key words' was more taxing, but I'd ended up with six phrases in all, I recall, 'heaven and hell', 'connected?' and 'smell the coffee?' among them.

The curves were quite spectacular but left me more confused than ever. Somehow all were now back in the frame, covering similar amounts of shaded area. Even Lincia, who came through strongly on the connections, was lagging only slightly, within the margin of error, while Candy, with her various parents and heaven and hell quotient boosted by a growing appreciation of both sides of the story, notched a solid set of scores that put her right up there.

I'd been so locked in I'd been barely registering the outside, but the rising hum of helicopters broke through. More than one, for sure. So loud now, like they were just above me.

I looked out the windows. A few guys darting past the bollards below, to the lights, others standing, staring above me, and there was definitely some human noise, concentrated, in the distance. Chanting, possibly.

Something was going down, for sure. I should get my ride to the rental's soonest.

I frowned at my paper, rather irritated, I confess, by it, by him, by now: I wanted this decided before I left to give myself the chance of settling it tonight. Funmi was there in case I needed her tomorrow, but to still be juggling everything in my head then would be cutting it too fine. I couldn't understand it. It shouldn't be so hard.

My fatigue came again as I padded back and forth, desperate for one last piece of science.

Only then did the Bible occur to me, I could not believe how belatedly. He'd written from it, hadn't he, given me the note? Use your flippin' nod.

The problem, and part explanation, was that I didn't have a copy. But the Net, fool, and, sure enough, there was chapter and verse.

The edition we had at school must have been abridged; that one seemed long enough but here was reams and reams of the stuff. I didn't bother printing off, just skimmed through what I could of the Old, searching for my line. If only it had come from the New; that was plenty shorter.

It was an odd feeling, speeding through the Good Book with this situation cooking around me, but I persevered to Chronicles, and zipped through 'Recommended Readings' before throwing in the towel. There was just too much: too many battles (just like I remembered), too many names. Perhaps Day Five was a bit late to be getting scientific.

Decisions, decisions. Just do it. I called my respondent Mona and asked if we could link tonight. She said we could if I fancied coming down to this independence anniversary dance she and her cousin were heading to. We arranged to meet by the ground floor bar there between 11.30 and midnight, otherwise I'd call her over the PA. I told her I would be alone, and dressed in black. She sounded pretty excited, thank God.

As she was giving me the club's details, with its south-central code, it clocked that this 'Atrium' might be the same place Candy had said she was going to. I couldn't remember the name but I was sure she'd mentioned an anniversary occasion as well.

Earlier in the week, such a coincidence might have left me in a flap, teasing out the superstition in it. But now I mulled it cautiously as I slipped on my shoes.

I didn't need to get ready ready. There should be enough time to pass back, clean-up and what-not when I dropped this off. The only query was my bucky: I'd feel safer with it, the way shit was shaping, but there'd be so many police around and what if I got stopped. Just then the first great shattering sounds of glass and flares streaking through the air settled it. If the beast stopped me, I'd show them my PI's licence and soft-soap them. It should be sufficient to prevent a search.

I did find myself dialling Ice Cream's digits on my way to the car. No big reason, but I might as well stay thorough and check on where Candy would be, if needs be, before she left for the night.

She was half out the door already. They had to call her back to the front desk. A pause, then those bullish, breathless tones. I'd half forgotten what an instant tonic she was. Maybe that was really why I'd rung. She and Caramel had had the best day, she volunteered, shopping then flop-out time in her room—

'Jesus!' I jolted behind the wheel at the sound of two successive explosions.

'What?'

Smoke was rising to join the big birds and there was fiery light off the main.

'It's happening, it's really happening.'

'What's happening?'

'Turn on the radio girl. Look at the telly, probably.'

I filled her in. She was a bit worried about her and her friend's welfare but I told her they'd be fine in that part of town. It was the Atrium where they were going. I kept vague about my own plans but said I'd probably see her there, around the witching hour.

'Wicked. I'll look out for you,' she said.

'Yeah-yeah, all right.' I was a bit short with her at the end. I was fast approaching the main and I needed full-on concentration. She said she would cross her fingers for me.

I was picking up the sights and smells now. Various guys, bandanaed and 'clavaed up, darting across the sideroad. One of them, extravagantly young and short and wielding a stick, tried to wave me down. I was thinking, How dare you play a leading role in this? I had slowed right down – you had to – but I accelerated past him.

Sammy's rental was half a mile down the main on the right-hand side, but I'd only got about a block before a group of armourless officers, hauling metal barriers across the street, signalled for drivers to go left, so it was back to the sides again.

The adrenalin started to pump as I steered past more masked ones, running to the lights and the line behind, returning pounds lighter, laughing, bigging up their strikes – men, women, they had no fear tonight. I was reassured by my piece, nestling in the pouch under my seat; right now I was just part of the flow, but it was too easy to turn target in these situations. I had already seen a couple of cars upturned and ablaze.

The police strategy seemed to be to try to contain their foes down these residential roads, lock off and defend the main. It made sense, there was fuck all for folk to mash up down here. I wondered if the strategy differed on the other side, home to our leafy avenue and successful street.

I couldn't get back to the main until two blocks beyond Sammy's, where I joined a single-lane snail's crawl of traffic being filtered off left, past the town hall and the great crowd that had gathered there, to greener parts. The right-hand lane, which would have allowed me to double back up the high, as I needed to, was closed off at the intersection, where a mighty phalanx of officers, in full riot cons, were spread back to back across the street. Up the incline beyond them, amidst sights of destruction, lurched an upended bus, smoking again, although I think the fumes may have been tear gas rather than vehicle-related for officers from the other side of the line were breaking out and running into the pall, shields and longsticks raised.

I blew hard: somehow I thought I could forget about Sammy's. I would do well just to get out of this. The lane I was in had ground to a halt, with the drivers at the front preferring to chat with the crowd, who stood – stringy-haired pamphleteers, akas and respectable types alike – most exultant, flinging the odd taunt at the protectors opposite.

I must admit I was surprised by the scale of it. I mean, it deserved to happen, and I knew MB and the PPP were popular but . . . I pulled my window down, to hear and be seen by any familiar face. There were no worries here; folk were just come for the crack.

It didn't take a moment for a couple of friends, laughing in a little group, to hail me and for all to troop over. It was quite funny actually; a line was being flung about that the riot had been orchestrated by mobile, and I found some onlookers – gazing at the phone on my dashboard, my nine series and my people leaning down – nodding at me respectfully.

Turned out the cause was more than I realised. Some trouble had started between a bus driver and some youngbloods. The driver had called our keepers, who'd come and dragged off a couple.

Sympathising passengers had refused to clear the bus, and a stand-off had ensued, with reinforcements gathering on both sides. When the frequent rumour spread that one of the youths taken in had collapsed with a 'heart attack', it had kicked off.

There was some perturb at the shortsightedness of these wrecking moves, but general grim satisfaction, with much citing of recent history, at the retribution exacted on those who'd been troubling blackhead-central. So, Greenland's, which had gobbled the grant only to recruit from the country, had been visited, and Bagel's, which had suddenly introduced chairs then said, if you weren't sitting, get out, most likely to join it. Even the Blaster's official house now had its blinds flapping. Netto's had been spared, Sammy's fate unclear.

I chortled the same as they but there was a familiar heaviness in me too: all these things – the changes, the consequences – they were the week-in week-out of my state briefs. *It's gonna blow*, that's what I used to write him, Caesar. I wondered what these would have done with me, if they knew.

A second channel of cars were now inching their way past the stationary vehicles and this I joined, unfortunately not quite quickly enough to miss a certain fool take the snake from his head and carry the fucker forth to the officers, like an offering.

It was only half ten; should still be just enough time to pass home before the club. There was a long, circuitous route back if I followed this street, which would certainly bypass trouble, but it should be quicker to throw a right, take a couple of the small roads off this side of the main, then cut across it at the top. I suppose I was curious too, to see a little bit more of the fallout.

Activities in this more commercial sector seemed, if anything, more brazen than elsewhere; against a cacophony of alarm bells and emergency sirens a number were calmly sampling the delights of window shopping, passing kettles, Hoovers and stoves on in little convoys reaching from busted fronts to waiting cars. Heads were braking hard in front, leaping out of their cars into electrical stores and coming out arms crammed. Boy, we do love technology. You could tell the respectable ones by their fearful glances up and down the street. I even braked momentarily myself but, really, with my present agenda, it would have been a rash thing to do.

I was just crossing Pitt Parade, the refurbished success story – fairly scathed, with some private security still guarding the PPP – when I heard another explosion and looked up to see a burning and folk fleeing the Clarendon, once a longstanding blackheads' dive, now an otherwise-leaning establishment, with a cover price. Such was the history, but to sling a device with punters still inside, well, obviously, that was poor.

I drove up to it; no one I saw seemed hurt – I think whatever it was had actually landed behind – but there was real panic and terror, the first I'd seen that evening, young ones stumbling blind and spluttering, jumping at the sound of you, as if they feared you were their assailants come again. I'd seen the two brers scuttling away; they hardly looked like heroes.

It was a souring scene, no question, older arrivals avenging themselves on these other for fifty feet of turf. Some of these bewildered were the same thrift-shop types as were leading the taunts outside the town hall. These would have stayed on here and thought they were safe. Not known the war was this messy.

I ended up taking this couple a few blocks down, away from the front lines. I felt embarrassed by the bombing, something more – a little deviation didn't matter. They were in such shock I think they thought I was a cab.

Reversing away from them, I turned to glare at a car parked interferingly close to a corner then got the shock of my night: that pale blue Granada – Caesar's car! The stitched cushion on the driver's seat, the 'BAT' plates – what the fuck was he doing here?

I scoped the cross-street and the alley I'd reversed into. It was just terraced housing up and down, barely anyone about. The cars here must have been ram-up with his Ford perched on the corner like that, but there were some spaces now so I guessed he must have been here a while. Who was he seeing? Who else did he know?

Fuck it, I would go to the club like this. I parked up as near as I could to the corner opposite. I'd give it a few minutes. This had to be useful information.

I took my night-sights out from my front compartment and had a look through what windows I could. Quite a few in the top rooms were staring out of them, towards the action. I doubted he was in any of these; I doubted they could see much either, but you could hear stuff still in the distance.

After ten or so minutes, when I was thinking of giving up, I saw a door open diagonally in front of me. Aha, there was Caesar, and a hand on his shoulder – what? Eb'ry Year, my would-be assassin! Eb'ry Fuckin' Year and Caesar! So that was the story.

I pulled my Tanfoglio out and slipped it at the back of my trousers. Didn't know what I was gonna do, just make sure I got him.

I waited 'til Caesar was halfway across the street, and the door shut behind him, before I stepped out, half shadowed my face and walked towards him. He had on his casual in-the-ghetto wardrobe – suede jacket, jumper, shoes with too much click for the impression he was trying to give.

'Hey, Caesar,' I said.

He paused, gazed hesitantly at me, then I was on him, my gun at his guts.

'Boy!' He was breathing shallow, arms raised. 'Boy?'

'Walk,' I beckoned him right. 'Walk, quick.'

I prodded him, just behind, up the alley, not giving him the chance to settle. He was one of these very smart types so you couldn't allow him that or he'd string some foxy story together.

'Didn't know you had so much friend down here.'

'Oh,' he cleared his throat.

'How d'you know him?'

'Mr uh—'

'Yes?'

'Mr Lambert, you mean?'

I turned him round. He stared at me, trying to gauge what he was dealing with. My eyes were hard as anything. I cracked him across the face with the butt. He cried and staggered.

'How d'you know him?'

'We – the same way I know you, that's all.' He cupped his hand around the cut and eyed me bleakly behind it.

I kicked his legs from under, then jumped on top, my chrome to the fore. 'You sent him to do me, isn't it, you little fuckhead! I know – isn't it?'

'No, Boy, I didn't, I swear – you gotta listen to me.' He gulped. 'Just to talk. It wasn't me. Someone else said we should send him just to talk to you. We'd tried everything else. We wanted you back, that's all.'

'*Talk?*' I snorted 'You're gonna have to come better—'

'Maybe to scare you a little, that's all. No more. So you'd see it wasn't safe and come back for protection. Come on, what would the point in more be, for us? You know that.'

'So he knows.'

He nodded softly, gazing his most fearful eye at me, aware that it was now or probably not at all for him.

I rose, a bit dazed, my interest in this man backgrounded a moment by this revelation. If Eb'ry Year knew, and his partners, how many others?

'Can I get up too?' His smart little ways returning. Thinking he'd gotten away with it.

He dusted himself and pressed a handkerchief to his temple. 'I understand there were shots. He had no business doing that, I assure you. He's a wild one, Mr Lambert, not with us long.'

'How many know?'

He contemplated me, and the tool dangling at my side. 'I saw an old mate of yours the other week. TK. T'Kalla, is that his—'

'What about him?' I snapped at the hook too readily.

'Oh nothing really. He seemed somewhat agitated with you though. I don't recall if it was something old or something new. Still, I believe he's out of operation for a while, though these things change sometimes, don't they? Phwuh! Now he's another wild one. Not like you. You got more sense than the two of them.' The smirk curling. 'Come back, Boy. I admit it, it's been a bit of a mess since – like this.' He gestured to the distance. 'Listen to them! They think we're impressed. We're not impressed, are we? There's nothing for you out here, Boy. Eh? We'll put you up. Somewhere nice. Even we're moving out: far west, a quiet, little district. The Minister's new offices. An old corn exchange. Corn . . .' he let the word linger.

I nodded and stuffed my weapon out of threat's way, just to really loosen him up, then swung venomously at his midriff and kicked him back to the ground. I kicked him for Eb'ry Year, for how he'd nearly killed me, for bringing TK back into my life; for his work, for Sports Day.

He was protecting his face, holding his hands up like mittens, whimpering in a well-bred way.

I kicked him one last, cold-blooded time. 'And that's for making me a cunt,' I said.

Most times, an outburst is like a good dump; it clears your system of the physical discomfort you've been feeling before and during, but not then. No great relief for me; I'd uncovered one spectre to find another resurrected. Someone would come for me at some point, if Caesar didn't have me arrested first. That side of it wasn't worrying me unduly – what could I do? – just what I was hoping to, leave – but it sure felt a sorry epitaph, to be run out by such as these.

My life. My faulty little life. I had been punished before for a disloyal act I hadn't committed, thought I'd gotten away with others I had, and all this week I'd been wondering which one this was. Something I had done, after all.

All too clearly now I saw the juice in the Race Man's words. *'Don't worry about that side of that matter . . .'* i.e. Eb'ry Year won't get you, but you're not out of the woods yet. Pay heed, there may still be consequences . . . Oh, very sly. Aren't we clever?

I felt faint, stomach back again, almost too fuzzy to drive. I wished I could just leave mine on the road and take a cab. But no time; I was badly up against time now, rushing to the bridges and beyond.

What consequences? Wasn't I paying heed? Still consequences? Fuckin' hell! When would I be allowed to finish that thing?

That was when my phone went, and I get Lincia, pleading for reinstatement. Can you imagine? She was in town herself, I could hear the sounds of a bar. She asked me why I hadn't called. I told her I'd been busy this last day.

'So you weren't gonna call?'

Silence from my end.

'You were just gonna leave it there. It wasn't all bad, our night, was it?'

'No, Lincia, not all.'

'Is it that mixed girl—'

'No, it's not, as it goes.'

'Huh. So what are you doing right now?'

'I'm working.'

'Still on the same thing?'

'That's right.'

'Why can't we meet tonight then, or to—'

'*No*, Lincia. It can't happen, you understand?'

'But—' her voice was breaking up bad now—'but I'm used to

being *adored*!'

Ah, Lord!

She got there in the end. Managed to extract the details of my destination. Said she wasn't far from there, anyway. I told her, 'Look, no promises. Definitely no promises . . .' as if that was me being strong. Try so hard to be strong, but I'm weak.

I remember how I was tingling that last stretch down: the faintness, Lincia's intervention, my lateness, this new information, plus a stop on the Elephant approach (the rads radioed in, peeked their torches for a scan-through, I'm thinking, Babylon's *burning* – ain't you got better things to do?), all contributing to a funny panic. I tried to focus on this last effort – this shouldn't be hard, even with two, maybe three, shouldn't be hard, if you're strong – but . . . it was the whole vibe of the night really, the sense that there were certain forces abroad, and that they weren't done with me yet. Wondering how they'll come again.

As I slowed to turn into the yard that fronted the Atrium, I could hear the screeching halt of a car ahead, then overheated voices by the door as I pulled up. Bouncers doing their stink again, I surmised, even at a jolly independence dance.

'Boy!' A woman came running to me as I clicked my doors shut. Oh no, not Lincia already.

'I thought it was you,' she said. 'I'm telling you, I'm not standing there any longer. That's looking to go off big-time. Security aren't letting this group in and they're not having it, and this young girl's trying to sort it all out.'

'Yeah?' I pricked up when she said that.

'Uh-huh. You wouldn't catch me! I don't think she's even one of the—'

Glass broke ahead of us, like the crash of a bottle against a head, and I could see scuffling, obscured by the queue around it.

Then a shout, and the queue scattering, and a bloodied-up punter peeling away to the side, two flight-jacketed men giving chase. Then Candy, and another man, standing for an instant, then fleeing too, from a third doorman behind, steel in his hand.

That's when I ran.

Shots thudded out. Screaming. She was still running, then she jerked horribly and fell. Candy!

I reached her, bent down. She was on her back, legs buckled under, grit and a graze on her forehead. I couldn't see a wound. But dark was there, seeping.

She saw me, eyes flickering. 'Look at me,' she forced out a whisper. 'What's wrong?' There was just puzzlement there.

'Ay, baby.' I ripped off my shirt, squeezed her hand, then felt about her. I wasn't sure – I didn't want to move her. 'Where does it really hurt? Can you tell me?'

A tiny nod. Her eyes were big, stared at mine; then they went.

'*No!*' I looked up, couldn't see for the film, '*No, Lord. Please, no!*'

part two

*'to discover the scheme
of things . . .'*

Eshu Elegba,
Master of Potentiality.
He's the tiny, tiny, tiny guy
returning with the last stragglers
from the market of the night.
He's close, close, close as the
shoulder of the road.

YORUBA INVOCATION,
BAHIA, BRAZIL

12

give me my wars

So this is where people come to thrive; I would have thought it a greater fcat to survive. These stone works where they come to wonder; I would have thought it a better place to surrender. Here, where the waters pass over; no cry, not a whimper.

Yes, you have won. Congratulations. No more – requests – I know when I ask you will take. But I did not ask for her, I did not even know to ask for her, yet still . . . Candy, dearest Candy, I'm so sorry. I'm so so sorry, I didn't know, I couldn't save you. What did you do? I'm so sorry. I brought you into my deserts, I didn't know.

These wars, these stupid, wicked wars. Here looks like a good place for peace. Here, we could meet . . . *Don't go there, meet me here, don't care if it's a rainy day* . . . Thrown stones, and flopped out by this bridge. But you had to take.

Haze, still hazing, every picture so slow and so true how will I ever sleep again? She just still, me tearing my shirt for the flow, a man and a woman bending down. 'Don't touch her!' but begging, looking,

Lincia, slipping her coat under, and security stepping back inside. Wicked, wicked man. The wickedness – what does he follow, that man?

For fuckries, foolishness. Because a girl gets facety with him in front of his people. Because three brothers come in a group to him, and he doesn't feel to let them pass. Because we don't care for us either.

Because I was late. Because I called, I told you I was coming and I was late again. Late for my mother, too long with T'Kalla, ten minutes with Caesar . . . So you come out to look for me; you know the door's stiff, and you thought you'd just check. For them and for me. What did I do? Five days and I did it.

They had the blood, but too late again. Never ever a sound, a smile from you again. You didn't smile down at us, when you could, save me this one good. Daah! because this place ain't no friend to grace. You ain't no friend, it's true.

All the worst stories, the pictures – her parents in the picture – in her heavy, lifeless room, hugging Caramel there, the photo and that first day: solid working hands, I'd noted, and her roundabout me, 'Chief'-ing and skittering away. Then it comes real home to you, it comes back fresh again. I couldn't speak to them. I spoke to the police, the worst again. I couldn't speak to them.

Sundays called. I don't know, an hour ago, maybe more. Hope is dead, he told me. Body found dumped up not far from the stadium. Debt-related, most probably. Of course Hope is dead. How can Candy dead and Hope not be?

'Hang on to the money,' I remembered. 'We'll need it to bury . . .' we'll bury the money, we'll throw it to sea. Take the money, take Your job, take your bleedin' mission.

I saw lights, other night sights, then the rushy-rushy people, the rides and the criss-cross. Speed it up, slow it down, in a haze. I see shapes, I see stone, I see all I have known. I see wars.

No way home. Can't have wars at work and wars at home. The bills are your own. You see, father, I don't forget you.

I see, this nearest thing to sea. Seeing you deep in your books and beckoning me; expecting stern instruction, but you only take my hand to this map, make a triangle with your own, and trace around the wash of blue. 'See this, this ocean. We own it, we do.' You look up then and your eyes are wet, so I'm scared, never seen you this way before: I don't understand, if we own it, why it makes you so sad. I see it, now (see how this life reassembles, piece by wretched piece!): see my country – is that the other side of here? The cruel partings and the crossings, and the wars that started there, the original that lies buried and the shook ones that inhered: from young ones through school ones, certain wicked ones, certain crossfire civilians . . . Oh, we've deep rights to it, we've earned it, these bills we brunt still, but what a cold, indifferent, graveyard thing to own! Forever, like the sea, like the hills they say you've grown to be. Not a home to own. Enough to make you mad.

And I'm not strong, Lord. You know my old man – Dean, Leschelle, they were strong and still they fell. So what could I possibly do, Lord? Can't fight the river, can't fight you. Tried. I tried harder and you took another. Just a mean collector, never any better. You don't smile down on us, and you could. Save me one war good.

Stumbling, dragging . . . was I not here just before? The shards by the rentals, the smouldering linger by the carpet store? Yes – it comes back, some while before, same grey pall – the Minister; the Minister, then a pack.

Hazing along, head up at the sound of steps, and the Minister, bare yards away, breaking into trot, hand outstretched. He found mine and shook it hard, beamed. 'I hope we can do something for you here.' I blinked at him, obviously I had nothing to say, then blinked some more as cameras snapped away.

It was all over in an instant. He strode on, and most of them fell in behind. A suit on a pushbike pursued me, though, hurling questions. It all comes back now. From they corner one of us, they want to know everything. Did I work at the rentals? Ever hear of a 'Hope Bonaventura'? A local doorman known as 'The Ninja'? My stare then served only to encourage him, for he took out his wallet, and badgered on. But another appeared, wailing, 'The next ones is to join him an' dyam cemetery full already! We kill our own! Skull an' bone, skull an' bone . . .' The suit pedalled in pursuit, and I was left alone.

I must have passed home then. Perhaps before. I found a letter from Cosmic by the door. I picked it, managed to scan it – written in her hand, as if these personal flourishes might count for something now. A long page she sent; hard to take in when it recharges the chain of events '. . . *You developed this sweet, fantastic story around me, and I didn't always have a problem with that . . . don't need to tell you that saying yes to some things isn't yes to everything . . . but at different times, in different ways, you were wrapping those dreams so tight, and I was trying to tell you I couldn't breathe . . .*' An absurd foolish age ago, that I had dreams like those; now the swirling, closing clouds that confound your every sense (the sights that come at night that you banish from remembrance?): I'm twisting, not falling, not flying – I can hear the rustle of their wings . . . No! it's swamp, it's quicksand, and I'm struggling, brown and leaves up to my chest. Candy is there, with friends in a field – why isn't she helping? I'm calling, not helping, then she turns and, aah, God! – there's someone on her face, the side of her face – dark sloping square, something so deep and horrible, bits of hair, it's stopping my heart, can't breathe, mouth bared, at my belly . . . THUM!

It's all right. I'm on brown ground, in the saloon. It's all right. No one even looks at me as I get up, replace myself on the sofa.

My belly is aching in the frequent place, but my belt and zip are not where they should be. I wonder if I have been interfered with – it would not surprise me here.

Perhaps at the 'bank. There is soil about me and dirt in my hair – perhaps that is what took me from there. I have been here some time, I think. On the table stand three dying glasses of my common brown drink.

Around me sit a handful of old man miscreants of the outlaw kind, their victims too, sufferers of the illest reverses and crimes, hunched over the same cups, mouths blank open, clothes no dignity, staring into memory. The sinisters grin suddenly, occasionally, the victims do not smile at all.

I had come here once, to this neighbourhood basement hole, tracking an unspeakable man. Seen the mildewed walls and shuttered windows, smelt the urine and broken menace; thought it the worst place, a good one to be alone.

A man holding a paper has been staring at me. Perhaps he is the one. Now he sidles up the sofa. Talk is rare but not unknown. He drops the paper beside me.

'Heh-heh!' he laughs, a deep, tobacco rasp.

My picture is there, from the street. 'The Minister reassures a concerned local' reads the caption. My face looks blotched. I put my hand to it – it is peeling.

'Heh-heh.'

He sits down, much nearer this time. Was he moving or would I have to fight him? It's me to go, now – just noticed the jungle scenes stitched behind us. Those things just set me off. Oh, but the ground, the brown sucking down!

It took me a little while, eyes closed, feet held safe inches high, before I could scutter across the floor, to the little room beside. No sofas, just stools here, fearless threadbare carpet and plain yellow walls, the palest light from the yard door, and four dotted hardcore. I thought I could be here a while.

A woman too, cleaning up, removing cups, the first in this place. Jobs indeed are hard to find.

I forced my mind there, to the future. It seemed unlikely. Where to, and for what? Yeah . . . unlikely. I just want it to stop.

Huh. The case. Never even got to see Mona. There were many evacuees after Candy, perhaps she was one of these. Lincia followed us to the hospital, and was good enough not to mention our matter anymore. It's finished now, time all but done too. I would ring my client when I could and explain, if I was still around.

And what would You do if I found her? You'd probably kill her whole family.

One early, aborted, breach of the peace. A giant man, who'd been fidgeting dramatically, got up and bore down, great waves of irritation with every roll, on the attendant. What for, I don't know; we all had our bottles. Certainly something unpleasant, perhaps filthy, for I had seen him grin briefly. The lady turned at his approach and said, 'Hi!' most brightly. It was the quality, it seemed, as much as the rude noise of it, that had heads rising and blinking, and that did for the giant. He sagged a moment, the wind quite knocked out, managed an abashed boy's mumble, and padded meekly back.

So I must have noticed her too, then, again, but it didn't impress, being lost still, seeking a way past this, but never beyond the pieces . . . hating me, and all these ones who'd made me, all that I'd followed that had failed me. But still a tiny fight in me, one sweet place to pass for me. Just lonely. Lonely for this only.

And I surely heard her too a while, but I thought it the sounds in my head; a song for the week, a song for the dead. A song from Ice Cream, and our first meet, for you, wrong, *what's wrong?*, on the street.

Lalalalala, what do you believe, boy—

Boy! That's what I heard, when I heard.

> —*heaven or hell?*
> *We don't believe in heaven so we're living in hell.*
> *What do you believe, boy, heaven or hell . . .*

I stared transfixed. Was it her, was it here? Yes, others are wondering too, our eyes exchanging for the first time. Scowly, jolted, quarter-smiles appeared. Music! Here?

She had her back to me, was washing something in the sink by the door; apron strings tied behind her long shirt, a cloth wrapped around her hair. Her voice was soft, I could not hear it all. It had a gentle rise and fall.

I got up then, stood a yard behind her. She was warbling, humming, a few words, but mainly excursions on the melody, an amateur's voice, breaking as she scaled and held the high chambers: '*Ah,ah,ah, ahhhh . . .*' A discreet, lulling, shade-tree voice, like a warm bath you could just sink into and lie, like these glasses. As she wiped them down, she turned around, and noticed me. She smiled.

She took a dry cloth and moved on, from room to room, back and forth, still the tune. I followed her.

'*Living in h-ell, living in he-e-ell, oh yeah, oh-oh yeah . . .*'

Slightly sad, faraway eyes in a peaceful face; years hard to say in the general way of our kind but, I thought, about mine.

'*. . . he's mad as hel-ell oh, ohoh oh wo, oh oh oh, what do you believe? Question?*'

She brushed, she touched up: the tables, the ornament (a framed portrait of one Ugolino. The landlord? I didn't know). There was a pool of something sticky, which she attended to on hands and knees. Pure diligence, much more than made sense, here. But at last she gathered her mop and her bits, took them by their place under the sink, and gulped a cooling draught. The work was done now, I thought. But then she sighed, gathered up her stuff and, with some difficulty, manoeuvred open the back door.

I want to do something, intervene on her behalf, find this Ugolino or whoever. She shouldn't have to clean outside. She had stopped singing.

She left the door ajar, and I followed her out, slowly mounted a couple of the iron steps.

It smacked me, I remember, just feeling the air, the passage of time again. Nearly dusk now, again.

She was in the little yard up top. Almost didn't recognise at first, she was – aah, how can I tell you? I'd never seen such a thing. She was holding her body in this lovely, proud, arc, leaning slightly forward, right leg slightly raised, her tools raised too in her arms like – so it seemed that first moment – an offering, and I found myself peering for someone to appear. But when I looked beyond her, followed her gaze, there was only the sky, the setting sky. Oh, what I'd seen of it had been a rainy day, but you could just make out the late, red gasp of the sun, framed by the focus her body gave and, really, when you saw that, very quickly you realised it wasn't an offering at all, but an acknowledgement, an expression of her relation to these natural things, of her alignment with these elements, and for this she was giving thanks. Not for her tools, these lowly tools, nor even in spite of it but, I understood, notwithstanding them, and she needed to show this before downing them. Even for me, then, it was thrilling, so powerful you knew it was true. And I was calmed.

Full fifty seconds she described that angle, before a slight lowering then final lifting of the head. I couldn't see her face, her back being to me, but I knew she was content then.

She turned, stepped back in momentary surprise when she saw me at the foot of the stairs, then came clanking down. She was almost past me when I croaked, 'Please, don't go.' My voice sounded strange to me, after all this time. 'I – I've seen—' *I've seen your power, seen what you do*, I wanted to say, but I only gawped at her, sighed hard. She looked puzzled, even nervous, but polite.

'The song,' I tried again, 'You sing "Boy" in the song. There's no "Boy" in the song.' She screwed her eyebrows at me. '"What do you believe, Boy".'

'*What do you believe, boy*—' she laughed, launching into it.

'Yes.' I put my hand to my forehead, closed my eyes, mouthed the words with her.

'. . . *heaven or hell? We don't believe in heaven so we're living*—'

'*So?*' I stared at her. I had said 'cos' to myself. 'It's "cos", not "so", isn't it?'

'Urrm . . . no, I don't think so, least not how I remember it.' She considered, put down her bits, still looked just mainly amused by these queries. But I was accelerating back to attention, thinking to my client's comment. *Right, that's nearly right.*

'They don't always say the same thing, do they, but,' she shook her head, 'no, it couldn't always be "cos", could it?'

'No?'

'No, because . . . because that would just be to hate how it is, but we have to think to the way it should be. We have to love that. Couldn't always be "cos".'

'You feel so?'

'How else could it be, get better?'

'Yes . . . I see . . .' then, quicker again, 'I see!' My limbs were loosing all over. I fell back against the rail, stared at her.

'Are you all right?'

'It's very . . . big of you. These places that you speak of, sing of – what do you know of these places?'

'I—' she seemed about to tell me something, then her eyes looked down. 'They are both close, and may be visited.'

'The good one too? It's possible?'

She nodded. There was firmness, a hint of defiance there.

Her pose, the travel in her eyes. 'Yuh,' I whispered. I meant, 'I believe you.'

'Who are you?' My eyes, painfully tight and crusted with whatever, were shining.

She laughed. 'What do you mean? You see me, I work here—'

'Is this all you do?'

She just held my gaze, looked somehow sad.

'Do you know what I'm going to say to you?'

'I – I think so,' she looked away from me, to the side. Now it was her voice that was trembling.

'I have a proposal. Do you understand?'

She didn't look but flung her arms around me. 'I've been waiting,' she said.

13

promised land

We just kept on grinning, we couldn't stop ourselves. We broke from our hug and faced each other; holding hands, a little giggle.

'Are you ready?' I asked, for something to say.

'Ummm,' she nodded and breathed in deep. 'It's just these,' she contemplated her tools. Neither she, I think, nor I, wanted to go back inside.

'I'll just leave them by the door.'

She rearranged her headcloth so that it became more a wrap than a bandana, slipped off her apron, folded it over the rim of the bucket, and snuck her bits back inside. She closed the door very softly, like this was a secret operation, which had us grinning again.

I could have linked her hand even then, I think. Her language suggested so as we contemplated one another a moment. But I, I don't know, I didn't want to risk disturbing anything, and we fell in side by side, out of the yard and on to the street.

She just had a thin, patterned shawl on top and the evening's chill had set in. I offered her my jacket, but she declined.

'Are you sure?' I asked. 'It's a good little walk.'

'I'm fine.'

'I just need to, umm, finish up at home. Clean up, grab my things, and then we can . . . we'll go.'

'Umhm.'

'Yeah?'

'Yes.'

'Hnn! There's so much – aaah . . .' I shook my head, smiled in nerves and wonder, '. . . so much to say.'

'I know. It's okay.' She reached out her hand and I gripped it gratefully. Yes. Didn't want to talk. I'd like to rest now. I felt I could with her. I'd inhaled deep when we hugged that first time – her neck and hair – heady, strong, like something of the earths I'd smelt before. So didn't need to gaze, didn't need to. I suppose again I didn't want to disturb.

People were staring at us but it was all right, I knew it was the last time. Oh, it was the most surreal, floaty walk, but my frame was strung out with fatigue and tingling, and I wanted to be home already.

We got there. I took her up the backstairs, inside.

I flicked on the lights, snorted. The room looked just the same: my graph and pens scattered on my desk top, a half-attended glass on the floor, the green shirt I'd been meaning to wear draped over a chair, the iron beside it. You hardly expected it to look the same.

'Not much of a place, I'm afraid.'

'You haven't seen *my* little hole.'

I took the cushions off the two chairs, either side of the desk, and pottered with them. They were for her, but I didn't know where to put them. Didn't feel she should sit on the chair – that would be like, business. Then a dizzy, vomitous turn – I think the change of air – threatened to overcome me, and I simply handed them to her.

'Make yourself at home, please – whatever you can find. I just need to lie down a sec . . .' I hurried to the cupboard and pulled out my pillow, wilting too fast for the whole mattress palaver, and lay down across from where she had parked herself, cross-legged and concerned, by the long certificates wall.

'Better?'

I nodded, regarding her anew, it seemed for the first time. Her lips were the red of cinnamon.

'D'you want something to drink? Something hot?'

'Please.'

She rose, moved past me over to the sink unit. I heard her footfalls, the gathering storm of the kettle, calming. My body felt less likely to embarrass me now, my stomach hurt dully but easily ignored. There were various questions, matters to sort, but soon . . . I was grateful she had made it as easy as possible for me.

I must have drifted, then. Not very long. I awoke blinking to find her leaning over me, smiling. It was quite dark – she had replaced the main lights with the desk lamp and the dimpled, backlit contours of her face were all I could make out for a moment. She jabbed her finger down, pointing to the mug beside me.

'Slip off your shoes,' she bade, moving towards them.

'No. It's all right,' I hauled myself forward, kicking them off, brushing by her. A tiny scent of her. 'I'm all right now. Thanks.'

I stood up, took my drink and some fresh wear, and padded to the bathroom.

God, it was a pretty horrible sight, the mess of me. A shower couldn't come soon enough.

The last hours played themselves out in dull, staccato fashion as I washed. Even the knowledge that I had found her, that I had solved my case, brought no great surge of anything. It was her, for sure, no question. I could call my client, and collect. Damn client, man. Blood on his hands too. He was the cause. Tchh . . .

No need for rush. Could call him tomorrow. Deadline day. If we, if we still wanted.

What I wanted . . . Very little now. Just – get away. With her, without . . . I don't know. She seemed so tender, a little while with her would be . . . would help me. Huhhuh, she'd already said she'd come hadn't she? I had forgotten that. But where could we go? I didn't even have the ride. Left it there by the club. Couldn't take it anyway. If I took it, I'd have to come back. If I took her I'd have to . . . well, we could see, tomorrow.

I turned off the head to hear the strains of music. She must have uncovered the stereo. Good for her. When was the last time I used that, anyway? A little while.

I clothed, stepped out a couple of paces, didn't go any further.

She was dancing, in a room that seemed only distantly related to the one I had left: a few adjustments and resurrections – the stereo, nestling on a cleared-up overspill table, the second lamp, long presumed dead, now atop the cabinet and turned against the wall so that it cast light and shadows along it – and the place looked altogether, ah, cosy. And bigger. She had moved the client chair and other bits to the side, freeing up the central space. And here she glided and twirled, eyes unseeing, all open fluid movements, to the tune. I didn't recognise it, it must have been something from the radio, from the old country; discreet marimba and high, chopping guitar.

She was one supple mover. I wasn't sure that her moves fitted the song, but that was hardly her point. She seemed, rather, wrapped up in some story occasioned by the song, and that story had someone else in it too, for she went through a range of expressions at fixed points in the distance, or else made these inchoate sways and sweep-downs, as if a co-protagonist was adding his part to them.

The song fell away into an ad break and she scootered over to the machine. She didn't hear me when I entered, started when she saw me.

'Yeah, it's a killer – that tea.' I was clutching the mug. 'What d'ya drop in it anyway? Some spicy somethings? My head's burning up a bit still, but this may sweat right through it.'

'Bad day, eh?'

I nodded very slowly. 'You could say that.'

'I hope you don't mind me changing up the room a bit . . .'

'No, no, not at all.'

She searched through some channels while I located my jacket for my cigarettes and plumped myself on my desk, legs dangling down.

'So, uh . . .' she turned when I began, '. . . we never finished our conversation, did we? In the yard. You said you'd been waiting.'

She regarded me intently but did not offer anything. I had to gesture with my hand to encourage her, and came again with my query before she, somewhat hesitantly, elaborated.

A man had come to the saloon a week ago. She'd recognised him – he'd come twice before, and left mighty, unheard-of tips. What kind of man? I pressed her. Different, she said, well groomed, tidy little beard, and a distinctive silver ring with – yes – like a monkey—

A pang shot through me then. My forehead dipped a little on to my clasped hands. 'Go on. Go on,' I said.

That day he'd paid up, really nicely as usual, and she'd thought he'd gone. But then she'd been outside at the end of her day and encountered him on the steps, just like me, on her return. He'd kissed her hand – that's when she'd noticed the ring. 'I hope to see you again, elsewhere,' he'd said. 'Someone may come for you, soon.'

'Oh, I couldn't tell you how happy I was after! I . . .' she took a big breath, '. . . it'd felt so long there. I was so relieved, when you came.'

Her eyes were shining. I don't know, maybe I didn't look sufficiently enthused for she seemed to hold on for something more from me.

'You know him, don't you?'

'Oh yeah. Yeah, I do.' My voice was flat as I mulled this clear confirmation of my client's peculiar, formidable, abilities, of the
strangeness of this whole enterprise. If he *knew* where to go
already . . . For sure it was him then, too, at Ice Cream . . . I was
mildly surprised to notice the extent of my irritation: at this feeling of
being played, being led around by the nose; kinda denied privacy.

'And you're to take me to him?'

'Yuh. That's the arrangement . . . But we can still spend a bit of time
first.' It was I who searched for endorsement then. 'Tell me something. What were you doing there? Why did you have to *be* there?'

Pain veiled her eyes. She shook her head and trembled a shrug.

I waited. 'I don't mean to 'set you.'

'No. It's just,' she sighed, 'today I'm gone from there and I just
want to feel different. You gonna allow that for me?' she asked almost
impishly, glancing back to the boombox.

'For sure . . . same here, really. Hang on a sec . . .'

I joined her at the cabinet, and sifted through the tapes and discs
in the bottom drawer. I found my favourite spaghettiheads, their
Fistful of Dynamite and *Once Upon a Time* tunes. I didn't know if she
would recognise them but I thought she might welcome those grand
sweeps and melodies and, at the first stroking of strings, she beamed,
beckoning me with her hands, and for a close quarter-hour we
danced together. In courtly styles, facing, hands linking, or else on
hips and shoulders, little patterns back and forth and sides. She tried
to get me to lead, but I would end up flopping around her, so more of
the time she would initiate something – she might arch back and
suddenly dip, for me to catch underneath, or else coil in with her
back for me to unfurl, at all points invited in to her story.

I tell you, it's amazing how two people dancing in symmetry mag-
nifies its beauty. We didn't say much. I'd pretty much understood she
wasn't much of a talker. I remember remarking how her cheeks were
on the child-bearing side. 'I store nuts there for winter!' she'd

winked before her eyes returned half-closed, serenely following the strings.

She liked *Fistful* too much she had to rewind – that's what woke me. I'd drifted away there, by her shoulder. But this time we barely moved, even as it galloped and giddied to its prettiest, we just swayed, 'til I was overcome and gently broke away; filmy, so frustrated at these glimpses of all I'd never had.

She continued, came to grab me for the fall, then saw something was up as I sat down heavily on the side chair, the palm of my hand against my head. She leant her arm across me.

'Come with me, please.' I wiped my eyes. 'Just tonight. One night.'

'Yes. I already told you, didn't I?'

'All right. All *right* then.' I jumped up, took her hands. 'We'll go away, I mean *away*! Look – I've got this mate, Visa, he does passports – he'll knock us up a couple, we'll go as far as we can get. Just give—'

'We don't need passports.'

'We're gonna. Or have you got—'

'We won't need it.'

'No?' She was very firm. I had heard about not needing documents for certain parts of foreign.

'And I don't want to go and see Visa,' she added. 'We must rush.' There was something plaintive in her voice. 'We must rush now.'

I wished she hadn't said that. She'd make me sad already.

She helped me remove my frames from the wall and dashed out to the store to procure some boxes. As much as possible to be packed, my fondest and essentials to go.

There wasn't so much anyway, and not so many friends to think of. I stacked away my files, left my computer and most of my little bookshelf for Dean, the bucky and other practically useful tools for Sundays.

'Is this to go?' She held up my cartoon.

'Oh definitely,' I replied, and directed her to the space set aside for specials.

I dumped some towels and sheets and clothes into a black plastic bag, and she tutted and shook them out and reattended to them with a space-liberating rolling technique.

It was all speedily, efficiently done, the one bone of contention being my blades. She urged me to ditch but I wanted to keep them, basically. She looked real disappointed, said she thought I wanted to get away from all this, I said of course I did, and I'd already ditched the bucky, hadn't I? (My shoulder sheath too, after the shower.) I wanted these only from the collecting, and the historic, aspects. They'd saved me once before, after all.

But she was most insistent, so I agreed to forgo them, but not before retrieving my prized red cherry blade and, when her back was turned, slipping it inside a jacket amongst the rolled-up baggage.

She flicked through my Epics tome, towering over the 'Specials', and I peered over her. 'Romance' she turned to, 'a quest for higher knowledge . . .' New information, a new spin on the Race Man's advice, and, though there was no mention of the Love-word, further strong indication.

It was just the final documents now. I wrote down a testament, my will, if you like, leaving instructions on settling outstanding accounts and the distribution of my chattels. To Dean I left any remainder, with direction that he should dispose of it as he saw fit, and a few names I hoped he might consider: I left the whereabouts of the ride as well, for him to convey to Sammy. All the money, the fifteen Gs I had with Sundays, I wrote he should keep, and I hoped it came in useful with his school plans.

I left money and details too, for Junior's headstone. Three Gs, most of what I had left. The rest we might need.

When it was done we double-signed it, as I understood was necessary for such instruments. Signed: *Boy*. In the presence of: *Girl*.

I managed to fit pretty much everything into my large rucksack, plus a little overspill string-bag she took for me. At the door I took a short look around, rested my eyes on my 'Reality Rules – *cos the city ain't pretty*' inscription, tapped my feet three, then seven, then three times on the floor.

Finally, I'm out. Nothing need bring me back.

On the main we took a minicab for our mainline station. We spent the journey in a delicious whirl: on the run, the two of us, night thickening, destination unknown.

I had enough money left to buy us a first-class sleeper compartment. We didn't even have to say where we were going; at the Willie level it's a flat rate.

Flowers and fine wine awaited us. We clinked our flutes, the train whistled and clanked, a gaze out and waves to no one in particular, she closed the curtains and it was just us.

I was really pleased now to have splashed out on the tickets. She was so thrilled with the luxury of our cabin and, I suppose, after such drudgery as hers, who wouldn't be? She jumped up on to the bunks, admired the various foldaway contraptions, gave a little 'Oo!' at the telly-concealing cabinet, and soon had that in operation. She got pretty quickly, loudly, wrapped up in what looked like your routine hospital drama. 'No! *No!* She's gonna show him the note! Serious! That's it, it's all off now . . .'

It made me smile, hearing her, as she reclined, feet off the floor, cushions packed behind her. This is how it would be watching telly with Candy, I was thinking. Like her, something of the child in her style.

I wondered why such as these brought out such positive feelings in me, and found myself tracing it back to Junior, to his early passing. Never thought about it before, never come across quite this response in me before, but yes, it was possible. Perhaps something, ah, tender in me that could be legitimately expressed with him had largely muted these years, lacking the image to wrap around.

Yes, I can see the different ways it might be. Her face, dark pools of eyes, those round spots. Not the likeness of my mother but the same territory . . . Huh, not such an unfathomable combination. These are the things that warm me.

We fell into talk soon enough, neutral stuff and, as the train entered a tunnel and began to get its groove on, some speculation.

I confessed it was my first time, and asked if she had been away before. She nodded. Of course, she had.

She did not elaborate or, if so, then obliquely, for she said she hoped there would be water where we were going and, when I pressed as to why, I gathered that she'd been something of a diver, of all unexpected pursuits, once. The beauties that she spoke of – dazzling oranges and purples in a red sea, grey hammerhead sharks ('So amazing when something bigger than you is right there in front!'), penetrating the bowels of a battleship ('Very odd, kinda spooky, diving into something manmade . . .') – I do not think that you find them here.

'Sounds pretty dangerous.'

'Oh yeah, can be. You've really gotta look out for each other, trust one another, you know.'

She stared into the distance and raised her brows in a 'that's life' grimace before meeting mine again.

'Right,' I said, wondering.

I began offering her something of myself. I wanted her to know everything, but got no further than the preamble – something about the ups then downs of a well-travelled friend of mine, I believe it was Leschelle – when I noticed her looking increasingly forlorn.

'What's up?' I broke off.

'No, it's funny,' she sighed. 'Everyone, and I don't even know her, but everyone, when you know them enough, gives you something to cry about.'

'That's true . . .' I nodded. 'It can take man a long time to recover from their business. And some people . . .' I shook my head. 'Boy! I – It's, it's taken me a long time, really, to put my shit together, but—'

She shushed me, 'I can see it all, in you.'

'You don't wanna h—'

She was shaking her head, a wry smile.

'Y'want some more of this?' I indicated the champagne as she grabbed a palmful of mixed nibbles from the table.

'Uh-uh. Don't really care for it actually. Ever since this guy I didn't much care for either used to buy it for me and go, "This is our drink"!'

I chuckled, got up. 'You didn't discover a gents in here, did you? No? All right.' I went to the door, unlocked it. 'D'you want anything?'

She shook her head.

Most of the other compartments had their curtains drawn, and there wasn't much action in the corridor neither. One or two bods, plus a gang of four playing what looked a tense game of cards with their blinds up; they took a good gander at me as I swayed a little past.

Rah! This train was going like lightning.

It felt like we weren't all that far away, though, folk still dressed the same. I found a toilet then embarked on a long bootless search for waiters with something hot to eat.

She jumped up a little on my return. I thought she'd been asleep but this she denied. Which did not stop her asking, 'Have we stopped yet?' We hadn't.

I sat by her on the bunk, shoes off, feet up. She was sat along the length of the bunk, head and back leaning on cushions, against the wall. I was flicking the TV channels, making some comments on them, when I looked and decided she was definitely dozing this time. But as soon as I stopped she opened an eye and said, 'Go on. It's nice, the sound of it. I like listening to you.'

Then she took her cushions from behind her – her position had looked slightly awkward – and placed them on my left leg, then curled down with her head there, facing out into the compartment. She turned her head to me, broke into a 'Is this all right? Yeah, I think it's all right' grin, and settled back down.

I prattled on: different stuff, Sports Day 5, and pretty soon I heard the rhythmic rise and fall of her breath. Her right arm had emerged from under her cheek, and was limp over the cushion, over my lap. I took it, held it in place.

How could she sleep on a night like this? Still, I didn't mind. It gave me time to contemplate.

I was, mainly, grateful. She had seen me when I looked like nothing, shell-shocked, stinking, and she had come. Oh, I know that she understood I was a conduit, but she cared something for me too, or she would not have come again with me here, surely. And look how comfortably she sleeps, snores. Long day, the both of us.

And yes, I admit, I did stare. There were curves, grooves everywhere: her face, of course, then her shoulders and the dip at the crook of her neck. The inward arch of her spine, the outward spin of the behind . . . Aah, geometrically, very fine.

The batty made the figure, no question. Made her up. High and fleshy and fitting, arch-enemy of those apologetic kinds. Gazing at it then, pressed firm against the bunched fabric of her skirt, was pretty sensational. A backside like that, man, just for starters, could keep me enslaved for years.

Huh. Who would have guessed it, to be talking about years again already.

The train slowed and pulled to a station. I wanted to open the windows to see where we were only I didn't want to move her, her hand in mine and her body weight tilted towards me. I made do with listening to the slamming of doors and indistinct shouts from the platform.

I didn't think it was us yet. A little while longer.

I may have nodded off myself, it's possible; at any rate, not much later I think, the train slowed again, then stopped, it sounded prematurely.

She fidgeted, blinked; that lovely waking moment when you don't know who or what's the coup, before she put it all together, appeared content.

'Have we stopped?' She scratched the back of her head.

'Kind of.'

She slid across, tugged at the blind, easing it up. 'Nice!' she exclaimed.

I drew up alongside. Outside was the deepest dark-blue sky, with a near full moon, black scuff marks on its upper half, whiting a little right part of it: illuminating, too, dramatic stretches of grey cloud, their wafery thin texture like the patterns of dirt on a dust brush.

'That's a bit of all right,' she murmured.

'Yeah . . . What's happening, anyway?' I went to the door.

'Wait up,' she said, gathering herself. 'How about these?' She glanced down at the bags.

'Erm . . . Take 'em. May as well.'

The corridor was dead quiet, our fellows' blinds still drawn. I left her with our things at the end of our carriage and continued a further newsless stretch before returning. She had pushed down the bar of the outside door and was poking her head out into the air.

I could make out a grassy verge a few yards from the track, glinting silver in the night, a lowish fence and what was probably waste land beyond. To our right, maybe five hundred yards down the track, we could hear a low babble of voices, which seemed neither advancing nor retreating. I thought maybe we were close to a station.

I blew hard. 'They never tell you anything on these flippin' things.'

We caught each other exchanging glances twice in succession, laughed.

'Are you thinking what I'm thinking?'

'Probably.'

Go on then, she dared me with her head.

I took hold of the string bag, dropped the rucksack out and jumped after. Shoes on stone. I held my arms out.

'Brace yourself.'

'Whoa!'

I half caught her as she pitched forward.

'Shame it wasn't moving,' she grinned.

'Yeah. But at least the tracks aren't electric.'

She peered past me, to the voices down the track. 'Come on then.' She suddenly hurtled up the verge, to the fence. I lumbered behind as quickly as I could. The rucksack was heavy.

She slowed by the fence, then found a hole and crocodiled through. She waited some moments for me then dashed away again. I followed but pretty soon I had lost her. I stood and rotated around in the grass, a little worried, trying to sensitise myself to this dark stuff. Then a rustling, swift footfalls, and she was charging me, head-butt in the midriff, toppling me over.

She collapsed on top and I held her loosely. We were both gasping.

'Were you scared?'

'Nah. Just about saw you coming.'

'Couldabeen someone else though.'

'Couldabeen.'

'We had to get away from those voices.' She fell to the side. 'Spooky . . . It's not too bad, is it? Not too cold?'

'No, no. Quite mild. No wind.'

We sat there for a time. She had recovered a bottle of water and two straw cartons of orange juice from our first-class comforts, while I retrieved my flask, with its lingering nips of brandy, from my specials. Not forgetting, to be sure, the herb. She partook of all. Which was nice. I wasn't sure she would.

It wasn't all that dark actually. The moonglow saw to that. You could make out near shapes but not the details, everything clothed in silver and shadow. Trees and bush ringed the top of our little hill. Beyond that street lights and a main, perhaps, or more country.

I stubbed out the butt, she packed up our empties, and we rose, excitedly, without discussion, to investigate.

Over the brow and it was country, country all over. No lights, apart from the stars so close and bright, just great sweeps of land. Around us was rocky, the lie rather jagged but, further, to our left, flatlands, as far as you could guess. Beyond that, she reckoned, was water.

'Smell the air,' she said. 'Damp. And listen . . .'

It took me some moments to hear a trickling nearby. We pursued the source, clambering down and right. The grass, first coarse and dry, began to squelch underfoot, and we found our pebbly spring. She splashed her face, drank from it as I stirred its sediment.

'I wonder if all this belongs to someone, or it's just land,' I said.

'It'll be light soon enough—'

'You reckon?' I looked about me, unconvinced. A shade lighter possibly, but within the bounds of acclimatisation.

'Mm-hm. We'll get a better idea then.'

She was right. Dawn came soon enough, it came brilliantly, setting off a mess of emotions in me. For I knew, of course, that day signalled the beginning of the end. That soon I must call. The gnawing inside started then, seeing it rise.

Aah, but it was beautiful! We'd been pottering, always rightwards, but not so far, I think, in total, lingering by the odd sight and scent, ambling on, buoyed by the freedom and adventure of it all, when morning broke with a swiftness that I'd never seen.

You could see its lustrous pinkness inching over the horizon. I mean, literally see the inches of it. At first the circle was distorted,

like an egg yolk that has begun to run, before it – congealed is an
ugly word, but it did this as it passed over, ushering pure colours:
bands of yellow and reds that faded into each .other as they rose.
There were pale blue scars in the sky beside it, white immediately
above, dark grey clouds bringing rain for somewhere far off.

It was covering the landscape in a clear, light haze and underneath the glories of our valley stood revealed: muffled, gentle hills
and bluffs, most nothing abrupt there. Below us were tree groves and
multicoloured rugs, beyond that a light blue lagoon. Around us,
streams were lapping all over, apart from one spring, to our right,
where the water was red with earth, and spurted like a geyser.
Anywhere you looked it was thrilling.

Her eyes were shining. I squatted down on my haunches looked
up again to the sun. 'It's so close!' I began. 'To actually see it all
happening . . .'

She came up behind and dropped her arms around my neck, leaning against my shoulder blades. 'Thank you,' she said.

'What for? I didn't do anything.' My heart was pulsing hard. I
almost wished she wouldn't do this. 'So where d'you wanna head
then?' I added. 'Let me guess—' and I pointed, correctly, to the
lagoon. She didn't move away as I got up, so that I had her perched,
piggy back style. We started in this vein, I as nonchalant under her
weight as I could be, wanting to impress, 'til I realised we had left my
bags behind and we turned back.

We shared the bag duties on the way down, our destination quite
a trek away. I imagined myself a gruff frontiersman, living on his
wits and the land. All we needed was a beast to be ripped and roasted
over a spit, and a horse or two, not that there was much that looked
nourishing, in the yellow-streaked, slightly daunting grassland, with
its hardy cactusy plants. We passed through it to some fertile, tilled
acres – cereal crops and great starchy tubers and others I could not
name – and on through a plain of auburn clay: the earth was so rich

and fine in your hands here. We looked behind us at our distinguishing trail of footprints and felt like the first ones who'd walked
on it; then another patch of green, and the shore.

Here we finally saw company: a boat of fishermen – different
kinds, ours amongst them – casting their nets far out on the blue,
gliding across, from right to left.

It was an important moment. Not that I hadn't been captivated
already by this fabulous space, but there is always a worry, a guard not
completely dropped, for me in the country. You wait for a certain man
to appear and regard you in a way; still others may follow and put it
to you blunter. I'd ventured there three times, twice on business
matters and once to watch a game and all these things had happened.

So to spy those fishermen there was even reassuring, removed
one of my naggings. If we worked here we could surely rest here too.

She was unbuttoning her top already. 'Something tells me we're
out of state!' she laughed.

'Just might be.'

She stood in a white undershirt, kicked off her shoes, then shot an
enquiring look, clicking her fingers for me to get started. I demurred
and she pressed, '*Relax* – you're allowed to. You deserve it. You don't
think you deserve it, do you?' I can't swim, I explained. 'That's all
right.' She didn't bat an eyelid, so what could I say?

I took my trusty tennis ball and two T-shirts from my bag, passed
her one, and stripped off. We left our things by one of the big rocks
at lakeside and went for it.

The water was bracing cold. I padded gingerly forth, searching for
soft ground with every step, while she hovered around me. When the
water was up to my chest she splashed away for a few yards, then
flipped over and stood, sputtering water out from her mouth, to indi-
cate the limits of my safety zone. Then she winked, turned and
swam out further, where the blue turned turquoise, and I skimmed
the ball after her, trying to ping her backside as she front-crawled.

You could look down to your feet in the silky shallowness; there were little pieces of coral, rocks with mossy seaweed on them, and thin baby fishes scurrying about. Deep browns and greys and blues; stayed cool down there too.

We threw the ball back and forth, flat, high, leaping to make the catches. She had to come a bit nearer to ensure her throws reached my vicinity. There was the odd tricky moment when I had to venture too far out to retrieve and found myself out of my depth, but I never panicked and would manage to bob my way out. I knew she would come for me anyway if she didn't see my head for a bit. The nearest we came to drama was when I went under one time – I must have hit a dip in the water – and just couldn't get back over. All sorts of nastiness was just pouring into, bloating up my lungs. I put my hand up, as we had discussed, but I couldn't be sure it was even breaking the surface. There was some fear then, certainly, as I reattempted some breast strokes, my nearest claim to competence. I finally emerged, coughing and everything, to find her a yard or so behind, looking utterly frantic. She urged me to stop there and then, but I carried on a little before I bowed out, leaving her to it.

I felt mighty chuffed as I lay myself down on the rock, lovely hot stone against my wet frame: I'd survived, nay, chilled in the ocean! This boy has no limits.

The fishing vessel was still out, moving further away. They honked, I suppose at us, and we waved back, then at each other.

This lady, man. Damn, this lady.

So much familiar . . . yes, those family triggers, but something more; the deeper glow of something that's quite precisely known to you, just as the way this week had been a lot of old news. In her, in here even. How could it be, here? That walk – aah, the clay was my favourite, so rich, but not that, that felt new. The lagoon? Hmm, not sure . . . No, the smell, the tangy smell!

I sat up straight, inhaled, stared back to our trail. That's the smell, the tang I'd smelt at the Race Man's. Yes . . . I felt I could see it: me so small, yellow grassland, everything flat and wide around. I am content.

A pure calm swelled within me. None of the frustration that had overwhelmed me when we'd danced, at those glimpses. It was a place like this where I was supposed to be. This time I would stay.

I've heard say that in the old country, people return to their ancestral village to die, to be buried. But what a thing to return to *live*! To start again and flourish. We could work the land, fish, whatever. We could—

She was back-crawling, head towards me, towards the shore. When it was shallow enough she stood, executed a couple of back-flips, then a handstand. Coming with the party tricks now, is it? Yeah, I believe you. You could have been a diver.

Yes, that was it, that's the spot she hit; what I've been struggling with all my life . . .

So much of me, I realise now, has been occupied with a certain physical aspect. I have craved a strength of movement in the world, and sought out those who possessed it. Perhaps, to begin with, it was little more than the physical prowess most boys seek to demonstrate and, later, more than likely, connected to a reaction against the interior, incorrectly armed life of my father, and Junior's death. That was the start of my moving with some older ones, and all the rest of it.

And, though there's been these thugries, that type of impact was never the point. Rather this relationship between our bodies and our space, and the place that we have within it, which I've so long had hints of, and whose understanding I've so coveted. Oh, it's been so distorted in me, but I've always been on its trail: hunched it would be graceful, like maths and my bridges, Cosmic's stage personas and cricket . . . Now, her. She was so physically articulate – not these party tricks, but she could move and you'd glimpse the power of her soul. That was why she was familiar, known because of my fondest aspiration.

So yes, of course it was her content but, really, what slayed me was her style.

By the time she stepped out I was – I wouldn't say resolved, but I knew definitely what I wanted.

She slipped inside my bag for a towel. 'Wish I had my mask, you know. It's so clear you can see all sorts down there. There were these little seahorses, like a slice of my finger!'

'Ahha,' I nodded.

'Hurrr . . .' she sighed contentedly. 'Did you call him yet?'

'Not as such.'

'What d'you mean?'

I shrugged. My look was light but a serious line crossed her brow.

'D'you want me to?' I asked her after a moment, sitting up.

'I think we should, shouldn't we? I said I would. And you too, didn't you?'

'Yeah. That's true . . . Do you, d'you know what he's got in store for you?'

'I have a fair idea.'

'And you're all right about that?' I asked, very even, laid back, but my heart was going.

'I, I think so. He seemed, yes, a good man and . . .' she paused, looked at me hard then away, 'and I'm alone!'

I nodded slowly, brought my hands to my chin. 'I'll sort it,' I said. 'We've still got some time.'

She deposited herself alongside and I steered the conversation to more amenable terrain, adding to my knowledge bit by bit. Not information, in my old way, but an increasing sense of the size of her. There were some tussles, from time to time, in our discussions, but these were strictly of the nourishing kind. One vigorous little exchange, I remember, concerned happiness. I was gazing around when a pang came again, and I remarked how it was funny how quickly even really nice things made you sad, knowing that they would not last for anyone and that I'd found it impossible not to have this slight contempt for those who went around expecting to be happy; and that, maybe, in the end, this had been what had come between me and certain women I had known. She reckoned both of our kinds expected to be happy same way, or else there wouldn't be so many unhappy but, yes, she knew what I meant about sadness not far behind, and what could you do? There's always ghosts at the banquet. But you could still make it worth it, and the deep happiness, the only one worth striving for, is the one that you feel in full view of the rest, notwithstanding any of it.

And I wondered again if she had done or been done to. I still could not quite make up my mind. From one or two allusions she made later, though, and from how she'd looked at me when I'd fallen under, in the lagoon, I put together a theory.

This is what I think her story was: she'd got a water-based job in some instructional capacity. Some terrible accident had occurred on her watch, for which she blamed herself, and thus I found her, in the saloon, doing penance for a sin of omission.

Lord knows where her water-love had sprung from. Perhaps she was born in the country too.

We talked and we walked that day away. Aah, I do not think I have adequately conveyed the splendour of our surroundings. I don't really notice the world about me too tough. I pick up on people and the vibes in a situation quickly, but I'm not great on the details of my exterior world. But there were plateaus and gulleys and fallen frangipani (she told me), red jasmine and jade and springtime shades. The light from the hills changed with the clouds above them, and came filtering down in strips and shadows in a leaf-carpeted wood that we found. Beyond, at long last, I met cherries in the flesh: an orchard of puffy pinks and morellos and these frail exquisite clusters of white blossom, crystalline in the air. We paused in a meadow nearby to keep them in sight.

There I rebroached the issue of my client, no longer hiding my urgency. Why go? I put it blunter: don't go to him. But I've promised, she insisted. You haven't promised, you're not promised. Did he ask you, this guy? He wants you – stuffed and served up on a platter, like you're his sacrifice. What gives him the right? How about what *you* want, where *you* want to be, your plans. You like it here, isn't it?

'You know I do.'

'Well then. Stay. Stay.'

She looked down and away, shaking her head, so troubled.

'How about me?'

Believe me, I would not have pushed it except I had the right. She had lain to rest before, on a towel where we sat. We were both a little weary – these exertions and no refuelling, but too hyped to nod off. I lay beside her, though, on my side, behind, my head by hers. She had taken my hand and pressed it against her chest; begun humming absent-mindedly, privately, 'til at last her head slipped down and she jerked back up.

So little information and already you were humming. What does that make you – a fan, I think. If we're both fans we can do anything.

She stepped up to me, beholding me, then suddenly threw her arms round, tips of her toes, and I gripped her for some seconds.

'I don't know. I don't know.' Her eyes were moist and she covered her face with her hands. 'You've come and – aah! I don't know, I just want to do it right. Thinking about the trouble as well. He seems powerful. From what you say and – everything. Plus I've got this feeling there's maybe even more than him involved, do you understand?'

I guessed what she meant; prayed it was true what a few maintained, that He wasn't as powerful as all that.

She searched my face. I looked pretty down, replied flatly, 'Fear's not a reason to do something.'

'No.'

'Well,' I said, after some silence, 'I'll do what you want me to do.'

She straightened up the towels and lay down, looking skywards, her palms under her head. The sun had begun its descent.

'What are we gonna do for food, eh, wiseguy? That's what I want you to do.'

My mind was elsewhere. I knew if I could just find us some viable alternative, I could convince her. Personally, I wasn't even worried about whoever or whenever. I knew that with her, it was like, it was never gonna turn into the kind of life that I'm scared of.

What? – gone already? Look at you! No one could say it was kidnapping or anything. We couldn't help ourselves. We found who we behaved best with.

Her head had lolled over. I stretched alongside. At my movement she stirred, and I pretended to be asleep. She cupped my head in her hands and wriggled up closer, her lips nudging up tight against the side of my face. We lay like we'd been together for ever. I waited until the sound of her snoring, and I was close to succumbing myself, before putting into train the other phase of my 'asleep' test, pecking her on the sensitive, dewy tip of the nose. She flinched, which had the superstitious in me going a second, but didn't properly wake 'til I did it a second time. Now she slowly raised an eye, saw that it was me splayed beside, smiled and returned easily to the world I had interrupted, back into her deep rhythms.

So, I tell you, I know she loved me. All the little things. She was even saying so in her sleep.

I could not believe there could be another one like her, for me. To think, once, I wanted C-C . . . Huh. Perhaps these things are partly a matter of gratitude. She, she was the first person I'd really wanted, who'd said yes, who wanted to. I'm not as confident a person as all that, as you've probably guessed by now.

I felt so proud to be involved in her serenity. To think that I might ever be the cause of distressing that – Jesus! – to wipe that smile . . . She just made me smile.

Just lie right there, my baby, lie right there. *And I will sing forever, my love. And I will smile fore-e-ver, my lo-ove, oh-oh* . . .

When we woke, it was dusk, and he was standing over us.

14

reunion

I was dimly aware of her body not being there, and I struggled my eyes open to find her inclined a foot or so forward, staring. When I peered beyond her I made out the big figure in the half-light and bolted forward, pushing down hard with my knuckles, trying to haul myself up to give us a fighting chance. But my co-ordination in these first moments of waking was lacking and as I fell back – peripherally aware, too, that she seemed very calm for an intruder – his goatee, his features fitted together.

'You found the place all right then. I'd been hoping that perhaps you were on your way when I didn't hear from you.'

I blinked, gazed nervously at him. Embarrassment at our blatant discovery had replaced the protection worry.

He, and I was thankful for it then, seemed unperturbed as per usual. He extended an arm to pull her up. I rose too. There seemed nothing to be gained from remaining grounded.

'Really good to see you again.' He kissed her on the hand. 'And Boy!' He embraced me warmly, arms high on my back, his soft-threaded garms ultra-fine to the touch. 'Thank you. Congratulations.'

He stepped back, sort of admired the two of us. 'You took the train, I take it. A long trip. You must be hungry.'

She nodded imperceptibly, muttered an assent. I had regained my composure, was thinking ahead.

'You'll join me for some dinner, I trust and,' he glanced towards me, 'stay a little.'

I watched as he helped her fold away the towels and they embarked on natter. Don't worry, it isn't far, he said. She told him we hadn't seen a house anywhere around. 'You may have missed it,' he chuckled, 'you can't spot it from here.'

He seized my bags and took us back down to the lagoon, exchanging pleasantries with her about the delights we had seen: how he had planted the cherry trees himself, and how we had come at the right time, for their bloom was spectacular but brief, and so forth. I walked a yard apart and fractionally behind. 'Tired?' he asked me at one point. I forced out a smile.

At the shore approach she turned, looked back. 'So this, all *this*, is yours?'

He lowered his head slightly, modestly. 'Technically I believe so, but everyone is most welcome. So what do you think?' he asked me. 'Did I do it justice when I spoke with you?'

I nodded.

Around the little crest of the shore, further than we had ventured, he had moored a dinky rowing boat. It looked as if it were from your basic end of the market, though again I don't know much about such things: wooden, with the bow curving out, slats running across it, and rope attached through hooks to either end.

We clambered aboard. He unhooked a slack of rope up front and pulled at it, then the boat stirred and dragged us away.

She went out front with him; pointing at shit, yapping. I don't know why she had to be so bloody wide-eyed.

The air had a bit of nip to it now. I could glimpse the spray of water we were churning up ahead and, beyond that, the grey glinting calm of the lake.

Finally, a smile from her; some puzzle in it too. At this acknowledgement of our own connection I came towards them.

The shoreline we were hugging was very thick, overgrown with vegetation, straggly creepers and such, wilder and sheerer than anything we'd seen. I asked him how long he had lived here. He replied that he travelled so much, as he'd told me, but that he'd been returning here a long time. I told him he hadn't told me, but Mr Development had. He professed puzzlement, but there was that old, knowing curl.

'Forget it,' I said.

He tugged again to steer us right into a narrow, veg-heavy cove, pulled in and guided us up the steep, rising bank. There were a series of stone steps cut into the hill. Even in daylight you'd have done well to spot them.

I insisted on taking my bags back for the ascent, and cracked a debut joke about his postman as I mounted behind.

There must have been close to a hundred of those steps, some deep enough for your calves to be feeling it, but at last we came to levelling ground, and a break in the trees, and a brown cabin, nestling there in the clearing.

It was far more compact than I'd imagined, most discrete and proportionate. Two lanterns were fitted in grooves on either side, with a third perched high in the growth behind.

The door was hardly your quiet kind. Had I been of the same breathtaking disposition as she I might have responded similarly. It was fashioned from the same red clay as the soil before but this in solid, pillar form, on which was carved three singular fetish figures.

The most man-like to the left, a ferocious foot-high spirit, wielding a cutlass. Opposite was a slightly daintier thing, clutching a bow and arrow. Between them, much smaller, hunched, even lame, and clad in strands of tiny, nicked, cowrie shells, was the third.

'They're my three warriors.' He turned the heavy handle, winking. 'They guard me.'

Inside, much like the Race Man's, was far roomier than you were expecting. He had us remove our footwear in the doorway and walked us down most of the length of it. I saw just the one door to the sitting room on the right-hand side, but three or four to the left. The place was built like a compound, most of the bits hanging off a central space, long and flat-feeling. There were three levels though: I noticed stone steps going down as well as upstairs to the guest floor, where he took us.

And most tastefully appointed it was too. The joint looked handmade, with sloping roofs and wooden beams in different shades of brown. Uncluttered, the odd old-country canvas on the landing and a few more choice carvings, in wood and ivory. The floors were covered in these buff non-stick shavings: they were thin, but they kept the warmth in.

He opened a door for her first, then ushered me further along the corridor.

'You're quiet tonight,' he said to me.

'Different things,' I shrugged.

He put a hand to my shoulder.

My room was plain, brownstone walls, but comfortable. I dropped on to the bed. Lordy! What a day, what a deadline day . . .

There was a lace mosquito net above me and music oozing, it appeared, from the walls. I couldn't see a player. Lifting lovers' rock, one of my favourite styles, and this one of my favourite tunes: '*Lovely senorita-a-ah, you really look so pretty when you smile at me, you're all I see-e-e-e-e* . . .' What was this – to goad me?

I sat up. Come on, Boy. What are you gonna do. Gotta do, say, something.

I had to speak with her. Know her mind and counsel.

I went to the door, poked my head out. It was quiet out there. I scurried down the landing, gave a soft knock and entered.

She wasn't there. I'd been so banking on speaking with her I felt quite crushed. There was a bathroom door quarter open at the back and I even checked in there, but no.

I pondered a moment, heart quickening. She had sounds too, on a similar vibe to mine. On the bed lay a flowing, green and gold gown with matching headdress. I hadn't seen it for a moment, under the net.

Something from him, no doubt.

I stood outside and craned my neck, but I couldn't hear anything from down below either. Maybe a murmur. Where was she?

A cigarette restored some calm on my return. Probably no great intrigue anyway – fuck, it was a big house.

A dark metal statuette had been contemplating me, presumably for some time, under half-closed, heavy-lidded eyes. On his face horizontal scarification markings were etched. His were a lot prettier than mine.

He resembled the cutlass spirit downstairs, albeit in fractionally better mood. In his hands he grasped a hammer, possibly an axe. To his left, a diagonal foot behind, loomed a thrusting piece of rugged grey stone, as tall as I. You felt they were connected, else why place it there? Everything else looked just so in here.

Who was he, this dude? A god of war, perhaps. Long-dicked, no doubt about that.

I went to grip the stone, tried to shift it – not this day of the week – and got a nasty shock when my fingers touched some wetness up top. Urrgh! – thick red oil. I stared at it, waiting for my fingers to fry or something, before washing it off in my en suite business and getting my arse in gear. He's probably waiting already.

Under the shower, my head full of her again, and the splendours of the day, I felt more positive by the minute. It *had* to happen. Such a laid-back guy, my client, maybe we could come to some arrangement.

I unrolled the green shirt and black trousers from my bag. Aah, dressing for dinner! I should have laid them out before . . . The shirt was a little creased and I flattened it as well as I could with my hands. Never mind, I'd sling my good jacket over and keep it on.

I took a big breath, nodded respectfully to my man, and killed the lights.

I checked her room again, then a couple of the siderooms downstairs. I was hoping to have a joint strategy worked out before we dealt with him. I finished up hovering by the basement stairs, but didn't go down there. I walked back up, knocked on the half-open sitting room door, and entered.

There were on the left-hand side, behind the door, down at the bottom. Candles and a fire crackling were the only points of light in a room that was almost as long and high as the house itself and that ended beyond them in great French windows. It was dark already, by the doorway, and the ceilings and the front end just disappeared.

I advanced towards them. I could see straight away how radiant she looked; totally made up, in her headdress and patterned gown, forehead high and oval curves, the gold against the brown. Truth say, he wasn't far behind, regal in his white silken robes and Fila cap, waiting easily with her, drinks in hand, by the fire. They looked, well, on another level.

I halted a yard in front. Behind me, the table, and rich aromas of stews. 'Suits you,' I said to her. 'Really does.'

I wanted to do something to re-establish the link. Too late to kiss her, I had to have done that already or not at all. Instead I glanced a slightly pained expression at my client.

'What can I get you, Boy? Wine, juice—'

'Whatever you're having is fine.'

I fixed her as he went to the cabinet. 'What are we gonna do?' I hissed. She stared at me, questioning.

He was on his way back. I gestured frantically, turned and took the glass he was proffering. He poured me a cloudy drink from the bottle, then topped his and hers up: a sweet palm wine, I'd had it before.

'A toast, I think, is in order.' We clinked glasses. 'To a successful conclusion,' he beamed at me, 'and a happy ever afters,' he beamed at her.

Well satisfied. *What a good little boy you've been.*

'Please!' he held out his arm for us to accompany him to the table.

A less stout wood might have groaned under the succulents jostling there: stews and yams and groundrices in silver-plated platters and tureens, resting on black grills cornered with candles, for the heat and the look of it. On a sideboard were all manner of fruits and nutty sweets. At the top of the table were three chairs with places laid, two facing and one at the head. I paused naturally, behind him, at one of the facing chairs, my back to the window rather than the great distance of the room, but he beckoned me forward, to the head.

'It's you who's done the work, the hard work. Tonight is in your honour.'

His eyes were transparent and kind but . . . tch! You always suspected some mockery there.

When we swapped places I instantly saw what was going on. Now he was facing her.

He clasped his hands and dipped his head in what I imagined was a silent grace. I looked at her but she had dipped sameway. Why would she not let me catch her eye?

'All right,' he said, thirty seconds on, and we sat, started cycling the pots. He handed me a tray containing fried doughballs and such. I took a couple but I am not overly fond of ground or minced eats.

She was heaping her plate with spinach and guinea fowl. I helped myself moderately to some too, and some fish, took two lusty mouthfuls, then fell to picking away. It was nice, but I wasn't in the mood.

'So when did—'

'Have you—'

They smiled at their synchronicity. 'Have you got any brandy actually?' I enquired in the gap.

He pointed me to a cabinet on the wall behind.

'Go on,' he continued to her.

'So you two met – when was it?'

'Last week – a week ago exactly.'

I found a bottle and a glass. Tried to tip some back, for the amount I'd poured was embarrassing. Ended up sending nuff of it down the sides, on to his pristine finish.

'That's right. And we last spoke – oh yes, at the end of the game the other day, wasn't it?'

I nodded, returning.

'And how has it been for you, Boy, since then?'

I shook my head. Why was he asking me this?

Still looking at me expectantly.

'You know how it's been. Two dead, that's how it's been.'

That sat them up a bit.

'What – the woman outside the club—'

'Candy,' I nodded, 'an' Hope too. Don't pretend you don't know.'

'Well, I read about the lady, a hostess I think she was, in the news—'

'Yeah. From Ice Cream. Ice Cream, remember?' I was almost glaring at him now. 'How d'you find us today? How d'you know my name an' address to begin with?'

I shot a glance at her. She was staring at me, looked surprised more than anything.

'A business acquaintance told me where you were. A lawyer – I have the name down somewhere. I can find it if you want. And as for today, I didn't find you, you found me, like a – like a homing pigeon.'

'See, you coming with your smartness still! I don't get no straight answer from you.'

None of us were eating. She definitely wanted me to stop now.

'Boy,' he considered me patiently, 'bear with me, please. You look at me as if I had something to do with it,' he gestured with his hands. 'I read about your lady and I was – orh! – devastated, of course. But it's happening, we all know it's happening. You both, better than I. It doesn't happen here.'

I closed my eyes, nodded in 'We can close the subject' mode. I had seen annoyance on her face, on my account, for the first time.

'She intervened, didn't she?' – it was he who wasn't letting it drop – 'to stop trouble for another. One of the greatest things we can do. Only matched, or surpassed, I think, when someone intervenes to bring about something deeply positive for another.' All these abstracts, when a top girl is dead. On our accounts. 'That – that is *grace*.'

And he gazed straight at her and she . . . yeah, she practically simpered.

And that was the way it was, for a while. Various chat, percolated with his pointed wisdoms, and her engaged and, for the main part, receiving. A touch deferential, I suppose polite, the way I had once been with him. I troubled my food occasionally, but in no way matched their enthusiasm for all.

She was pretty taken, I remember, with his latest pictures. What I could make out of the rest of the room it had been bare, just pan-elling, but down here there were pieces in dyes and resins, of a similar style to those we'd encountered already, only these took more of a narrative bent, with vivid scenes depicted. There were more humans around too, though the one I found the chilliest – a winged sprite with a full-grown face, and a hole where its teeth should be, adrift in swirls of thundery sky – didn't feature any. She seemed to know of a couple of the stories and I was irked because I had so many legends under my belt, but not these. She hazarded details past him, and they got into an animated exchange over the true acts attending one battle portrayed. He was saying that this chief lieutenant to this king, this Alafin, had been killed there while she was maintaining that in the version she'd heard he had not died at the front, as shown, but elsewhere.

'The Alafin of Ife, and his best man!' he said gravely. 'Love rivals. A mad little episode. Imagine destroying your greatest warrior by setting him an impossible task! Do you know the story?' he asked me.

I shook my head. See how he loves to rub my nose in it.

'Isn't history one of your things?'

'Well,' I did not hide some sharpness, 'I don't know that one.'

'I hope that Alafin got his deserts,' she smoothed the pause over. 'Mashing up man's life like that!'

'Poor, without question. To be fair to the Alafin, his lieutenant had been most *disloyal*, don't you think? Trying to steal that which his Lord held most dear. So our lieutenant deserved a big task. However, you still have got to put it on a level that he can reach otherwise—' he tossed his hand carelessly—'it's not on, it's not fitting—'

'True.'

I looked sullenly at her. Every so often, like just now, she'd thrown me a personal glance, but these were puzzled frowns, a trivial 'What's up? Are you okay?' worry in them. She didn't seem to be picking up the pace, the real issue in the situation, all his little jibes, the urgent problem that we faced. Rather she was cosy, almost colluding with this man. Yes, we'd had our discussions too, before, but it seemed to me she was at least as thralled now.

'. . . Like the symmetries between people, or water always finding, reaching its level. And gifts,' he fingered his ring, ladled a little more of his brown, gummy soup, 'as well as burdens, have to come right, you know. They have to be dressed appropriately, in fitting clothes. Otherwise the one you're intending it for, they may not even *see* it, even recognise it . . .'

This man, with his land and collats and sensitive chat. His beautiful things, and his powers, giant blocks of stone in upstairs rooms – how could I compete with this man? Fuck it, everybody knows it. If a Willie wants what's yours you can't do jack.

'Boy?'

'Urh?' I looked up. They were staring at me.

'My little token for you,' he continued. 'I was wondering if you wanted it now, or later? Better now, I think,' he rose, 'it may cheer you.'

He walked down to the fireplace. 'I bet it was the water, you know,' she said. 'We went swimming in the lake before, and this one ended up emptying half of it down his throat! You may have caught a bug or something.'

'Ahh. And here was I thinking it was just the toll, the exertions of the week,' he shouted over his shoulder.

I leant forward to her. 'You're not helping me,' I hissed. She searched my face, as if trying to estimate my mood, then squeezed my hand: 'After. If we have to, after—'

'There won't *be* an after.' Can't you see? Please don't deny me. 'We've gotta move now . . .'

I looked anguishedly at her as he returned and she took her hand away. It was just so frustrating, you know, we had no privacy from the moment we found him above us.

He handed me his blue-wrapped, rectangular token, hovered beside. I attacked the covering – it felt like a picture frame.

'I don't mean to make light of the week you've had,' he smiled at me, 'but I thought you'd enjoy this. It can stand beside your "dropped catch" cartoon, on a new wall.'

Inside was a blown-up, red-treated photo of a kind of Last Supper scene, with the nine members of the Wu Tang, the singers of his song, grouped, some standing, others seated around a table. Only instead of viands and such, the table was crammed with the fruits and hardware of a mafia's pharmaceuticals empire: spoons, beakers and distillation tubes, wads and fine wine magnums exultantly brandished. Along the bottom, in that sloping script, ran the words '*What do you believe, Boy, heaven or hell?*'

What was this, the consolation prize?

'A little reminder,' he said, 'of how far you've travelled.'

She came excitedly to see, nodded a grin, and hummed the refrain as she slid away to take a closer peek at his wall pieces.

'You dropped something,' he said to me. On the floor was an envelope. Inside was a cheque, in my name, for sixty thousand folds.

'What would you say,' so much plea in my eyes, I glanced over to her, 'if I gave this back to you, told you I wanted something else?'

'We have an arrangement, don't we?'

'Have you asked her?'

'I don't need to ask her.'

'God!' She pointed to a face in a picture. 'Have you noticed how this one's in all of them? He's kinda surfing the sky there, he's guarding the crossroads here.'

He looked. I didn't bother.

'That's right,' he said.

'You knew where to find her. So why ask me, pay me to find her?' Even as I was asking I knew there was no point to it. Information would not stop his intent.

'Why indeed?' He met my entreaty with a poker face.

What did he mean? My head dropped, my brain was thudding under the pressure. 'I've had enough – I've had my fill of your games, y'unnerstan'?' I burst out.

'Come, Boy.' He watched as she made her lissom way back. The thought of him being with her, knowing her, just turned my stomach.

'A sportsman, a riddle-man, like you! We're so near the end; don't you think it would be a shame to stop now? What? Would you have me walk you to the door? And where's your glory then?' He turned his back, sauntered to his seat, and rebellion, which had been flashing so much, overran me.

Next to me again. But she ain't looking.

'I knew there was something going on in those pics,' she said. 'And it's the same one, the lame one, on the door, isn't it?'

'Ouuh! Getting warm!'

I'm holding this cheque, helplessly, unconsciously slip it inside my jacket. What's this? Something slim, something long.

Something else about this man, like I understood that first time he came to the bar. These pictures, they're more than just his pictures. What's he saying? What he's come for? He's *telling* us, in his way he's telling us . . . Not for me, that's for almost sure. I'm not feeling that. Can't you see that?

It would be so easy to do. No one knows we're here.

'That's my favourite one right there. The animals-with-human-heads one. I'm not mad keen on spiders, but monkeys – they're my weakness!'

He may have a ride. Or just steal one somewhere. We'll be hundreds of miles away by the morning.

'There are three of the same there. Did you see?'

Fly-away scenes. Something above and beyond about him. I don't know, I think they really are *his* pictures. Very stable. It's like he's not just visiting where he is, he's there, properly there. He's something you might come to at the end. Not in the middle, like me. Or Boy. Boy! It's you I love. You I know how to.

Sweetheart! He's not catching my smile. Where is he, hand in his pocket – is he with us at all? I know, sometimes, boys don't listen.

It slips nice and easy from its groove. So lucky, I didn't forget you. I'll give him a chance to forgo his claim. I'll give him two. But from he don't, from the moment he don't – well, I'm sorry.

'Have some fruit,' he gestured at the sideboard behind, 'or chin-chin – do you know it?'

'So let me just get this straight,' I cut in, shaking my head in false weariness. 'Sorry I'm a bit slow today. The deal remains the same?'

He frowned at me, finally, glanced a little embarrassedly at her. 'It would be nice to finish the dinner in peace. Without private matters—'

'Oh but I need to know.' I rose. I might have been pottering to the fruit. 'Hardly private, is it?'

Spiders. Spiders and snares. Snares and . . . hunting? The bow and arrow on the door?

He put his hands together, as I slipped mine inside, behind. Pronounced slowly—

Toying with his ring. The monkey ring. The monkey up there! Cheeky, tricksy. Tricksy and snares . . . unclear. The crossroads: place of . . . potential. Left or right, for better or worse – *unclear* . . . Messenger flying through the skies . . . I know him . . . Yes! Riddler Divine!

'The arrangement *is* the case, the test. You must remain loyal to the deal. Only then can we know of your suita—'

My left arm curled around his neck in a lock as my right arm came down over the chair, spearing to his guts. His muscles were slack, surprised, the cherry blade ran in deep like butter. Two time.

He moaned from deep in his stomach, clutching it, turning shocked at me. Her sound was the same, but sharper, more desperate still, mouth agape, eyes unbelieving.

I don't know what I expected from her.

Hearing that wretched echo . . . aah, boy – I regretted it then.

I stood there a moment, looking at her, the blade in my hand. I couldn't understand – there was no blood on it, no blood from him. For a second I thought I might be saved, but then he fell back and tumbled off the chair.

She screamed and ran to him. 'Eshu! Eshu!' she cried.

He was on his back, still holding his stomach, breathing shallow, trying to push himself, prop himself against the table leg behind. She helped him, gently parted his hands. He had eyes only for me, he looked so sorry.

'I came for you, you don't see. I was sent, I came for you. I am yours. Aah!' he gritted his teeth, and something came out at last, but water, a clear water.

Who *is* he?

'Oh it hurts, it hurts! He did not tell me it would hurt so much.'

She turned her head to me, frozen there. Her eyes flashed anger and grief. She put her hand up and whipped off the tablecloth, sending everything scattering. She ripped off a little piece, began wrapping the rest around his middle, as cloudier water began to spurt.

Horrible déjà vus of Candy, lying there. Lord, what have I done?

'It's all right. It's all right,' he croaked to her, then slumped further. Blood was starting to trickle now.

'Eshu!' She hugged him. 'Eshu, don't go.'

Eshu? Did I once hear somewhere . . . the fallen's patron saint?

My legs were jelly and my face streaking with tears. I had been blessed, more than most any. A god, a god come down for me. How could I not see it?

He managed a smile and beckoned me. Man's blood is like claret, but his was brighter, burgundy.

'I was looking forward,' he said, 'to your happiness. And our new work. With the Race Man. Like your family before.'

I was shaking my head, crying, shaking my head. Been blessed, been so blessed.

'Closer, closer.' I came, crouching down. 'Inside.' He had his hand to his back trouser pocket. Hesitantly, I put my hand by it. He nodded. 'Inside.'

There was a piece of paper there. '*One man amongst a thousand . . . but a woman amongst all those . . .*' His original.

He opened his right hand, and I placed it there. He took my hand in his left, hers in his right, and joined ours together. Her hand was stiff, reluctant, she could not look at me, but he kept us there. His eyes closed, then faintly opened.

'I go back now.' There was peace there. 'Go back . . .'

A man may come for you, he had told her. I should have seen it.

'Please. Forgive me,' I blurted. I wanted to explain someway. 'It's just the message, the clues – they're so hard to figure from this place of yours.'

His eyes flickered, his mouth still in this pained, upward turn. I think I saw him look beyond me, to the window and the dark outside, before his hand fell away from ours, fell forward, and his whole physical frame lolled.

I stumbled away then. How could I stay, I who had done it?

I felt outside my body, apart from everything. Dully charting the blood towards the note, and her, the girl I loved, cradling and hugging him, like lullabying.

Desolately eyeing my underachievement.

All the patterns, the chronicle of my fail foretold. Everything follows you.

Just one more trusting moment. It could have gone either way.

People will hear. They'll think I did it for his money. But, you know, it wasn't the money, it wasn't the money at all.

I had to look away. My gaze caught the picture of the sky. What a ferocious thing.

It was a rumble first, but it grew awesome. We both looked to the windows, to the dark. Then the most blinding flash and dazzle of gold, red and green. The girl screamed, the rainbow streaked the room asunder, and I fell.

acknowledgements

To my mother (I don't forget you ever), to my father, and all my (growing) family; to Ellen Ochu, and the Big Bonsu, 'l'homme qui aimait les femmes', once again.

To Skip Gates, whose 'Canon Confidential' in 'Loose Canons' got me thinking. . . ; to the Wu Tan Clan, especially Ghostface and Raekwon, ('Cuban Linx' – all bow, but "one novel a year," bro, what's happening?!); to the older gods, Donald Barthelme, Ishmael Reed, Amos Tutuola, and all my peers out there.

To Alex Lahood, Ian 'The Thunderer' Cook, Imtiaz H and Boysin for Port-of-Spain '94 (Ambrose 6 - 22 . . .); to Winston Scott; to Size and co. – the chess dons! To Jacquie Juceam; to Hamza Walker, at Chicago's Renaissance Society, for turning me on to Kara W, (now what was the name of that Delfonics tune again. . .?).

To the professionals: my editor Lennie Goodings, my agent Jonny Geller.

To all the ones who, at times and in ways they may not know about, have encouraged me.

Thank you.

SOME KIND OF BLACK

Diran Adebayo

With its world of Afro-bohos, Nubians and the
Love Has No Colour Brigade, *Some Kind of Black* stakes out new
terrain for the urban novel. A coming of age story about Dele, a
young student, and his sister Dapo who glide through violence,
love and politics, Diran Adebayo's debut is funny, street-smart
fiction which puts language through hoops and back again to
create an exhilarating odyssey through the London scene.

'Has the rare, incandescent energy of a story that's
never been told. A classic coming-of-age-tale . . .
marks the debut of a serious talent'
GQ

'A gloriously capable and confident writer . . . *Some Kind of Black*
is thoughtful, witty and moving . . . it is refreshing to read
something so extrovert and alert . . . I urge you to read it'
The Times

'Dissects British race relations with a scalpel wit that leaves every
stereotype begging for mercy . . . a sophisticated examination of
what race can mean in millennial London'
The Face

'Sharply written and exceptional'
Daily Telegraph

Abacus
0 349 10872 2